A GAME OF DECEIT AND DESIRE

A STEAMY LESBIAN FANTASY ROMANCE

GIRL GAMES
BOOK THREE

RUBY ROE

For all the girls who love to win... This one is for you.

Note for Readers

This book is intended for adult (18+) audiences. It contains explicit lesbian sex scenes, considerable profanity and some violence. For full content warnings, please see author's website: rubyroe.co.uk.

This book is written in British English.

If you would like to read the free *steamy* prequel to book 1 sign up here: rubyroe.co.uk/signup

CHAPTER 1

REMY

The alchemical formula for love is perplexing.

Sex I understand. It's all orgasms and carnal pleasure. But love, that's something more. If I were to reference academic literature, it would tell you the base chemicals are hormones: oxytocin, dopamine, norepinephrine, and serotonin.

Perhaps I find it baffling because I've never been in love. But it simply shouldn't be possible. And yet, I've watched Scarlett and Quinn fall for each other. And that's without mentioning Stirling and Morrigan. You simply can't explain what they're experiencing with chemical equations and hormones.

Love, it seems, is something that no magical mansion, castle, palace or academic can explain. Well, no matter that I can't decipher it, there's only one thing I need to know: love isn't for me.

I don't have time for it, not if I want to keep my reputation intact and complete this mission for Morrigan and

Calandra. I have to stay focused. Besides, there's only one woman I could have ever loved, and given what her parents did to me, that has put an end to that.

I hold my favourite book—*Runes and their Magical Applications*—close and stare out the window as the carriage rattles along the road. My fingers rub the edge of the spine, its cloth fabric frayed and worn thin from both my fingers and overuse. But I can't bring myself to part with it. Marcel, my mentor, gave it to me. It contains all the original runes—the old magic language we've bastardised and heaped technology onto. I keep it to remind myself that while I work with new magic, there's merit in the old ways too. I open the cover, let my fingertip skim the inscription. It's written in a code, and even after I found the key scrawled in the corners of pages, it took me weeks to decode:

May the old ways keep us together. Love, your big brother.

The carriage lurches as we move over cobbles. The Runic Games are located in Lantis Palace, a revered building that resides in the heart of our realm between the six cities. Accordingly, six bridges lead to the palace—one from each of the cities. What I love most is that each city has a different magic. The academic in me would love to spend years studying them all. But perhaps that's for another life, another time.

Lantis Palace is sacred to us all. Though none of the other cities are participating in the games, they frequent the palace as much as we magicians do. It's home to us all and home to cross-city negotiations too. It's considered unseemly to fight on the grounds. Some of us call it the

Peace Palace for that reason. Ironic, really, that we're running a competitive game from here.

It's rare I leave Imperium. My stomach aches for home as the carriage judders over the bridge cobbles. I try to comfort myself that I'm doing this for a reason. Morrigan asked for my help. But it's more than that. After I built the security grid perimeter keeping Roman jailed, it flung me into the limelight. He's the most notorious criminal in the city—one who went after both my friends and the crown.

The fact I'm the one keeping him locked up has led to a sharp increase in my own notoriety. To say that I'm in demand is an understatement. Which is why the pressure to perform at these games is acute. But I'm no legacy magician. I don't have centuries of familial lineage attesting to my worthiness. I just lucked out facilitating his incarceration and now my reputation feels... unjustified. Thus, I'm at the games trying to live up to the perception the city has of me.

And honestly, I don't know if I can do it.

I'm just some inconsequential magician from the Borderlands who struck lucky and made a fortune. I need to win this competition to cement my reputation. Prove that I am as good as the rest of the legacy magicians. Prove that I am worth the accolades the city has bestowed upon me.

Outside the carriage, the horse's hooves clack against the bridge cobbles. Lantis Palace is situated in the bay of the Lantis Ocean—hence the name. The position of the palace was a tactical choice, I suspect—to make it harder to attack. I scan the bay, spotting each of the six bridges.

Hungry waters and frothing waves mar the surface of the ocean. I wonder for a moment whether anyone has studied its properties.

There are stories that say the water is alive. That should

a magician stray alone to its shore, they'll be swallowed and turned into merfolk and creatures of the deep. Though whether that's a myth, I cannot say. The scent of fish and salt drifts through the window. I can't decide whether I love it or hate it—a little fresh, a little acrid.

The carriage slows as the palace towers up, piercing the sky like a stem full of thorns. We draw to a stop and the driver opens my door.

"Good luck, miss. Hope you give 'em hell," he says and tips his hat at me.

I give him a handful of coin along with a hefty tip. The courtyard is bustling with magicians, suitcases, carriages, and families.

Before I've even hauled my case off the carriage, a young magician with enormous ears runs up to me.

"Oh miss, are you Remy Reid?" he says.

"Yes, I am."

"The same Remy that imprisoned *the* Roman Oleg?" He bounces on his feet as he exaggerates the words.

I smile, trying to quell the unease in my gut. "I just made the security grid, but yes, if that's what you're referring to, it was me."

"Amaaaaazing. Will you sign my schoolbook?"

I glance down as he thrusts Level Three Runes for Young Magicians at me and a pen.

"Sure." I sign the book, hand it back, and he runs off to his parents.

Somewhere in the chaos is the rest of the team. Morrigan and Stirling are no doubt already inside preparing to open the games. Scarlett is probably working with the guild assassins on securing the palace. And Quinn is going to arrive later. She went back to the Borderlands to see

Malachi and Jacob. The boys are staying in the Borderlands permanently, so Jacob won't make the games.

The boy's loud squawking at me has attracted a gaggle of other magicians. I sign three more items: an arm, a notebook, and a water bottle then, finally, I'm on my own.

I head to the entrance, but a hand grabs my shoulder and hauls me into an embrace. I laugh into the ribbed jumper, the scent of leather and tobacco filling my nose.

I disentangle myself and give him a broad grin. "Marcel..."

"Ms Reid." Marcel's grey eyes beam at me. His hair has faded to the same shade as his eyes since the last time I saw him.

"I see you're more silver fox than tall, dark, and handsome these days."

"I'll have you know I am still dapper enough to have my share of the ladies. Come here, you..." he pulls me back into a hug, and this time, I drop my case and fling my arms around him.

"It's been too long," I say.

"Far too long," he says into my shoulder. When we break apart, he keeps his hands on mine. "I hope you're going to win."

"Of course. How can I lose? I had a great teacher."

That makes him huff out a laugh. "Oh, fuck off with your flattery. I've got to help the other Games Makers, but let's catch up while you're here. I'd love to hear all about the famous Remy Reid, prison-master extraordinaire."

My face falls, tension leaking into my jaw and cheeks. His face crumples.

"Life not all it seems at the top?"

"I..." I don't want to confess my insecurities in a public

courtyard, but especially not to Marcel. He was kind and incredible as a mentor. But he was also a tough old bastard, more stiff upper lip than hugging you while you sob type.

I shrug. "It's a wild ride, a little overwhelming at times. I'll be fine."

"Of course you will. I'm proud of you. Can't wait to see what you do."

I smile and give him an awkward, single laugh. The fact Marcel is proud I locked Roman up does not come as a surprise. I don't think even Morrigan hated him as much as Marcel did.

I remember one competition, Roman was there cheering his apprentice, Bella on. Marcel was there cheering me on. The two of them ended up in a fistfight over the adjudicator's ruling. I stand by the fact Roman started it claiming the adjudicator was biased in my favour. Unfortunately, Marcel threw the first punch. Roman tried to strangle him in return, and three adjudicators had to pull them off each other. As much as it was mortifying, it wasn't the least bit surprising. It was always like that.

I grab my bags as he saunters off into the crowd, barking instructions at stewards in neon jackets and Games Makers in Lantis Palace robes.

That's when I see her.

Bella.

My body reacts, my stomach tight, heart racing. This is the one woman I could have fallen for. I very much did not fall. And let me tell you, I'm glad I didn't. I dodged a bullet with her and her rotten, cheating family. Speaking of which...

She's alone.

Where is her family? When we were apprentices, her

mother and father would always be at the competitions. Granted, we're adults now. But still I find myself curious. A group of young magicians walks past her, whispering. Bella stiffens, gives them the middle finger, and then turns back to the registration desk. There's a twinge in my chest. I shouldn't feel for her, she kept working with Roman long after she should have left. But no one wants to be gossiped about.

She leans over the registration desk to sign forms, her plump ass forming a heart shape. I swallow hard. The sight of her exquisite bottom does things to me. Things it shouldn't.

Look, it's not beyond me to confess that I find the woman deeply attractive. Always have, much to my chagrin. All throughout our apprentice years, I was equal parts infuriated and infatuated with her. But she's about as legacy as you can get, and I am really not. This is the problem, this is why I've dodged a bullet.

And yet, there was the kiss.

The kiss she gave.

The kiss I stole.

My lips tingle at the thought. A shadow of cherry-flavoured balm drifts over my tastebuds.

Disastrous really—to be attracted to your biggest rival. Not that it matters. If that kiss taught me anything, it's that we'd never work.

Besides, our rivalry is a decade old. It's etched into the marrow of who we are. We only know how to exist on opposite sides. Our history is long, bloody, and heated.

But that is exactly why I'm here. It's why Morrigan begged me to come.

If nothing else, I'm looking forward to is this competition putting our history to bed.

I'm going to prove that I am the better magician.

And as for that kiss, it's ancient history. She probably doesn't even remember. We're both busy adults—I'm very busy. I have a huge busy company to run, an important mission for Morrigan and her mother. And I'm sure Bella probably has a wife or partner. Not that I'm interested.

I'm not.

Obviously.

I don't even care whether she's single.

She stands, her fingers lightning quick as she lifts something from the Games Maker's robe. I roll my eyes. Still up to her usual tricks then. Another reason we'd never work. She's far too quick and loose with her morals.

Tight jeans show the curve of her thighs, her equally tight top shows the contour of her waist, and her push-up bra the mound of her breasts.

Gods.

I swallow again.

She catches my eye, her expression narrowing. Fuck, she caught me looking at her. The corner of her lips quirk into a smug grin.

She inclines her head at me and mouths 'you wish'.

The illusion bursts, and the warm rush of lust is replaced with the hard heat of irritation.

Oh, I wish alright. I wish for the day when I can fuck the little brat into submission.

She knows she's riled me. I can tell by the way her eyes curl into a smile. She saunters off inside the palace, and I swear to gods, she pushes her hips a little wider and wiggles her butt a little further, just to piss me off.

I grit my teeth and march to the registration desk, a single truth settling in my gut.

I am going to enjoy beating Bella Blythe once and for all.

But first, I need to explain how I ended up here. Let me take you back twenty-four hours.

CHAPTER 2

REMY

I swig the dregs of morning coffee from my cup when my apartment door buzzer goes. I pick up the orb, and the doorman's head appears.

"Yes?" I say.

"Fella in the lobby, Ms Reid. He's, er... summoning you," the doorman says.

"Summoning me? What? To where?"

There's a scuffing noise, and a new face appears in the orb. It's Benedict, the palace chief of staff.

"Benedict? How can I help?"

"Her Royal Highness, Princess Morrigan, requests your attendance at the palace."

"Okay... I can be there at 1pm."

Benedict shuffles in the orb, his expression twitching. His cheeks are flushed, the rouge running down his neck and under his damp collar. Did he run here?

"No, ma'am, that won't do. It won't do at all. She requests your presence immediately... please, and, umm...

thank you," he adds as if he's giving me a choice, when clearly, this is a command.

I sigh. "Fine. Give me a moment, and I'll be down."

"There's a carriage waiting out front." Then he vanishes.

I gather my bag, sling my coffee mug in the sink, grab a jacket, and head down to the carriage. Half an hour later, I waltz into the palace. It greets me with a wash of pressure over my body, the scent of lilac and mint and clean air. Like all buildings in the heart of New Imperium, magic thrives in their foundations and their connection to the land, the palace more so than any other. Magic is spawned and grown through our buildings. Magic twists through every mansion's walls ready to choose which magicians to bestow its gifts to. These powerhouse mansions and castles will always be a wonder to me. The way the palace's magic glides over my skin, it's a kiss and a caress. I swear the most magical ones are sentient. The way it greets me is like an old friend's hug.

The war room is in the palace's heart, so I make my way down the long corridors and through the warren of grand rooms dripping with opulence. Scarlett and Stirling appear. Scarlett leans against the wall of the war room. She's holding a short blade and using it to pick her nails, clearly more relaxed than Stirling, who's pacing up and down the corridor.

"Finally," Stirling says. "Morrigan has been in a horrendous mood this morning. What did you do?"

"Innocent, of all charges, my friend. I got summoned half an hour ago. Came straight from my apartment. What's going on?"

Scarlett pockets the knife and kicks off the wall. "You're

both innocent, don't worry. The intel the assassin's guild received has unnerved her."

Stirling fires her twin sister a vicious stare. "And you didn't think to enlighten us about this fact earlier?"

Scarlett shrugs. "Come on." She opens the door and guides us in.

Morrigan and Queen Calandra sit at the head of the table, the pair of them a yin yang of black and white. Morrigan's dark fringe is blunt across her forehead, as midnight black as her jeans and top. Unlike her mother's sweep of blonde hair, which is a luxurious match for her crisp cream suit. I've always appreciated Queen Calandra's taste in suit wear. I prefer a waistcoat, but I still admire the tucked lines and darts of a well-fitting suit. And Queen Calandra wears the best.

They stand as we enter, and I bow my head in deference.

Queen Calandra gestures for us to take a seat at the long oblong table. There's a fruit bowl in the middle, tea and coffee.

"Thank you for coming at such short notice," Queen Calandra says.

Morrigan pulls an orb I made out of her pocket and it flickers to life, Quinn's face appearing from one of the rooms inside the old palace in the Borderlands.

"Hey, what's up?" Quinn says and settles into a chair.

"Are you in a secure room?" Morrigan asks.

Quinn's shimmery head turns. "Hold on, I'll shut the door." She vanishes and reappears a moment later.

Stirling and Scarlett take seats next to me. I catch a look pass between Morrigan and Stirling, one that spells of unspoken understanding. My legs cross and uncross of their own volition, as I lick my lips. I don't like this.

Morrigan turns to her mother. "Do you want to start?"

Queen Calandra threads her fingers together, her expression grave.

"I'm sorry to have pulled you in so suddenly, especially because you're all packing for the Runic games tomorrow, but we have a situation." Queen Calandra nods to her daughter. Morrigan waves her arms at the far wall, and a screen drops down.

A string of runes appears.

"We've intercepted some encrypted messages," Calandra says.

I squint at the screen, piecing the code together, reading the runes.

Oh shit.

My mouth opens, forming a little 'o'.

"Quite," Queen Calandra says.

"Who sent these?" I ask.

Morrigan folds her hands. "We're not sure. They were encrypted with an erasing rune, so while we caught a snapshot of what they said, our security magicians didn't have time to trace the source of the runes because they erased themselves as they passed through our server."

Stirling kicks back in her chair, rocking on the legs. "For those of us illiterate in runes, could someone elaborate?"

"It's a message about Roman. It explains the location of his prison," I say, a shiver running through my words.

"Oh," Stirling says and plonks down onto all four of the chair's legs.

"Oh indeed," Scarlett says.

Hovering above the orb, Quinn's shimmering face falls, a little gasp bursting out.

Scarlett turns to Quinn. "We're going to need you here."

"I'll leave straight after the meeting," she says.

This is exactly what I've been afraid of. I may have coded the security for the grid trapping Roman inside a cottage with no magic, but the weight of responsibility that comes with that is enormous. Yes, I'm being deluged with praise, but should anything go wrong, the liability lies with me. A terrifying prospect.

"What does the guild say, Scarlett?" Queen Calandra asks.

Scarlett leans forward, resting her elbows on the table. "The timing is too coincidental with the games starting tomorrow. The guild suspects, with the theme of the games this year"—she turns to me. "This is confidential information as part of this mission. It doesn't go outside of this room."

"Not a problem," I answer.

Scarlett continues. "The theme is prison security. The nature of brainstorming the theme of the games means we don't know who suggested it, and we can't know if that person is working in league with Roman, or if it just provided Roman the opportunity he needs to use the games as a cover."

I sit bolt upright, my stomach bottoming out.

"A cover for...?" Stirling says reaching for an apple in the bowl in the centre of the table.

Scarlett raises an eyebrow at me.

"For a prison break," I answer.

Stirling pales. Morrigan rubs at her temples, pulls the sheaves of paper in front of her into a neat pile as if she can't quite bring herself to face this. Not that I blame her. None of us wants Roman to escape. But Stirling and Morrigan have the most reasons to need him kept locked away. Morrigan's parents arranged for her to marry him shortly after she was born, as is the case with princesses and political alliances. When it was clear she had no intention of marrying him, things got nasty. Stirling actually worked for him for a period, but that led to her double-crossing him, and while it was a team effort to imprison him, I'm the one keeping him trapped.

Stirling stands abruptly. "No."

All eyes fall on her.

"He can't be allowed to escape. Can you imagine the consequences?"

Morrigan raises her hands up, "He won't escape, will he, Remy?" Her dark eyes are like fire boring drill holes into me.

I sincerely hope not.

But I put on a confident smile, hope it reaches my eyes, and say, "No, I used the most up-to-date tech. The perimeter is iron proof. There's no way anyone can infiltrate his prison."

Queen Calandra shifts in her chair, tension seeping into her eyes. "You're certain?"

I uncross my legs. Well, no, not fucking really. My throat dries and I can't quite make the word 'yes' emerge. So I nod. All the while, I'm running calculations. Lines of rune code appear in my mind's eye as I check and recheck the program I wrote. There's no way. It would take someone extraordinary. That, at least, calms me down enough to get control of my vocal cords.

I clear my throat. "I'm certain. There are only a handful of magicians capable enough to out-rune me."

Queen Calandra's shoulders sag. She glances at Morrigan. "Show her the next message."

The screen at the back of the room flickers and shifts. And another string of messages appear.

"Oh, gods," I breathe.

Stirling opens her mouth, but I answer the question on her tongue.

"It's only half decoded, but it says *friends at the games*. The next line is destroyed and then it says. *Already decrypted half...* then the string runs out."

"So, when you say only a handful of magicians, you're referring to the handful of elite rune magicians at the Runic Games starting tomorrow?" Queen Calandra says, her tone void of humour.

I mouth the air, unable to formulate a comprehensive sentence.

"Fuck," Morrigan breathes and balls her fists on the table.

Queen Calandra blanches at her daughter's outburst and turns to me. "Remy, you're lead investigator. You're going to the games anyway. But now you're going with a mission. Scarlett—" She cuts herself off.

"I brought the list of attendees as requested." Scarlett pulls a scrap of paper from a bag and pushes it across the table.

Morrigan examines it. "I don't recognise many names on that list. I'm sure you'll know more, Remy, but there is one that stands out."

She passes the list to Queen Calandra, who scans the page and then passes it to me.

My eyes run down the names, my gut churning harder with each successive one. And of course, I don't need to speculate on which name is familiar to her.

Bella Blythe.

My childhood rival. The same woman who was apprenticed to Roman, who, even after her apprenticeship ended, continued to consult for him and run the odd job, including using her lattice magic to cover all his imported magic. It was frankly ingenious. She weaved a series of runic symbols into a physical mesh and then fed the sequence of runes into the RuneNet—our digital communication system. She connected the physical mesh to the digital rune code and it rendered the lattice invisible through a kind of mirage where the runes bent the light around them. Super sophisticated, and a nightmare to undo.

"Bella?" I say, forcing as much calm into my voice as I can. Beneath the table, though, my leg is tapping up and down.

Morrigan nods. "Wasn't that the woman we suspected was working for Roman?"

Stirling pipes up. "Yes, I ran into her at the auction so Remy could check. Despite the fact her lattice magic was protecting Roman's imports, by the time we convicted him, everything she'd created was gone." Stirling shoots me a surreptitious glance. I swallow.

And here we have the problem.

The reason all traces of Bella's magic were gone is because I erased it to ensure there was no evidence of her wrongdoing. And yes, we can debate the hypocrisy of me contesting Bella's moral ambiguity after that little confession, but...I had my reasons, and they seemed highly logical at the time. What's worse is that I confessed to Stirling at her and Morrigan's beach-house BBQ. I told both Stirling and Quinn that I was the one who'd erased it. Thankfully, no one else knows. But I hadn't anticipated this mess then.

And of course, now I'm sat at this table, the tingle of panic setting into my fingertips, I'm questioning my sanity over the whole affair. But here we are.

I shift in my seat, a line of sweat running down my neck. Stirling won't have told Morrigan, would she? As if she reads my thoughts, she squeezes my hand under the table, and I release a little sigh. The palace doesn't have rune magicians competent enough in the palace to figure out it was me. Which means this conversation can't be about that little... what shall we call it...? Faux pas of mine.

"But Bella *was* Roman's apprentice. That's a matter of public record. And now she's attending the games. Suspicious, no?" Morrigan says.

"Well... I..." I start and stop.

None of this adds up. Yes, Bella consulted and did the odd job for Roman, but she isn't a fool. Her parents are legacies and reputation-oriented legacies at that. I doubt she'd be stupid enough to entangle herself with him after she narrowly escaped jail. She's got looser morals than most, and a habit of petty theft that would impress even the most hardened of street urchins. But she's not a bad person. So it must be someone else.

"How well do you know her, exactly?" Queen Calandra says.

"I... I mean. Well enough to think it's highly unlikely she's tangled in this mess," I sputter.

"Really?" Morrigan says. "And yet, we know she worked for him on his imported magic. Don't you think that's highly suspicious?"

"I think it's inconveniently coincidental... for her, that is." I'm feeling more and more like this is an interrogation than a team meeting. Another bead of sweat bubbles on my neck, wetting my shirt collar.

"Come on, Rem, we need your help. What can you tell us?" Scarlett says, putting her hand on my arm. The tension in the room eases.

I glance at the list again, scanning names I recognise: Gabe and Alba Merrick.

They're legacies, but only just. Their attitude stinks like

it too, clinging to what status they can get. But work with Roman? I don't buy it.

There's Eli Winters on the list, but he's an old boy now. I assume he'll be organising or adjudicating the event. I can't think that he'd have anything to do with Roman either. He's always been on the straight and narrow.

There are a handful of names I'm familiar with but none that have ever stepped over the line, law-wise.

Which leaves Bella.

I frown.

"It could be anyone on this list. The Merricks are hardly upstanding legacies," I say, but there's no force behind my words. I don't believe them anymore than anyone else in the room does.

"Yes, but they don't have any known association with Roman. What about Marcel? He was your tutor, no?"

I nod. "I was his apprentice. He has enough magic, sure. But there's no way."

"Why not?" Morrigan asks.

I laugh because the thought *is* laughable. "I mean, if Roman had been murdered, I'd suggest he was your prime suspect. But help the man out of prison? No way. They…"

I try and finish that sentence, wrack my mind for the origin of why they hate each other and I simply can't find it. I mean, I know Roman fucked us over multiple times, withdrawing my applications to competitions, encouraging Bella to steal my work. I know Marcel fought back just as hard. Under his tutelage, I once snuck into Roman's apprentice warehouse and hid a rune bomb in there. Not a big, explosive one so much as a stinky one. They had nowhere to train for weeks. I'd hide at the edge of the forest as they'd train on fields, watching Bella get drenched. The way her curls would stick to her face as she'd huff about flinging runes and defensive shields at the other apprentices.

I circle back to my original thought. I don't actually know why Roman and Marcel hated each other, just that they did.

Morrigan huffs. "Fine, not Marcel, then. But Bella does have a connection to Roman," Morrigan replies.

I'm yanked back to the present. I suppress the urge to grit my teeth because I can see her point. Still, something in my gut is screaming no. I just don't think Bella is like that either.

"Bella, then?" Queen Calandra says.

I shake my head. "Not Bella. I've known her since I was sixteen. She's always had quick fingers, she flouts rules, is moderately unhinged at the best of times, but... jail breaker? She's more petty crime than traitor to the crown. I can't put the two together," I say.

Besides, Bella is as hellbent on the role of Royal Rune Master as I am. Morrigan's old Rune Master just retired so she figured rather than interview for the role, she'd add it to prize pot at the Runic Games. But it's the role Bella and I— and pretty much any other rune magician--have trained and lusted after for a decade. There's no way Bella would jeopardise that by jumping into bed with Roman again. Not when I gave her a free pass, erasing her magic from his crimes.

I want to argue, I want to lay down a million arguments why it can't be either of them, but it's clear the only thing that will persuade anyone in this room is evidence.

Queen Calandra's expression hardens. "Remy, I'm officially assigning you the team's next mission. You all need to attend the games and find the perpetrator behind Roman's potential jailbreak. We cannot allow that to happen."

A man knocks on the door and indicates to Morrigan and the Queen that they're needed. They stand.

"I'll leave you to discuss the details with the team. I have another meeting I must attend, but I need you to handle this discreetly," Queen Calandra says. She leaves the room, taking Scarlett and Morrigan with her.

When it's only Quinn and Stirling left, Quinn speaks up. "You like her, don't you...?"

I adjust my position in my chair. "I er. No. It's not that. It's—"

"Remy, you're not under investigation. We need you. We need your help. Be honest with us," Stirling says.

"Well, I mean. When we were sixteen, we shared a single kiss. But that's it. It's not like I'm in love with the woman. We don't speak. I don't have a relationship with her above competitive retorts and frequently thrown scowls."

"So you'll have no problem investigating her, then?" Quinn asks.

My whole body is suddenly hot. I adjust the collar of my shirt, undoing the top button. Do I have a problem with that? Honestly, it feels wrong to spy on her, and I'm not sure why. It's not like we have any kind of relationship.

"No. I don't have a problem. I just... appreciate her skillset. Yes. That's it. A deep, but firmly academic, appreciation of her skillset. And I truly can't see a motive."

"Remy...?" Stirling says, raising a single eyebrow at me.

"Her skillset, *Stirling*. I promise that's it. The woman is annoyingly good at what she does."

She narrows her disbelieving eyes at me, but I turn away. There's a soft knock on the door and Morrigan sticks her head back in.

"Sorry about that, I am going to have to say goodbye.

But I just wanted to make sure you're happy with what you need to do?" Morrigan says. "By any means necessary? We must find the perpetrator no matter what. I guarantee you someone knows more than you think. You must put aside any feelings you have for them, Remy. This affects more than just Stirling and I."

That catches my attention because, of course, this is what I've feared most. From what I know of Roman, he doesn't just want to end you. He wants to watch you suffer. Take down your friends, your family, everyone and everything you've ever treasured. Which means he won't just come for me and Morrigan. He'll come for the whole team. Our families. And if he comes for Morrigan, then what is Calandra going to do? Who is she going to blame when I'm the one who built the prison keeping Roman imprisoned? If it's hacked, if he escapes, everything I've built, my entire reputation will be destroyed.

And it won't matter if I win the games or not, I'll never be able to repair the damage his escape will do.

I'll be ruined.

CHAPTER 3

BELLA

Was it petty to wind Remy up the first moment I saw her?

Definitely.

Was it worth it?

Thousand per cent.

Her uptight shoulders, her puckered little mouth. Gods, her distress was exquisite. I'm still laughing to myself when I saunter into Lantis Palace. It greets me with a wave-like rush of pressure. I close my eyes against it, salty, fresh and warm, like I'm on a crystal beach. *Well, hello to you too, honey.* I shoot it a little magic to say thank you for the kind greeting and head to the welcome room.

It's breath-taking and cavernous, stretching wide and long like the maw of a monster. The air is frigid, no doubt because ocean winds buffet the palace. There's usually a storm just off the coast, and by the looks of the vast smear of billowing black on the horizon, we're due one soon.

I glance up. The ceiling is high enough my neck aches. Along the walls are thin windows cut out of the stone like the scrape of desperate nails.

Ahead of me, a crowd of magicians mingles in front of a raised stage and set of seating, all of us waiting for the Runic Games to kick off.

Three weeks. Three rune-magic challenges. One fight to be crowned the best rune magician in the city. The greatest honour, especially now they've added the prize of Royal Rune Master. A job and honour that is going to be mine.

Several sets of eyes follow me as I stride further into the welcome hall. Glances that descend into whispers.

Bastards. I know what they're saying without hearing them. The same shit my mother is freaking out about. I'm one of Roman's apprentices. My name is tarnished because of his foolish decisions.

Some legacy girl with fiery red hair and a nose obsessed with the sky strolls up to me. "You're brave," she says.

"What is that supposed to mean?" I snap.

She sniffs at me, her shoulders shift and she leans in conspiratorially. "You might come from one of the oldest legacy families, but there's nothing Mummy can do to help you here, not now your rune-daddy's in jail."

Before I can scruff the bitch, she spins on her heels and walks away. It's fine. I'm fine. They can think whatever the fuck they like. I can deal with the open harassment. It's what's been happening at home I'm more concerned about.

There's a stage at the back of the room, no doubt for the organisers to conduct the welcome talks from. In front of the stage is a set of seating, though most of the chairs are empty, people too busy milling around, talking catching up. The air is alive, buzzing with excitement and anticipation. I wish I could feel it. But I'm wound too tight.

Someone here is fucking with me, I'm sure of it. That's why I invited Red. I'm just praying she can come. She's a Hunter, a trained killer, and she's the only one I trust to have my back. I stand off in the corner, behind the cover of a pillar and survey the room.

Two weeks ago, my RuneNet was hacked, and I've traced the fucker to the games. Someone is after me—and I know it's because of Roman because none of this shit happened before he was put away.

I pull up my RuneNet screen now. Just a small screen for now—I don't want to be noticed. It hovers between my hands, semitranslucent. I cast onto the Net, forming rune symbols. They swirl in the air, coppery and shining before I send them into the screen. They vanish and reappear as lines of symbols and code on the screen.

It's the greatest magical advancement ever made in New Imperium.

Of course, half the old codgers in the city can't get on board with the new ways, but I'm not being left behind. I create a new string of runes. They pop into existence in front of me before I guide them into the screen. They shoot off across the screen to scan the area for the runic signature. But no luck. There's only a handful of people on the RuneNet right now, and none of their signatures match the one I'm looking for.

Fucking data breaches, attempted hacks, the works. I've had to tighten my security encryptions to eye-watering levels. I have my suspicions of course: Remy fucking Reid has enough reasons to hate me, and she's the one who imprisoned Roman, so my bets are on her. Marcel Corbin— her old mentor, but I don't know why he'd be coming after me. Unless... Did Remy put him up to it? And the Merricks.

But I doubt they have enough brain cells between them to come for me.

A woman walks across the stage. I disconnect from the RuneNet, shut my screen away, and focus on the room around me. The new princess is at the back of the stage. I shouldn't say new. She was always the princess, but new to us—her lowly subjects, given she recently had her investiture. She's striking, curvy, with sharp cut hair, and every inch of her exposed arms and chest are smothered in Collection tattoos. I suck in a breath.

To gain a Collection tattoo, you have to study a mansion, master its magic before the building will choose to bestow a permanent connection with it to you. I'd heard the princess was powerful, but with that many tattoos, she must wield a colossal amount of power.

The room is packed with magicians. Some I know, many more I don't. I sniff. Most of these pathetic try-hards don't worry me. Even the ones I do recognise, like Aurelia, Jezebel and Valence, can't come close to touching my skill.

Neither mother nor father had the time to bring me here. They used to take me to competitions when I was training—when they cared enough about my results to place their expectations on me.

'Now, Bella, you understand your results reflect on us. You must try your best, child.'

I suppress a shudder as mother's voice rings through my head. Today, they couldn't care less. I have my own reputation to uphold—or fix, I should say. I'm not sure what's worse, the fact they used to care too much or the fact that now, they don't care at all. All this is to say, they're no longer vying for parents of the year publicly, but the weight of their expectations is still a giant pain in my arse.

No matter, I will win the Runic Games, and then they'll

have to acknowledge the fact I've finally achieved something, finally made something of myself.

My pocket vibrates. I pull out my video orb and clench my jaw for two reasons. One, my childhood rival made these fucking orb devices and, much as I hate to admit it, they're deeply useful. And two, because I'm about to have my ear chewed off.

I wave a hand over the orb, and mother's face appears.

"Mother," I say through gritted teeth and head to the side of the room and out onto the balcony before anyone can overhear our conversation. I pull out a set of earbuds and connect them to the orb just to be doubly sure no one can hear.

The sea air whips around me, making a shiver wash down my back. There's a short coffee table and a couple of chairs in the corner, so I sit in one, rest my feet on the table and pop one of the mints I lifted from the Games Maker at the front desk into my mouth.

"What do you want? It needs to be quick. They're starting the welcome talk in a second." I practically growl the words.

"Now dear, is that any way to speak to your mother?"

I glare at her, waiting for this charade to end. She won't have called unless she wants something.

Her eyes harden, and her mouth forms a little pinch that reminds me of the tightest arsehole I've ever seen. Here we go.

"We need to discuss a transgression that has been brought to my attention."

I open my mouth to protest that I only trapped Lady Gwendolyn's micro pig in a lattice cage, popped it on a raft, and left it to float about Lake Montagu because I thought the boring bitch could lighten up a bit. But I close my mouth when I realise she could mean the fact I stole Lord Shenley's latex thongs and gimp mask and strapped them to the front of his carriage like summer bunting.

What? It was funny.

Then I remember a string of other shit I've done and realise I have no idea which of the many indiscretions she could be referring to.

"How could you deflower Lord and Lady Pembridge's daughter?"

Ah. That.

I snort out a laugh. "Deflower? Gosh, mummy, you must be so proud of your daughter for being a horticultural pervert."

She bristles. "Well, I... er..."

I roll my eyes. "Lex is nearly thirty. The fact she's unmarried and still a vir— sorry, *was* a virgin has nothing to do with me. It's not my fault she prefers pussy over peen."

"Beatrice Blythe, you wash your mouth out immediately. Vile, crassness." She wipes her hand over her mouth, mortified.

I have to bite the inside of my lip to stop my mouth twitching. Gods, she's so easy to wind up. Something shifts in her expression. A sneer spreads across her lips and funnels right into her eyes. It unnerves me and I am never unsettled.

"Now you listen to me, you ungrateful little shit. Your father and I have had enough of your nonsense. You will win this competition or—"

"Or what?" I snap. And I know I shouldn't. I know damn well I'm antagonising an already irritated woman, but for fucks sake, her unfulfilled dreams and expectations are exhausting. Perhaps she should worry more about maintaining her own reputation rather than assuming I will do it for her.

Her expression turns to ice. "You will win, Beatrice. You will restore your reputation, wash all this Roman nonsense clean. Or we will disinherit you."

My heart stops. She wouldn't dare. No. This is just her usual bullshit designed to push me to my limit, make me work harder, shine her fucking reputation a little brighter. I throw a mint up in the air and catch it straight in my mouth. "Actually, Mother, there's no evidence connecting me to his crimes. It's all rumour and circumstantial hearsay. I can't be convicted of shit."

Which is convenient for me. I still don't know who my goddess in shining armour is—because there was, in fact, ample evidence connecting me to Roman. And I should definitely be in prison.

"You know damn well how insinuation can damage a family." Her lips are all wrinkled and pouty.

"Do you have a point, or are you just calling to berate me?"

She huffs. "As I was saying, you will win, or you will be married off to a reputable Lord and produce an heir that will represent our family in a manner becoming of the Blythe name."

This makes me sit up. Now, I've always known a political marriage was my destiny. You don't grow up in a house like mine, with the weight of two thousand years of legacy without knowing your marriage will be a political bartering funfair. But whenever it came up, mother always agreed I would have a say. I'd be able to at least influence the short list. To take that away...

"You wouldn't dare," I breathe.

"Try me. I don't care who you fuck in your own time,

daughter. But I've had it up to here with your debasing of our family name. I'll have it no more. You will toe the line or you will give me a grandchild who will. The choice is yours."

I start to protest, but the orb goes dead.

"*Fuck*," I scream and kick the table across the balcony.

I stand, shove the balcony doors open and drag my case with me. My raging is interrupted when I slam into someone and stumble. Before I hit the deck, a hand grabs me.

Remy.

Oh, well, this is just delightfully fucking wonderful. I yank myself out of her grip ready to give her a mouthful, too, when my skin prickles and I realise she wasn't the one to knock me over. She just stopped to help—a fact that irritates me further and I can't finger why.

"Well, well, well. Look what legacy trash we have here."

"Alba Merrick. What a displeasure seeing you here," I sneer. I glance at the stage, hoping the organisers will hurry up and start. While the seats have started to fill, the stage remains empty, which means I'll have to deal with Alba.

She steps up to me. "Oh honey, the only thing you'll be seeing is my back disappearing over the finish line. I can't believe they let wasters like you enter."

I smile, really pouring in as much sweetness and delight as I can. Then I grab her collar and push my lips onto hers, giving her a brief kiss. She freezes up in a way that screams of repressed denial. So I lean into her ear and whisper low enough only she can hear.

"See, I think you have a secret penchant for trash like me."

She shoves me off. "Go fuck yourself Bella."

"A-plus comeback there, Albs," I smirk and glance at

Remy, who's possibly even stiffer than Alba was. Gods, what is with everyone today?

A pale man with hair as dark and feathery as a crow sidles up behind Alba. Outstanding. One Merrick wasn't enough.

"Gabe," I spit.

"Miss Blythe," his nose and mouth point like a beak. Yeah, it definitely wasn't them who hacked me. You can tell there's fuck all going on between their ears. It's the dazed and vacant looks that give it away.

"I'm amazed Lady Blythe is even letting you out in public. How you're related to her I'll never know," Alba sneers.

"Gods Alba, I know my mum's a MILF, but if you're that desperate you should have just said. I'm sure I can arrange a date."

Her nostrils flare so wide I swear she'll take off. Next to me, Remy shifts, stands a little taller. All my least favourite people in one place. Exactly how I wanted to start the Runic Games. At least I can train my sights on them all.

Gabe looks down his nose at Remy, his lip curling as if he can smell something gross. "If it isn't New Imperium's latest celebrity Borderling."

Alba sucks in a little gasp as if even she's surprised he'd use the word. Borderling is an awful insult. I might dislike Remy but I'd never call her that.

I step right up to Gabe, not giving a flying fuck that I only reach his chest. And I stab a finger into his solar plexus, the hum of magic frizzing at the tip; a threat, a warning, a promise.

"Jealousy is an ugly look, Gabe. But then I suppose it matches your personality."

"Well, isn't this pleasant? Should I commiserate for you now or after I win?" he says and steps away from me.

Alba sticks her beak-nose in the air. "Must be awful for you," she says.

"What's that?" I ask, indulging the wench.

"Knowing you're only here because of your parents' money. Not because of your skill."

I want to punch her. It takes every ounce of self-control not to lash out. Not because of her pathetic jibes, but because she hits a little too close to home. My parents would never pay for me to enter this competition, gods forbid. But there is this little sliver of doubt that likes to play with me. What if I'm not good enough? What if I actually can't meet their expectations? Of course, it's all psychological bullshit. I'm beyond brilliant. But we all have our off days.

Remy steps between us, as if trying to calm things. Trust me, Remy, I am calm. Calmly plotting their fucking demise.

"Oh, Alba…" I coo. "It takes legacy trash to know legacy trash. Let's not be name calling, hey?"

She narrows her eyes at me, but her brother tugs at her arm.

I blow her a kiss.

She spins on her heel and vanishes into the crowd.

I scan Remy's face, trying to work out if it's her that's been fucking with me. Someone wants access to my RuneNet, access to me. The Merricks might enjoy the smack talk but what reason do they really have to hate me? No. Remy is far more likely the one fucking with me. I narrow my eyes at her. What I want to know is why. Is it because she knows I was working with Roman? She is the city's sweetheart after she jailed him. To my surprise,

Remy's lips are twitching like she's trying to stifle laughter.

"You can fuck off too," I snap.

"Now, now, we all know you like me more than the Merricks..." She raises an eyebrow at me.

I'm sorry, what? Perhaps she's taken the rod out of her backside at last and that is quite the unexpected turn of events.

I round on her, take a sudden step forward. She hesitates, steps back as if my proximity to her is unsettling. Good. I like her unsettled, means I'm more likely to win. Her bottom lip drops, her breathing hitches.

Oh, I can have fun with this. Does she have the hots for me? I thought we had left that in the past. Is that why she's hacking into my accounts? She's obsessed with me?

I step into her personal space. She flinches like she's going to move back. But then she surprises me again me by holding her ground. We're so close I can smell her perfume. The rich scent of bergamot and vetiver. I close my eyes, lean in, and inhale. Remy's breath hitches another notch.

Oh gods, this is fun. I do enjoy knowing I've unnerved her. Though the knowledge sends a pulse of electricity right to my clit. How inconvenient. I thought at least *I'd* left that in the past. Suddenly this isn't so fun.

I snap my gaze to hers. She runs a hand through her ice white hair. Her throat bobs.

"You can be a real dick, Bella."

I let my tongue run over my lips and hold her dark eyes in my gaze. "Perhaps. But we both know that's why you've always wanted to fuck me, *Remy*."

Her jaw flickers like she's going to challenge me.

"Nice to see you're appreciating your freedom." Her top lip curls.

There's no way.

"I have no idea what you're talking about," I whisper.

This time, Remy is the one leaning in. Her breath trickles over my ear, sending shivers straight down my spine and into my pussy. I loathe this woman. I'm not sure if it's because of her genuine brilliance with runes. Our long-standing must-be-better-score-higher-kick-your-ass rivalry, or that despite years of competing both on and off the digital field, she is the only person with the lady balls to play me at my own game. She also happens to be the only one who won't stand for my bullshit. And isn't that the turn on? Not that I'd admit that, either.

"You owe me, Bella Blythe. And I always collect my debts."

She leans back; her perfect smug lips drawn into a pout that could break hearts. For the first time, I'm stunned into silence. Not least because she's referring to the kiss she stole from me... The one I stole back...

Okay, okay, okay, fine. That was a lie. She didn't kiss me first; I kissed her. But I swear it was because I was under extreme stress. So yes, I caved and kissed her—but that's a secret I will take to my fucking grave. And I'll gut any bitch that says different. And no, I don't want to talk about this right now.

Anyway, back to this revelation: I'm stunned silent because it was *her*. Remy fucking Reid is the reason I'm free?

Why the hell did she do it?

I'd half wondered if Roman had gone and lost his head, had a moment of genuine moral conscience and had someone cover them for me. But I put paid to that notion when I got the first note. But that is a story for a different day.

But Remy?

Remy? Miss moral and upstanding, do-good professor, on-the-side-of-her-extremely-busy-business-Reid?

That is unexpected.

Which begs the question why?

Remy's hand comes to my chin and pushes my mouth shut. There's a moment between us, her hand still on my jaw. The realisation of what she did, the fact she broke the law to protect me, crashes into reality and my expression bugs wide, wide, wide.

What the ever-loving fuck?

Our eyes lock, and an intensity that's suffocating passes between us. I can't breathe. I have to know why she did it. Why she'd take a risk like that for me?

"But you hate m—" her thumb silences me, pressing my lips shut.

"You're welcome." And then she's gone, vanishing into the crowd, and I'm left standing there, my heart pounding between my ribs with the knowledge that Remy fucking Reid is the one who saved me from prison.

CHAPTER 4

BELLA

Remy strides to the front of the crowd near the stage. The seats are almost full now, the hubbub of excited chatter waiting for the welcome speeches to begin reaching fever pitch. Remy flings her jacket over her shoulder like she's all chill, and winding me up hasn't flustered her.

She forgets. It might be vicious warfare between us on the rune field, but I've known her a long time. Remy fucking Reid can't hide shit from me. See, I've watched her form runes, I've watched her compete. I know the way her hands move and vibrate around magic. I've memorised the precise way her runes form in the air, the swish and wave as she threads them into the RuneNet. I can recognise every eye twitch, the quirk of her lips, a shift in her constantly stiff posture.

Just like I knew something was wrong at the intercity games. She came third in the qualifiers. Just couldn't form her runes quick enough. I'd heckled the shit out of her. But she didn't heckle back. Remy's far more gracious than me, so she didn't always bite, so it wasn't the lack of smack talk that gave it away. It was the curve of her eyes, something buried behind them.

I went to her after the qualifiers were over. It was one of those strange moments in the dorms, just us, no one looking, no mentors or competitors and we talked. I asked what was wrong, it took a little nudging. Her father had abandoned them when she was young, but she'd found out that morning he'd died before they had a chance to reconcile. I held her.

It was one of those moments that just happened and we never spoke about again. Like a secret we'd both rather forget. Only the bitch must have felt better the next day because she kicked my ass. My point is, I know her.

Remy halted mid-stride as someone fawns over her. She smiles, gracious, and signs a piece of paper. I roll my eyes. When the fan girl leaves, she takes a seat in the front row. I tut. "Geek."

I make my way to the rear of the welcome hall. It's too stuffy near the stage. Too many people, too close to the truth of what Remy just told me. I stride down the aisle between the two sets of seating and towards the marble pillars at the back of the room. I stand next to one and crack a window; sea air rushes in and calms my mind. What the hell was Remy thinking?

I dislike owing anyone a debt. Least of all her.

It does leave me with a question. Who is helping Roman try to get to me? There aren't many other people here who have motive or means.

Remy glances over her shoulder. Her big brown eyes find mine, and she grins. Dick.

Her big, stupid, dark eyes glimmer at me and then she has the gall to mouth "You owe me," and grin.

I ball my fists. The only solace I take is the fact that those same big, stupid, dark eyes give everything away. Probably why I used to beat her at card games when we were apprentices. Because competing all day wasn't enough for us. All I had to do was stare into those big stupid eyes and I'd know whether she was bluffing. It would incense her.

I smile to myself as magicians, games makers and dignitaries walk on stage. Marcel Corbin is at the head of them all. My fingers twitch. The urge to hurl a poisoned lattice cage at him on stage is overwhelming. But alas, I sit on my hands instead. I've got to win this competition. I can hardly murder one of the judges before the thing has even started. Not that I would. I'd make his balls fall off or something less lethal.

Shame, though. It would be fun to watch him writhe on stage. He caused Roman and I no end of problems while I was training. I swear, sometimes it felt like we were in a pantomime. To this day, I'm not sure who despised who the most: me and Remy or Roman and Marcel. He strides across the stage and takes a seat. He waves at the crowd and nods at Remy—his ex-apprentice—on the front row.

I have a fleeting moment of sadness that Roman isn't here. But that fool should have let things lie. It's his own fault he's in prison. He let revenge blind him. Took everything too seriously. He should have listened to me when I told him to let the crown go.

Speaking of which, Morrigan sweeps to the front of the stage and stands in front of a plinth in the centre.

She opens her arms, and the crowd falls to silence. Those that were chattering and standing all sit.

"Magicians, friends, family, legacies, and honoured guests. Welcome to the ninety-ninth Runic Games."

Applause breaks out around the room until she raises her hands for silence. There's a woman behind her in the corner of the stage, shoulder-length hair, leaning against the staging in the shadows. She's staring at Morrigan with a look of longing in her eye.

I wonder.

There are rumours sweeping the Daily Imperium gossip columns that the princess bats for my team...The palace hasn't confirmed or denied anything, only promised a grand ball to announce a royal wedding later in the year.

Something about the way the woman looks at her tells me the rumours might be true. She's awful familiar, too. I wrack my mind, trying to remember where I've seen her, and then it clicks. She bumped into me at an auction at the end of summer. Same day I met Remy. Pieces slot together, connections forming in my mind.

That's how Remy knew I was responsible for the lattices protecting Roman. My gloves were off, she would've seen my Collection tattoos.

Son of a whore.

I do owe her a debt.

Morrigan interrupts my thoughts.

"For those of you who aren't Daily Imperium readers, my name is Morrigan, and I am the princess heir."

There are a couple of short sharp gasps from those magicians living under rocks, and the rest of the room breaks out into applause.

"I am honoured to be opening the games this year, as well as presiding over the competition. And I'll be presenting the winners with their prize at the end of the challenges in three weeks' time."

She takes a sip of water and continues.

"The grand prize is fifty-thousand coin, and a personal addition this year: the coveted role of Royal Rune Master. A role that will serve the crown and me personally for the next five years until the next games. It is the most sought-after role and highest-ranking security position in New Imperium, standing even above the Assassin's Guild Master."

An audible ooh and ahh ripples through the room, and it takes a significant effort to stop myself calling out to all these peasants to 'give up now fuckers'. That role is mine, and no one is going to get in my way. Yes, it's partly a fuck you to my mother, but also, it's for me. I want this role. I've worked myself to the bone for the last ten years to reach this competition. Don't think I've ever wanted anything more.

Morrigan calls for silence, and when she gets it, continues her welcome speech.

"Each set of games has a unique focus. This year is no different." She glances down at a scroll on her lectern.

"The last games focused on mansion security. It bought about the invention of the mansion network—the communications system connected to the RuneNet that many of you living in the newer areas of the city now benefit from."

Remy nods aggressively at the front of the seating area. Gods, she's so keen, it's almost cute. *Almost.* If it weren't for the ridiculous way her hair spikes up, the coif bobbing up and down with enthusiasm.

She kept me out of prison.

Fuck. The thought won't leave.

I glance back at her. Remy was just as keen when I met her a decade ago. I'd only been with Roman a month. Can't have been more than sixteen or seventeen at the time. I was on a busy New Imperium street. I forget which, but it was for a club Roman wanted to *'acquire'*. He'd been struggling to broker a deal. The club was overpriced, according to him, but the seller was reluctant to go lower.

So Roman sent me to hack into the club security system. He was planning to have his men burgle the property to discredit the owner and force the price down. Regardless of your ethical code, give Roman credit. It was a smart idea. Albeit not the best way to train an apprentice.

I didn't mind being thrown into the deep end. I've never enjoyed learning theory—unlike Professor Remy, who spends way too much time in the books and not enough doing the do.

Anyway, it was close to midnight; I remember because Remy was wearing a set of white overalls, and as she stepped out of the darkness and under a spotlight on the building's roof, I was stunned. For a second, I thought an angel had come to tell me to be a good girl and not break into the club. It's mortifying to admit—and I never would in public. But I mean come on; she is pale as water, wearing white, with snow-coloured hair. What the hell was I supposed to think?

Of course, she opened her mouth, and I realised immediately the mistake I'd made. Three paltry words that annoyed me enough they sowed the first seed of irritation... and alright, maybe a little bud of lust.

Fucking Marcel had sent her to update the club's security systems. I guess the owner must have had some smarts because he went out of his way to protect himself, knowing Roman wanted to buy what he was selling.

I stood there blinking at Remy, knowing she'd beaten me to the club's data wall, and I wasn't going to be 'adjusting' any security after all. Her hands were white hot, vibrating at the data wall, runes flying off her, as she worked so fast I could barely keep up.

She was everything. I was consumed, mesmerised. I couldn't work out if I wanted to be her or be fucking her. She was adding layers and layers of runes that I was only just learning about. Runes I couldn't even read, let alone code.

That was before Roman taught me the old language. The old language is a bit like a runic cheat code. If you can read and spell those base runes, then you can do anything. Too bad for new apprentices they don't teach it anymore.

I realised fast that even if I convinced her I was there innocently, it would have taken me all night to decode her security. And that was if I was even capable—which I absolutely wasn't with her standing right there.

Those big, stupid dark eyes caught sight of me, and she grinned wide as she finished the line of runic code, not even looking at the runes she was creating.

Show off.

She genuinely waited until she was done, like she didn't have a care in the world. Finally, she turned to me. "Are you lost?"

You have to understand, what happened next was because I panicked. Not because she was tall and svelte and slightly masculine, with her hands all dirtied up from working on the data panels.

Or the fact I was a blossoming, fresh-outta-the-closet lesbian with a vagina so horny it would've put even the most virulent of bachelors to shame.

No. Nothing to do with any of those things.

As she approached, towering above me, her allure swallowed me whole. What can I say? I lost my fucking mind.

I threw my hands up like the ridiculous teenager I was and... gods, I can't believe I'm admitting this. I giggled.

Giggled for fucksakes.

Can you imagine? Me? I do not giggle. I stab and swear and fuck. I don't fucking giggle.

Whilst I was doing this onetime only—I swear—giggle, I managed to cough out, "Yes. Lost."

"I see," she says.

"I—er. Was in the club and all my friends decided to get some air, and I must have drunk too much because I ended up here instead of down there." I pointed over the roof and smile up at her.

She stepped into my personal space, smelling like desire. The waves of bergamot were paired with something citrus back then, but it washed over me and made my eyes roll shut for just a second.

"I'm afraid I couldn't possibly let such a deeply attractive young woman like you stay lost on an evening like this. Perhaps you'd care for me to show you the way out?"

I *blushed* for fucksake. Pathetic. I blushed so hard it flared up my cheeks and ran all the way down to my toes and maybe between my legs.

"I... I mean... yes. Thank you, that would be great." I was a dithering idiot.

I hate what happened next. She had the gall to turn around and say, "All it will cost is a single kiss."

My mouth dropped open. It's rare I'm taken by surprise. I pride myself on being the one to do that to others. Stupid teenage hormones. I'd just come out, but until that night, I'd only ever kissed boys and that one non-binary magician from a previous rune competition. But never a girl.

And a single kiss?

Such a small price.

I figured one kiss couldn't hurt.

Of course, I'm groaning now, because that's why the fairy tales warn you that a single kiss can break a curse, heal a heart, save a life. It can change everything.

"A single kiss?" I breathed.

"Mmmhmm."

My brain shut off. My feet had already pushed me onto tippy toes, my hands found their way up her shoulders and around her neck.

I wanted her.

All of her, right there on the roof. I coveted her skill; desired her mouth, craved the smell of her. I'd have given her whatever she commanded. She'd dared me to kiss her. Shocked me with the request. That was the worst bit. Everything about her was surprising.

She leant down, the air full of her heady perfume, filling my senses with hunger. Her lips parted. The noise of the street below and the club goers inside fizzled into nothing. The stars above us winked out, until the only things left in the entire of New Imperium were me and her and the anticipation of a kiss held between us.

She hovered, waiting for me to close the gap, to give her permission. It was my debt to pay, of course, my kiss to give.

So I tilted up a millimetre further and placed my lips on hers.

She kissed me like I was the entire universe, wrapped in a single breath. Like I was every star in the sky, and every diamond in the earth. Like she was starving and hungered only for me.

And fuck, I still remember how she tasted.

Like gold and clouds and summer evenings.

Like heaven and addiction.

Like the end of something and the start of everything.

One kiss ruined everything.

On stage, Morrigan claps her hands, snapping me out of my memories. "This year, our theme will be prison security."

Something about that unsettles me. But I assume the crown has insisted on the theme, what with Roman's recent imprisonment. Perhaps they want the greatest minds working on upgrading Remy's latest invention. Gods, she's such a relentless overachiever.

"Gathered here are fifty of the best runic magicians in New Imperium. We expect great things from you. But be warned, you will be tested to the limits of your abilities. You'll have to think outside of the realm of possibility and push yourselves to extend your powers. There is one change to the normal proceedings this year."

Her expression grows grave as she scans the audience.

"Due to the nature of some of this year's challenges, you'll work in, as well as be scored as teams."

The crowd erupts into a cacophony of jeering and gasps. The only two who don't seem to mind are the fucking Merricks, who high five each other like the children they are. Pathetic.

How will this work? Two people can't be Rune Master. There can only ever be one winner. My chest flames hot. My neck burns, fists ball. Who the hell am I going to be paired with? They better not be dead weight. I've got my hands full winning this competition without having to shepherd some half-baked magician with me.

Morrigan bangs the lectern hard enough the room responds. "Settle down, please. To explain. There will still only be one winner. Each contestant will be scored individually as well as in their teams. Meaning, those more adept at teamwork will score points easier, pushing them up the leaderboard and closer to the coveted prize."

I scan the crowd, trying to establish which competitor I want to be partnered with. I'll have to choose strategically. Someone who will submit to my way of doing things but also be a good team player and not a complete fuck up with runes. I cut my thoughts short when the woman who was lurking at the back of the stage strolls up to Morrigan, holding a glass bowl with cogs in.

"Oh, holy mother of magician gods, no." I stand. Sit. And wipe my mouth, horror widening my eyes.

They're picking pairings out of a fucking hat? The woman holding the bowl hands it over. Morrigan's fingers skim hers and I know then, for certain, the rumours are true, and this will be the royal wedding of the century.

Morrigan dips her hand into the bowl. I can't look, so I cover my eyes. As if they're not letting us pick the dead-weight we have to carry. As long as it's not the Merricks or Remy, I think I'll be okay.

"The first team will be Jezebel Eldric and Macy Lins."

The teams come thick and fast. She calls pairing after pairing, and with each successive pairing I grow more tense. The Merrick siblings get called and predictably end up together. I actually feel relieved they're not partnered with me.

"Aurelia Fitzgerald and Octavia Kendleton form the next team."

My heart races, blood pounds in my ears. I catch sight of Remy turning in her chair, a frown on her brow. She's trying to work out who's left. I know because I'm doing the same. Her eyes meet mine and widen right as Morrigan calls.

"Remy Reid, you'll be..."

Time slows. I can't breathe. In fact, I'm pretty sure my

heart ceases to beat. There's only the roar of blood in my ears and the piercing stare of Remy holding my gaze. She closes her eyes in slow motion as if she's resigned herself to her fate. As if she already knows who she's being paired with and hates it.

What are the chances of it being me? One in—I glance around do a quick calculation—twenty-five? Close enough. The odds are in our favour. It won't happen.

Remy opens her eyes, and her gaze never leaves mine.

Time snaps back and Morrigan flips the cog open. "Partnered with... Beatrice Blythe."

Ah, shit.

CHAPTER 5

REMY

Well, this is unfortunate. Of course, I knew as soon as Stirling stepped onto the stage and handed Morrigan the bowl that this was a setup. I'm not sure whether I'm more distressed that Morrigan failed to mention the level of proximity she was forcing me into, or that I'm now teamed up with the most infuriating woman in New Imperium.

I'm here to win this.

I understand the severity of the Roman situation, and that she wants me to investigate Bella... but this is my career, my business on the line, and I absolutely cannot work with that woman. What the hell is Morrigan thinking?

I glance over my shoulder to find Bella turning a deep shade of plum. Her normally plump lips have thinned into a furious line, and the look she's giving Morrigan is akin to a furious rottweiler.

Except, I can't take Bella seriously.

I'm going to have to revise my former statement.

I'd say she was more like a very angry poodle. Sort of cute but frazzled around the edges, with teeth.

My heart rate elevates as I stare at what I can only describe as a murderous rage descending over Bella's features. By the warmth pooling between my thighs, I'd say I was rather aroused by the whole debacle. I might not want to work with her, but there's something wild and feral about angry Bella. It creates a burning need in me to tame her. Make her get on her knees like a good girl and do as she's told.

Bella lets out something between a huff, a growl, and a suppressed scream, grabs her bag, and storms off as the final sets of names are called out.

Movement, as new teammates gather, shake hands and make acquaintances. They exit together at the rear of the room where the Games Makers dish out envelopes and keys.

Marcel jumps off the stage and gives me a playful nudge. "Unfortunate luck of the draw, hey?"

"Reminds me of the good old days. If only I had you to help me strategise against her."

"You don't need me anymore, Remy. You're the city's latest highflyer." He gives my arm a squeeze and heads off to help some of the other teams. But his words sink into my veins. I know what everyone thinks of me, and that makes it worse.

When the hall is more than half cleared, I notice Quinn strutting into the room. She waves me over to the balcony, so I drag my bag to meet her. I step onto the balcony, and a frigid breeze whips under my clothes. The sea is murky, a whirling maelstrom of darkness frothing beneath us. In the distance, three tall ships hover on the horizon under a stormy cloud. I shiver and glance back. The giant chamber is more or less empty now. Marcel waves at me as he leaves, and I nod to him.

It will be nice to catch up and perhaps have a gin or two with him one evening. It's been a long time since we had more than a few fleeting sentences exchanged at an event. My dad left when we were young, and in a way, Marcel stood in for him. Not that he'd ever admit to it, and not that I'd ever place that burden on him. But it was one of those things I knew from the way he'd slip me a couple of extra coin on the weeks I'd head into the Borderlands to see Ma. Or the way he'd push me through extra hours of training. No other apprentice trained as hard as I was... save maybe Bella.

But Roman is and always was a bastard. He trained her hard because of his thirst for more, rather than a desire to see her do well. Maybe that's why I always gave her allowances. No one ever seemed to treat Bella right. Even as a teen, her relationship with her parents seemed fraught. Not that she'd admit it, but I observed enough to know.

Marcel was just as secretive about his background as Bella, but I wheedled enough out of him to understand he and his Ma were on their own too. He hated his father—not that he talked about him much. I think that's why Marcel took such a shine to me. We shared a hurt that couldn't be put into words. He collected people, *family*. Made them family. A brother here, an old mentor uncle there. He created the family he didn't have growing up.

"Hey, Rem," Quinn says and nods in the direction Bella took off in. "That went down well, then."

"Did you know Morrigan was going to do that?" I ask.

She stares at the floor. "I mean, after the meeting yesterday, I'd guessed."

I shake my head. "I should've known. Morrigan owes me big time."

"At least you'll be able to get the most evidence this way. You can watch her every move."

Quinn toes a stained spot on the balcony floor. "I remember the way you looked at her in that auction, the way you kissed her hand."

My heart clenches. "I told you, Bella and I shared a kiss once when we were teens. It was nothing. When I was apprenticed to Marcel. We actually spent a fair bit of our youth together. Marcel and Roman put us through the ropes, trained us hard, expected us to attend every competition and trial and workshop we could. Which meant we spent an excessive amount of time together. Much as we dislike each other, I know her better than most. But like I said, it means nothing. It's all old history. I can't risk my reputation. I won't. Not for anyone."

Quinn's brows furrow and release, a slow smile building on her lips. "So, you didn't monologue a giant justification to me just then because you *don't* feel anything for her?"

"Must you be so trying? Everything is fine. Calandra and Morrigan were clear. We need to find the culprit. I am objective and professional. I won't put Morrigan and Stirling's safety at risk. Let alone my reputation and therefore my livelihood."

I'm saying this with all the confidence I can muster, but inside I'm all twisted up. I want what I'm saying to be true.

I'm so distracted I have to ask Quinn to repeat herself. She leans back, folds her arms. "So you just objectively find her attractive?"

"Right exactly. Wait. No. What?"

Quinn buckles with laughter, panting the words between laughs. "Love how you're not actually confirming or denying one way or another."

I purse my mouth, refusing to comment.

So Quinn continues once she regains her control. "Okay, okay, I'll leave it alone. You still don't think it's her, then?"

I shake my head. "Someone here is out to destroy the crown, and I will find out who, but my gut says it's not her."

"You're sure?"

"What's the motive? You and I both know she dodged a bullet with the Roman debacle. Her parents are proud legacies—you know the types. Why would she risk it?"

"I take your point. I guess… just be careful."

I laugh. "I'll be fine. Bella might be deeply petty, an incessant pest, and completely unmanageable. But I—"

"Says the most ostentatiously pompous academic I've ever known," Bella barks from the balcony door.

"Oh delightful, her royal highness is back," I say, noting the fact that thankfully, she didn't pick up on me calling her attractive.

I am going to find whoever is trying to help Roman escape. I'm going to win this competition, bolster security in his prison and win the role of Royal Rune Master. Maybe then I'll feel like I've earned the reputation I've got.

Bella shoves a hand on her hip, narrows her eyes at me. "Oh, so you have a thing for princesses now?" She fires a glare at the stage.

"Gods, no."

She sniggers, and I take a long, deep breath, pushing what I hope is patience down to the bottom of my lungs.

I straighten myself up. "Look, there's obviously been some kind of mistake. Her royal highness is still there.

Perhaps there's an opportunity for us to rejigger the teams, a little swaparoo?"

Bella guffaws. "Swaparoo? What are you, twelve?"

"Well, I don't see you trying to fix this," I snap.

Quinn raises a single eyebrow so far up her forehead I'm amazed it's still attached. "I highly doubt Morrigan will bend to this, but you don't get anything if you don't ask."

The hell was Morrigan thinking? I am clearly capable of spying on Bella from inside this competition. I just need to track her digital rune activity. It's as simple as that. Morrigan doesn't need to torture me by forcing me into a team with her. I glance at Quinn. Her eyes are wide as orbs, her shoulders rocking in silence, a rhythmic wheezing slipping from her throat, each one forming a little mist-cloud in the ocean air.

Marvellous. I glare at her. But she shakes her head at me, unable to help.

"For the love of gods, tell me there is a way out of this —" I gesticulate in Bella's general direction.

But Quinn just wipes a tear away and strolls back into the hall.

"This? Who are you calling 'this'? Run out of big words, have we, Reid? If anyone needs a way out of this, it's me."

"Reid? Resorting to last names like savages, are we, *Blythe*?"

This can't be happening. I march into the hall and up to the stage and growl at Morrigan under my breath.

"Are you fucking kidding?" I say.

She hops off the stage and smiles sweetly, her lips barely move as she answers.

"Now, now Remy. You know what we discussed yesterday."

"Yes, but there was no mention of being on the same team.

It's completely unnecessary." I'm snarling, with absolutely no mind to the consequences of how I'm talking. She might be the heir to the throne, but this was a dick move as my friend.

"Think of it as additional precautions. We're not taking any risks."

Bella sidles up next to us. Morrigan exaggerates as she opens her arms and clasps Bella's hand in it. "Bella, dear. Lovely to meet you."

Bella, to my utter shock, pulls the sweetest expression I've ever seen. It's sickening.

"Your highness," she curtsies.

Curtsies? Bella? What am I even seeing? The fake smile I understand, but a curtsey like a fan girl?

"Call me Morrigan, please," Morrigan's expression is as pleasant as Bella's, only I can tell she's tense by the tightness of her eyes.

"An honour, Morrigan." Bella bobs into another curtsey, and I have to bite my lip to stop the hysterical laughter from spilling out.

"Your highness, there must have been a mistake. Remy and I... well. We don't exactly get along. We've a long history of, umm... well, decidedly not getting along. Our mentors were rivals, you see, it was bred into us."

Morrigan presses her lips together and nods, sage and calm. This performance is priceless. "I understand, but the drawing was done randomly, and the pairings are final. Perhaps this is a chance to settle old quarrels. It would be a shame to see you leave the competition at the end of the first round because you can't make it work. Now please excuse me, I have a prior engagement to attend." She pats Bella's hand like an aged monarch and disappears.

Bella mumbles something under her breath, which I'm

certain should not be repeated in polite company, and then storms off to the exit and snatches our envelopes and keys off the Games Maker.

"Well?" she barks. "Are you coming or not?"

She slices open the envelope, snatches her bag up and vanishes out the door. I trot to catch up with her. Bella veers out of the main room into a dim corridor, lit by lanterns containing ice flames hung on the walls at intermittent junctures.

The entire palace has a blue haze. Every winding path we take, every corridor is some shade of blue, from glacial pale to ocean deep or vibrant sky on a summer morning.

We approach the heart of the palace and a winding circular staircase that, when I crane up, makes my vision blur it soars so high. It twists and spirals and disappears into a speck in the roof. It's like a hallucinogenic illusion.

Bella powers up the stairs. Five minutes of climbing later though, and she's slowed down as much as I have. We're both glistening with the hint of sweat. A line traces down the edge of her temple and onto her jaw, and I have the urge to wipe it clean. I resist when she fires a poisonous glare at me.

When the burn is too much to manage, Bella finally pulls off the staircase and onto a floor. I notice a lift at the other end of the hall at the same time she does.

"Oh for fucks sake," she mumbles.

"Next time, I'll navigate," I say, taking the palace map out of her hand.

She pouts at me; her plump lips forming a perfect shape to kiss. I look away because her expression shoots a bolt of electricity right into my clit.

I don't know what's worse, the fact she's aggressively

annoying or that despite the level of irritation, I still find her exorbitantly attractive.

The thought crosses my mind that we're going to have to share a room for a month. Perhaps if I could just fuck her once... put her on her knees and make her lick my cunt dry, then all these inconvenient desires would simply evaporate? I'd be far better placed to focus on digging up evidence on her.

But it's faulty logic, of course. One can't just fuck these things away.

Can they?

It's not the most farcical idea I've ever had. Perhaps I could set a hypothesis and test—

I'm distracted by Bella taking the key out of an envelope and shoving it against the door fob.

"Let's get one thing straight, Reid. I'm not picking up after you. Pull your weight, keep shit clean, and do half the cooking."

"You're aware there are daily cleaners and a canteen on the first floor?"

Her nostrils flare. "Whatever." She opens the door, slides inside and slams it shut in my face. I try the handle and realise it's definitely locked, so I suck up what little patience I have left and knock.

She opens the door. "What?"

"Are we really going to do this? It will be a long three weeks."

"Maybe I like long weeks." She shoves the door open and turns her back on me.

I make my way to the sitting room. The apartment is an open plan space. There are two doors on the back wall. The two bedrooms, I assume. A huge kitchen with an island in the middle, a balcony with glass doors, a table, chairs, and sofa. Plush sofas in the living room space and a cute glass coffee table. Last, there's a workspace doubling as a dining table the other end of the room. It's more spacious than I expected.

I stow my case, slide onto the sofa, kick a foot up onto my knee, and lean back. I sit up as Bella reappears with two bottles of beer, two shot glasses, and a bottle of rum.

Intriguing.

"Kitchen's stocked." She shuffles on the spot, not quite meeting my eye. "Peace offering…?"

She holds a bottle out to me.

"You sure about that? Sounds more like a question."

"Are you taking it or not?"

I do, in fact, take the glass and the beer.

"For what it's worth, I dislike you intensely, and nothing about this competition is going to change that," Bella says.

"Feeling's mutual, darling," I say and pour both of us a shot. She snatches hers up as I grab mine, both of us slamming the tumblers down simultaneously—like necking shots is a competition.

It's not. But if it were, I wouldn't let her win. In a decade, nothing has changed. Still competing on and off the field.

"I can't believe we're stuck with each other," I say.

"Agreed." She pours our second, third, and then fourth shots, and we sink them in aggressive succession. Each one faster than the last. I win two rounds, she wins three.

I reach for the beer as a haze of alcohol descends over my vision. I need to slow down.

We sit in silence. The warmth of booze settles in my stomach, words form on my tongue. They're hot and thick and so wrong.

I'm not sure what possesses me. It's not the objective professionalism I promised Quinn. Perhaps it's the way she's sitting there on the sofa, her heart-shaped hips, legs crossed, breasts for days. Fuck... the words tumble out before I can retract them.

"You know... you only hate me so much because you want to fuck me."

"Says the kiss thief."

"Oh please, you wanted to know how to get off the rooftop. That was the price. Some would say you gave that kiss willingly."

She shivers, and I'm not sure if it's rage or lust, perhaps a little of both. And this is the real reason I tried so hard to persuade Morrigan away from this course of action. Why I tried again before we came up here. Because as much as this woman infuriates me, even she can't deny the sexual tension between us. It was there that first night on the roof. It was there the night by the lake when I definitely did steal a kiss. It was there in the auction house when I bent and kissed her hand. She knows it as well as I do. And being in close proximity to her, when my reputation is on the line, knowing the crown is watching, is excruciating.

"The last thing I'd ever want to do is fuck you," she says.

"And yet, your breathing has increased, your pupils are dilated, and you were absolutely the one to kiss me first."

She stands up. Sits down. Stands again.

"For an irritation, you're intensely attractive when you're cross with me."

Here's the thing. I might not have time for love, but I most certainly do have time for sex.

And if I'm going to have to room with the most attractive woman I've ever met and I'm not allowed to touch her, then well, I guess me and my hand are going to be well acquainted by the end of this competition.

"And your jaw gets all chiseled when you're trying and failing to flirt." She downs the entire beer and says, "Goodnight."

She retrieves her bag, opens the first door and mumbles, "Oh. Bathroom." Then she walks over to the other door, which she wrenches open, and she freezes.

"You have got to be fucking kidding me."

CHAPTER 6

BELLA

"Where's the other one?" I say, my voice higher, whinier, and definitely drunker than I'd like. The sunset streaks through the room, auburn beams highlighting our problem in a stark, single spotlight.

"Other what?" Remy says from the couch. She stands up and comes to the door. "Oh."

I glance from her to the bed.

She does the same.

There's a pause. A single beat in which our bodies tense. Calculations made, probabilities weighed.

And then there's an explosion of arms and legs and limbs and hysterical screeching and thumping as we collapse on the only bed in the apartment.

"Get off me," I snarl, digging my elbow into her ribs. I shove her, hoping she'll fall off the bed, but she's looped her foot in the bedrails and stays put.

"And what do you plan to do now?" She says, smirking at me. Her body is far too close. I'm hyper aware of where her legs cross mine, where my arm is stuck under her ribs.

"Oh, because you're the pinnacle of maturity, are you, Professor?" I roll my eyes at her.

"I jumped on the bed first."

"And I'm Queen Calandra." I glare at her, pouring as much vicious poison into my stare as I can muster. "Look, you'll have to sleep on the couch."

She snort laughs. "And what, precisely, makes you think I'd do a thing like sleeping on the sofa, when this appears to be a perfectly acceptable bed?" She nudges my shoulder, but not hard enough to knock me off the other side.

"Er, how about the fact that this is a single bed and we can't both fit on it?"

"Yes, that much is evident."

I snap my head at her, my eyes wide. "So... be a gentleman, and get the hell out." I throw my arm toward the door.

She doesn't get off the bed.

"Aww, does the pretty legacy not know how to sleep on a couch?"

I mock shock and cover my mouth. "Aww, the border trash thinks I'm cute."

Her eyes narrow. But she doesn't budge. A scream of frustration builds between my ribs.

"Also, how very fucking dare you. I slept on the floor the night we got trapped in that godsforsaken shipping warehouse. Between naps, you spent the night teasing me while I tried to fix the fucking runic cypher that unlocked the door and got us out. I always clean up after you...?"

She continues to stare at me in silence. Gah, she's infuriating.

"Remy," I hate the way I say her name. Like some bratty sub. Why does she have this effect on me? "I'm not sleeping on the sofa. It's well and truly your turn."

"Do you always remember the nights we spend together?" Remy says with a grin.

It sends flames into my chest. She leans in so close heat pools between us. It's like wildfire in summer. I'm supposed to be angry. I'm supposed to loathe this woman. And I do. I really do.

But every cell in my body is urging me to close the gap, remember what the taste of her lips was like. Just one little kiss won't hurt. Will it?

"Perhaps I enjoyed watching you bent over struggling to hack the data panel, Bella."

Oh my gods, the way she purred my name like molten lust. I can't cope. I want her to say it again. Half of me even considers getting off the bed, until...

She reaches over my body and taps my arse twice—and not in the I'm-going-to-make-you-go-blind-coming kind of way either. "Now, be a good girl, and get on the floor.,"

Is she fucking kidding? The lust turns to boiling fury in a snap. "You patronising, chauvinistic pig."

She's leans back, her head rocking with laughter, and the crosser I get, the harder she laughs.

Fuck her very much. I'll fucking show her. There's no way I'm getting off this bed now. I yank my shoes off.

She glances down at my now shoeless feet.

"You're still sleeping on the floor." She then proceeds to one up me by undoing the top two buttons on her crisp white shirt. She's wearing a dangling necklace that slips between her cleavage and under the still-closed shirt buttons.

I swallow hard. My cheeks flare hot, my body heating alongside. It's rage. It's rage. Must. Hold. On. To. The. Rage.

My eyes drop lower. That's when I notice she's not wearing a bra.

Motherfucker.

It's also when I notice how hard her nipples are. I grit my teeth. She doesn't get to have *that* kind of effect on me.

"If you think looking all hot with your half-open shirt and tailored suit and... and those..."

"Those what?" she says, raising an expectant eyebrow at me.

My tongue slides over my lips. I drag my eyes away and up to hers. "Nipples."

Remy tilts her head at me, an amused curl tugging at the corner of her eyes. "You like my nipples?"

I huff out a frustrated cry and slide my hands to my trousers. I will not lose this bed. It's not even about the sofa anymore. It's the fucking principle.

I unbutton my trousers, yank down the zipper, and shuffle myself out of them. All while precariously clinging to the bed rail and hoping I don't fall off the bed onto my arse. It's not like there's a lot of room.

"What are you doing?" she says as I finally haul myself back to her sightline.

"Upping the stakes, duh. If you won't leave willingly, I'll scare you out."

That makes a laugh erupt from her belly. "You—You—You think getting naked is going to make me leave this bed?"

I open my mouth. But words seem to have vanished. Well, it seemed logical at the time.

She's bolshie now, but she won't be when I'm naked. I

haul my top off. Because clearly my trousers weren't sufficient.

This time, instead of Remy laughing, she's gone as still as death.

I win, motherfucker. Now... off you pop.

But still. She doesn't move. Her lips part, form a thin 'O'. I glance down, wondering what's made her reaction shift. Oh shit. The underwear I'm in is lace, and my nipples are very definitely standing to attention.

Fuck.

I fold my arms over my chest. "Well?" I demand.

Her face darkens. Her eyes glimmer at me, threaded with hunger. "As if I'm backing down that easily."

My eyes glide down her neck, her chest, down, down, down to the slit in her shirt. I swallow hard. My pussy is tight. My jaw flexing. This is not at all going the way I planned.

The urge to reach out and flick open another of her buttons is overwhelming. My fingers twitch with the pressure of resisting.

I love sex, hell, even a one-night stand. But not this. Not with her. I don't trust Remy.

"Bella," Remy says, breathy and deep. My name in her mouth is electric. Goosebumps rise on my skin. As her grin deepens, she unbuttons another notch in her shirt.

She takes her time, as if she's enjoying this. As if she's in control and I'm not the one who upped the stakes.

As if she wants this.

I don't even know what this is.

"You shouldn't look at a girl like that. Gives her the wrong impression," I say. But my words are barely above a whisper.

"Oh, and what impression is that?" she says and shucks

her shirt off, exposing her breasts. They're small and pert and look utterly suckable. Heat floods between my legs. Shit. Shouldn't have thought that. Why isn't there a memory erasing button in our brains? I can't seem to unthink it.

This is all wrong. Remy is annoying, and far too academic and petty, and yet... I can't look away. Obviously, she's my type, if it weren't for her whole personality. Sure, we've kissed once. Okay, fine, twice. But that's a world away from wanting to fuck her.

But... umm... that is... it seems, what I want.

It must be the booze. It has to be. We don't even like each other. We've spent a decade tolerating each other at competitions and meets and the occasional torturous job we found ourselves on.

And yet, and yet...

She's staring at me with that same expression. I shift my body and my bra strap slips down my shoulder. Remy's nostrils flare.

"You're staring at me as if you want to fuck me," I say.

Even saying the words tastes illicit. I suck my bottom lip in, as if that can take my words back. But like my thoughts, they don't erase.

Blood throbs through my body, coalescing where it shouldn't. If she touched me, I'd melt.

Somewhere in the depths of my less-than-sober mind, an alarm bell is ringing. No, scratch that, it's screaming that I should stop. That it will be a mistake, even if it doesn't feel that way now.

"And if"—she waves her hand above the bed—"in some alternate universe, that was true, that even though we dislike each other intensely, I still wanted to fuck you... what then?"

She's looking at me with a ferocity that could evaporate an ocean. Her fingers find their way to my arm, skim my Collection tattoos all the way up to my bicep and under my bra strap. Her touch is lightning. Every inch of my skin she caresses flares golden and hot and electric. She pauses, with her fingers under my strap, like she's waiting for a response. Waiting for me to push her away or pull her close.

Just like she did on that fucking rooftop.

Her fingers are warm, the pads of her skin soft. I want to pull her hand up to my mouth, suck her finger between my lips, and then slide it down my body and into my cunt.

Oh my gods, these thoughts. What the hell is wrong with me?

I don't understand how we ended up here.

Except, when I think about it, that's a lie. Because like the fairytales, I kissed her a decade ago, and everything changed. Was our rivalry wrong all these years? Was it really repressed desire? Suppressed need? I scoff silently. Of course it *wasn't*.

"What drunken bullshit you're spouting!"

"Is it?" the intensity of her expression takes my breath away.

It's just sex. You're an empowered woman, Bella. You can fuck whoever you want. Even your most dedicated rival. Means nothing.

I inch forward, nudging her fingers down my arm, pulling the strap. "If it's not, then...in this hypothetical alternative universe, we would find ourselves in a deeply confusing paradox."

"I see. So a paradox where we dislike each other and yet..."

"And yet we still want to fuck," I finish for her.

"Well, if I were another kind of academic, I'd suggest it

was worth the scientific research to do that. To evaluate the cause and effect... on the, umm, nature of this paradox..."

She leans so close to me that her nose skims down mine, leaving a wake of tingles in its trail. Her lips are millimetres from mine. The *shoulds* and *shouldn'ts* don't seem interesting anymore. I'm far more consumed by this paradox.

I inhale and find my air is filled with the scent of her. Of bergamot and vetiver and books and leather. My eyes seem to shut by themselves. It's deja vu. Like ten years ago, I'm the one that closes the space between us and feather-light touch my lips to hers.

And just like the first time, my world shatters.

She grabs me hard and crushes my body to hers, as if my kiss broke all her barriers. Hard nipples press against my chest. The sensation of her breasts against my lace and skin drives me wild. My knickers stick to me as desire throbs through my body.

Want mixes with the booze, and everything becomes a haze. It's like I ripped the bandages off a decade of frustration.

She kisses me like she's starved. She kisses me like nothing else exists but me. And it's intoxicating. Her hands run down my back, sending skitters of exquisite static down my back. I arch into her.

I want more.

I need more.

I need everything she can give me, and still, I don't think it will be enough.

Gods, if she's not driving my mind to insanity, she's sending my pussy that way. My hands slide to her trousers. I unbuckle them, unzip them. It's only then that she breaks apart long enough to yank them down to reveal boxers. She kicks her trousers off the bed, slides her arm around my back, and unhooks my bra in one swift motion, all the while peppering my skin with kisses.

She slips her hand between my thick thighs and draws her palm over my pussy. I freeze, knowing she will feel how wet I am. It's like a secret I've kept.

And now it's out, I don't know how to cope.

"But you hate me..." she says and nips the fleshy skin between my neck and shoulder.

"Hate is a strong word, Remy. You infuriate me. You frustrate me. You fuel me to want to do better. To beat you."

She snuffles a laugh against my neck.

"We're going to regret this in the morning, aren't we?" she says, bringing her mouth down between my breasts.

"Mm-hmm." I run my fingers through her hair, pushing her head lower, lower. She resists, focusing on my breasts, pulling my bra the rest of the way off. Her hand cups one of my bosoms as her tongue sweeps over my nipple. It hardens instantly. She grins at it as if she's proud of her work. And then she blows cold air over the peak. I lean back, the pleasure mixing with the frigid ache of her breath. It makes my nipple tighten to an almost painful point.

My mother's words ring in my mind. One builds a reputation carefully. You only let them see the pieces you want. I try to hold everything in. Try not to let Remy see how she's making me feel. But a whimper of pleasure slips out.

Her eyes darken with a ferocious hunger. "So we're agreed, this is all for scientific purposes?"

"At this point, Reid, I'd be willing to agree to anything if you'd shut up and fuck me."

She hesitates, "Ten years I've waited for you to kiss me again... I guess it's my turn to steal an orgasm from you."

And so she does.

She climbs up my body, pushes her mouth over mine in a bruising kiss. A kiss made from the bones of a decade of yearning. And I think, even in my drunken stupor, that I believe her. That despite all the rivalry, maybe she wanted me all this time.

Maybe I wanted her.

Her breath is sweet as her mouth moves over mine, her tongue hard and then soft as she savours every mouthful of me I give her. Everything around us disappears into the press of lips and the ache of her fingers slipping under my knickers and pulling them down.

Somewhere deep inside, a part of me is bellowing that I want this. I've always wanted this. Four little words, enough to start a civil war inside me.

It's only sex. Just drunken, foolish sex.

Isn't it?

I want her.

I hate her.

I'm a liar.

All I know is that right now, I want her close enough I can drown in her. She loops an arm around me and rolls me onto my back. Then she slides down my body, dragging her tongue over the fleshy mound of my belly and over my thighs. She shoves my legs apart and looks at my pussy. I'm so exposed. The vulnerability is over-whelming. And yet... and yet... And yet, adrenaline threads through my system, mixing with need and hunger. I tilt my pussy up at her. Daring her to fuck me, to lick me, to suck my clit between those filthy, tempting lips of hers.

"Are you going to fuck me, or do I need to do it myself?" I slide my hand over my pussy and rub my clit.

She snaps, her hand gripping my wrist.

"Your pleasure is mine, Bella. You don't touch yourself unless I tell you to. Do you understand?"

I raise an eyebrow. Losing control isn't something I'm used to. But to my surprise, it sends bolts of pleasure to my core. Knowing I could fuck myself right in front of her, and not being allowed to... it's intoxicating.

I grin and submit... for tonight, anyway. I remove my fingers, bring them up to my mouth, and suck them clean. All the while, I hold her darkening gaze in mine.

A devilish grin spreads across my lips. It's a dare. A taunt and a tease.

A muscle flickers in her jaw. I'm affecting her, and it brings a deep sense of satisfaction that only serves to make me even wetter.

Finally, after what feels like a tortuously long time, she lowers herself between my thighs and draws a slow swipe of her tongue down my slit. The moan she releases is unbridled.

"Fuck, you taste amazing," she says, but before I can respond, she crushes her mouth to my cunt and worships me.

She licks long, lavish sweeps of her tongue down my heat. Pushes her tongue in my hole as if she can't get enough of me, as if she wants to consume every ounce of excitement I can give her. And fuck, I want to give it all to her.

She moans as much as I do, as if giving me pleasure is driving her wild, too. She focuses on my clit, working me hard and then soft, fast and then slow. It winds me higher, twisting my body tighter.

She pushes a finger into my pussy and thrusts it into me.

"More," I pant. "I need more."

She slides another one in, and I almost come apart in her hands. Her fingers are long and thick for such a svelte body. She fills me, her fingers pushing against my walls, rubbing in all the right places.

I gasp as she curls the tips of her fingers against my inner wall.

"Gods," I cry. "Remy. Please. I'm so close." My hands find their way into her hair, it's just long enough to grip on and allow me to rock against her mouth.

That drives her harder. "Use me," she says into my pussy. "Fuck my face until you come."

My head rolls back as I rock my hips into her face, ride her until my body is so tight I can't see. My eyes squeeze shut, my clit throbs against her tongue, and I soak her fingers with excitement as finally, she swipes one hard lick over my clit, and I tip over.

My pussy clenches against her fingers. She thrusts once, twice, two more times and the clit-gasm ruptures and spreads to my pussy making me come harder.

I cry out as shivers rip through my body. She pulls out of me, leaving me bereft and empty. A sudden panic crawls over me that I'll never feel full like that again.

But she clasps me in her arms and makes her way up to meet me. She kisses me long and deep.

"I don't think there's anything sexier than tasting my orgasm on your lips."

She grins and plunges her mouth over mine.

I kiss her over and over, until both our mouths are sore and our lips are swollen. I kiss her until I can't kiss her anymore. Until both our eyes droop and the squawk of dawn gulls over the sea drifts through the window. One last thought passes through my mind before I nuzzle into her neck and fall asleep.

"I'm calling this round a draw."

CHAPTER 7

REMY

I wake up realising two awful truths.

One: I'm never drinking again.

And two: I fucked up, in a big way. Morrigan wants to meet me this morning with the rest of the team to talk tactics while we're here. And to reiterate all the shit she's told me, no doubt. Of which, remaining objective was the most important.

I could badge this as getting close to the enemy. Pitch Morrigan the line of seducing the enemy and fucking the secrets out of her. I wipe a hand over my face. She'll see right through me. But I also hate lying. I'm a terrible liar. I could omit the truth instead. Yes, plausible deniability works. I'll stick to my hypothesis. Fuck once to get it out my system and then go back to absolute objectivity.

I ended up undeniably drunk. My mind claws through the memories. We argued and then there was booze and it was a peace offering and then there was this stupid single bed. Who the hell thought that was a smart idea?

I slip my arm out from underneath Bella and tiptoe out of the room, closing the door behind me. Thankfully, my case is still in the living room. So I pull out fresh clothes, dive into the bathroom, and turn the shower on.

The water does nothing to help the splitting headache ringing between my ears. I towel off, throw on some slacks, a clean shirt, and try to scrub the acrid taste of day-old booze off my tongue. I tiptoe out of the apartment and into the lift. It judders the whole way down, sending throbbing bolts of pain through my head.

I can't do this. Morrigan is going to have to find a way to change the rules, bend them, break them, but find a way to partner me with someone else. I'll observe Bella from afar. Last night was a mistake. Not because I hated it, because I loved it. The way the lace fell from her breasts, the way she tasted, how her back arched as she came.

I traipse through the lobby of the palace and out the main doors. The courtyard is fresh, and I immediately wish I'd bought a jacket with me. The sea breeze cuts through the air and drills straight into my head. Though it makes eradicating the memories of last night significantly easier.

If I don't get a coffee and some painkillers soon, I'm going to have to sacrifice something. I knead my forehead as I walk around the back of the palace and find the stair-case down to the underbelly of the building. It spirals down a sharp cliff, and if I didn't already feel queasy this morn-ing, this would have made my stomach turn. I grip the stone and wonder at the magic that carved the stairs out of the rock itself.

The closer I get to sea level, the less wind there is, and the higher the staircase stretches. I can't see over it anymore, but it continues to twist beneath the ocean. A fascinating construction indeed. Ice blue lanterns hang on the staircase walls as I descend beneath the surface and into the bowels of the palace.

Finally, I reach the bottom and step into a circular room with arched doors positioned at regular sections around the room. Stirling is leaning against one of the doors to my far right, eating a donut.

"How can you eat that shit at this time of the morning?" I mumble.

"Bad night?" she asks.

"Tell me you have painkillers and coffee in that room."

Stirling grins. "The team is in there. But I'll be back. I know a girl that can help with your predicament." She opens the door for me and then vanishes down a corridor on the opposite side.

I step inside the room and gasp.

There's a small table with a tea and coffee tray, but that's not what makes me gasp. The ceiling and the far wall of the room are made of glass.

I don't quite understand the physical dimensions of this castle. They built the palace out of a rock island. I assume we're positioned off to the side of the island, buried under the ocean. This room, like the stairs, is carved into the rock and sealed shut with magic glass. It's breath-taking. On the other side of the glass is the ocean bed. Orb lights shower the sand with light. Schools of fish scuttle past. Larger creatures swim by lazy and relaxed. Other creatures with dozens of legs and limbs zip past.

"Wow," the word slips from my mouth.

"Quite," Morrigan says.

"Here you go, bud," Stirling says, grabbing my shoulder and handing me a small circular pill.

"I owe you one." I squeeze her shoulder.

Quinn and Scarlett are in the corner, Quinn pinned

against the glass, Scarlett's arms locking her in place. I'm not entirely sure if they're arguing or trying to fornicate. But then, you never can be sure with them. I'd assumed that once they were together, the bickering might stop, but I suspect it's actually their love language.

And as I have the thought, Scarlett leans in and kisses Quinn's neck. I pull my eyes away and locate the coffee.

"Tea, black one sugar?" Morrigan asks.

"Gods no. Not this morning. Coffee. Make it a double."

Morrigan blinks at me, but says nothing, making me a strong black coffee as requested. I hold it like the life-giving miracle cure it is and sip the scalding liquid down. The painkiller feels like a bowling ball smashing into the sides of my oesophagus. Not that I'm complaining. I'm grateful to Stirling, grateful that we could be three cities away and that woman would still know a girl.

"Rough night?" Morrigan asks as Scarlett and Quinn finish whatever they were 'discussing' and sit at the table.

Stirling shoves her chair out and kicks her heels onto the table. Morrigan slaps at her feet, but she doesn't remove them. Instead, Stirling rocks back on her chair and sips her piss-water coffee. Never understand the amount of milk that woman puts in her coffee.

"Something like that."

"Is there something you want to say?" Morrigan asks.

Yes. A lot. Why is there only one fucking bed in our apartment? And while we're at it, you can't trust me not to fuck her into oblivion, so perhaps you should swap me out of the team after all.

"No. I don't think so."

"Are you sure?" Stirling asks, her eyes scanning my body language. Fuck, that's the last thing I need—Stirling reading the fact we fucked last night out of my expression.

I take a deep breath and choose my words carefully. "I wonder whether being in such close quarters is a good idea? The logic of needing to have me near her makes sense, of course. But do I really need to be in the same team? In the same room?"

Morrigan's eyes narrow. "I'm afraid we can't change the teams at this point. Not without arousing suspicion. Unfortunately, you are stuck with her. And as for changing rooms, I'm sure you can retreat to your bedroom when necessary. But this way, there's no point in which she can do something without your knowledge. It's the perfect cover."

"And the one bed? Was that someone's idea of a practical joke?" I ask, my tone less than impressed.

Stirling coughs, but I'm not a fool. She's stifling a laugh.

"One bed?" Scarlett asks.

"We have a single bed in our one-bedroom apartment."

Morrigan's fists ball. "And you slept on the sofa? That nothing untoward happened? We can't afford you to be compromised. We all understand you have history, but we need you on our side."

My heart slams against my ribs. I fight to prevent my eyes from growing wide as moons. My chest is tight, my mouth dry. I take a sip of coffee to buy myself time. Then another. My heart rate slows enough I can catch more than a single word with my tongue.

"The apartment has other furniture that can be commandeered for sleeping."

Not a lie. There's a sofa. Not an answer either. But Morrigan doesn't seem to notice. Quinn though, narrows her eyes at me a fraction. Enough to suspect she's on to me, even if the others aren't.

Fucking Quinn.

"I know a girl in maintenance. I'll see about getting another bed put into your room," Stirling says.

"Appreciated, my friend." I dip my head to her, and she gives me a wink back. Morrigan folds her hands together, and it reminds me of her mother when Queen Calandra means business. "Did you pick up any intel last night? Did Bella do anything untoward? Anything useful you can tell us at all?"

I shift in my chair. This is going to be far more complicated than I anticipated. Past Remy is an absolute buffoon for accepting this job. What was I thinking?

"No, we mostly argued about being placed on a team together. Drank because we were both annoyed. Slung accusations at each other and then rowed over who would get the bed."

Quinn's mouth twitches, Stirling scratches her face--conveniently covering her mouth--but I know the pair of them are suppressing laughter. Bastards.

"I see," Morrigan says. "Well, did she access the RuneNet in your presence?"

"Not last night."

She huffs.

"I'll attempt to hack her RuneNet the first opportunity I have."

Stirling drags her feet off the desk and leans in to Morrigan, pulling her hands apart and clasping one. "We'll find the perp, babe. This is day one of the competition. The contestants haven't received their first challenge information yet. There's time."

She pulls her hand out of Stirling's. "I can't believe you're so relaxed over this. If he gets out—"

"He won't."

I know I need to follow Bella's movements, but at the

bottom of my heart, I don't think it's her. "I've been thinking we need to widen the scope of the investigation. Of course, Bella is our main suspect. But it would be foolish of us not to investigate every contestant here, don't you think?"

Scarlett nods, "101 of assassin school. We need to know who we're dealing with. Find any and all connections, and eliminate people one by one. Bella might be our prime suspect, but what do we really know about everyone else?"

Morrigan's expression tightens.

"We can't be blinded because we have a suspect," Quinn agrees. And I want to hug her.

Scarlett nods. "She's right. What if Bella is just a distraction?"

Morrigan's whole body sags. "My gut still says she's involved, but I take your points, and I agree. We can't take anyone for granted. Which brings me to you, Remy. You obviously have something in mind?"

"Well, it's hard to say without knowing what the first challenge is," I say.

Morrigan smiles. "We can help with that. Stirling?"

Stirling's grin is even deeper than Morrigan's. "Let's just say I '*acquired*' this."

I give her a suspect glance but take the envelope she's holding out to me. It's white, luxurious thick card, and on it, emblazoned in gold, is the phrase: CHALLENGE ONE.

I open the envelope and pull out an equally luxurious piece of card with gold writing embossed on it.

I read the note out to the team.

♛

Esteemed contestants,

Your first challenge awaits you. This challenge is poised to be formidable, pushing your skills and resilience to their limits. Brace yourselves for a battle of wits and prowess in the realm of digital warfare. In this challenge, the fate of half of you hangs in the balance, and only the top fifty percent will continue.

Prepare for a relentless race to the finish line. Here's the mission: hackers will attempt to breach the impregnable fortress of our chosen bank's main rune database. Should they succeed, they claim victory. But you'll be pitted against another team: the patcher team. If the hackers succeed, the patchers will be eliminated from the contest. However, if the patchers can stand their ground and thwart the hackers for the full six-minute duration, they will emerge as the victors.

This is sudden death, and there is no room for error. The clock will be your harshest adversary, ticking away precious seconds as you defend or assail the digital fortress. It's a test of your mettle, your adaptability, and your strategic brilliance.

Remember, only the most resilient will prevail. Prepare to give it your all, for the outcome of this challenge will shape the destiny of your journey in this competition.

May the most tenacious team emerge victorious.

Yours with anticipation,
The Competition Organisers

♕

I look up at the team. "Banks?"

"One, criminals have to store their money somewhere, and two, we want to make sure the prison's banking systems are secure," Morrigan says.

I nod. Makes sense.

"What opportunities does this afford us? Every contestant will be using the RuneNet to access the bank's security," Morrigan says.

"Surely you can do some higgery-jiggery fancy shit with Runes and track the contestants?" Scarlett says, gesturing at me.

"Why yes, I'm actually an expert in higgery-jiggery runes," I deadpan.

Quinn and Stirling laugh.

"Quite the linguist this morning, Scarlett," I say and wink at her.

She gives me the middle finger and reaches for the tea and coffee tray.

"But yes, I can write some rune code before the first challenge and, umm... how do I explain this simply?"

The team waits... all of them staring at me as I wrack my throbbing head for the right words. The painkiller is kicking in, thank the High Magician, but there's still a severe ache at the top of my skull.

"Essentially, I will program a series of runes to act like a virus with a homing beacon inside them. They'll target specific rune signatures and attach themselves to the contestants."

"Will the other contestants know?" Quinn asks.

"Not if I do my job effectively. I'll have to go in through the subnet to stay invisible. But I think I can do it. There's only a couple of people who have the skill to discover what I'm doing..."

"Bella?" Scarlett says as she takes a sip of freshly poured black coffee. I shove my empty mug at her across the table and she pours me a second cup.

"Indeed. But hopefully, they'll be distracted enough they won't notice what I'm doing."

"Big hope, no?" Stirling says.

"Where's your faith?" I jab back.

Morrigan sits up straight, her face a little softer and more relaxed. "Well, it sounds like we have a plan. We track all the rune signatures of the contestants and if any of them do anything suspicious, we'll know."

"And if they're not using the RuneNet to break Roman out? What then?" Quinn asks.

"They will be. Even if they're communicating another way, the magic system I set up around the cottage he's in uses the RuneNet to run. Thus, in order to break him out, they will have to enter the RuneNet or they'll never hack the security grid," I say.

"Shouldn't we be looking at other options, too?" Scarlett asks.

"Yes, I think we're making a huge oversight here. We all need to keep our eyes and ears low to the ground, search for any suspicious behaviour. I will bug various rooms with secret recording orbs and audio devices. I can collect and review footage at night," I add.

"Someone here will know something. I'll woo some new friends," Stirling smiles.

"Scarlett, gather some guild assassins and set up patrols. If there's a visible security presence here, it should put the perpetrator off, unsettle them, perhaps. And in the meantime, you may find something suspicious," Morrigan says.

Scarlett nods, "Done."

"Quinn, I know it's not really your specialty, but perhaps you could liaise with Mal and Jacob and see if they can do any investigations in the Old Palace. Look at records, see if they can find any connections between contestants?"

"Do you have that list of attendees?"

Scarlett nods and pulls out a sheet of crumpled paper from her pocket and hands it to Quinn.

"Perfect. Then we have a plan. Let's reconvene in a couple of days," Morrigan says.

And for the first time since they gave me this mission, I feel better. Like the target is easing off Marcel and Bella, and I stand a chance of finding who is really doing this.

CHAPTER 8

BELLA

When I wake, the thin strip of bed that Remy occupied is cold and empty. I should feel relieved. And I do. But there's a twinge in my chest that I don't want to admit exists. Of course I'm not disappointed she left. I don't give a shit. I mean, what was I hoping for? Snuggles and morning coffee with someone I've spent ten years rowing with?

Obviously not. That would be pathetic. And I don't do desperate. I roll onto my back remembering one year at a competition in a different city. I'd pissed Remy off—for reasons I forget now—and she put itching powder in my sheets, so I woke her up by throwing ice cold water over her. I cackle at the memory of her scream and then wonder how the hell last night happened.

I shove the cover off me and clamber out of bed. My knees give out, and I have to grip the mattress so I don't collapse. A thundering pulse rips through my head, nausea claws through my gut.

"Oh f—" I cut myself off as my stomach rolls again. I race to the bathroom and grip the edge of the toilet and hurl my guts up.

I lie on the floor, grateful for the cool press of tiles against my skin. My orb trills out a godawful noise, the sound of it drilling into my skull.

"Shut up." I crawl out of the bathroom and rifle through my clothes until I find the irritant. I slap the orb, hoping it shuts up, but instead, it answers.

"Oh hello, bestie!"

"Ugh, Red," I mumble into the carpet where my face seems to have landed. As much as my stomach rolls, my heart swells hearing her voice. I just hope she has good news.

"Hello to you too. And fuck, you look horrific, I'm glad this thing doesn't have smell," she says.

"I'm never drinking again."

That makes her snort a laugh. "That bad? Tell me you did something awfully naughty that we can gossip about."

I groan into the carpet. Which only makes Red snort louder.

"Now listen, I do hope you can find it in yourself to get up and get that stinky body of yours showered and changed."

I roll over so I can see her face in the orb.

"Why would I do something horrendous like that? I don't need to be anywhere until this afternoon."

There's three sharp knocks at the flat door, each one like a hammer to the head.

I wince. If that's Remy, I swear to the High Magician I'm

going to beat her to death and forget the competition entirely.

I clamber up, pulling clothes on while Red is still talking at me. I groan with every movement.

"Wow, things are really that bad? Almost like you need someone to bring you coffee and painkillers."

I stagger through the apartment, waiting for the rolling of my gut to cease its infernal sloshing.

"If only I were that lucky. Why are you calling at this vile hour? What is it anyway, like six?"

I open the front door.

"It's eight, *actually*," she says and her voice echoes through the orb.

I leap at her, flinging my arms around her neck and immediately regretting it as my head screams in protest.

I pull back, take a good look at her beaming face and yank her into another hug, squeezing the life out of her.

"You made it. How the hell did you negotiate your way here?" I finally release her. I'd hoped and prayed she'd make it but with her living in Sangui City, the vampire capital, it can be complicated.

"One, my best friend asked me for protection. Like I'd let you down. And two, how could I let you compete in the biggest competition of your life and not come and watch?"

I grin. "You're the best."

"Oh, I know." She holds out a brown paper bag.

"If that contains what I think it contains, I may just reconsider my life choices and marry you instead of finding a nice wife."

She laughs, "Don't be vulgar. It's far too early. Now, get plates, and find some painkillers. I'm afraid I didn't know you'd drunk yourself silly. While I have your favourite entirely pretentious coffee and bun, I didn't bring painkillers."

She holds out the bag. I reach for it, but she snatches it back, her nose wrinkling.

"Why can I smell sick?"

My eyes skirt to the bathroom door.

"You are a depraved specimen of a magician. Go clean yourself, and then we can have breakfast."

"I'd rather be a magician than a hunter." I stick my tongue out at her as she gives me the middle finger. I retreat to the bedroom to collect my belongings.

Red doesn't come from New Imperium. She lives in Sangui City. Her magic is wild. I don't really understand it or how the hell her city works, but we met on a job. Roman sent me to steal a vial of blood. And, of course, there's no stronger or more magical blood than a vampire's. But here's the thing, sending an untrained apprentice magician into a vampire den is like encouraging a lame bunny with a gaping wound into a lion's cage. It was never going to end well. Lucky for me, Red was hunting the vampire I was trying to steal from, and she is trained.

She staked the bloodsucker, got me the vial of blood I needed, and invited me to buy her a pint to say thanks. I did, obviously, and we hit it off so well that we stayed in touch. I've visited her, she's visited me. It was tricky at first, as relations between our cities aren't the best. Magicians don't much like vampires and the feeling is mutual. But she's not a vampire, she's a hunter, so border guards are less huffy about her crossing into our city.

I unzip my suitcase and grab fresh clothes and my wash bag. I'm about to shut my case when I spot the note. I throw clothes on top of it and check over my shoulder. Red's in the kitchen, so she didn't see.

I don't want anyone to know, least of all Remy, given her fame and fortune. She'd probably sell me out to the princess. I pull the note out and flip it over. It's still sealed. Delivered to my doorstep before I left for the games. Motherfucker. Sealed with a wax stamp, so I knew exactly who had sent it.

The seal is still perfect. I refused to open it. Don't need any more trouble at my door. I vowed when I got away with covering up Roman's illegal magic, I'd never meddle with him or any illegal business again. Not just because of my mother's banshee wailing about our family's standing in the legacy community, but for me. I want a life. To achieve things. And I can't do that when Roman is a weight and noose around my neck. Every time I take a step forward, he, or someone I've pissed off because of him, drags me back under.

I bury the note at the bottom of my case, zip the thing shut, and put it to the back of my head. I don't have time to deal with it today.

"Taking your sweet time, aren't you?" Red shouts just as I turn on the shower.

The water rinses away most of the nausea. I crank the temperature down low enough that the icy chill destroys most of the headache, too, though I pop a pill to rid me of the rest, since we'll be receiving our challenge information today. I need to be at the top of my game.

A few minutes later, I'm dressed, and my face and hair are done. I pull open the bathroom door and my blood turns to ice. I legit squeal.

"What the hell is wrong with you standing there grinning like a psycho?"

Red buckles over laughing, almost spilling the takeout

cup of coffee. I snatch it out of her hand. "Must you be such a dick?"

"Couldn't resist," she says, wiping a tear from her eye. "Why are you so uptight this morning? Normally you're the one pulling the practical jokes."

On the kitchen counter is my favourite muffin: whole-grain lemon with poppy seeds and a drizzle of lemony icing. A treat for the morning.

Red takes a bite out of an identical muffin and chews. "Your muffin is as pretentious as your coffee."

"Mmm hmm, and my friends are as high maintenance as my coffee, it appears."

She ignores me and takes another bite. "Fuffking good fo," she says around another huge bite.

"Did you really come here just to support me?"

She shrugs. "Of course, you idiot. And to protect you. You've had me worried. Have you worked out who tried to hack you?"

I shake my head.

She purses her lips. "Well I did have to negotiate my way out. I suggested the academy consider upgrading their security systems. And would you believe it, the magicians in New Imperium happen to be running the Runic Games. How convenient for me to come here and watch the games to see if we can buy a new security system." She winks.

I grin. "Unbelievable. You're good, I'll give you that."

"I try. So tell me what's been going on."

I take a slurp of coffee. "Someone has been trying to hack my RuneNet account. I'm not sure why because they're never stealing information."

"Then what are they doing?"

"I have no idea, they're leaving runes *in* my system, not taking info out."

"So you're being set up?"

I open my mouth but stop. "Shit. Possibly. Maybe something to do with Roman. He's been sending me notes."

"Speaking of notes, someone handed this to me in the corridor."

I reach to take it and freeze. The blood in my fingertips turns cold.

"Who gave you that?" I say the first signs of a tremble edging into my fingers. I don't take the note, I can't bear to touch it.

"I'm not sure. They had a hood on. Shoved it at me as I knocked on your door and then they ran. I only realised it was for you when I flipped it over."

She turns the note over. *Beatrice Blythe* is scrawled in ink on the page. But it's the wax seal on the back that has me wound tight.

Buried in the wax seal are the letters R and O.

Roman Oleg.

"Fuck. I destroyed the first two I received without opening them. I thought he was sending me grief for being out."

"Are you going to open it?"

I hesitate. At least with the seal unbroken I have plausible deniability, but deniability from what? There's obviously something he wants, or he wouldn't have reached out again. Knowing Roman, if I don't respond, he will keep trying in more aggressive ways until I do.

"Fuck," I say and crack the seal.

Dearest Bella.

I understand you're free. Incredible that you didn't get caught. We'll discuss that when I'm out. For now, I need a favour.

You'll help your dear old mentor, won't you?

You know it will please me if you do.

I hear you're at the Runic Games. Should you be willing to help your favourite mentor, I need you to borrow some blueprints for me... For the underground tunnels beneath the city, the ones connecting New Imperium to the other cities. During the second challenge you'll have the opportunity, see that you take it.

Once you've retrieved them, leave them under the bridge, you'll find an exit on the second floor under the palace, where the bridge workers go for maintenance. There's a loose brick on the third pillar, four bricks above head height. They'll find their way to me.

Do this for me. I'll accept it as your apology.

Good luck with the games. I look forward to hearing from you.

Yours,

R

I look at Red; she looks back at me.

"What the hell are you going to do now?" she says.

"I have no idea."

We're silent for a while before Red pipes up. "I can protect you physically. I'll be at every challenge. I can stay in the shadows and guard you during the day. But if you're being hacked and this is magic-based I don't know that I can help."

"Just being here helps. Knowing I have someone to talk this through with helps."

"What do you already know?"

"Only that I traced the hacker here."

Red shrugs and sips her coffee, "Well you know what they say... follow the money."

"That's actually a genius idea."

Red smiles at me as I file away the thought for later planning.

"So did you catch her yet?"

Her face darkens. She knows exactly who I'm talking about, an ancient vampire she's been hunting for years. Steel and poison pass through her gaze. She rolls up her sleeves. Her forearms are even more covered in red marks than the last time I saw her.

"Fuck, how many creatures have you killed now?" I ask.

"Fifty-six. Just had the most recent kill tattooed last week." She points at a dash nearest her elbow. "But no. Still not caught her."

I squeeze her hand. "You'll get there."

"Who's the teammate then? Was that who you got shit-faced with last night?"

I shift behind the kitchen island. Red knows all about my history with Remy; funnily enough, we met around the same time. Not that Red has ever met Remy. But she's heard me complain about her over the years—mostly the times I lost.

"You'll literally never guess," I say, challenging her.

"The crow looking girl can't remember her name, real bitchy sort."

"Alba Merrick?" I say.

She nods, "That's the one."

"Nope. Guess again."

"That absolute rando from the ice city we stole a blood charm from?"

I shake my head.

She throws her hands up. "I give up."

"Remy fucking Reid."

"*No*," she gasps and then the corners of her lips quirk

once, twice and she huffs a laugh out. She pops the last bite of muffin into her mouth and licks her fingers one at a time between words. "I. Am. So. Glad. I. Persuaded. The academy to let me come and 'buy security'. This is going to be the best month ever."

"You are a dick of the highest order, and you're lucky I love you."

"Does this mean I get to meet the infamous Remy?"

I cover my face with my hands. "Can you not? The painkillers haven't kicked in."

Her brows pull into a frown as she jerks her head back. She scans my face, her eyes narrowing. "Well, shit."

"What?" I say, a little too defensively.

"It was her you got drunk with last night, wasn't it? And don't even think about lying to me."

I fold my arms on the counter and lean against them, covering my entire head from view. "We're no longer friends. Goodbye forever, Red."

"*It was*! I fucking knew something was up with you. Tell me everything? Was it a blazing row? Did you set her straight?"

"Really don't want to talk about this," I mumble into the counter. If I protest enough, maybe she'll leave it.

"Bitch please, don't make me sing, very loud and off key. I can tell how bad that hangover is."

"I dislike you so much."

"No, you don't. You love me like I'm blood, and you know how important blood is in my city. So, the only reason you'd be protesting this much is if something happened. Did you... oh, I dunno... confess that you secretly find her attractive?"

I groan into my arms, and then I pull myself up so she can see my expression.

"It's worse than that, isn't it?" she says, her eyebrows wiggling up and down in delight.

"Do you need to take so much pleasure in my pain?"

"Abso-fucking-lutely. It's my prerogative as your best friend."

I bite my lip and nod. "It's worse."

"Did you kiss?"

I scrunch my face up.

Her mouth drops, "You *fucked*?"

I give a barely perceptible nod.

"I need to know everything immediately." She walks around the counter and flicks the kettle on.

What's important to me is winning this fucking competition. Then I can shove it to my parents, shove it to the Merricks and to everyone else who's doubted me over the years.

Besides, I've had plenty of one-night stands before. That's all Remy was. A meaningless one-night stand. And now we've fucked, I can move on and forget it and we can go back to... to whatever we were before. Mutual disdain and occasional destruction. See? Healthier already.

But Red just glares at me with that deeply irritating expression only a best friend can give you. You know, the one that calls you on all your bullshit with one hideous glance. The kettle clicks as it boils over.

Red holds her hand out. "Give me that takeout cup. I'll re-fill it, and we'll go for a walk."

"It means nothing, Red. It was a mistake, and it won't happen again. Besides, she left this morning without a word. She must think it was a mistake, too." The words slip out of my mouth. "I'm not upset. Like I said, I don't care."

"Sure, Bella, and I'm in love with a vampire."

CHAPTER 9

REMY

I take a stroll on the beach after the meeting with the team to clear the rest of the headache. A necessary act before I face Bella and the rest of the contestants for the official challenge briefing this afternoon. I stroll for an hour or so, leafing through my copy of *Runes and their Magical Applications,* trying not to let the old book fall apart in my hands. It's pointless reading it, I've memorised every word. It's more habit than anything else. I slip it back into my pocket when the wind picks up and collect shells instead, putting them down in exchange for stones or pebbles. I find a stunning blue shell that reminds me of the colour of Morrigan and Stirling's beach house.

Eventually, a few minutes to twelve, I find my way back to Lantis Palace. The crowd has thinned since last night. The parents, friends and family have left, though they'll return for the challenges I should imagine. The courtyard is so much quieter than yesterday, it's almost eerie.

I make my way through the giant wooden arched doors.

The palace greets me with a wave of fresh sea air, pressure that tickles like the foamy brush of shallow waves. The palace is in a good mood today.

I head up to the apartment first. Bella isn't in here, so I cast onto my RuneNet and locate her avatar. She's not active on the RuneNet right now which means I have a small window of opportunity to try and hack her account.

I cast several precision runes into my screen and guide them towards her RuneNet account. Of course I face an immediate barrier. A mesh flashes up on screen in bright warning-red. I sigh, spell several more runes, connecting them in the air, their coppery bodies swelling as they link, before pushing them into the screen. That manages to hack the first lattice, but my RuneNet screen screams, a hideous siren sound blaring out around the room.

"Fuck. Fuck." I disconnect from her account, withdraw all my runes as fast as I can and shut my screen down. My heart is in my mouth, blood rushing through my ears, my cheeks flame red.

I have to get out of the apartment.

When I've calmed down, I spend a bit of time hunting out the training rooms and hiding audio bugs and camera orbs. I place another couple in the corridor with our apartments, more in the canteen. They'll run a daily recording and then send the data to my RuneNet. I'll create a program to hunt for key words rather than trawling hours of footage.

When I'm done, I head to the main welcome hall. I'm late for the announcements today. Morrigan is already on the stage. I glance around but don't see Bella. I breathe a sigh of relief as Morrigan taps on the mic and clears her throat.

"Good morning competitors and Games Makers. I'll keep this brief. This morning we are handing out not one, but two challenges. Both the first and final ones. The first because you have less than a week to prepare before you go up against each other. And the last challenge because you'll need a considerable amount of time to prepare for it."

She beams at the room, but I can tell she's tense. It's written in the sharpness of her eyes.

"Games Maker Marcel and Eli are in the two corners of the room. Please go and collect your challenge envelopes. We've provided a training and preparation centre on the tenth floor...should you want to practise working together. Or if you want to create different tech and rune solutions once reading your challenge cards."

She opens her arms up and smiles. "I'm afraid the New Imperium Palace calls. So I'll be back in time to preside over the first challenge. Good luck, and see you all in a week."

There's a smattering of claps and she disappears off to the back of the stage and out of sight. I catch a subtle wave of Stirling's hand at me before she slings her arm around Morrigan and pulls her behind the stage.

They reappear at the foot of the stage, a queue of magicians building in front of Morrigan. Stirling and Scarlett stand on either side of her, ensuring the queue is orderly.

My neck prickles, and I know before I locate her that Bella is watching me somewhere in this room and she is furious.

I left without saying a word. I had to meet the team, but I'm not sure how I'd feel if she'd done that to me. It's not like we're dating or owe each other anything. The fact is, we don't even really like each other. She probably doesn't care, probably hasn't even considered the fact I was missing.

And then I spot her snatching the envelope from Eli's wrinkled hand and marching across the hall to Marcel. I stride over and take the envelope from him before she can do something she regrets.

"Thank you, Marcel."

He beams at me. "Drink later?"

"Tomorrow?"

"Sure. Do you remember the eccentric millionaire magician we installed home security for?"

"Umm... no?"

"Okay, no matter, he wants an upgrade and I can't remember the encryption key we used to lock all the code up, and of course, I can't find it in my records."

"Wait, was that the guy who had the lake you taught me to fish in?"

"Yes," he beams.

"I'll have a look through my records when I get a chance and send over anything I find."

"Super, thanks."

I head away from him, and Bella barrels right up to me with the force of a pitbull and snatches the envelope out of my hands.

"Glad to see you look as hideous as I feel," she says.

I grimace. "The hangover was bad. I needed air."

She narrows her eyes at me, but nods. "Like I care. I had a coffee date with a friend."

There's something about the bravado that makes me wonder.... "I'm sorry I left this morning."

She touches her throat, a flush of red runs through her cheeks before vanishing.

"What I care about is your focus on this team. Some of us are here to win. Not fuck all night." Her tone is far too loud and some of the contestants glance over.

I bristle. Morrigan's eyes find mine, and her expression thins.

Shit.

"Quiet," I hiss at Bella.

"Don't you quiet me," she barks, louder than before. I hustle her away from Morrigan's field of hearing.

"I'm just saying there's nothing between us. It's not like fucking is on our challenge agenda...unless it involves fucking over the competition, that is."

"Oh, my gods. Can you stop saying fucking? Let's not do this here." I snatch the envelope Bella's holding just fast enough she flashes red and follows me.

"I will put your hands in a serrated lattice and cut them off if you don't give those back," she swats me, trying to grab the envelopes, but I hold on tighter.

"You weren't complaining about my hands last night." I shoot her a grin and wheel out of the welcome hall and into a side corridor. There's a library at the end. I swing open the doors and pull both of us inside.

The library is vast. Shelving painted the darkest blue stretches high into an arched ceiling as far back as I can see. In the middle of the room is a set of wooden tables, painted the same ocean-bed blue. Scattered around the tables, a few people sit, half hidden by piles of books and quills and scrolls of paper. The room is dim, lit by a handful of lanterns hung on the wall and only table lamps for those studying.

I grab Bella's hand and lead her down an empty aisle.

I can't afford for Morrigan to realise what happened. I can't let her find out I slept with Bella, or she'll think I'm compromised, or worse, that I'm involved with Bella and trying to break Roman out.

I'm neither of those things. We're adults, we can keep this platonic. Last night was fun, surprising even, but it was definitely a one off. It won't happen again.

"What the hell do you think you're doing snatching the envelopes like that? This is teamwork. Or did you forget that little piece of information?" Bella barks.

"I didn't forget." I hand her one of the envelopes back. "But I do require you to calm down."

A wave of pure rage descends over her eyes. Oh dear, that was clearly the wrong thing to say.

"Calm down? Calm fucking down? You patronising son of a—"

I cut her off by placing a finger over her mouth. "I apologise. For everything. For coming on to you last night and for not being there this morning. I do, in fact, want to work with you as your teammate."

Her posture sags a little. "I donff care abuff lasth nighff."

I pull my finger back, a little stung. "Liar," I say. "Besides, now you owe me twice."

"And how exactly did you calculate that, Professor Reid?" she says, shoving her hand on her hip.

I hold up my balled fist, ready to count off the ways in which she owes me. "One, I saved your arse from going to jail."

"We should talk about that..."

I pause my counting. "Go on..."

She fidgets, pulling her top this way and that. "I guess... I guess I wanted to thank you. I would be where he is right now if it weren't for you. And just so you know, I'm all the way done with him and his bullshit now."

"Well, I'm pleased to hear my judgement and deep sacrifice didn't go to waste." I gesture liberally just for effect. But she rolls her eyes at me.

"You just did it to get one up on me and prove you can undo my magic."

I hold up the finger on my still-balled fist. "Not true."

"Then why did you do it?"

Because you're too talented to rot in jail... Because you're a petty irritating thief, but not a bad human... Because I'd be bored without you annoying me constantly... Because maybe I like looking at you...

That's not a conversation I'm ready to have.

"I see," she says. "Go on then, hit me with the second reason I owe you."

I lean in close this time, let the heat of my face warm her neck. "Two is the giant orgasm I gave you last night."

She inhales a sharp breath and stands upright.

I grin at her, a piece of me questioning myself. The sane, rational piece that's a member of Morrigan's team. Why go there when I can tell from the way she wets her lips that she wants me as badly as I want her? This is a dangerous game to play.

"Way I see it, those are two enormous debts," I say.

"You're an arse," she says and gives my arm a playful shove.

The movement makes something inside her snap and shift her body language. I freeze, wondering if I'm going to have to defend myself. There's a feral intensity washing over her eyes, and I'm not sure if it's anger or lust. A little of both, I think.

She grabs my neck and pulls me down until I am millimetres from her mouth.

"I'm afraid we have a problem then, Professor."

"We do?" I say my heart ratchets up a notch. This close to her, all I can smell is the scent of sweet lavender and coconut shampoo or soap or... whatever it is, I want to bury my face in her neck. Drown in the intoxicating sweetness of her skin and hair.

She yanks me down another inch. "I can't have you holding that many debts over me. So one of them is getting repaid right now. And given you're not in imminent danger of being jailed, I guess that means you're about to get fucked."

I stiffen in her grip. "Bella, we're in the middle of the library."

"Then you'd better keep your mouth shut, hadn't you?"

"We shouldn't," I say, and it's true. There are half a dozen Morrigan shaped reasons we shouldn't.

"Shouldn't we? Are you telling me you don't want to?"

"I want to more than is reasonable."

She swings me around until my back crashes into one of the bookshelves. Several tomes clatter to the floor. I flinch as a handful land hard on their spines. The urge to bend down and pick them up is intense until Bella steps up to me and grabs my waistband.

"We agreed last night that this wasn't a good idea," I say, but my words are feeble.

"Yes, and then you pointed out that I owe you. So now you're going to reap what you sow."

I want to say no. Need to say no. I should get a grip of the situation. Fucking Bella last night wasn't sensible. It goes against everything Morrigan has told me to do. But Bella has nothing to do with Roman's breakout attempt and what if, while we're busy pointing fingers at her, someone else breaks him out?

Bella's tongue slips over her lips. She sucks in the corner and glances up at me, a question in her gaze.

I should say no.

But I don't want to.

Right from that first kiss, from the moment the world stopped turning on that nightclub roof, I wanted her.

Wanted every piece of her, and I've spent a decade denying myself. Telling myself she's annoying and petty. Reminding myself what her parents stole from me.

But the way she looks at me, long curly lashes fluttering over deep brown eyes, I'm done for. I think I always was.

What's one more kiss? One more fuck? When challenge one hits, I'll still release the trackers and one on Bella, too. And then I can prove Morrigan wrong and find the real culprit.

I reach out, take Bella's hand and bring it to my buckle.

She grins deep, unclasps the belt and pulls me forward as she fiddles with the button and zipper. She glances left down the aisle and then to the end of the shelving.

She slips her hand into mine and drags me into the shadows a little further, then pushes me against the shelf and holds her finger to her lips.

"Not a sound. Understand?" she says, her eyes glimmering.

I nod. Her hands come to my hips. She dips her thumbs into the waistband of my jeans and pulls them down. The press of her fingers sparks hot and tingly. I want more. I thirst for her touch. She slips her palm against my thighs and tugs my jeans and boxers down just enough to get to my core. She kicks each foot apart as far as my jeans will allow, the fabric digging into my knees, protesting against the strain. Then she lowers herself to meet my pussy. I shiver against the bliss of her touch.

I shouldn't want her.

I'm not allowed to want her.

And yet I can't bring myself to stop.

She leans so close to my cunt her breath trickles over my skin.

"Ready?" She looks up at me.

I nod and a deviant grin peels across her features.

She leans in and swipes her tongue over my flesh. My nostrils flare at the pressure of holding in a moan.

Somewhere in the back of the library, a chorus of murmurs echoes. Then a woman with a cracked voice hisses, "Quiet." And the murmurs stop.

Bella grips my thighs and slides her tongue between my folds. Her eyes dip closed, and she swipes once, twice, three times at my clit.

My legs instantly rebel. The desperate urge to spread wider to give her full access to my pussy is overwhelming. But my jeans won't stretch any further. I try to spread my feet, but the fabric bites into my legs. It burns, but the frustration sears hotter. It melts into the pleasure of Bella's tongue and creates a tantalising mix of pleasure and pain.

The restriction makes the pressure of her tongue against my clit even more intense. She moves rhythmically until a whimper escapes me and she stops.

She wipes her mouth. "I told you not to make a sound."

My teeth clench. This is excruciating. The restriction of my legs, my voice. She's turning the tables on me, taking control. The power she wields over me threads into my veins, heightening every sensation.

Her fingers stiffen against my thighs, her head snaps to the central aisle. Someone walks past, but we're so far into the shadows they don't notice us.

"Be quiet," she growls.

I lean my head back against the shelving unit and close my eyes as she drags her tongue between my wet folds. I have to bite down on my lip to stop myself from crying out. My fingers find a shelf. My legs shake from the pleasure building between them.

There's nowhere for my whimpers to go, nowhere for

my body to move or arch. And so the blood floods to my clit instead. Every slash of her tongue against my pussy feels like sunlight and glistening diamonds. It's too much. I can't stay upright.

One of her hands slides between my legs.

Oh gods.

She palms my pussy, wetting her fingers against the slick of my excitement, and then she circles my hole, the nerve-endings already alight from her tongue at my entrance. I can't help but whimper again. A breathy half moan I shut off before it's complete.

She stops licking my clit. And I glare down at her.

"What did I tell you?"

"I swear to the High Magician, if you continue to edge me, I am g—"

"Going to what?" she says and cocks her head at me.

I growl and shove several more books off the shelf. Annoyed at myself at the sacrilege and utterly desperate for her to finish fucking me.

"Now, now, no need for a temper tantrum."

I grab her hair. It's braided in a long plait today. I wrap it around my fist and use it to pull her towards my pussy. "If you leave me hanging, you won't like the consequences."

"But I love consequences." She grins at me, but I use her braid to close the gap and she releases a sigh of pleasure as she slips her tongue over my clit.

This time, finally, she pushes two fingers inside me, and thrusts slow and firm. Waves of electric sensation pulse deep into my body. A climax builds. I glance around, knowing I'm close to coming and desperate not to be disturbed. We could be caught at any moment. This is a public library.

She pumps into me, curling her fingers until she finds

the spot that makes me clamp down on my tongue to prevent myself from screaming her name.

I use her hair to press her head into my pussy, desperate for more, for her to fuck me harder. She knows, because she responds by thrusting and pumping faster.

She drives into me so hard I have to grip the edge of the shelf, knocking another section of books off. It makes a loud clatter, as my body knocks rhythmically against the shelving unit.

"Shit," I hiss.

She responds by speeding up the pace of her tongue, flicking and licking and drawing long, luxurious swipes over my clit and between my folds. My legs tremble at the building climax, as she pumps her fingers inside me at an ever-increasing pace.

I grip her hair tighter. It's all I can do to prevent myself from collapsing. My eyes squeeze shut as waves of pleasure throb down my thighs and shiver through my core.

She thrusts once, twice more, and then I come undone. My legs shake so badly I lose my grip on the shelving unit.

"Shit," I hiss as she breaks contact with my pussy and we collapse onto the floor, her piled on top of me.

"What is going on here?" the same cracked voice says from down the aisle.

"Fuck," I breathe.

Bella's shoulders rock from suppressed laughter as I wriggle to pull my jeans up and fasten the buckle and belt between our bodies. She's still laughing as the woman strides down the aisle.

"Nothing, nothing," I say waving a hand at her, "I fell over."

Bella rolls off me as I finish doing my jeans up and haul myself standing.

"I... umm... I fell into the shelving unit, you see. I do apologise for having knocked so many books down."

The librarian huffs at me, and flaps her hands until I leave, dragging Bella with me and picking up the abandoned envelopes.

I glance at back at the librarian, but when I glimpse Bella, my cheeks heat.

"What?" Bella says, frowning.

I make a gesture indicating she should wipe her mouth. And that makes her crack up all over again.

"What if I want to wear my prize with pride?" she pushes open the library door, and I scamper after her, grab her shoulders, and wipe my arm over her mouth and chin.

"Such a spoilsport," she tuts and opens the envelope, revealing challenge one. "Now, let's see how I'm going to beat you next week."

"In your sweetest fucking dreams, Bella Blythe."

She gives me the broadest grin I've seen yet and pulls the card out.

CHAPTER 10

BELLA

Once the hangovers are gone, Remy and I make our way to the training room together. But by the fifth floor, I'm blowing hard. "Who the hell has a training room on the tenth floor?" I grumble.

"Struggling, darling? Is this a sign of how I'm going to absolutely trounce you in the warm-ups?" Remy says.

"No," I fire, refusing to rise. But I give her a poisonous stare, and then pick up my pace, driving my legs up the stairs as fast as I can.

Remy falls behind and I can't help the smug grin spread all the way to my warming belly.

Not that I'm racing her...

But I like being ahead, even if my thighs are screaming and there's still four flights left. This makes sense. It's how I understand us. Always bickering, always fighting. Always one-upping. I don't understand the library. Or last night.

That's... just...

I'm not sure I want to figure it out. It's just fucking.

That's what it is. Basic rubbing of bits together, shagtastic emotionless humping. I already feel better.

My back heats as Remy appears at my side and matches me step for step.

Shit.

I don't know if I can climb any quicker. A line of sweat trickles down my spine. My calves are already protesting, but I tilt onto tiptoes to make myself lighter on my feet.

Remy gives me a side glance, holding my gaze as she leans in.

Daring, tempting.

She inches ahead. It takes every fibre of my being not to reach out and grab her elbow and yank her back.

I gulp a huge breath in, hoping the oxygen floods to my dying thighs.

I draw level again as we pass floor eight.

Ha, winning.

But every muscle in my body is screaming and I'm pretty sure I'm causing some kind of serious musculature illness I'm never going to recover from. Step after step, we forge on. Every foot is a little faster. I'm puffing hard. I sound like a pregnant elephant in the throes of childbirth.

Remy, though, despite the sweat forming on her fore-head, is still smiling like a psycho, as if it isn't excruciating to climb seven thousand steps at the pace of a fucking cheetah.

I blink at her, wondering if she's properly delusional. And she just smiles back. Wider this time, all toothy and clown like.

Yeah.

She's lost her mind.

This was one petty competition too many.

That, or she's in so much pain that the only thing she

can do to stop herself from hollering out a death rattle is to clench her teeth and give me a horror movie grin.

I'm about to cough a lung up halfway up floor eight, when bold as brass, the bitch winks at me and bolts, practically running up the stairs.

Motherfucker.

I pray to any of the gods who will listen that I don't have a heart attack and dig deeper than I have ever desired to dig. I unleash a war cry and sprint up the last floor. I surge past Remy.

YES!

Only to find myself suddenly stationary as Remy is, I shit you not, flinging herself through the air like a bird, past me.

Oh, no you don't.

I leap a split second after her. Arms out wide, latching on and pushing her back as I throw myself tits-first through the training room door.

There's a tangle of limbs and muffled shouting. An elbow in my ribs. A grunted sound rips from Remy's chest, my knee sinks into something deliciously soft, and then I'm on my back facing the ceiling of a new room and there's a crowd of people leaning over, looking down at us.

"What in the ever-loving fuck?" a familiar voice says.

"Red?" I say, squinting at her from the floor.

She reaches down and offers me a hand. I take it and she drags me standing. She gawps at me and points at the pile of Remy still on the floor. She nudges me out of the way and offers Remy her hand.

"Thank you." Remy dusts herself down, trying to wipe a smudge of grime from her top.

"You must be the infamous Remy," Red says.

Remy's eyes narrow at Red. She looks her up and down,

a frown appearing between her brows. And I get it. Red doesn't dress like a magician. She's in hunter gear, her sleeves rolled up showing a line of tattoo marks that are wildly different to the Collection tattoos we have. She's practically an alien in this city.

"Remy, this is Red. Red, this is Remy. Red is my best friend, she's from Sangui city. Remy is, unfortunately, my teammate for the games. She's also—"

"The same Remy who tortured you in your teens?" Red says, smirking.

"That's an exaggeration. It went both ways," Remy mumbles.

"She's joking, Professor," I say.

"Oh, well—" But Remy's cut off by Games Maker Eli moving to the centre of the room and clearing his throat.

It's only now I take in the room's vastness. Glass window-walls on three sides. This room must take up the entire floor. Sunlight streams through the windows, making the space bright enough it makes me wince. The floor is marble stone that mimics the look of ocean waves. Scattered down the left-hand side of the room are rows and rows of workstations.

Wires, cogs, and floating RuneNet screens hover by the desks. Some of the competitors have already chosen desks and stand in front of their screens, their arms out wide, gesturing and pointing at various runes floating in front of them. Some have code strings filling their screens, others have their heads bent over their desks.

Games Maker Eli steps in a circle and raises his voice. "Welcome contestants. This is your practice room." He points to the space in front of him. He draws a rune in midair. It puffs into existence, a coppery swollen symbol, and then he touches his index fingers together followed by his pinkies. He snaps them apart and the rune erupts into a giant screen in the middle of the room, hovering a couple of feet above his head.

"This is the warmup scoreboard. Today and for the next three days, we'll run practice trials. We have a virtual simulator of a variety of banks. You'll take it in turns practicing your strategies—and teamwork—in preparation for the real challenge in just under a week's time."

"The scores are public?" Alba Merrick says from the corner of the room. All eyes turn towards her.

"They are indeed," Eli says, beaming. "Nothing like a bit of transparency to heighten the competition. Speaking of which. This screen..." He repeats the same rune and movement, and a second screen appears. He then holds his hands out and guides both screens to the back wall—the only one not made of glass.

"Is so that you can watch the live hatch and patches."

A ripple of gasps circles the room.

Everyone can watch us? I swallow hard. That seems like a lot. I glance at Remy and we share a concerned look.

She leans into my ear, our recent stair challenge forgotten. "How are we supposed to strategise if everyone can see everything we're practicing?"

"I have no idea."

Eli turns back to us. "Should you wish to practice, I will divide your teams into two groups: hackers and patchers. Each day, the groups will spend half the day hacking and then you'll swap to patching and vice versa. Signup forms are on the first desk."

Before he's even finished speaking, the room is a scramble of magicians all clamouring to get to the signup forms.

Remy sighs and heads over for us.

Red turns to me, "So, what exactly was that?" she points at the staircase.

"Oh. Umm."

"And why is your plait all ruffled and out of place?" she narrows her eyes at me.

I'm not quick enough to respond.

"You didn't...! You fucking did, didn't you?" Her hand claps to her mouth.

"Red?"

She turns to see who the voice belongs to and gasps all over again. "Stirling? No freaking way. What has it been? Four years? How the hell are you?"

And then she's gone, Stirling slinging an arm over her shoulder and the pair of them descending the stairs.

"Stirling. So that's her name," I mumble, recognising the woman that was behind princess Morrigan when she opened the games—the same woman who fell into me at the auction.

Remy appears with two mugs of water and nods her head in the direction of a free workstation. She puts the cups down and pulls out the challenge envelopes.

She opens the first, skims it again, and hands it to me. Then she does the same with the final challenge, only this time, she reads it aloud.

♔

FINAL CHALLENGE

Esteemed Contestants,

The culmination of this competition approaches, and it promises to be the ultimate test of your strategic genius, magical prowess,

and innovative thinking. Prepare yourselves for
the most epic showdown of this journey - the
Final Challenge.

In this thrilling contest, each team will be
entrusted with a sacred duty: to defend a
prison like no other. Your task is to fortify this
prison with an ingenious blend of security
systems, magical runes, and your collective
skills to render it impenetrable. The canvas is
yours to paint; you can craft entirely new security measures, or adapt what exists. We want
you to draw upon your vast knowledge and
creativity to safeguard your prison.

But here's the twist that makes this challenge the pinnacle of your journey: two Games
Makers, masters of the arcane and the digital
realm, will be pitted against you. Their sole
mission is to infiltrate your prison's defences.
Your goal? To keep them at bay for a gruelling
thirty minutes. If you can withstand their
relentless assault and protect your prison,
victory will be yours. However, should the
Games Maker breach your defences, the ultimate
prize will elude you.

In this challenge, your ingenuity knows no
bounds, and the sky's the limit when it comes
to crafting intricate security systems and magical
runes. We'll be awarding marks not only for the

complexity and originality of your systems but also for the level of challenge they present to the Games Makers themselves. Your creativity will be your greatest weapon.

This is the moment you've all been working towards, and only the most innovative, resourceful, and resilient team will emerge victorious. The fate of this competition rests in your hands, and we can't wait to witness the awe-inspiring systems you'll design to defend your prisons.

The Final Challenge awaits, and the destiny of our future champions hangs in the balance.

With the highest anticipation,
The Competition Organisers

♚

"We're third up, by the way. There's a team I don't know going first, and then the Merricks and then us."

"Did we get hacking or patching first round?" I ask.

"Hacking."

Good. That's my preference, anyway.

"How should we do this? If we're hacking, then my lattices are the most efficient way of penetrating a system."

"Says you," Remy says.

"Yes, actually. They suffocate the system from the outside."

"And while we're sitting on our arses, letting the lattice do its thing, everyone else is hacking in."

I shrug. "I'll build a defence system into the lattice."

Remy kneads her temples. "We need to be more strategic than that. I have a precision rune I use for hacks."

"I've seen that in practice. You can't finalise the code script until you know what you're hacking. You'd have to live-code the runes. It's not efficient."

"But it's the most effective way because—"

"Remy Reid, Bella Blythe? You're up," Eli shouts from across the hall.

I glance up at Remy. "I guess that's time. And we have absolutely no agreement on how best to run the simulator?"

We walk across the hall together.

Remy's expression is severe. "Well, we do. My strategy is flawless. You let me run my precision rune. It will enter the bank RuneNet through the subnet, and then it's a simple case of coding the right cypher to decrypt the rune keys, and poof, we're in."

"No, that is not the best plan. Like I said, it will take us too much time to figure out the code script we need. If we overlay a lattice mesh made of spelled runes, we'll be able to suffocate the system from the outside in. It will destroy their entire network."

"Ultimately, the precision rune is faster because it will go straight to the key we need, rather than having to take down every rune wall and security measure with the lattice. It's like you want to use a sledgehammer when a needle could do the job. It's so crude. I thought you were more sophisticated than that."

"What the hell? How can y—"

"*Ladies*? Are we participating or am I calling up the next team?" Eli says, his arms folded.

I fire Remy a shitty look and saunter up to the Games Maker.

"We're ready. Aren't we Reid?"

Remy appears next to me. "Yes, Blythe, we are."

"Er. Okay. This way," Eli says, his eyes flitting between us.

How do we go from mind blowing orgasms to rowing, again? I thought maybe we'd put our differences behind us.

I check the score screen before following him. The first team didn't complete. But the Merricks completed the hack in four minutes twenty-eight with only three firewall alerts. That's not bad.

They know it too, by the looks of their shit-eating grins as we stroll past them. Great, not only do I need to waste energy convincing Remy the lattice is the best course of action, but now I have to put up with the Merrick's ego if we don't beat their time.

Eli leads us over to the far corner of the room where there's a walled off section and he opens the door, plunging us into a dark room. His voice echoes around the dim chamber.

"You'll have exactly five minutes to hack into this bank. We're starting with a low-level security system. Have fun. Simulation starts in three. Two…" his voice drops out, and the simulation appears on a huge RuneNet screen in front of us.

Remy's hands are already out in front of her, vibrating so fast they're a blur. Her eyes shift too, first to grey, then deepening to black.

"Oh for fucksake, don't worry about working with me or anything. No, it's fine, you go ahead," I snap as I throw my hands out and cast on to the RuneNet. I unleash a series of runes. Symbols and shapes fly through the room and vanish into the RuneNet screen, absorbed and converted into digital magic. They reappear in the rune code simulation in front of us. I pluck and weave and thread symbols together, meshing them all into an enormous lattice.

A visual of the bank's security system appears on the side of the screen and then Remy's precision rune appears on a third screen, logged into the RuneNet.

"I said no. It's much more efficient to hack the system with a lattice." I fling my arms out, drawing them across the screen, reworking rune codes and strings as fast as I can to finish threading a lattice into the system.

"And I said a precision rune is the best option," Remy snarls.

A timer appears in the centre of the screen. Ninety seconds have already elapsed. She hasn't stopped working on her runes and neither have I. I glance at her. She glances back, both of us pushing more magic through our fingers. Working harder. Faster.

"Gods, would you listen, Bella? I'm not saying a lattice doesn't work at all. We all know they work very well... don't they?" Remy growls.

Oh, no, she fucking didn't.

"We're on camera, remember?"

The bank rune code shifts and several lines of my lattice melt away, evaporating into dust.

"You know what? Fuck you, Remy."

"Like I said, this is faster and more efficient. Why use a sledgehammer if you can pick a lock with a hairpin?"

I clench my jaw and focus. Fuck her. I'll win this for us. I move my hands faster, weaving lines of rune into a mesh so fast my chest pounds with the beat of my heart. This is faster than I've ever had to mesh a lattice together. But what do I expect? Remy is one of the best. To my absolute rage, the faster I weave, the faster Remy feeds her runes into the system.

I will not lose this.

"Remy, please be reasonable. Look how much energy you're expending. The lattice is the least amount of work. All we have to do is thread it into the system and it will do the work for us."

"How basic."

I swear I blow actual fire and steam from my nose. How fucking dare she.

"It's not basic, you pretentious fucking jobsworth. It's called efficiency. Why overwork when my intelligent rune can work for us? Oh, and you missed a fucking string," I say, lifting her rune, pulling it out of the RuneNet and throwing it at her head.

"Huh?" she says, and her focus slips as the rune poofs into a thousand particles against her temple.

I cackle as I finish weaving the first layer of lattice and thread it into the bank security system.

Boom, done. Thank fuck for that. "Now we let the lattice do its job."

"Bella," Remy fires a warning at me.

"Yes, Remy?" I say.

"Why can't you work with me for once?"

"Because you need to work with me. We were losing time. Three minutes have elapsed already. Let the lattice run. There's less than ninety seconds left if you want to beat the Merricks."

"Oh, don't worry, I will beat them for us, and quicker than your sledgehammer," she says.

She huffs out a loud nasal breath and turns back to the screen, her focus zeroing in on the rune code lines.

"Second rune wall down," I say. As I lazily watch my lattice suffocate the prison system. I fold my arms and just let it do its job. Remy sweats and grimaces as she fights her way through the system.

I examine my fingernails because I'm petty like that. "Having fun?"

"Working hard for the team, I see," she says, her eyes never leaving the screen.

"Third rune wall, and I do believe that's three out of three for me."

Remy's eyes narrow as she locates the source runes for my lattice. The vibration of her hands shift and she buries a string of runes into the lattice, destabilising the code.

"What the hell did you do that for?" I shout, pushing off the wall and casting back on to reach for my runes again.

"It was slowing me down. I needed it out of the way. Now quiet."

"Remy! We hit *four minutes*. There's twenty-seven seconds left for fucks sake. You ruined our shot."

"Not if you hush your gums for one gods damned moment."

Her brow furrows as she leans forward, her hands practically buried into the screen as runic code flies from her hands, shimmers against the screen and buries itself into the codes on screen. There's nothing I can do. Not in ten seconds. We've lost, and all because she sabotaged my lattice.

"We would have had this," I moan.

"We do have this. No thanks to you," she snaps.

"Five, four, three, two... one..." I count down.

"I've got it." She releases a final string of code and the whole prison security system disintegrates. But I know before it dissolves on screen that it was too late.

The simulator door opens and Eli stares at us, his eyes

wide. "I think we might need to practise our teamwork, don't you? Hmm?"

I can't even bring myself to respond. I'm so annoyed. If only she listened to me.

"For fucks sake, I had it before you flung the lattice and suffocated my precision rune. I was halfway to decrypting the entire prison's Rune walls. You needed to be patient," Remy says, leading us to the scoreboard.

"Oh yeah, and what? You expected me to sit back and do nothing? Let you take the reins, should I? Don't fucking think so. We're both scored in the real games. There's only one Royal Rune Master."

She lowers her voice leaning into me. "So if you think for a second just because we fucked that I'm going to roll over and let you steal the position, you're sorely mistaken."

"Let me steal it? Bella, first up, we're meant to be a team. And second, I'll fucking win it because I'm better than you."

"Better than me?" She's bellowing again.

The other contestants are giving us uncomfortable looks.

To my horror, Alba skips over to us, smirking. "Gosh, you guys make a great team."

Remy and I snap to her and shout, "Fuck off, Alba!" simultaneously.

Alba sniffs, but to my relief, walks away.

"Well, Remy. I hope you're happy. Alba might be a bit of a cunt. But she's not wrong, is she?"

I stab a finger at the screen and our blinking time: four minutes, thirty-one seconds.

We came second.

CHAPTER 11

REMY

The next four days pass with horrifying speed. I can't say I've been at my finest. Bella and I can't seem to find a happy medium.

Red, on the other hand, is a delight. Most evenings after practice, Bella leaves with Red. Sangui city is so different from ours. I'd love to have a deeper conversation with her about how their magic works. Though when we'll get time, I'm unsure, because she's here to buy security for her academy. I suspect having an academic chinwag on the merits of blood magic isn't one of her priorities.

When Bella and I aren't fighting over strategies, we're duelling in simulations, or squabbling over which runes will work best for the final challenge. Which means, between practices, trying to develop a digital tracker that will be untraceable to everyone here, reviewing security footage my orbs and audio bugs have recorded and meeting the team, I'm exhausted.

But fighting is exactly what we're doing now, less than fifteen hours before the first challenge.

"Ugh, Remy, please see reason. I get that your runes are 'works of art'." She waggles her fingers at me. "But the lattice would be a more effective barrier to the Games Makers. These guys are the best there is. They're training us. They're going to be able to get through any rune code we use. That's the point of us doing something new."

"And you think they can't smash their way through a lattice?"

"Not one of mine," she replies, folding her arms.

The lights in the training room flicker on, lanterns on the wall throwing dark shadows and orange glows over the workstations.

"You're being naïve," I say, kneading my temple.

"And you're being pigheaded. How can I put this so it will go through that thick academic skull of yours? Your code, while it might have acute accuracy, is like a system of roaming lasers. Complex and difficult to evade, yes. But if you're light with your fingers and adept enough, you can dance right through it."

"Oh really? And that makes your lattice system what?"

"A solid 20ft wall of granite." She beams at me like this is obvious, and that what we're discussing isn't a philosophical debate about rune principles. I'm not uncultured enough to realise there is no right or wrong answer. Of course there isn't. Both our systems are fine. But if we're talking fucking principles, then I'm not budging on mine.

I roll my eyes. "Brilliant. So all I'd need is a big rune bomb, and I'd be able to blow it apart."

She pouts at me and folds her arms. "I'd like to see you create a bomb that big."

"So to summarise, we still don't know how to work with each other for tomorrow's challenge and we have no great ideas for building an impenetrable security system for challenge three, either?"

The Merricks pack up their station and walk past us smirking.

"Enjoy tomorrow ladies, we will," Gabe says.

Bella opens her mouth to spit jeers, but I reach for her hand, and she flinches.

"Let's leave it all on the field. We can show them what we're made of tomorrow."

She snatches her hand away. "What if the smack talk turns me on?"

I tilt my head at her. "If Gabe Merrick turns you on, then I've made an egregious error in my summation of you."

She shakes her head at me. A curl falls loose. My fingers twitch to push it behind her ear. But we're in the practice room. And anyone could walk in.

"Lighten up, Rem. Someone's got to put the Merricks in their place. That someone is me, honey." She scrunches her shoulders and gives me a mean girl sassy wink.

"I think I just puked a little in the back of my mouth."

That, at least, elicits a laugh from her. "Much as I would love to go irritate the Merricks, I promised Red a stroll on the beach. I'll see you in the apartment."

She leaves. My eyes drop to her arse; hips wiggling like that should be illegal. I'm about to castigate myself when she looks over her shoulder, understands precisely where I was looking and kicks her hips out further.

That woman will ruin me.

I reach into the cupboard of the workstation. I've been storing books here. Every night, I stay late. I've had no choice. Not if I want the trackers to be ready. Building them is the easy bit. Figuring out a way to release them into the system is proving harder than I anticipated.

I open one of the new tomes I gathered from the library earlier and scroll through the pages.

When you have fifty teams all looking for rune anomalies to either hack or patch, how the hell do you hide what is tantamount to an anomaly? They'll be on a search and destroy mission for the very thing I'm trying to release. So how do I hide in plain sight?

I lean over the books, head in my hands, trying to think, to dig deeper than ever. I desperately don't want to let Morrigan down. Can't risk her security or Stirling's by allowing Roman to escape. And that's without what the Daily Imperium would do to me. I might be their darling right now, but what happens when they find out the truth? Oh, I'll still have a paparazzi problem, but it won't be to find out where I've been or who I'm dating. The paps will claw through my past, hunting for anything they can use to take me down. They say an underdog story is popular, but a fall from grace? That story eclipses them all. And if I can't release these trackers, that's exactly where I'm heading.

"You're here late."

I startle and look up. "Marcel, hey."

"Good evening. Studying hard, as always."

"You know me too well." I smile and he hands me a mug of hot chocolate.

"Ooh, my favourite. You even remembered the marshmallows."

"As if I'd forget."

"Did you get the specs I sent you for the job you asked me about the other day?"

He nods at the mug. "My way of saying thanks. What

are you doing in here this late?" he asks. He scans the books on my table and the mini RuneNet screen I have hovering above the desk.

I wave a fast hand over the screen, shutting it down, hoping none of my code strings were visible, and shake my head at him. "Just studying. I need to win this for so many reasons."

"Do you? Your reputation precedes you. You imprisoned our favourite piece of shit, Roman Oleg. Quite the list of accolades you're accruing."

I shrug. "I mean, I provided the crown with the magic, sure. But come on, Marcel. We had to fight him and Bella for every single win. A takedown like his wasn't a one-woman job."

"Aren't you miffed that they didn't slot you into the role of Royal Rune Master?"

I frown at him and lean back in my chair. "Why would I be upset? That would be an unprecedented move."

"It was an unprecedented capture."

I hadn't really thought of it like that. "I thought it was a nice touch adding it to the prize of the Runic Games. They're such an ancient tradition. And... there's a small piece of me that needs the win."

He sits on the edge of the table. "You feel like an imposter?"

"I chose a field of study dominated by legacy magicians. Who am I to come in with no family backing, no money to my name, nothing, and foist my way to the top of the industry?"

"You are a worthy magician. That's who. You're my greatest student, Remy. Your background doesn't matter. Tradition doesn't matter. Fuck the legacies. What matters is your skill, your power." He reaches up to place a finger against my temple. "Your mind."

I smile, but my insides don't warm. There's something about his words, the aggression in them. I decide it's Morrigan and the team. They're making me doubt everything I know to be true. Finally, the smile reaches my eyes.

"There's my girl. Now, I won't bother you anymore. I can see you're working hard. I wanted to come and say hi and remind you that you have someone here who believes in you. Go get em, Remster."

He ruffles a hand over my head like he used to when I was shorter than him. I stare after him while he walks away and think back to those early days. The way he used to make me learn the old language, archaic rune magic before all the new stuff.

The other apprentices didn't bother with ancient rune theory. They never had to learn how to weave old runes that had no place in today's magic. I would kick and scream and protest and still he'd make me study. My eyes flit to my first edition of *Runes and their Magical Applications*.

'If you don't understand the old language, Remy, you don't truly understand the new. History matters, my girl.'

Marcel's voice runs through my mind dragging an idea with it. If I code the trackers using ancient runes, they're more susceptible to being hacked. But equally, they might appear old enough and benign enough that no one bothers to check them during the challenge either. After all, most rune magicians don't even learn this shit, let alone how to hack it.

Yes, this is it. This is how I get the trackers into the system. I reopen my screen, expand it and push my sleeves up. It's going to be a long couple of nights.

♕

The morning of the challenge, Bella is up and bouncing around the apartment. I, however, feel like a dried-up necrotic husk of a magician.

I stare at myself in the mirror. Bags hang like bruised plums under my eyes. My skin is paler than a ghost and even my hair looks lank.

Wonderful.

But it will be worth it if I can release the trackers safely and secure a top-ranking position for us in the challenge.

"Here," Bella says, handing me a mug of potent coffee. I wince as I take a sip. It tastes more like fermented carriage oil than coffee as it slides down my throat.

"What did you put in it?" I ask.

"Back in the city, there's an apothecary called... er... like Quinn's something. Meds? Remedies? Anyway, doesn't matter. She sells the most ferocious herbs, best in the city if you ask me. And the ones I dropped into your mug, they'll have you feeling bright and sparky in no time. It's like coffee on steroids. You're welcome, by the way."

I stare down into the mug and make a note to check with Quinn what she's selling and whether it's legal.

I sigh, a heavy lump of a sound and sag onto the stool by the kitchen island.

"Something on your mind?" Bella says and sits opposite me.

Yes, where do I even start?

"No," I say. But I can't quite bring my eyes to hers.

"I might not be your favourite person, but I have known you for a long time, and you're a terrible liar."

"Fine. Yes, I'm bothered. Our practice sessions haven't exactly gone well, have they?"

She juts her chin up. "Yes, well, if you'd listen to my logic, then perhaps that wouldn't be the case."

I pull my hand over my face. "We've gone through this. We need to compromise before the challenge, otherwise we're going to end up fighting each other rather than the other teams."

"This is the most ridiculous set up for a competition I've ever heard of. Who puts people into teams when there's only one prize for one person?" Bella says and picks at a smudge on the counter.

"Sadists. Though I suspect that's part of the point. The role of Royal Rune Master requires teamwork. If we can't work together, how do we lead a team?"

She opens her mouth to protest and promptly shuts it. "I see your point."

"So we're agreed?" I say.

"That my lattices are the more efficient method to use? Sure."

"Bella!"

She grins at me. "Gods, you're so easy to wind up when you're tired. Fine. We have to work together. But this job is as important to me as it is to you. I want to earn as many points in this challenge as you do. So which one of us is going to bend the knee? Cause I can assure you, it isn't me."

I want to scream at her to stop being childish, but I'm not ignorant enough to recognise the fact that I am behaving the same way she is. We both need this for very different reasons. It doesn't matter that my reasons are superior, I can't ignore the fact that if we don't work together, neither of us are going to win.

I open my mouth to propose a compromise, but there's a soft knock at the door. Bella bounces on tip toes and opens the door.

"Red," she smiles.

Red steps into the flat, and a voice hollers down the corridor.

"Wait."

Stirling.

Bella holds the door open. "Hi umm, I'm sorry. I forgot your name."

"Stirling, and I'm mortally offended you didn't remember me."

Bella's eyes widen.

"I'm kidding. I'm actually here to see your teammate. Oh hey, Red." Stirling strides in.

"Wait. You know Remy *and* Red?" Bella says.

Stirling grins. "Interesting story, that. I met Red in a different city, if I remember rightly."

Red gives her a nod. "A city in the north."

"The fae city?" I ask, frowning.

"Yeah, I can't even remember why I was there now, but Red was looking for a specific Fae weapon that's deadly to vampires, and I happened to know a girl who had stolen it out from the Fae years back. So I hooked Red up."

Red nods along, "And very grateful I was too."

"And then, when I needed to start importing Sanguis Cūpa for Claude, I used a magician colleague who had contacts in Sangui City to reach Red. Red's been sending me bottles ever since."

"Small world," I say.

"Anyway, need a word," Stirling says and tilts her head to the bedroom.

Bella's eyes narrow as she glances between Stirling and me. As I gather my mug of coffee-extra and follow Stirling, I realise that Bella won't have seen us together before. At best, she'd have seen Stirling and Morrigan. She closes the door and pulls me close.

"Are you ready?" she says under her breath.

"Yes, but I am relying on everyone else being too distracted to notice what I'm doing."

Stirling grimaces. "I hate that I need to ask this, but what do you mean?"

"You have a group of fifty teams, half of which are there to hack the prison, the other half are there to look for runic anomalies and seek and destroy."

She looks at me blankly.

"When did you leave school? Don't you know anything about runes?"

"One, rude. Two, why would I need to? I know a girl... that girl is you, by the way. Now who's smart?" She taps her nose like she's a secret genius, and I honestly don't know what to do with her.

Exasperated, I continue. "Morrigan's asking me to feed an anomaly into the system with half the teams--twenty-five highly competent magicians--hunting them."

"Right. And did you find a way around this predicament?"

I give her a look that suggests she should reconsider the assumption that I'd fail.

"Okay, okay, so how are you getting around it?"

"I used an archaic form of runes to code the tracker. It's called Runata Majora, and I'm hoping it's innocuous enough that no one would think it was interesting. Essentially I—"

Stirling holds up her hand. "Good job, bud. I've heard enough. Give the details to Morrigan. You know how she loves to nerd out."

Stirling heads back to the kitchen. "Come on, Red, I can get you one of the best seats in the house if you like."

"Fuck yeah," Red says and trots after Stirling.

We head out, following the pair of them down into the central foyer where we find Games Maker Eli. He's standing with an orb in front of his mouth. He clears his throat and his voice booms around the foyer.

"Magicians and friends, this morning marks the first of our challenges. We're going to head under the ocean and into the bowels of Lantis Palace to its Rune Server room. Good luck to you all, and may you all cast true. Let's go, the princess waits."

I glance at Bella. For the first time since arriving here, she looks hesitant. Her eyes flicker across the foyer, scanning our competitors. She periodically chews on a nail. I swipe her hand away from her mouth, but she huffs at me and puts it back.

I glance around, but Stirling has vanished. Morrigan, I assume, will be in the palace's Rune Server room by now, and I don't see Quinn or Scarlett. I slide my hand into Bella's.

"It's going to be fine."

She glances down at our hands, and I think she's going to pull away, but she doesn't. Instead, she rubs her thumb over the back of my hand. "Thanks."

We stroll along behind the throng of contestants following Games Maker Eli and descend into the belly of Lantis Palace. Like the spiralling staircase in the heart of the building that we traipse up daily, there's an identical one burrowing into the earth beneath the palace. It turns and turns and turns, drilling deeper under the ocean until the air is suffocating and heavy and a little bit wet. Lanterns burn crystal blue flames on the walls, casting eerie glows and shadows over us as we file into the base of the palace.

We step into a large circular room, similar to the grand room above us. Only this room has doors and tunnels veering off it. The Games Maker doesn't wait. He continues his trudge through the warren of tunnels.

Finally, we pull to a stop. I'm no longer sure if we're really in the Lantis palace. The air has changed. My ears popped on the way down, but they've popped again now, as if we've climbed back up out of the ocean.

"Welcome to the Lantis Palace Rune Server," Eli says.

I guess we are still in the palace then, or at least in a connected room.

"You'll wait here in the green room. Inside is a select audience, including her royal highness, who will preside over the challenge. I will set screens here—"

He raises his fingers and forms hovering screens for us to watch contestants. Then he forms another for live scoring, just like the training room.

"Two teams will be called in at a time," he says.

There's muttering, and he holds his hands up, seeking silence.

"This first challenge will, in some ways, be the toughest. By the end of this challenge, only half of you will remain. This is a fight to the finish line. If the hackers successfully hack into the bank's main rune database, they win, and knock the patcher team out of the running. If the patchers successfully keep the hackers out for the full six-minute timer, then the patchers win. This is sudden death. And half of you won't survive."

Bella glances at me, her eyes harden, and she straightens her shoulders. "We're going to smash this."

"Yes, we are."

The first contestants are taken through the largest arched oak doors I've ever seen. They must be three times my height and I'm not short.

The hovering screens flicker to life, and the Rune Net appears. It zeroes in on a prison system. I expected to see the room and the contestants themselves, instead, we get to watch their code.

Four avatars appear: the patchers in white, the hackers in blue. A clock in the top right-hand corner. The second screen shimmers and their names and a six-minute timer appears by them.

The timer starts and the teams burst to life. The screen fills with rune codes. Dozens, hundreds, thousands of runic symbols scroll across the screen. Hackers always have the advantage. It's easier to destroy code than it is to write and create it.

But if you're a skilled patcher, then you can create some preset strings of secure runes that you can weave together faster than writing from scratch. Anyone with any sense will have prepped in advance. I suspect that's what this team did because the patchers are fast, like really fast.

They're dissolving the hacker's aggressive runes quicker than the hackers can cast more runes into the system.

"Basic Mesh Runes," Bella whispers in my ear. "The hackers haven't got a chance. It's complex rune magic. I studied them during my apprenticeship. The problem is, if you don't know how to use a de-threading rune, you don't stand a chance."

Sure enough, two minutes later, the timer runs out, and the hackers' lights go dark. The second screen flashes, and the patcher winners appear.

It goes like this for almost forty minutes. Ten teams go in, five come out smiling. The Merricks are called.

Predictably, they win, and in quick time, too, shaving a minute off the previous winning hack.

"That's our target then," Bella says.

And I glance up at the clock. Three minutes, fifty.

It's fast. Too fast, especially since I need to release the trackers. But I can't worry about it anymore. The doors slide open and Eli holds his arm out for us to enter.

CHAPTER 12

BELLA

I have only ever been in one other Rune Server room, and it was as breathtaking as this one. I have to force my mouth closed.

In the heart of the circular room is the server hub, a vast set of concentric circles. One set on the ground, the other hanging from the ceiling. Between them, the connections to the RuneNet shimmer in glistening threads beaming between the circles. Runic symbols float at speed up and down in spider-like beams. Around the circles on the ground is a casting table and two sets of seats opposite each other.

The floor is dark slate, and carved into the tiles are gilded runes—the old language. Above us around the edge of the room is a circular balcony. In the centre sits a throne, with princess Morrigan looking regal and emotionless. To her left and right are a group of magicians, most of whom I don't recognise. A little further down, Red sits. She catches my eye and smiles.

The walls are the same gilded slate as the floor, and every few feet, there are arched glass windows that peer out into the ocean. Fish and creatures swim lazily by.

"Take your seats," Eli says.

I follow Remy to the table.

"Ready to cast on?" Games Maker, Eli says.

Morrigan and the magicians all stand and move to the edge of the balcony. This is it.

Eli offers Remy a choice of two cards. She pulls one and flips it over. It has a golden H on it.

"Congratulations, you'll be hacking," he says and moves around the other side of the table to hand the patcher team their card.

"Timer!" Eli shouts, and the strings flowing between floor and ceiling of the Rune Server swell. A shimmering clock pops out of the strings to hover in the air like a bronze omen.

"Hacking team, you have six minutes to hack into Blackmont Bank. Patchers, you have six minutes to stop them. Ready your runes."

He pauses while we hold out our hands.

Blackmont? That rings a bell. Why does—? That's Roman's bank. An idea twitches in my mind. It's risky.

"Three," Eli says.

Remy's wearing an expression I can't quite place.

"Two."

She seems skittish, her cheeks flushed, but even as I stare at her, eyes shifting to black, hands vibrating, I decide it's probably just nerves.

"One."

I take a deep breath, sink into my magic, and cast on to the Rune Server.

Being this close to the server is like standing in front of

an engine powered by the sun. Runes fly through the ether and latch into the system. Threads disconnect from their pulsing beams and wiggle through the air to connect with my arms. It takes a second to steady myself. It's like I've spent my life paddling in ocean shallows and they've just thrown me into the middle of the ocean in a hurricane.

The patchers' avatars appear in white on the screen. Remy and I are in blue at the bottom of the screen.

"The exterior rune wall is a basic four-rune code lock," Remy says.

"On it," I answer and draw out several runes. There's no point using a lattice or weaving now, not until we're inside the system.

It breaks in seconds. The runes dissolving. I glance at Remy's side of the screen and she was...what the hell was she doing?

"Are you helping or relaxing?" I bark.

"Helping, gods. I was assessing the internal Rune walls." She says it so casually I almost believe her, but my gut bottoms out like something isn't right.

I use a lock pick rune to hack the next layer of bank security, but as soon as I'm in, the patchers appear.

"Remy shit, watch out," I shout.

But she's already on it, flinging exploding runes into the bank security and annihilating the avatar of one of the patchers.

"Oops," she says without a trace of remorse.

"Cold. Ice cold, hun." But I'm cackling at the lead we're amassing. Adrenaline threads into my system, the wild force of it melding with my magic and augmenting my power. It's extraordinary. Addictive.

The bank's infrastructure appears and dislodges the

conversation I had with Red... *follow the money*... Well, this is Roman's bank. It would be stupid not to take advantage. But can I do this without being caught?

I split my hands--one continues weaving the challenge lattice, the other spells a new set of runes. I weave a micro lattice to cover the new code and thread it into the system. I won't know if it worked until later. But if it does work, I'll have found the bastard who hacked me.

"I want to win," Remy says breaking me out of my distraction.

I glance up at the clock. Shit. "We're already a minute in. How many layers left?"

"Three," she says, "but we're only combatting one patcher now."

Remy fires a set of intricately spelled runes. Later, I'll tell her they're exquisitely spelled, like a master artwork. They weave their way into the system and unpick everything the solo patcher is throwing at us.

Something flashes across the screen and disappears into the subnet. I frown. We're not using the subnet. It vanishes, and I can't decide if I'm seeing things or if it really happened. It was an ancient rune. A simple spell, something I haven't seen used in any tech, ever. I wonder if it's a bug or an artefact from a previous iteration of the bank system. Without knowing how old this bank is, I can't be sure.

I shrug it off, deciding it was nothing, and follow up behind Remy's code. But it makes me want to shield us from any bugs. Create a defence system as we push through the bank's code.

"I want to try something," I say.

"Oh, now is a great time for experimenting."

"I'm doing it. You need to trust me."

And I weave. Threading a double lattice, one layer to cocoon us in and protect us from the patcher and a second layer that will slowly expand out. It will eat any code the patcher or bank can throw at us.

"Wh—what are you doing?" Remy says as we approach the final set of runic security measures.

"Protecting us. What does it look like?"

"Bella, drop the lattice," she says, her voice a hiss.

Deep lines carve into my brow. "What the fuck is your problem? This will keep us from any security runes the patcher releases on us." I'm growling.

"I know. But...I—I need you to drop it. I can't cast any more code from inside this lattice."

"You don't need to cast anymore, Remy." My voice is low, a warning. "The lattice will do the job. This is a compromise. Besides, I can't do anything now. The lattice protecting us is woven into the lattice currently eating up the final security wall. Or are you distracted enough you're no longer even reading the rune code?"

I glance over. She wipes a hand over her face. "Please understand, I'm sorry."

She releases one of her rune bombs, only it doesn't speed into the patcher's code. It nestles in a line of code right at the knotted mesh of runes forming the structural support code for the lattice.

I gasp. "Remy, what the actual fuck?"

There's a ripple of drawn breaths around the room. I peer up and all the audience members are leaning over the balcony railing as if trying to get closer to the screens. I turn back to ours, realising the patcher has gained on us. Then the rune blows a hole eighteen code lines deep in the lattice.

"Fuck me. What the hell are you doing? I can't lose this. Talk to me for fucks sake, Remy. The patcher has us cornered. Shit, the code, the code. We're not going to get out of this."

My skin prickles, my stomach writhes. I feel sick. Something is going on, and we're going to lose this fucking challenge. "We can't both get out of this."

Remy grabs my hand so tight it hurts. "We can't, but you can. Please trust me."

"What?"

"Trust me. Fire your lattice up and let it finish the job. I have to... Listen, I'm going to sacrifice myself, so you can still finish. But I need you to do something for me," she says, a line of sweat dripping from her brow.

"I don't—"

"Just listen. There's a string of Runata Majora buried in the subnet. Execute it. Use me as a shield and get into the bank's data core. Okay?"

I nod. My breathing is heavy. The stricken expression pouring across Remy's face tells me she's deadly serious, that something is very wrong, and I should listen. For once, I do.

Remy's avatar races out of the carcass of my lattice and I re engage, weaving a new lattice so fast my fingers burn with the pressure.

Remy's avatar shields me the entire way. The clock ticks down. I release the final thread and the lattice charges forward, demolishing the last lines of code as Remy's avatar evaporates. There, buried in the disintegrating dust of her avatar, is the link to the subnet. The patcher hasn't seen it. She's racing for me, battling against the lattice.

"Bella," Remy hisses next to me.

My lattice is almost through the remaining wall. If I

don't hit execute, the challenge will finish and whatever Remy is doing won't complete.

"Please," she breathes. "Bella, please."

I hit execute just as the screens go blank.

CHAPTER 13

REMY

I wipe the line of sweat from my forehead and thank the gods that Bella did what I asked for once. I really didn't believe she would execute the Runata Majora. But she did. I have to find something I can say that isn't a lie without also confessing that I am working secretly to track all the contestants.

I swallow hard as we traipse out of the Rune Server. Our time flashes up onto the scoreboard. A cheer erupts from the corner of the waiting room the Merricks are standing in.

The clock reads three minutes fifty-six.

Dammit. The Merricks beat us by six seconds. At least we made it through. But second place is starting to grate.

Bella seems less than impressed. She gives the Merricks the finger and marches out of the waiting room and into the corridor we came from.

"Wait," I say.

But she's already gone.

Stirling appears. "Morrigan wants to see you." She leads

me around another corridor and up a flight of stairs and through a door that leads to the balcony.

Below, another set of contestants are already battling. It looks neck and neck right now.

Morrigan and Quinn stand.

Morrigan reaches out and shakes my hand as if congratulating me. I bow my head in deference, playing along for anyone watching.

"Were you successful?" she asks.

"I was, but I won't have any data until tomorrow at the earliest."

"Okay." Her lips press into a thin line.

"Everything okay?"

She shakes her head. "There was a break-in at another prison. One on the other side of the city."

"Did anyone escape?" I ask.

But it's Scarlett that answers. Stirling steps out of the way as she appears with a sheet of paper.

"No. We're not sure if it was a red herring. No one escaped and nothing was stolen. But the story will run in the Daily Imperium tomorrow."

"Dammit. That will only shine more light on the competition and any technologies coming out of the games," Morrigan says.

"Can you prevent it from running?" Scarlett says.

Stirling shakes her head. "I—I don't think so. I know a girl who works for the paper, but I already asked her for a favour when we were working on the Roman case. She wasn't too pleased after... Look. Point is, I can't help with this one."

"Could always poison the paper staff. A spontaneous case of the squirts for the entire department," Quinn shrugs.

"Too obvious," Stirling says as if it weren't a ludicrous idea and she'd genuinely considered it.

"We have to let it run," I say.

"You never know, it might force the perp out into the light," I say.

But Morrigan doesn't look convinced. If anything, her skin pales. "Update me on the tracking data as soon as you have it. Have you found anything on Bella yet?"

I shake my head. "She's clean. But I guess the trackers will bring something to light if there's anything there to find."

"And if there's not?" Quinn asks.

Scarlett shifts her footing. "Then we narrow our search. After the ball tomorrow night, there will be half as many suspects to deal with. Quinn, can you pull files together on the remaining contestants?"

"Sure, I'll start once the challenge is complete and we know who's left."

By the time I get to the apartment, Bella is already in the shower. I make us both tea and wait for her to finish. While she's faffing, I pull up the data from my bugs. The programs running are meant to highlight any suspicious conversations or behaviour. I pop an earbud in and listen to a conversation between the Merrick siblings.

It's mostly inconsequential, though it seems like their parents are harbouring debt. I can't help but feel a little vindicated after what they called me on day one. If their parents go bankrupt perhaps they'll understand what it's like coming from the Borderlands. Much as it's juicy gossip, it doesn't connect them to Roman.

"Oh, hey," Bella says as she comes out of the bathroom with nothing but a towel covering her body. I slam the RuneNet closed and stall out. Water drips down Bella's skin in rivulets that I want to run my tongue over and lick up.

"H-Hi," I say.

My hand skims my book, *Runes and their Magical Applications*. Bella nestles in next to me.

"That thing looks like it's about to fall apart," she says and lifts the cover. The book falls open to the inscription. "May the old ways keep us together. Love your big brother." She reads the inscription.

"How did you decode that so fast? Took me weeks to figure it out."

But Bella has gone pale. "We should talk about the challenge" she says, but turns her back on me and walks into the bedroom.

I follow, grateful that finally, after a week, they've changed the bed. Although instead of adding a second one, they've replaced the single with a double.

"Oh my gods, how can they get furniture this wrong?" I say.

"Can't get the staff," Bella says and just like that, whatever was wrong has vanished from her face, the colour pouring back into her bronze skin.

I'm going to have to explain what happened in the challenge. I don't want her thinking I jeopardised our win.

"Thank you for helping me," I say.

She huffs and sits down on the bed. Her towel splits, as she straightens a smooth brown leg and rubs moisturiser over her skin. It's distracting.

"Sure," she says but won't look at me.

I never used to care if we communicated, but I can't bear the wall building between us. It makes my whole body rigid with unease. "I can't deal with this...Whatever this is. I need to know what the issue is. You're being weird and it's uncomfortable."

She glares up at me with the intensity of a volcano.

"My issue? I'll tell you what my fucking issue is. You—!" She stabs a finger into my chest. "You're my problem, Remy. The better part of a week you kept pushing me to compromise. And then you what? Throw some bullshit in your runes, slow us down, nearly cost us the fucking challenge, and for what?"

I fold my arms. "Are you finished?" I say.

"No. *Fuck you*... Okay. Now I'm finished."

I sniff to muffle a laugh, and scratch at my face to hide the curl tugging my mouth. Her face cracks as if she wants to laugh but then she forces it back to fierce.

"You better not be laughing. I swear to the High Magician, you cost me this contest and I will end you. What the hell were you doing, anyway? I didn't have time to read the code. Who even uses Runata Majora code like that these days, anyway?"

This is the moment I was dreading. What the hell do I say? I don't want to lie to her. But I can't tell the truth without betraying Morrigan.

Before I can answer, she continues.

"It looked like.... But why?" she's mumbling talking to herself.

"Go on..." I say, hoping beyond hope she hasn't figured it out. How long was she reading the code before the system shut us out? It couldn't have been more than a second or two.

She picks up a brush and runs it through her wet curls.

"It looked like a tracking code."

Fuck. My mouth runs dry. I blink at her. Once, twice. She inhales.

"Gods, it was, wasn't it? Remy. You sly fucking dog. I didn't think you were the type."

I start to deny the accusation when she stands up, her towel dropping to the floor, leaving her stark naked. It takes every ounce of my strength to keep my eyes on her face.

"You fucking genius. If you were going to track all the contestants, why the hell didn't you tell me? Now we'll know all the strategies they're using. We'll know all their weaknesses. Any strengths or advantages they may have."

She jumps up and down, her breasts bouncing. I try to process what she's saying. But the distraction of her bronzed flesh, the curve of her stomach, the roundness in her thighs, all of it bouncing. Fuck. I don't give a shit about the tracking code anymore. My pussy is drenched and all because of the sight of her.

"You're, er—" I point down, keeping my eyes trained on hers.

But she isn't paying attention either. She bouncing on her toes. Once, twice more, and then she's jumping into my arms.

I catch her. She laces her arms around my neck and brushes her lips against mine. My hands cross under her arse and thighs, holding her in place. But I can't help but feel the heat of her pussy pushed against the hard plane of my stomach.

"You absolutely cannot be naked like that." I glance down. She tilts her hips up so I can see the bare flesh of her pussy.

"Why? Do you see something you like?" she purrs.

"Bella," I say, my voice low and edged with need. But she licks her lips, her eyes twinkling at me, full of teasing and wanting, and something snaps in me. I swing her around and walk us until she slides on top of a chest of drawers. It puts her higher than me. She cups my jaw with her fingers and tips my chin up at her.

She hitches her arse forward to the edge of the furniture and then she spreads her legs, baring her pussy to me, keeping her eyes locked on mine the entire time.

"I think we should celebrate your deviousness, don't you, Professor Reid?"

"Oh? And how do you think we should do that?"

Her hand slips from my chin to cup the back of my head. She pulls me up onto tiptoes and to her mouth. Soft lips caress mine, our mouths gliding over each other. She kisses me deeper, hungrier, pulling me tight to her body.

My hands glide over her naked thighs and up the damp skin of her back. I run a delicate finger down her spine, and she breaks the kiss, arching into my body as goosebumps shiver across her arms.

I barely have nails, but I slide what I do have over her damp skin and it makes her arch even further. This time, her nipples peak into exquisite brown buds.

"I need you," she breathes. And her words are enough to make me crack, to make me get on my knees and worship her.

I lean close to her, inhaling the coconut and lavender soap on her skin. It's all I can do not to salivate as my breath trickles over her skin. My hands find the curves of her body, slipping to her waist. I close my eyes and lean my forehead against hers. Gods, this woman drives me wild. I want to taste her, hold her. I want to fuck her more than I want to breathe right now. But things are shifting and changing between us. If I keep doing this, how unbiased am I going to remain?

How much longer can this continue without Morrigan or Stirling or Scarlett, or gods, even Quinn finding out? And what happens if they do?

"Remy," Bella whispers and she takes my hand from her waist and drops it to her knee. "If you don't fuck me..."

She guides my fingers towards her pussy, closer. Closer. She pushes two between her slick folds, nudging me lower until I circle her hole. Then, as I dip inside her warmth, she pulls me away, dragging my hand up her body and placing my fingers in my mouth.

"Do I need to fuck myself, or am I sweet enough to tempt you?"

I crack.

Every ounce of me needs her. I grip her ass, tug her to me, and lower my mouth to her wet pussy. She moans and grinds her hips against my face. I lick long, greedy swipes over her clit. I suck her into my mouth until she moans against me.

"Fuck, Remy."

I pull away, reach up to her mouth, and kiss her. Our tongues dance a waltz. My fingers find her core and I thrust inside her. She grips my arms; her nails long enough to scrape as she digs in and reclines her head. My arms will bear her marks tomorrow, and I don't care. I want them. I want her to mark me so I remember, so she remembers.

I drive my fingers harder into her pussy, hard enough it makes the chest of drawers knock against the wall. A rhythmic thumping , a beat for the melody of Bella's pants and moans.

I kiss my way down her neck, nipping the skin to elicit those carnal sounds that make me as wet as she is.

"Wait," she says.

I pull out immediately and go still.

"What's wrong? Did I hurt you?"

She blushes, her cheeks deepening. "No. Of course not," she kisses me and when she pulls away, there's a glimmer and a flutter in her eyes that are full of lust.

"How do you feel about straps?" she says.

"Did you bring one?"

"Top of the case."

I stroll over to her suitcase, take off my trousers, and pull it on over my boxers. I pick up the bottle of lube. She doesn't need it, but it won't hurt either.

"What do you think?" I grin.

"I think I'm about to come all over it."

"I can't wait. But..." I hesitate, unsure how to say it. Not wanting to ruin the moment.

"Never on you?" she asks.

I shake my head. "I—I don't like them."

She nods, and the bit of tension that had found its way into my shoulders evaporates.

"You have to get down, though. I'm tall, but not that tall."

I grab her hand and help her down.

She struts ahead of me, swinging her arse deliberately wide. She cocks her head over her shoulder.

"Enjoying the view?"

I tense, lust making me impatient. "Get on the bed, right now."

She slides a knee on the bed, then another, 'til she's on all fours, her head at the top of the bed, her pussy on display. She slowly inches her knees wider.

I climb on the bed behind her, pour lube over the cock, and then smear it with my fingers, which I promptly slide down her more than soaking pussy. She leans into my fingers.

"Use my hand. Get yourself ready for me," I say.

She grins as she rubs and grinds against my palm. I've had enough, though. I want her pleasure under in my control.

I pull my hand away and she gives me a mock pout until I slide the hard cock to her entrance. Her lids droop with hunger. She sucks the corner of her lip into her mouth and tilts her hips an inch, so the cock pushes into her entrance. Then the little brat grins at me, knowing precisely what she's done.

"Did I say you could have me yet?"

"I—"

I shove into her, silencing her. She scruffs the bedsheets in her fingers, as I thrust until my thighs meet hers.

"Fuck," she mumbles.

"Yes," I say, drawing out of her, "I plan to."

Our words slide away then, as I pump inside her, drawing her pleasure out. I angle my hips so the cock grinds against her front wall. It elicits a whimper that makes excitement pool between my legs.

I lean over her back, palming her breasts and tweaking a nipple. She drives her ass into my thighs, riding me harder. I leave her breasts and slip a hand between her thighs, finding her clit.

"Remy," she gasps. "Fuck. Fuck."

"Something you want to say?"

"Faster, touch me faster. I need more."

I acquiesce, though I have to fight the urge to slow down. Desperate to draw this out, wring every drop of pleasure out of her.

I pull out, flip her onto her back, and pull one of her legs up and over my shoulder. I re-enter her and pump hard. She pulls her leg closer to her chest, drawing me down and angling the cock deeper.

Her head rolls back, her eyes closing under the pressure of pleasure. I lean my mouth against her knee, skimming kisses against her soft skin. My teeth glide against the flesh of her thigh. I nip and bite as I slide my palm to her clit, adding just enough pressure to create friction.

Her hand grips my wrist, holding me in place. She digs her nails in as she cries out. Her body twitches. I drive the cock deep inside her until her back arches, her mouth open in a silent scream.

"I'm going to—" she cries, but the rest is inaudible. She gasps as shivers wrack her body. She lies flat and motionless, her breathing heavy. I draw the cock out and unstrap the buckles, letting it slide to the floor. I move up the bed and pull her into my arms.

"Oh, don't think just because I'm spent that I don't have the energy to fuck you silly," she says.

"And here I was thinking I'd won this round."

"Please. As if I'd ever let you give me a bigger orgasm than I give you."

I raise an eyebrow at her, but she's already on her knees, scrambling out of my arms and pulling at my boxers.

I hitch my bum up and help her yank them down. She continues until she slides off the end of the bed and pulls them off my feet. Her fingers wrap around my ankles and she pulls my legs until my bum is on the edge of the bed.

"Sit up," she demands and then lowers herself to the floor. She sits back, feet under legs, hands palm up on her knees.

Gods.

She's submitting herself to me. I swallow hard. It makes

my whole body ignite. "I didn't think you had it in you,"
I say.

"Had what in me?"

"To be a good girl."

Her bottom lip parts, a slow breath drawn in. I know my
words have the intended effect. Her goosebumps peak over
her arms.

"Do you like it when I call you a good girl?" I ask. My
voice is low, commanding.

She looks up at me. "Try it outside of this room, and I'll
gut you before you can finish the sentence." She flicks her
hair over her shoulder. "But in here..." she shrugs, as if she
can't quite bring herself to say it. Because telling me means
she submits herself to me, to my control, and that is the
antithesis of who we are to each other.

"I see. Well then," I scoot the last inch to the edge of the
bed and open my legs, displaying her prize to her. "Be a
good girl. Come over here and lick my cunt."

Her eyes flash, and I'm not sure if it's lust or desperation
or some unbridled concoction of both. This is new for us.
Hell, it's new for me. But there's something about her. I
want to own every inch of her. She makes me want to get
on my knees and pleasure her until my last breath. She
makes me want to give her everything she needs. And if
that includes me keeping her safe in the bedroom, then I'll
die before I let her come to harm.

She shuffles forward, places her hands on my knees,
and then draws her tongue along my thigh, licking and
sucking and nibbling at the skin. I'm soaking by the time
her tongue flickers over my pussy.

It takes a monumental effort to stay upright as she
draws a hard lick down my slit.

I hiss as my clit tingles. I lean back, exposing more of

myself to her. It only encourages her to lick rougher. She slides her tongue into my opening. It makes my head drop back, a growled moan billowing from my chest.

"Fuck," I say.

She moans into my pussy, drawing slow licks from my entrance all the way to my clit. I lean down, slide my hand into her hair, and hold her mouth to my pussy.

She releases a whimper, her eyes closing with pleasure as I rock my hips against her mouth. She grabs my thighs, pushing herself harder against me.

"Mmm," she says. And then she pulls back, sliding her hand between my legs.

I slow my hips to a stop, enabling her to push a finger inside me. She looks up, locking eyes with me, and the world evaporates. She holds my gaze like I'm her everything and it scares me. This moment is too much. We can't be like this. It's dangerous. I don't even know if I can trust her, even if I want to. In this moment, I feel like I can.

But what if Morrigan is right?

My chest is so full I can barely breathe. She pumps her finger inside me until I'm wet enough and relaxed enough she can slide a second in and all my thoughts give way to the pleasure.

My pussy throbs as she creates a rhythm with her fingers, her mouth, all of it pulling waves of pulsing pleasure through my body. I glance down at her figure between my thighs and I don't want it to end. I want her between my legs now and always.

Staring at her winds me tighter, electric pulses erupting from my clit, throbbing through my pussy, making me pant. My hips move again as her tongue ravishes my clit. As my whole body tightens, she pulls her tongue back; the pressure easing on my aching clit. But she thrusts her fingers harder.

Her tongue softens, teasing my apex with light licks as she rides my cunt with her hand. The softness of her mouth, her lips massaging my pussy against the hardness of her fingers, makes my entire body tremble against her, my walls tighten.

"Bella," I pant. My hips jerk forward, and I tip over into the bliss of orgasm.

I jerk my hips against her face. Her remaining hand grasps my thigh so tight her nails dig into my skin, sending pain-pleasure waves through me.

She slides her fingers in, out, in again.

"Bella," I growl. It's too much, the pleasure swelling in giant waves.

She just grins at me, and slow and steady, pulls out of me, but not before she gives me one last lick that makes my whole body quake under her touch.

She stands but wobbles; her legs gone dead under her. She pulls me standing, and wraps her arms around my shoulders and kisses me deep, her hands caressing my shaved undercut and my neck.

She tastes of sex and longing. But laced in the kiss is a twisting in my gut. I can't keep doing this. At some point we're going to get caught, or worse, she'll find out I'm tracking everyone, including her, and not cheating. And something tells me she'll never forgive me.

CHAPTER 14

BELLA

I wake curled in Remy's arms. My hair is loose and spread over her chest, my face buried against her side. I fit. Right here, wrapped in her, and that is the strangest thought. Every cell in my body wants to wriggle closer, breathe in the smell of her and stay wrapped in her arms all day. But I can't.

I head to my suitcase to grab fresh clothes; loungewear shorts and a hoodie will do. My fingers skim over the envelope at the bottom of my case and I flinch. Gods, I let Remy pull my strap out of here last night. What was I thinking? What if she'd found it? The second note that Red gave me is hidden between two jumpers. I push both of them to the bottom of the case and pile clothes on them.

Remy gave me the final piece of the puzzle. I still can't believe it. I need to check the code I inserted into the RuneNet banking system during the challenge. But I have no doubt now. I know who's doing this.

I shower, change and take myself out of the palace and

down to the beach. I sit against the curve of a cliff wall so that I can see anyone approaching. I take my shoes and socks off and let my toes sink into the cool sand. The cliff is cold and hard against my back and it takes a few adjustments to find a ridge I can settle against.

As I pull up a RuneNet screen and cast on, the ocean laps against the shore, serenading me with a melody of crashing baby waves. I create a sequence of runes and push them into the screen. They hunt down the code I planted during the challenge and pull it onto the screen.

This bit takes some finesse. I hack into the bank's system and hunt for Roman's account.

There.

I widen my screen and allow it to populate with all the coin transactions.

There's one account that pops ups regularly. Big amounts, small. I single out the data, pull it onto a new screen and clear away the rest. The transfers date back decades.

Something vibrates against my thigh, I squeal at the sudden sensation as it snaps me out of my revelation. The vibrating grows more insistent. I sit up, irritated at the interruption, and dig my orb out. I hit reject, but it buzzes again. My fingers reluctantly pull the screen out. It hovers above the orb, shimmering in the morning light. A message appears.

I'm coming to the ball, there's much to discuss. Meet me in the foyer at 11.

Mother. Shit. What the hell does she want? She said they wouldn't come until the finale. Fucksake. I shut down my RuneNet and head back to the apartment.

By the time I arrive, Remy is bent over several orbs and

the RuneNet, with two screens hovering in the air above the living room desk. Her hair, usually in a neat up-do, is fuzzy like she's been pulling her hands through it.

"Everything okay?" I ask, switching the kettle on and pulling mugs out.

"What did you do to the Runata Majora?"

"Nothing, I released it using one of the lattice threads."

"Ah, well, could you disconnect the lattice, because I'm trying to draw data from the trackers, and I think it's blocked by the thread."

"Someone's keen to spy on the remaining contestants."

Remy looks up at me and pouts.

"Alright, alright." I drop two scoops of coffee granules in the mugs and a sprinkle of Quinn's powder. Once the kettle finishes, I pour us coffee and carry it over to her. There's no other chair, so I sit on her lap.

Her hands curl around my waist, and my back presses into her warm torso. I didn't think about it, but now I'm sitting here, her arms holding me to her, the warmth of our skin pooling between us. It feels... intimate.

I hand her the coffee.

"Thanks."

"Welcome. Now, what's the issue?"

"Look." she points at the RuneNet screen at a line of rune code. The symbols, to the untrained eye, are jumbled and matted into my lattice. But I know exactly what I'm looking at. I fist my hands, call my magic, drawing it up from deep inside me, and cast onto the RuneNet.

I steeple my fingers, tap my index fingers three times and pull apart. Three sets of rune code strings flow into the knot. The symbols tremble and then ease out across the screen like flowing silk. Then the tracker runes shoot off the screen.

"Simple, and sorted," I say and pop a kiss on Remy's forehead.

"You're rather sexy when you're in problem-solving mode," she says and leans up to kiss the back of my neck. I pull away, turn around and slide back onto her lap, facing her. Her fingers tiptoe up my thighs to the hem of my shorts. I'm wearing loungewear and nothing underneath it.

Her hands paw and knead at my thighs, as her lips explore my throat, my collarbone. Her fingers inch tantalisingly close to my pussy.

"Remy," I say, my voice low.

"We need to wait an hour for the trackers to find their hosts. I need to entertain myself."

She slips a finger over my core and jerks back. "You're not wearing any underwear."

"How convenient for you," I say. She stands, picking me up with her and placing me on the workstation.

She leans forward, pushing me back as she sweeps the desk clear. The screens evaporate as we glide through them, and I lie on my back. She slips two fingers through my excitement, rubbing between my folds, teasing. She circles my clit. Flicking and rubbing until I'm bucking on the table. She grins down at me and hovers at my entrance.

"You deserve a treat for helping me," she says and pushes both fingers inside me.

I gasp at the sudden feeling of fullness. My hands scramble to find purchase on the table. She hasn't even removed my shorts, just thrusting inside me through my short leg. There's something illicit about it. About the fact she needs me so much, she's not even bothered to undress me.

She uses her other hand to tug the shorts aside and

drops her mouth to my clit. She swipes over my already swollen nub, and I whimper in response.

I wrap my legs around her shoulders, tugging her tight against me as she drags a leisurely lick over my clit. She doesn't rush, as if she's savouring every ounce of me, as if drinking me down is her only purpose. I moan into her as my clit swells and my pussy tightens under her consistent pumping.

Waves of deep pleasure pulse from my core through my body. I slide my hand under my shirt and tug at a nipple. The movement seems to drive Remy harder.

She speeds up, swiping longer, faster caresses up and down my pussy. I can't take it anymore. I need to come.

"Remy," I beg. "Please."

Her fingers curl inside me as she hooks into the shape I need and rubs against my g-spot.

"Oh, gods."

Everything heightens, my body tenses, my pussy clamps. The shivers of bliss start in my clit and sink into my core. A blinding orgasm floods my body. My eyes slam shut. I gasp as wave after wave of pleasure rush through me.

She kisses my clit, drawing a last lick down my pussy as if to taste my orgasm. Satisfied, she slides her hand out of me, leaving me empty but satisfied.

"I could do this all day," she says, leaning her head on my lap.

"I wouldn't complain about that," I laugh. And I really wouldn't. She barely had to try to make me come this time. As if she's learnt my body, knows exactly how I want to be touched, how I want to be spoken to.

"Neither would I, but..." I stroke a hand through her messy hair.

"But we have a ball to attend?" she says.

"Unfortunately."

Things get busy after that. I'm dressed and out of the flat before she's done in the shower. I have Mother to deal with.

Outside, the air is warm for how close we are to winter. The sea breeze caresses rather than scours my cheeks as we walk into the courtyard and to the edge of the bridge. In the distance, the beach is busy. Several groups of people walking, some in gaggles, others sets of twos. I can't make out who they are from this distance though.

Mother strides across the courtyard. She's stopped twice, a legacy lord dipping his head to her and a palace staff member curtseying. I shake my head. She might have a long familial line but her shit stinks like everyone else's. What has she done to deserve the respect?

Mother approaches me, tight lipped, dissatisfaction lines gouging wrinkles around her mouth.

"You'll die with a mouth like a cat's arse if you continue frowning like that, Mother."

"Watch your mouth, Beatrice."

I roll my eyes. "Why are you here? The terms you gave me were crystal clear. Win or I'll disinherit you. Something like that, wasn't it?"

"Yes, and it appears not to have made a difference."

It's my turn to glower at her. "What is that supposed to mean? I made it through the first challenge. Fifty per cent were eliminated."

"But you didn't win."

"That's not. I—" I fall silent. My stomach sinks, my chest tightens.

"I expect better, Bella. You're a Blythe. We have a reputation to uphold. You're not here to swan along. Your association with Roman has caused irreparable damage to our family name. I warned you to fix it. Or give me an heir who will."

"Oh sure, and you expect to be able to marry me off to someone who can actually do that? Who's going to take me with a reputation in tatters?" I'm so tired of this conversation.

She hands me a note, our family sigil stamped in wax on it.

"What is this?" I ask snatching it from her.

"A list of potential matches, should you fail to win."

I shove it back at her chest, as if it burned me. But her arms remain at her sides and the note falls to the floor. It rests between our feet like a curse. I drag my eyes back up to hers.

"How?" I whisper.

She smiles. "Money can buy anything, dear. Even a husband."

"I don't want to marry a man."

"Your wants ceased to matter when Roman was sent to jail and your association lost your father three separate million-coin deals. If you don't fix this, our family will be ruined."

"So I'll work hard. I'm still free."

"Your freedom matters little when your reputation is in tatters."

Nausea rolls around my stomach. I won't marry a man. I can't.

"If I fail, I'll agree to marry a woman."

She scoffs. "I want an heir. That's the price for your fuck up."

I glare at her. "You know damn well there are ways and means."

"If you win—and that's not looking likely at the moment, is it—then, I'll consider a marriage to a female as long as she's a legacy with a line longer than ours. Good luck with the second challenge, dear. I'll be watching."

Longer than ours? What the fuck? There's only like four families older than ours, for fucks sake. I've always known I'd have to have a political marriage. That was something I accepted growing up. But it occurs to me for the first time that I don't want to marry just any woman.

What happens if the woman I want to marry isn't a legacy at all?

I wrap my arms around my body, suddenly cold, suddenly alone. Suddenly so many things I can't explain. I glance down; the note discarded on a bridge cobble.

I kneel, my fingers trembling as I pick it up and place it in my dress pocket.

Winning just became a thousand times more important.

CHAPTER 15

REMY

By late afternoon, shortly before the ball is due to begin, I'm in luck. The tracking runes have attached to their hosts and sent back the initial set of data. I give it a scan, hoping to find something useful. And while it's not what I thought I'd find, there are some interesting anomalies I'll need to tell the team about.

I pull on black trousers and a white shirt, leaving a button too many still open. Black waistcoat next, fastening just below my open buttons, and last, my jacket and shiny brogues. I take a dollop of hair product and slick my hair into its usual updo. The sides are still nicely shaved, gel is all it takes to polish the look.

I do, however, add a swipe of eyeliner and mascara. It is a ball, after all. Bella's been missing all day, but I assume she'll find her way. I need to meet the team, so I can't wait.

I make my way into the foyer and find Bella's friend Red, sat cross-legged beneath an enormous painting, a sketch book open in her lap and a set of paints.

"Hey," I say.

"Hey yourself," she replies and stabs a needle into her finger.

I wince as she squeezes the tip and drops two beads of blood into each pot of colour.

"Should I ask?"

She smiles. "Hunter by day, forger by night."

I stand and watch as she mixes her blood with the paint, and something strange happens. The colours glisten, an effervescent glow illuminating the blobs. She lets her hands hover over the paints and then moves to the sketchbook.

She contorts her fingers through the air almost as if she's weaving, all the while staring at the huge painting hanging on the wall. It's of the palace in Lantis Bay on a stormy day, the bridges covered in foam and spittle from the frothing waves.

And as her fingers move, the blobs of colour lift from the palette and bleeds into the sketchbook. I gasp as the palace reforms on the page, an identical likeness to the one on the wall.

"Bloody hell, you're incredible," I say.

She laughs, "Thanks, it's a pastime really. My ma used to paint. Made some money on the side forging works, passed the skill on to me. I do it for fun now, and I guess because it reminds me of her."

"She'd be proud," I say, and then spot Quinn on the other side of the foyer. She waves me down and I head towards her. "Catch you later."

She waves and returns to her painting. I give her once last look over my shoulder. Until now, the thought hadn't occurred to me, but is she really here to buy security? Bella might know her well, but they're from different cities. How good friends are they? What if she's here working for Roman? What if she's a proxy now Bella's on our radar?

Quinn glances up and down and whistles at me.

"Oh, stop it," I bat her compliment off. "Is everything okay? You look stunning too, by the way." And she does. She's wearing a deep green ballgown, floor length, tight at the waist and ruched skirt with a wicked corset studded in gems. Her hair is like mine now that she's shaved an undercut in, though hers is super curly on top. I bend down and kiss her cheek and offer my arm.

"Where's the team?" I ask.

"Waiting for you."

"Ah, so you're the messenger?"

"Something like that. Morrigan asked for us to meet. So here I am. I have a suspicion Queen Calandra has been putting pressure on her to deliver. We're a third of the way through the competition and we don't have suspects. You know?"

I sigh. "Or we have all the suspects. I guess Morrigan has a scapegoat at least."

Quinn glances up at me as we approach the foyer.

"Little touchy aren't you? How are you coping, staying in such close quarters with her?"

"Keeping it professional."

Quinn stares at me. She sniffs, checks around us and then lowers her volume. "You know you can't bullshit me, right? And if you try I'll drop truth serum in your coffee."

"I don't know what you're talking about."

"I'm not going to tell her—Morrigan—I mean. As long as you are actually doing your job and investigating Bella as well as everyone else, I don't care how you manage the situation."

"Quinn," I hiss.

"I'm just saying. The rest of us are swanning about. I'm working with Mal and Jacob. Scarlett's working with the guild, but you're the one doing the actual work on this mission. If you need someone to talk to about... her... About your past..."

"Quinn?" Stirling's voice echoes from across the foyer.

I glare at Quinn, and she shrugs at me. "I'm here... if you need it."

I nod, and squeeze her hand, but I'm grateful when Stirling approaches and we have to drop the conversation.

The foyer isn't busy yet. There are only a few party goers. I suspect most are still getting ready.

"This way, Morrigan is already down in the ballroom."

We head to the heart of the palace and down the same spiral we took to the first challenge. This time, though, we veer left and down a short corridor that opens into an enormous cavernous space under the ocean.

My mouth hits the floor. It's even more stunning than the server room. The entire domed room is constructed of glass walls. My hand reaches out to touch the wall as a fish floats past. Outside, on the sandy ocean bed, up-lights shower dark waters with an eerie blue glow. Fish glide through the beams like dust motes.

The room itself is the grandest thing I've ever had the pleasure of experiencing. Along the edge is a ring of ancient pillars connected by arches. Under the pillars is a walkway stuffed with tables and twinkling lights hanging from the ceiling. The walkaway and tables stretch the entire way around the ballroom, leaving space for a dance floor in the middle. The domed roof is a mosaic of connecting marble vines shaped like the prettiest seaweed branches. Hanging from them are chandeliers made of crystal fish. The effect is breathtaking.

"She's through here," Stirling says and leads us under the pillar archway and out into a balcony. She shuts the door behind us. The balcony is similarly contained by a dome. There's a set of table and chairs, and in the corners, tall seaweed lights decorate the space.

"Sit, please," Morrigan says. "I thought we could have some dinner before the ball."

Scarlett sticks her head around the balcony door. "Sorry I'm late," she says and joins us at the table, pulling her katanas out of her back straps and sliding them into braces at her thighs so she can sit.

Morrigan sags in her seat. "We've been all business, all missions, all fucking sovereign responsibility since the investiture and I miss my friends. I just want to sit in my cottage and eat pizza and talk shit with you all. So..."

She waves a hand at the balcony door and a server dressed in white comes in holding three enormous pizza boxes.

"I did the next best thing and brought the pizza to us."

My stomach twists. I swallow hard. On the one hand, I'm doing my best to be a good friend and investigate, but on the other, I'm fucking the prime suspect. How can I marry those two actions and come out unscathed? All things considered, I'm lying to everyone.

She opens the boxes and spreads them across the table so we can all help ourselves. The server returns with napkins and plates and then retreats.

"How are you, Morrigan?" I ask.

"As well as can be expected. Mother is fussing over the ball later in the year when we'll announce Stirling officially."

"And how do you feel about being announced?" Quinn asks.

Stirling rocks back in her chair, resting it against the balcony railing as she takes a huge bite of pizza. She shrugs, swallows. "They'll love me, obviously. Everyone always does."

Morrigan huffs. "Glad someone's relaxed about the whole affair."

"Honey, there are already rumours in the Daily Imperium. What was it? Princess Pussy? I don't think it's going to be a shock to anyone."

Morrigan pouts and I stifle a giggle.

"How's Jacob?" I ask Quinn, changing the subject.

"Well, him and Mal are finally official."

Stirling snort-laughs and holds her hand out. Scarlett huffs, reaches into her pocket and hands over a coin.

"We had a bet to see how long it would take them to be official. Stirling won." Scarlett twirls another coin around her fingers, half of it red, the other gold, then slips it back in her pocket.

"I'm pleased for them," Morrigan says.

"Me too," Quinn adds. "I haven't seen Mal this happy in a long time."

"How's the shop?" Morrigan asks.

Quinn pulls a hand over her face. "Painfully busy. I've had to hire help, what with the missions, the back and forth between the city and Borderlands. But growing steadily, I'm happy to say."

"And the Guild?" Morrigan asks, turning to Scarlett.

"It was difficult at first. None of them trusted me, and it's a bit of a boys' club, truth be known. I've had to fight my way back to the top. But they're toeing the line now. And I only had to cut one finger off and break three noses along the way."

"How shocking for an assassin," Quinn says.

"It's how it goes. Scrappy bastards, the lot of them," Scarlett says, reaching for a second slice of pizza.

We fall into chatter and gossip from the palace for a while. Once most of the pizza is consumed, Morrigan piles up the boxes and pops them by her chair, freeing the table.

"I wanted to update you on the trackers," I say.

"Ooh, are they working already?" Morrigan says, her dark eyes lighting up.

"Not exactly." I pull up my RuneNet screen. My hands vibrate, moving code strings across the screen, pulling out data and information.

"It's too fast," Quinn says.

"Don't worry, I'll talk you through it. I'm just lining everything up."

When I'm done, I start with the original fifty teams. "This was the list of people who entered. And this is who is left."

I wrap my palm over my fist and pull it away and half the names evaporate.

"But that's not the interesting part." I draw my hands across the screen and the names slide away, replaced with a new screen of moving shapes.

"That's making me nauseous," Stirling says.

I draw three fingers down my hand and tap them against my palm. The avatars halt on the screen and blink instead of moving around.

"What do you notice?" I ask and glance at the team.

"Er," Quinn says.

Stirling shrugs, Morrigan raises an eyebrow, and Scarlett blinks at me.

"Gods, and you lot are a crack team? Count the avatars."

I wait.

I wait some more.

Stirling and Scarlett both swear as they fuck up, miscount, and have to start again.

It's Morrigan who gets it first. "There are too many avatars," she says.

"Bravo," I clap.

I circle my fingers through the air and draw the additional avatar out, expanding it until its runes and source code fill the screen. "This is an anomaly. This is our culprit. I've been tracking its movements and it's been fishing in architect guild files as if it's hunting for something."

"What is that on it?" Morrigan asks as the code creating the avatar swirls across the screen.

"It's an encryption rune. It needs hacking to see the real source code beneath it," I answer.

"Have you managed to break it?" Quinn asks, a hopeful note in her voice.

"Not yet. I'm working on it. But my point is that this is an additional avatar. Which indicates there's another party here. I'd like to get a list of all guests resident in Lantis palace. Chances are, it's not a contestant."

"Or it is, and they're using an additional avatar to cast onto the RuneNet," Morrigan counters.

"Perhaps, but I don't think so. The code is different from the rest of the avatars. This is much more complex. I won't know for sure until I can read what's behind the encryption. But everything in my gut tells me it's someone else..."

"What are you not saying?" Scarlett asks, her eyes roaming my posture.

I shift in my seat, knowing this idea isn't going to land well. "I was postulating a potential theory about mapping. You see, if I could bring Bella in, get her to create a lattice in the subnet, it would be a foundation. I'd then be able to map the movements of the avatars across the lattice to an incredible level of accuracy. It would lead us right to the perpetrator."

Morrigan sits up in her chair. "Not if the perp is Bella. No. Unacceptable. I mean, great idea, but you need to find another way. Or find me unequivocal evidence that she's innocent. I don't want to take any risks here. It cost us enough to imprison him the first time. I'm not trusting anyone, especially not a colleague of his."

"What if I could turn her?" I ask.

"So, she is working with him?"

"That's not what I—. Never mind. No, she isn't far as I can tell. Her digital signatures don't indicate anything either."

Morrigan sits back. "That's progress. A good sign, though it takes us further away from having a suspect."

"Scarlett, can you get a list of everyone who had access to the RuneNet server room over the last week up to today? See who came and went through that room prior to the challenge," Morrigan asks.

"Hold on, I can do that now," I say and sweep the hovering screen clean and cast on to the RuneNet. I hack into the palace security system in less than sixty seconds and pull up the database for the server room.

There's a list of almost a hundred names. Most of them are Games Makers, they would have been setting up and preparing for the challenge. There's palace staff in the list by the looks of their identifiers. There's all the contestants. But no one unexpected.

"Which either means the perp is accessing another way, or it's someone inside the palace," Quinn says.

"Ugh, this isn't getting us anywhere," Morrigan says and shoves a napkin across the table.

Stirling slides an arm around her shoulder and pulls her

in, kissing the top of her head. "Isn't it? We know the culprit accessed the RuneNet from that server room. Look."

I pull up the ghost avatar and its source code.

"It's time stamped to the day before the challenge. And that string of runes there is the source code for that specific RuneNet server in the basement."

"And for those of us illiterate in geek?" Stirling says.

"The person responsible for the ghost avatar is in that list of names. If I can hack the encryption, I can access all of its historical data and map it to the times of who entered the server and then we catch our criminal," I answer.

"And in the meantime, can you track it?" Morrigan asks.

"Sure," I shrug. "In the last four hours, it's mostly been seeding code into the architect's guild."

"Why would it do that?" Stirling asks.

"Blueprints," Scarlett says.

I nod. "Can't break that bastard out without the building blueprints. But given it's a non-magical building, I'm betting they only have physical scrolls buried in some forgotten basement of the guild's archives."

"Hopefully we don't need to worry then. But perhaps I'll get some additional security on the guild," Scarlett says.

"And in the meantime, let's party. I need a drink," Morrigan says.

CHAPTER 16

BELLA

As I step into the ballroom, I'm handed a challenge envelope. My hands tremble as I open it. Roman's note said I'd be able to access the blueprints during one of the challenges. The first has already happened. The last is more about our creation. Which means whatever is inside this note holds my fate. I crack the seal and pull the card out.

♕

Esteemed Contestants,

The next challenge awaits you, and your prowess in security and strategy will once again be put to the test. You are to physically infiltrate the highly esteemed Architect's Guild. Your objective: to secure prison blueprints housed within its protected sanctum, without drawing attention or raising the alarm.

You will find that the guild has an intricate labyrinth of protections and securities, each more cunning than the last. Not only will you be required to bypass the various security measures, but also navigate the complexities of the guild's vast architectural expanse, and all of this, whilst maintaining utmost discretion.

The winning team will be determined not only by their stealth and the successful acquisition of the blueprint, but by the swiftness of their operation. The pair who can infiltrate the Guild, secure the blueprint, and exit the premises in the quickest time will be declared the victors.

However, heed our warning: you must not be caught. If you draw the attention of the Guild's security and are captured, you will face immediate disqualification.

This challenge will test your cunning, your precision, and your teamwork. We look forward to observing your strategies and methods in overcoming the formidable security of the Architect's Guild.

May the best team prevail.
Yours with anticipation,
The Competition Organisers.

Fuck. What the hell am I going to do? Either I'm going to do what Roman asked and risk everything, including the challenge, or I'm not and risk my life and potentially everyone I love, if he escapes. I need a drink before I overthink myself into a panic.

The bar is rammed, people jostling and milling around trying to get served. In the corner of the room is a group of musicians, stringed instruments playing lilting melodies that drift through the room. Dancers fill the floor, magicians in the arms of each other. Some swaying next to each other. I nod to Red at the bar. She's talking to someone but I can feel her protective eyes on me even after I get a drink and hide behind a pillar. Despite her managing to watch the games, and keep an eye on me, the academy is working her hard. Still, I'm grateful she's here.

I spot my mother halfway across the ballroom, a horde of legacy ladies following her. New ones curtseying as they say hello. I want to bellow across the room: *you're not the fucking princess mum.* But what good would it do? She's probably beside herself at the displays of respect.

"Hey you," a voice says next to me.

"Wow," I say, facing Remy and looking her up and down.

She smiles, "Thank you. You look impossibly beautiful this evening."

I glance down at my short black dress and back to her black suit. We match. Shit, a week sharing a fucking apartment and we're in the throes of the lesbian urge to merge. We're not even dating for fucksake.

"Imperium to Bella," Remy says, cutting through my thoughts. "Where did you go? Everything okay?"

I nod, pat down my frankly obscene dress. It poofs out around my waist, but if I were to lean over, you'd see my arse. If I bent a little further, you'd see the split g-string I'm wearing. Nothing like easy access or that's what I thought, and now I'm questioning my life choices. I need to do something to get out of my head.

"Care to dance?" I say, grinning.

She hesitates, that same expression I don't recognise flickering across her features.

"Oh, you don't have to. It's fine. I don't even like dancing."

She tugs me under the pillars and walks me halfway around the ballroom to a balcony in the far corner.

"In here," she says and tugs me through, shutting the balcony door behind us. The music immediately mutes to a soft humming melody.

She offers me her hand.

I take it, and she pulls me in tight, and for a while, we stand under twinkling lights, turning in a slow circle, from ocean side to ballroom, the view spinning with us. My head rests on her shoulder and, to my surprise, it's comforting.

Even if I win this thing and my mother lets me marry a woman, there's no way she'll accept anyone but a legacy. Not that I'm ready for marriage, or Remy, or--. Gods. I need to fuck this nonsense out of my mind.

"By the way, I'm cleaning the debt slate. Given I helped you with—"

"Not here," she says, untangling us from the slow dance.

I huff, "Well, you're welcome."

Her eyes darken, desire dancing through her expression. It's always a game between us. And gods I want to play, really I do. But this is dangerous. The balcony has glass doors, and mother is wandering around in there.

"Why did you do it?" I say. "Protect me... I mean. Erase my magic?"

She sighs, threads her fingers through mine. "There's not an easy answer for that."

"Try."

"The simplest answer is because I didn't like the thought of you locked away... from me. Because while you're a constant thorn in my side, a nightmare to work with, and the pettiest magician I've ever met, you're also singly the most talented magician too. Because I'd be desperately bored without you in my life... Because you fascinate me as much as you frustrate me. Because watching you work is like observing a master and maybe... just maybe because I'm rather fond of looking at you..."

I mouth the air for a moment, so taken aback I'm stunned into silence. That was unexpected.

"I don't think I've ever wanted someone more than I do you right now..."

Remy leans down and grazes my lips with hers, it's so sweet and so tender I melt in her arms. The balcony door shudders behind me and I flinch. Fuck. "My mother is here, and she would not approve. We shouldn't..."

"There's a lot of things we shouldn't do, but you dressed like that for me. Didn't you?" Her words are deep and filled with controlled lust.

I want to say no. But it would be a lie, and she knows it. The same way I know those additional buttons are undone on her shirt for me. The hint of her lace bra is for me the same way my split g-string is for her.

I suck the corner of my lip in, trying to decide what to say when Remy takes the decision out of my hands.

She slides a hand around my waist and spins me around until I'm facing the ocean, driving me forward until she stops me a millimetre from the railing.

I gasp. The sudden swing, the sudden lack of control, the exquisite precision of her domination over me sends an electric bolt to my core.

She leans into my ear, the heat from her cheek radiating against mine. "That's a very short dress you're wearing, Blythe."

The trickle of her words slides down my neck, the tease inching down my spine. Goosebumps rise over my skin, my pussy tightens, as if she has command of that too.

"Yes, it is," I breathe. "It would be a travesty if I were to —oops." I lean over the balcony, bent forward enough that air brushes my arse cheeks and I know exactly what she's seeing.

I shift. Slide my legs apart just a touch.

There's a sharp intake of breath. Remy's self-control evaporates. The dome protecting us from the ocean heats, the air fissures with unspoken want.

"You're wearing those on purpose. Aren't you?" Remy says.

I cock my head around until I can see her. "I have no idea what you're talking about." But I can't keep the smirk from my lips.

"Lies," she says.

Her fingers caress the back of my thigh, sliding along until it grazes the lace of my knickers, the pads of her fingers drawing a feather-light touch over my core. And then she pulls away, and the quick movement leaves me cold.

Fuck. I want this. I want her.

I face her and drift to my knees.

"Is this what you want, Professor? For me to be a good girl. To do as you say, suck that pussy of yours right here on the balcony until you come?"

I slide my knees open, my dress barely covering my pussy, but the intention is clear.

"We can be seen," she says.

I reach around her legs. "I guess you'll have to be discreet, then."

She grins down at me, her dark eyes molten and burning. Behind us, the ballroom music rumbles a rhythmic beat, dancers' bodies forming patterns and shapes on the floor. But no one attempts to come onto the balcony.

Remy untucks her shirt, and uses it to cover her arse, unclips her trouser button, pulls the zip and her boxers down low enough her pussy is accessible.

Then she curls her palm around the back of my head and yanks me to her cunt, my mouth instantly on her clit. Oh gods. She holds me to her pussy, tight enough I'd have to struggle to escape but not so tight I feel trapped and fuck... It makes my whole body shiver with need. I slip my tongue out and over her clit. She stiffens under my touch. I grab her thighs, using her body as an anchor as I press my tongue into her pussy.

"Show me how discreet you can be," Remy breathes and rocks her body, tilting her pussy into my mouth. She keeps me pressed against her. She is the only thing I can breathe and taste and swallow. Fuck, I savour every drop of her because it's like dreams and golden sunbeams and everything I've ever wanted.

I'm acutely aware that we could get caught at any moment. But that only makes me hotter, makes my pussy wetter, the tiny strings drenched between my thighs. I struggle not to moan against her. The short sharp breaths tell me she is suppressing the urge to cry out too. And that knowledge heightens every sense in my body. It sets every nerve alight and I store away the idea of fucking in other public places.

I suck at her pussy, tilting her hips so I can swipe my tongue along her wet folds. She might want me to be discreet, but I can still take my damn time.

And I do. I lick her pussy, inching from her hole to her clit in slow, deliberate strokes. Every lash I swipe over her sends a bolt of pleasure to my clit. And lucky for me, the slit means easy access. I remove a hand from her thigh and slip it under my dress.

"Did I say you could touch yourself?" Remy says.

I pout at her.

She grits her teeth. "Fine. But you're not allowed to come. Only I get to give you that pleasure."

My finger finds the split in my knickers, and I press through the wetness and use it to rub my clit.

It's going to be impossible not to come immediately. I remove my hand and put it to better use. I pull Remy closer, let my tongue focus on her swollen clit and push a finger up into her.

She gasps. Her thighs shudder as she tries to hold herself up against the building pressure of an orgasm.

"Fuck," she whispers and leans forward to clutch the balcony behind me. "Fuck, Bella. You're going to make me come."

Her words make me snap. Something wild and unhinged unleashes inside me and I lap at her pussy faster, slide my finger in and out, in and out.

She grips my head, her fingers tangling in my hair hard

enough it pinches over into pleasure. She rams her pussy into me, using my name like a swear word until her knees give and I have to use all my strength to keep her up.

I stand up. She's watching me, and it makes me want to give her something to look at.

I put my finger in my mouth and suck it down to the knuckle. Her nose flares as my eyes close and I lick her juices clean from my fingers.

She steps up to me, kisses me hard, her tongue pushing into my mouth, but then her body loosens and the kiss becomes more of a caress, her tongue softer than before.

"You taste of me," she says and places another soft kiss on my lips.

"Then I must taste good. Shame you're distasteful the rest of the time, Reid."

She laughs, pushes my curls back into place, her fingers as gentle as her kiss. "Sometimes I forget why we spent so long as rivals, when we make a great team in bed. If only we were that good at the challenges." She kisses me again.

Her nails graze over my arms and then she grips me tight, breaks our kiss and whirls me around to face the balcony.

"Now, I'm going to bend you over and fuck you from behind, and you're going to be silent."

I shrug, nonchalant. A glint of deviousness running through my expression. "The door's shut. We managed fine for you."

I know what I'm doing.

Tempting.

Daring.

Pushing us further. But I want it, need the danger. It's a fucking drug and I am an addict.

She narrows her eyes at me, steps back, reaches for the door and opens it three inches.

"Remy," I hiss.

"Now, you're going to be a very good girl and stay quiet. Do you understand?"

Her tone is clear, commanding. It makes my entire body melt. I'd kneel at her feet and fuck her all night if she talked to me like this. I nod, my stomach fizzing with anticipation. I hate she can make me lose control like this. How can I resent her so much and still want her to fuck me into oblivion?

She grabs my hips, her fingers holding me tight enough I feel owned. Tight enough, the shadow of her imprint will linger for hours. She pushes her body into me, bending forward so she's leant over me.

"Don't come until I tell you to."

I suck in a sharp breath. "Fuck." I'm already quivering with need. How the hell am I going to be able to hold myself off?

The pressure on my ass eases as she steps back, but then her hand caresses over my thigh, down my hamstring. The touch is so light I shiver, my skin flashing with cool tingles. When I'm about to cry out for her to touch me, her hand slips between my legs and down the slit in my underwear.

"Remy," I breathe as her fingers draw up and down the split in my lace knickers. I'm soaking wet. She pulls her hand away.

"I told you to be quiet."

My teeth grit. Heat blooms in my chest. "I'm trying to be quiet, but it's fucking hard when you touch me like that."

"Quiet. Or no orgasm."

My jaw flexes as I grind my teeth, but I turn back to the ocean and dig a little deeper and finally, Remy resumes touching me.

Her finger slides down my core, she focuses on my clit, circling and rubbing until my breathing is so ragged I can hardly keep myself standing. My knuckles are white where I'm gripping the balcony. Gods, I want to scream. The pleasure builds and builds until my legs are shaking.

"Remy, please. I'm close."

"No. Do not come until I tell you."

My body winds tighter and tighter. Waves of pleasure crash through me, rippling from my pussy to my toes.

Inside, I'm screaming and panting and the pain of holding it in only adds to the pleasure. It's consuming.

Remy must sense I'm barely clinging on. She eases the touch on my clit, drawing back and spearing my cunt instead, thrusting a finger inside me, and then another. She slams into me, shunting me forward to the edge of the balcony.

A squeal of pleasure bursts from my lips as I lose my grip on the rail.

"What did I tell you?" Remy says and then she slides a palm over my mouth while she continues fucking me with her other hand.

It's too much. I moan into her hand. My pussy clenches and spasms as she fucks me hard up against the balcony.

"Please," I mumble into Remy's palm as the waves strengthen and build until they're in my tummy, in my toes, on my tongue, my breasts. I am alight with sensation, going blind with it.

She releases my mouth, lifts off my back and slides her other hand to my asshole, and it's too much. The sensation so alien, so wrong, so fucking good.

She thrusts her fingers harder inside my pussy, and curls them to exactly the right spot. Her other hand teases my asshole, and I can't hold on any longer.

My eyes squeeze shut. I can't see anyway, blinded by building orgasm and the exquisite tingles wracking my body.

"You can come," Remy says and dips her thumb into my ass and my world explodes. My pussy clenches around her fingers, and I thrust back onto her fingers, riding the orgasm higher, higher, the softest gasp escaping despite my best efforts to stay silent. I grind on her hand until I really can't hold myself up anymore. Remy pulls out of me and scoops me into her arms.

Her figure is slender, but she's strong. I tremble in her grip; it's all too much. I've never come like that and I'm still drifting down from the high.

"It's okay," she says. "It's okay." She brushes loose curls out of my face and kisses my forehead. Still in her arms, she slides us down the balcony wall. She holds me until I stop shivering. She holds me while the ocean serenades us with a school of dancing fish, and the ball plays us a melody of stringed revelry.

And for the first time in a long time, I feel safe, content. I feel like I have everything I need, and that is the oddest part of it all.

Remy tilts my chin up with her thumb and leans in to kiss me, her lips tender on mine. I'm so distracted with her mouth on mine that it takes me a minute to register.

There's a clatter and someone stumbles through the balcony door.

Remy springs apart from me so suddenly, a rush of cold air wraps around me. She's already on her feet while I'm trying to work out what happened. Shit, shit, what if it's my mother?

I locate the person who stumbled through the door, and my blood turns cold.

"Marcel," Remy says, her eyes skittish as they dance between me and him.

"Remy, how delightful," Marcel says, but the jovial tone of his voice doesn't match the darkness in Remy's eyes.

Wait. That gives me an idea, because while I might want rid of Roman, Marcel hates him more than anyone else in this city.

I leave the pair of them talking, Marcel's eyes follow me as I scoot out of the balcony. I push my way through the dance floor. Drunken hands grab me, try to encourage me to stay and dance. But I have a mission now. The music picks up its beat, thumping drums join the stringed instruments as well as brass instruments now.

By the time I find Red tucked under the pillars at the ballroom bar, I'm shaking with excitement. This is how I take the bastard down.

She's talking to some guy about the potential of integrating blood magic into a security system. He looks as confused as I feel trying to understand how the mansions work in her city.

"Here," Red says, "got you a drink." She hands me a glass of wine and I take a sip. It's a rosé, sweet and a little dry. I love it.

"Thanks," I say.

She frowns and turns back to the chap she was speaking to. "Sorry, I'd like to continue this. But duty calls. Can I meet you tomorrow? I have buyers interested in increasing security at the academy, but we'd need it to work with our magic."

"One o'clock?" he says.

"Super, meet you in the foyer," she says and shakes his hand.

I pull the challenge card out of my dress pocket and hand it to her.

"Ah shit. So you have a decision to make. What are you going to do?" She asks.

"At this point, I don't have much of a choice. He knows everything about me, my family for fucks sake. There's nowhere I can hide from him. If I get caught helping him, I go to jail. If I don't at least look like I'm helping him and he does manage to escape I'm in a different world of trouble," I groan.

"Then you'll do it?"

"I don't want to. But..."

"You don't see another way?" She hands me the card back. "Did I ever tell you what those tunnels are for?"

"Erm..."

"They're hundreds of years old, pre-vampire-magician wars."

"What were they used f...?" But before I finish my sentence, I've already worked it out. The tunnels are underground and connect all the cities. I haven't visited Sangui city as often as Bella has New Imperium, but when I have, it's always been a bizarre experience. The sky is a shifting mosaic of dark umbers and molten fire. The sun never rises into the midday sky like it does here. It's always some kind of dusk or dawn, but never bright, never hot, only warm. Who would need transport like that?

"The vampires..." I finally finish my sentence.

"Yup. It gives them free roam across the realm at any time of day. Only the wars stopped them being used, or at least the magician tunnels aren't used. They still use the tunnels to other cities. No wonder Roman wants the blueprints. It's the perfect escape, no one would even know," Red says.

"How quickly can you create a forgery?"

Red's face breaks out into a grin... "Well, now, that depends."

CHAPTER 17

BELLA

I lay in bed the following morning. This habit of finding myself wrapped around Remy's limbs has become a comfort. I hate the mornings she's already awake, head bent over her RuneNets at the living room table. But I'm in a dangerous position.

Her mentor is trying to fuck me. Her mentor lied to her. He's lied to the whole city. He's Roman's fucking brother and she doesn't know. But worse, I can't tell her. Not without incriminating myself or breaking her heart. And if I do, then whatever this is, all these warm mornings filled with her long limbs and safe embrace... they all go away.

I have to go to Marcel. I pull the duvet tighter losing myself in memories. I still remember the first time I encountered Remy and Marcel in a competition, Roman was not pleased. We talked and chatted; me blushing hard the whole time. It was only a few weeks after the rooftop kiss. I found Roman, a whisky in hand, sat in the competition bar after Remy had gone to bed.

"I see you made acquaintances," he said.

I nodded enthusiastically. But my face fell when I saw his expression. It was stiff and cold, his dark eyes a fathomless void. He sipped his whiskey.

"I wouldn't get too close to them."

"Remy?" I asked

"And her mentor Marcel."

"Why not?"

He sniffed, a twisted sort of smile now I think back. "Because, Bella... She hates you. And I suspect Marcel does too."

I was crestfallen. My heart sank, my eyes stung. If I think about it now, it was all a fucking lie. He was manipulating me just like Marcel was with Remy. And for what? Their own brotherly rivalry? Because this is their fucked up way of having fun? Bastards.

I shuffled on the spot, desperate to prove him wrong. "You don't know that," I said.

"Of course I do. I heard her and Marcel talking..."

"What did they say?"

"Said your parents were liars and cheats and the only reason you were even in this competition is because they'd have paid for your place like always."

I gasped. How could she think that? My parents would never. But Roman continued to dig the knife in.

"I've known Marcel forever, practically his whole life... and that man is manipulative. He will be encouraging Remy to get close to you to steal your methods and magic."

"That's awful," I breathed.

"Which is why I want you to stay away."

That was how it began. A tangled tale of punches thrown an eye for an eye that escalated for years. I tried, at times, not to listen to Roman. The nights when group card games would start and end with only Remy and I. Those were the evenings I saw through the rivalry. Roman was right about one thing though, Marcel was as bad as him for pouring poisonous stories into Remy's head.

But this is why I think this will work. Publicly, if there's anyone who will help me escape Roman's clutches, it's Marcel.

I manage to escape Remy at lunch. She's staying in the apartment to go through the tracking data apparently. I don't get why she's putting so much importance on it; I doubt she'll find much about our competitor's plans, but whatever makes her happy.

I'm in the main foyer, about to descend the staircase towards the bars when I bump into my mother.

I hesitate. Part of me is convinced she'll help. Mother is desperate for me to rid myself of any association with Roman. Surely if I explain that I'm in legitimate need of their support, she'll help? My parents love me. They want me safe. Right?

"Hello dear," she says.

"Did you enjoy the ball, mother? I didn't find you." A moderate white lie.

"Oh, I saw you. But you were busy mingling with that Borderling."

"Mother!" I hiss. "You can't call people that. It's a disgusting word." I glance around us, but there's no one in the hall thank the gods.

"Then don't associate with people like that. Don't you ever consider what the other legacies would think? Gods, Beatrice, our heritage goes back two thousand years. We have a responsibility to keep that lineage pure and intact."

This was a mistake. She's a stubborn, ignorant fool, only interested in nepotism and keeping up appearances. If

I tell her Roman is in touch, she'll probably disown me here and now. I chew a nail, buying thinking time. But she bats my hand down.

When I don't respond to her, she speaks again. "I'm not expecting you to listen to me. I'm aware of your new age leanings, Beatrice. But I'd appreciate some compromise on these matters, okay?"

"Is that a crack I see in your reputational armour, Mother?"

She scoffs, but I can tell she's trying to suppress a laugh. Perhaps a night out at the ball did her some good, and she's in a better mood today. I chew my bottom lip, trying to work out if I should put my trust in her. If I should ask for help.

"Is everything okay?" She says and I almost spill. It's on the tip of my tongue.

"I..." the words lodge in my throat. How do I explain this?

"It's Roman... you recall him... Handsome chap, dark hair, built like a mansion?" I can't help the snark, I at least need to be consistent. Besides, for all mother's irritation with his repeated fuck-ups, she always appreciated his... physique.

She rolls her eyes. "Yes, dear. How could I possibly forget that failure of a legacy who's ruined our last few months?"

Mother's projection shimmers against the lantern hanging on the wall. Before I can continue, she's already off ranting.

"It's a good job that you're no longer associated with him, isn't it? Could you imagine what Lady Bembry would think? Did you know she ousted Lord Wentworth out of our legacy luncheon group for associating with the new officials in the old palace? Malachi Adams, I think it was. Anyway, he's a Borderling too."

"Mother. That word, for fucks sake."

"Sorry," she huffs. "That is what he is, though. Anyway, I couldn't believe it. Lord Wentworth's standing is irrefutable. And kicking him out, well, he has a lot of clout with the legacies. I was amazed Lady Bembry secured the votes, to be honest. But goes to show you can't underestimate the importance of your reputation."

My shoulders sag. Fuck. This was pointless. She's never going to help.

"Now, dear, I saw the challenge envelopes were given out at the ball. What can you tell me about the next challenge?"

I sigh inwardly. She doesn't care about what I want, not really. What she wants is to look like she cares. She's concerned with appearing to be a good mother, rather than actually being one.

"I don't have a plan yet, but I'll speak to Remy later today, and we'll figure something out."

"See that you do. Can't have a repeat of the first challenge."

"Mother, we came *second*."

"Yes, and I prefer it when you come *first*. Now I have a luncheon to attend, with lady Talulah Wildensteen, the mother of the young Charles. Who, I might add, is very interested in you, approaching thirty, and of prime age for children. I'll speak to you later."

My neck blazes hot. I'm about to hurl protests but she wheels around the corner and is gone.

Motherfucker.

Every damn time I speak to her, I want to win this contest more. And part of me hates the fact that's what she wants. Like what twisted mother winds me up to get what she wants? That same furious part of me wants to rebel and sabotage the whole thing, to fail the next challenge out of spite. But the only person that hurts is me. Maybe I should vanish on a boat to some other realm.

I rub my face, trying to smear that conversation away.

I head down the stairs remembering a rumour about the Games Makers having a bar they frequent to get away from the contestants. The first two bars are duds. One isn't even open yet. So I make my way to a pub two floors under the main welcome hall.

It's dimly lit. A fire roars in the corner, wood crackling and spitting embers up the chimney. Salt and fire and a hint of the ocean outside drift in the air. Wooden tables fill most of the floor space with a larger area on one side with plush sofas. I'm in luck. Marcel is in here. Unfortunately, that's where my luck runs out. The Merricks are chatting with him.

I consider leaving and think better of it. Fuck them. I ask for a lemonade and take it to a seat. I stare at the challenge card, trying to calculate the best way to both work with Remy to complete the challenge and escape long enough to steal blueprints.

By the time I'm finished thinking, the bar has filled a little more, and the Merricks have vanished.

I'm not sure what makes me finally decide to talk to him. Insanity? Desperation? But I find myself standing at the foot of Marcel's table. He glances up from strategy papers—clearly he was giving the Merricks a mentor session. Though given Remy's current proclivity for tracking the progress of our competitors, I'm not sure I'm one to talk about what's fair or right or wrong.

I must have got lost in my head, because I've stood here long enough to make things awkward.

"Can I help you?" He draws the papers together and slips them into a bag at his feet.

"Marcel..." I say his name, but it comes out more of a question.

"Yes, Miss Blythe? What is it I can do for you?"

He's softer than I imagined. Politer too. I'd go as far as to say friendly. That's unexpected and so different to Roman. I'm not sure what I expected because I've only ever known of Marcel from afar and what Roman's told me of him: that Marcel was a cheat, a fraud. Instead of earning his —and Remy's—way into all the trials and competitions, he used to defraud his way in. That he stole strategies and runes from other contestants.

Still, standing in front of him now, his dark eyes are much softer than I remember. They're like pools of midnight instead of the cold voids Roman has. His face is more open, warmer.

"Miss Blythe? Are you okay?" he says, jarring me out of my thoughts.

"What? Yes. Sorry. I... Could I ask you something?"

His expression furrows. He gestures for me to take a seat and then folds his arms. I sit, fidget with my hands, rolling a ring around my middle finger.

"You hate Roman," I start.

He doesn't respond, so I continue.

"I'm not sure why you dislike each other so much."

Marcel leans forward, his eyes narrowing at me. "What's going on?"

"I need your help. I don't have anyone else to turn to and, given you hate him, I figured you'd have all the reason in the world to ensure he stays incarcerated."

"I'm listening."

"Roman has been sending me notes, trying to contact me from prison. And now he wants me to do things for him. Favours. I have no idea what he's planning, but it can't be good, and my gut says he's trying to get out... but if he gets out, then... Gods." I lay it on thick, innocent girl desperately in need of big strong man help.

Vile. If I didn't need to pull this off, I'd be gagging on the misogyny. Marcel grabs my hand, stops me picking at my ring.

"Slow down. Hold on a second." He releases me, places his index finger and middle finger together, whispers words I can't hear, and pulls his fingers apart. The sounds of the pub mutes. Almost like I'm underwater.

"Tell me again, slower."

I take a huge, shuddering breath and start again. "You're aware Roman is in prison? He tried to attack the palace. It failed, and Calandra jailed him."

Marcel gives me a curt nod. "Who hasn't heard! Although we had a rivalry, he was an excellent business-man. That much I can admit, and it's a substantial loss to the runic community that he's no longer training apprentices."

It's funny, while Remy and I have always had a rivalry, I can't say anything bad about her skills. She's incredible at coding and encrypting and hacking runic security systems. I might have disliked her, but I absolutely respect her abilities.

Disliked? Past tense?

Huh.

I stow that away for future consideration.

"And you're aware I was working for him? Even though I'd completed my apprenticeship. After I created my security consultancy business, he used to contract me for certain more... delicate jobs. When he was imprisoned, I started receiving notes with his wax seal emblem on them."

A line furrows between his brows. "What did he want? What did he say in the notes?"

I shrug. "I destroyed the first two I received. He was in prison. I didn't think there was any point in opening them. Calandra jailed him for life, and my parents, they're..."

"A lot?" There's a smile tugging the corner of his eyes.

"Exactly," and for the first time since sitting down, I smile.

"Most legacy parents have high expectations of their children. I understand your logic to ignore the notes. But what does this have to do with me?"

"I received another note yesterday... and he's raising the pressure. The favour he wants me to do is..."

"Is...?" he says and his eyebrows rise.

There's no other way. I need to show him the note. I pull it out of my pocket and hand it over.

He reads it, his eyes narrowing. "I see. And you want my help to what, exactly?"

"I have no idea. I figured maybe you could advise me on the best course of action. Should I go to the crown with this? Should I do what he asks? No, that's stupid, of course I shouldn't. But if I don't and he gets out, he will kill me."

He chuckles, full on, eye-crinkling chuckles. "I'm sure you're not going to die."

"You don't know him. Not like I do. Trust me. If I don't help him, and he escapes, I am already dead."

Marcel's stills. "You're truly afraid. You're shaking."

And I realise he's right. There are very few things that terrify me, not even my mother's wrath. But I've seen Roman lose it. I'm seen him bleed a man to within an inch of his life, torture him until his soul cracks, murder his family in front of his eyes and break his mind. You do not fuck with Roman Oleg.

"Roman was an incredible mentor. But he doesn't take kindly to betrayal and while I didn't betray him exactly, you've read the note; he doesn't see my freedom as anything less."

Marcel is quiet for a moment. He rubs his chin, scans the bar, and then leans forward. "Okay. If you want my advice, I'd respond to him. Tell him you'll help."

"If I do that, if I steal the blueprints and hand them off... Gods, why? If anyone found out, I'd be tried for treason."

"And if you don't, and Roman gets out, then what? And let's be honest, when has Roman ever not succeeded with his goals? Then what happens?"

If I don't help Roman and he does get out, I'm fucked. Revenge is Roman's middle name for fucks sake.

Marcel shakes his head, takes my hand in his and squeezes. "If I know anything about Roman, it's that he doesn't stop. If you don't do this for him, someone else will. I'm not telling you to aid and abet an escape. Just keep him strung along for a while. Perhaps we can catch his colleague, whoever is on the outside helping him. I can help you do that. The point is to try to foil his escape. But you can't do that if you don't respond to him. And you definitely can't do that if you leave those blueprints in the guild for someone else to steal."

"What if I'm caught?" I tremble.

"You won't be. That's how I'll help. I'll assist you in any tasks you need. I can liaise with contacts to find anything I can about what he's planning. Don't worry, Bella. I won't let you go down for this."

"Isn't this a dangerous game to play, though?" I ask.

"Isn't what dangerous?" Alba says, sliding into the chair next to me. Gabe sits next to Marcel. The air fizzes and whatever muting magic Marcel had over us evaporates.

"Nothing. Sorry for taking up your time. I should leave."

Alba's nose wrinkles as if she can smell something poisonous. Her lip curls at me. "Are you really so worried you're going to lose that you're trying to steal the tips we were getting?"

I smile, and when I do, I make sure it's far more poisonous than whatever she's smelling. I sneer hard enough I bare my teeth. "When I beat you, Alba, I'll be too busy celebrating to give a fuck what you think."

Her expression drops.

Good. Fuck her. She looks away, scratches her face. Gabe snickers.

"Oh, what are you laughing at moron?" she snaps at him.

I finish my lemonade in one enormous gulp. "I take it our discussion will—"

"Remain private," he nods.

"Marcel, good day," I say.

"Miss Blythe."

I leave, my stomach churning, and not because I downed half a glass of fizzy lemonade on an empty stomach. Or the lack of sleep, but because of the terror of what's coming. On top of the fact that I have to win the next challenge and simultaneously steal valuable blueprints.

I walk past the palace reception. It's empty, so I acquire a pen and blank sheet of paper and then I stroll into the courtyard and locate the bridge and the stairs to get to the maintenance area. As I ink my words of agreement onto the page, my stomach twists in knots, nausea licking bile up my throat. My chest grows tight and I wonder if I am making a catastrophic mistake.

But I can't be. This will protect me and my family in the long run. But I go back to his words: *Do this for me, I'll accept it as your apology.*

I don't have a choice. This is my way out from under him for good.

This is the right choice.

I'm sure of it.

I slide the note under the third pillar, four bricks above head height, but my fingers refuse to let go. I recognise this as one of those fundamental moments. The ocean drifts, careless waves pushing and pulling in an endless cycle. I wish on them, hoping that one of those mythological sea gods will rise out of the ocean and bestow a truth upon me. Give me the answer I'm seeking so that I know I'm making the right choice.

But that's not how this works, is it? We only have ourselves, the best choice we can make in the moment with the information we have.

I let go of the note, wipe my hand over my face, trying to sweep the exhaustion of the last couple of days away.

When I look back up at the ocean, I second guess myself. "What am I doing? This is stupid."

Roman is in a prison without magic. One of the highest security prisons in New Imperium that Remy herself built. There's no way he's getting out.

I reach up to take the note back, but it's vanished.

Shit.

CHAPTER 18

BELLA

I don't go back to the room straight away. I wander the beach until dreary storm clouds hang over the horizon and the first crack of lightning cuts through the gloom.

By the time I get back to the palace, I'm drenched. Remy pulls open the door and gasps. "What happened to you?"

"Ocean storm."

"Why don't you have a shower and warm up? I'll put some food on."

Once I'm showered and dressed in thick winter socks and a tracksuit, I slide onto the sofa to be greeted with a mug of hot chocolate and a tray of picky foods. Biscuits and cheese, fruits, sausage pieces, rolls of salami, nuts, and dips.

"Thank you," I smile at Remy.

She shrugs the appreciation off as if it was nothing. Except it wasn't, was it? How different we are with each other compared to almost two weeks ago.

I swirl the chocolate around the mug, my mind spinning over the truth that we're not who we used to be to each other. And it makes me wonder.

"Remy...?" I ask.

"Hmm?" she says, distracted by the RuneNet screen projected in front of her.

"Can I ask you something?"

She closes the screen and sits up.

"Why you don't... or I guess, why didn't you like me? Because you've had a problem with me from the start."

"Not from the very start..." she says, raising a single brow.

"I still maintain that you kissed me first on that rooftop."

She shakes her head at me, but her eyes are smiling, so I push on. "I mean it. Tell me."

She opens her mouth and then squeezes it shut. She breathes out heavy through her nostrils as if exhaling a huge burden.

"That bad? Gods, it's not like I killed someone you love... Or did I?" I finish when she doesn't respond.

Her eyes narrow. This time she examines my face, like I've spilled hot chocolate on my chin. The urge to rub my face is overwhelming, but I realise that's not what she's looking for. I frown. Finally she answers.

"The Royal Academy of Runic Magicians," she says, as if that's an answer in itself.

My frown deepens into a scowl. "What has my child-hood school got to do with anything?"

Her jaw flexes once. "Yes, exactly. *Your* school."

"I don't understand. For the love of my sanity, use more words."

She looks away. "Please. Like you don't already know."

I must look like one of those dogs with all the saggy

skin because my entire face has scrunched up. "Know what? What are you talking about?"

She raises her mug, her index finger pointing right at my chest. "Your parents stole my place."

"I don't under—"

Her lips press thin, colour rushing up her neck. "I didn't take you for the sort to play dumb."

Well, that's gone and pissed me right off. "Hold on a second. I have exactly no idea what you're talking about. What the hell have my parents got to do with you not going to my school? I got into that school based on my entrance exam. It's not my fault you didn't pass."

Remy wipes her free hand over her face and when she looks at me, her expression is so cold it makes me shiver.

"I did pass, Bella. That's the point. Your parents stole my place because they paid for it. You scored lower than me in the entrance exams."

It's rare I falter or lose the ability to speak. But I am speechless. She's wrong. She has to be.

"No. There's no way my parents would cheat me into RARM. The thing they pride most is their reputation. They would want me to get in based on my skill. Otherwise... Otherwise..." I harden. "Just because I'm better than you, Remy."

I expect her to lash out. To throw insults at me, to undermine everything I say and disregard my truth. But she doesn't. She doesn't snap. Doesn't even attempt to fight, and that's more shocking than anything. She gets up, goes to the kitchen and brings back wine and glasses.

If she was lying about this, she'd be defensive, so even though there's no way this can be true, part of her must really believe what she's saying. But it's impossible, my parents would never.

Her eyes soften. "Perhaps you're better than me now. But I promise, you weren't then."

Heat flickers in my chest. I'm trying to compromise more, to bend and pick my battles, same as she is. But this is one I won't back down from. I can't imagine what mother's legacy ladies would say if they discovered she bribed her daughter's way into RARM. My throat dries. There's no way. Remy gives me the bottle of wine and a glass.

"You'll need this," she says.

Then she opens her hands, bends her fingers and pulls them apart, flinging a holographic RuneNet screen filled with lines of code into the air between us. She swipes over the screen in a rapid movement, runes and code strings appearing and disappearing.

"I've given you access to my Rune subnet. Hack the school. Check the records. You'll find all the evidence you need."

"Fine. But when I find absolutely nothing, you can admit you're wrong and stop holding it against me. Perhaps we'll stand a chance of actually winning this competition."

She sits back down. Takes a long glug of wine and lies down, kicking her shoes off and scooting her whole body onto the sofa. I stare at her, horrified momentarily that she's taken her shoes off and is that relaxed around me. It seems like such a small, intimate act that it takes me a moment to register what's happened. The fact that we, Remy and I, don't do this. We don't relax around each other.

We throw sarcasm and jokes, and snipe at each other. And once... okay, probably several times, we fuck. Was it more than several? How have I lost count of the amount of times we've fucked? Gods. What is happening?

She flings a dramatic arm over her eyes and nestles into the sofa.

Right. I stand and roll my sleeves up, drag my eyes away and to the screen. It's a different setup to mine, but it works as well. I crack my neck and fingers and then get to work casting on so I can thread and build lattices across the screen. My hands vibrate, faster and faster as my magic weaves through the air and into her subnet. She's deactivated all her security. For half a second, I consider feeding a broken rune into her system. Infect it. Fuck it up.

It unnerves me how uncomfortable I am at the prospect of causing Remy's disappointment. I decide I focus on the fact we're on the same team. If I fuck her up, I'm only fucking myself up. Yeah, that makes me feel better.

I locate the school and hack into their records. It's over in seconds. The school doesn't have much by way of security. A few simple encryption runes and as soon as I released a lattice mesh, it was all over. It drowned the school's simple runes, and I was in.

"Are you finished yet?" Remy says, peeking out from under her arm.

"Quiet, I'm concentrating." I take a sip of wine and continue.

She tuts at me, "Slacking in your old age."

"Go fuck yourself, I'm—. There." The records spill across the screen, and I fly through them discarding the ones that are too new or too old. I slow down as I reach the years around when I joined, and that's when I see it. All our entrance scores...

Remy did beat me.

And not by a point or two, but by *nine*.

Doesn't mean shit, though. I huff out a frustrated breath and hack into the financial records.

"No." One little word. Two letters cutting through everything I thought I knew.

But it's right there in black and white. The lie I believed. The truth I don't want to face.

Shit.

I plunge into the chair and stare at the screen. I down the entire glass of wine in one gulp.

"I take it from your silence you've found enough to accept I'm not lying," Remy mumbles from under her arm.

I can't breathe. I can't speak. How could my parents do that? How could they risk their reputation like that? And after everything they've thrown at me about upholding my reputation. What if someone had discovered that I wasn't there on merit but because they paid my way in?

I press my hand to my mouth. My eyes sting so much it turns to acid and instead of falling down my cheeks, the tears turn to fire and the sadness to rage.

Fuck. Them.

Fuck her.

How dare she? My whole life, she's preached about earning my reputation. Make something of myself. On and on she'd go, about preening and primping and perfecting oneself. But it was all a fucking facade, wasn't it? All to prevent anyone from seeing under the pristine, perfect mirage because, if they did, they'd find us rotten to the core.

The whole time they were lying to me. They predicated everything I have worked for on a lie, and now they have the gall to marry me off for not adhering to their expectations.

I reach for the wine bottle and take a huge swig.

Remy pulls her arm off her face and raises an eyebrow at me. "I mean, I get that it must be a shock to you that I am exceptional. But I'm almost offended you didn't realise I was a worthy opponent."

But I'm not listening. I can't do joking, not now.

"They're going to marry me off." I'm not sure what encourages the confession, but it's out before I can stop myself and then words come tumbling out. "Unless I win. They're going to force a marriage to some mundane lord to produce an heir that will meet their insane standards."

"Oh," Remy says and sits up. "I had no idea. I'm sorry."

"Are you?" My gaze clamps onto hers.

She looks down. "I'm sorry your parents don't think you're worthy of their standards. They're wrong." She stands up, closes her Rune subnet down, swipes the screen away, and comes to sit next to me on the sofa.

"I was the one who was wrong. Wrong about them. About everything I thought I was," I say.

"You're not wrong about this…" she tips my chin until I'm looking up at her. "You are exceptional, Beatrice Blythe. Your lattices are some of the most ingenious craft I've ever had the hassle of undoing."

I huff, but it makes me smile at least. "Are you ever going to let the fact you saved me from prison drop?"

She shrugs. Leans down and kisses me so tenderly and warmly that I feel the kiss all the way to my toes.

"Maybe after another orgasm or three."

"Why Professor, I didn't think you had it in you."

She leans in, caressing her lips over mine. The shadow of a kiss. I want to kiss back, be in the moment, but I'm still trying to reason why my parents would have done that. Am I really that much of a disappointment?

"You really didn't know what your parents had done?" Remy says, a single line crinkling the space between her eyebrows.

I shake my head.

She takes the bottle from my hand, swigs a huge mouthful and hands me the dregs back.

The edges of my vision are a little hazy, but I'm still sober enough to know that my chest hurts in a way I can't quite explain.

"I'm sorry," she says again.

"What for now?"

"For telling you. For giving you a truth I'm not sure was my place to give. And for ruining something between you and your parents. I never want to hurt this." She places a single finger in the middle of my chest over my heart. "That...that wasn't my intention."

My eyes sting again, but I bite the inside of my cheek until I taste iron and the sting in my lids goes. I refuse to cry in front of her. I hate crying. Mother always said crying was for the weak. But maybe that isn't true either. I'm not sure what is true anymore.

"Don't," she says.

"What?"

"Don't hold the hurt in. I'm not judging you. If the shoe was on the other foot, I'd be upset."

"All this time you thought I'd knowingly taken your place?" I ask.

"Can you blame me?"

I guess not.

And then the most surprising thing happens. Remy throws her arms around me and pulls me into her body. The scent of warm skin and bergamot fill my nose. I wriggle against her, trying to escape, but she grips me harder, and I realise I need this.

Need the comfort, the hug. And despite the fact I resent her for knowing, resent her for giving me exactly what I need, I can't help but fall into her arms and burrow against her collarbone.

We're silent for a while, and then she laughs. "Things I never expected to do..."

"Fuck your childhood rival? Shatter her relationship with her parents or be teamed up with her for a solid month?"

She tilts down until her mouth is on top of my scalp. "All the above... and one more..."

"Yeah?" I ask.

"Not hate any of it..."

"You shock me," I fan an exaggerated hand over my mouth.

"Would it surprise you to know I've thoroughly enjoyed every moment of the last couple of weeks... Especially the sex?"

She kisses the top of my head and my body melts into her.

"You tell anyone about this..." I wave a hand. "This moment of weakness I'm having, and I will stab pins under your nails." There's no malice in my tone. In fact, I can barely summon the rage I was feeling for my parents a moment ago. What is happening to me?

"It's the booze, right? Making us enjoy this...?" I ask.

"So you admit it then."

"The booze, Remy. It's the booze."

She laughs, leans into my neck and nuzzles the soft fleshy skin. "Bella..."

"Yeah?"

"I don't like seeing you sad."

"You don't?" I purr. "Well, you should do something about that then..."

"Oh, I plan to."

CHAPTER 19

REMY

Bella loops her arms around my neck, her lips dancing over mine. She's kissing me like she needs me and it makes my whole body tight with desire. I want her to need me. I want to give her everything and more.

I break the kiss off, sweep my arm across the coffee table, and knock everything on the floor. I pick Bella up off the sofa and drop her on to it.

She sits up, grabs my belt, and pulls me between her legs. Close enough she can unbuckle my belt. Her fingers work my button and zip. She reaches in, slipping her hand, not down my pants, but under my shirt and up the hard plane of my stomach.

"You know what would make me feel better?" Bella says, fluttering her eyelashes at me.

Our whole lives, Roman and Marcel taught us to hate each other. To best one another and yet I find myself desperate to touch her, taste her, inhale the scent of coconut and lavender skin.

I smirk. "What's that?"

Her tongue flickers over her lips. She removes her hand from my stomach and places a kiss on my crotch, a glint in her eye that tells me exactly what would make her feel better.

I'm instantly wet. I crouch down and hook her tracksuit bottoms off and fling them away. Her jumper bra next. She's naked but for her lacy underwear, laid on the table like a treat all for me. She leans back and spread her legs.

"Are you going to fuck me or tease me?"

"What would you prefer?" she grins.

"I'd prefer, *Bella*, that you be a good little girl and fuck me instead of teasing my cunt all night."

She bites her lip, looks up at me. "And if I spend too long teasing you...what are you going to do about it?"

Heat flares between us. It's as molten as my core.

"Then I'd take the strap out of your suitcase, bend you over the kitchen counter, and fuck that sweet little pussy of yours until it came all over me."

My eyes widen. "My, my, Remy... I think we ought to rename you the Naughty Professor. And you say I have a mouth on me. When no one's listening, you're pure filth."

"You're listening. Now put that pretty little mouth of yours on my pussy, because you have a date with that kitchen counter."

She sits up, slides her fingers under the hem of my boxers, pushing them between my wet folds to circle my clit.

I lean back, bliss rippling from her fingers through my body. My breathing increases, my eyes roll shut as my head droops. She nudges her hand deeper into my boxers until she finds my center and pushes in and out. Shallow little dips that radiate shudders of bliss through me. She moves faster until she elicits a moan from me.

Then she pulls out, leaving me frustrated.

"Clothes. Off," she demands and grabs my neck, tugging me close. Her lips press against mine, her tongue caressing its way through my mouth as she devours me with hungry kisses. My hands are all over her soft skin. She fiddles with my shirt until the buttons fall loose. Her hands slide up my chest, under my sports bra, and pull that off, too.

"You're beautiful," she says, her eyes casting over my body.

She stands suddenly, spinning me around and pushing me down onto the table. But it's only a small coffee table and I have a long body, so she pulls my hips to the edge. She drops to her knees, slides her hand along my thighs and encourages my legs apart. My pussy is wet with excitement. I know because the air rushing between my legs cools my skin.

Her tongue swipes over her lips again as if she's eyeing a delicious meal.

"What have I told you about teasing me, Bella?" I say, lifting my head so she can see me.

"What if I want to be punished, Professor?"

My lip curls, oh I'll punish her alright. She grins, giddy on her feet as if the threat is exciting. She kneels in front of the coffee table, slips between my legs and nips and bites at the lean muscle. Her lips are gentle against my hard lines and pointed limbs. Her mouth finds the hard bone of my hips. She drags her mouth across the V of stomach muscle. Tongue gliding over my skin, each moment drawn out.

"Bella," I hiss. "I swear if you don't put your tongue on

my clit right now, you won't walk for days after I'm done with you."

"What delights you promise."

She plunges down to my centre, sweeping a long, delicious lick through my wetness. It sends hot pulses of liquid sensation through my body. My hand grips the edge of the table, my eyes squeeze shut as she picks my legs up and rests my feet on the table. It means I'm spread impossibly wide for her. She lowers her head to my pussy, her tongue focused solely on my clit. With every swipe, my clit swells, hardens, the pleasure growing more intense. Wetness seeps out of me and she licks up every drop like she's starved.

She slides a finger inside me, moving slow and steady. I could come right now, but I don't want to. I take a deep breath, try to force the control back in. She must sense what I'm doing, that I'm trying to slow things down, because she slides another finger inside, driving up the orgasm. It makes my back arch off the table. A moan of pure, unadulterated ecstasy rushes out.

This is a game of desire: who can hold out, who can tip the other into orgasm. She's going to win. Her focus is on me, on my pleasure, on ravishing my body exactly the way I need.

"Fuck," I say and grab at my nipples, pinching hard, trying to force myself to hold on, delay the gratification a little longer. But I'm so aroused it has the opposite effect, and a bolt of electricity rushes straight to my clit.

She reaches her free hand up to swat my fingers away, and then she grabs my nipple instead. She tugs until I moan, and then she drags her nails down my side and I cry out as tingles run over my skin.

Bella knows I'm close. She speeds up the thrust of her pumping, pounding into me, drawing every ounce of pleasure out. She shifts her fingers, drawing them down my front wall, and it's all over.

I tip over into the precipice of bliss. The world comes apart. My body stiffens, pussy clenches, and spasms of bliss curl all the way to my toes. I lay still, spent and satiated. She peppers my clit with three more tantalising licks, each one making my body twitch.

Finally, when I can breathe and my body has come back down from ecstasy, I sit up and look at Bella. She's grinning at me from under her lashes.

"Do I get punished now?" she smirks.

"You'd like that, wouldn't you?"

She slowly nods at me. I clasp her chin, pulling her to my mouth and shower her in kisses. When I'm done, I suck her bottom lip in between mine. She groans in pleasure. I let her go and take her wrist, leading her to the kitchen.

"I wasn't lying. Put your hands on the counter and don't move." I thread command into my tone, I want her to understand I'm serious. I leave her bent over the counter and head to the bedroom to locate her strap.

It's nestled beside a pile of notes with wax seals. I pick up the strap and find her with her hands still planted on the counter.

"It seems you can be a good girl," I say.

"When it's in my best interests, sure."

I run my hands down the long curve of her back. Her skin is warm and smooth and it makes me want to worship her. I hook my thumbs in the lace of her underwear and slide it down her thighs. She steps out of the knickers, all the while keeping her hands on the counter.

I nudge her feet wider to access her pretty little cunt. She tilts her backside up, giving me a view of how soaked her pussy is. I stand there waiting, watching her bent over the counter, splayed ready for me.

"Remy," she whines. "Please."

"Please what?"

"Don't make me beg."

"Maybe I'd like hearing you beg."

"My legs are shaking. I need to come so bad."

"Yes, and making you wait is clearly working." I glance at her pussy, the excitement sliding down her thighs.

"I'm not going to come if I die of need first."

I step up to her backside. She responds, her fingers curling against the countertop, her breath hitching.

My hands find her hips, I give her arse a little slap. She squeaks as she rocks forward.

"Oh gods," she pants.

"You liked that?" I ask.

"YES. More."

"More what?"

"More please."

"That's a good girl." I pull my hand back and slap her arse again, a little firmer this time, but not enough to mark.

"Fuck," she cries out, a long exquisite moan of pleasure.

I bend over her back, start at her neck and lick all the way down her spine, lower, lower, until I reach the little dent between her arse cheeks. I pause long enough for her to look over her shoulder.

"Don't stop," she says.

So I don't.

I continue drawing my tongue between her cheeks, over both holes and down till I reach her clit. Her thighs are quivering under my touch. Her hands have moved from being flat on the counter to holding the edge to support herself.

I lap at her clit until she's panting and her knuckles are white. My fingers grip and squeeze her ass as my tongue swipes long strokes after short on her clit. I shift, drawing heavy strokes from clit to ass until she's shaking.

"Do you want more?" I say.

"Yes. *Yes*. I need more," she pleads.

I stand, slide the head of the cock down between her cheeks and all the way along her pussy, rubbing her clit for a few short swipes.

I pull back, circle her hole until she moans, "Remy, *please*."

I push the cock inside her an inch, pull out, push in another inch, pull out. She's wet, but she's also tight, and I forgot the lube, so I have to work my way inside her. Once I slide the cock in to the hilt, I withdraw and slam in hard.

She shunts against the counter and cries out. "More."

I readjust my grip on her hips. I focus on her entrance, short sharp pumps, teasing, caressing her pussy. And then I thrust all the way in. She stumbles forward but slams back against me, driving the cock in deeper, harder. Taking everything I give her and still demanding more. She pants with every thrust.

"Touch me, please," she begs. And I'm only too happy to oblige.

I lean over her, my fingers finding her clit, rubbing and sliding over and over. Faster and faster I pump into her, keeping in time with the movement over her clit. Her nipples slide over the counter with the force of my drive behind her. I know she's close because her spine bends with pleasure, and goosebumps swell over her skin as her body winds higher and higher.

My fingers move faster over her clit until her legs tremble. I pull her off the counter; I slide to my knees on the floor and pull her down to sit on my lap, her back against my chest, the cock buried deep in her cunt.

"Use me, make yourself come," I say.

I slide my legs apart, which pushes hers open, and I reach around to palm her pussy. She bounces on my lap, her hands reaching up and pulling her hair away from her face as she slams into me. My palm rubs friction over her clit as she drives into me, once, twice and then she buckles. Reaching for one of the stools to hold her up as her body succumbs to the orgasm. She cries my name and I shiver with the pleasure of hearing it.

I keep hold of her, as she slides trembling off the cock and turns around to sit on my lap, facing me. I hold her tight, shower her neck in kisses as she leans in.

"I've got you," I say as she sinks into my arms. And I really have. I could watch her come over and over and I'd never get bored.

CHAPTER 20

REMY

We spend most of the following day in the practice room. We start by pouring over the final challenge card and discussing the options for creating an impenetrable security system. While we've not bickered about anything, neither of us are overly enthused about the options we've come up with either.

It's late now, they'll be serving dinner downstairs in the canteen. You can always tell because the practice room thins as the smell of roasting vegetables and meat drifts up the stairs.

I push my sleeves up. "Let's leave this. We have time. Shall we look at the second challenge instead?"

Bella nods and pulls the card out and hands it to me. For once, we've already discussed and agreed on what we'll do if we're on the defending team. Which just leaves the need for an infiltration plan.

"Right. Our plan of action will need to be meticulous.

The Guild is highly protected, and it's not just runic security that's the issue. The very structure of the building is designed to confuse."

"Someone has done their research," Bella says, giving me a sassy hand on her hip. I glare at her.

"I did, as it happens, and I also found this..."

I sweep my hand over my RuneNet screen and turn it horizontal. I slice my fingers through the air in a cutting and dicing motion and a 3D model of the guild appears.

"Woah, where the hell did you find that?"

I shrug. "Can't reveal my sources."

My sources are, in fact, Stirling's sources; she knew a girl in the guild who happened to enjoy rendering 3D models and persuaded her to sell me one. Nothing in the rules that says we can't use them. So here we are.

"This is a to-scale replica of the building, but it's much more than that too." I draw my hands in a cutting motion and the building splits in two.

Bella's mouth opens, her eyes all big and round and it's kind of adorable. She's so much softer and sweeter with me than she was at the start of the competition, and I like it. A lot.

"This model is an identical replica, even down to perfect ratio specifications of the Architect's Guild. You can cut the model in any direction and you'll be able to see inside the building. Of course, the building is extremely old, so their more modern traps and security are missing. But I suspect this is a good start, don't you?"

"You're a clever bastard." She holds up her hand for a high five, which I dutifully give her.

"How should we approach this?" I say.

Bella does a circle around the building model. "Directly,

of course. We'll need to go in through the front door, but in disguise."

My eyes startle wide. "But that's so brash. Do we have to talk about sledgehammers again? There's no way we'll get away with that, not with the level of camera security they have in the guild. We'll need to be more discreet."

Bella's cheek flush. And I realise I've fucked up.

"Wait. I'm sorry. I didn't mean to dismiss your idea," I say.

She nods at me; the heat leaving her face, but her words are still a little sharper than normal.

"Well, come on then, *Professor*. What do you suggest?"

I run a thumb along my jawline, trying to assess the best options. Bella paces around the model, moving it in different directions.

The castle has three main concentric circular structures, the inner of which is where the blueprints will be stored. The centre of all magic buildings is always where the highest concentration of magic is and therefore where the most precious items are stored—like the blueprints.

I reach out with my magic, the tingle of the model's runes locking into mine flows through my fingers. The building judders while I try to adjust to its controls.

Several runes slide between my fingers, and I lock in, grinning. I flip the building onto its side to examine the roof. I pull sections out, expand them so we can see the detail, every air vent and door and fire exit.

The circles are only joined in three places. Three glass, tube-like bridges that connect the circles at uniform points, making the building look like a wheel spoke from above.

"That's going to be a problem. Any smart ideas about how to get through glass sky-bridges without being detected?" I say and rotate the building back to flat.

"Our first problem is getting in," Bella says.

She's right. There's no point worrying about traversing the building if we have no solid plan for getting past the exterior defences.

"I'm going to assume that most of the contestants will try entering through the roof. I noticed vents at the top," she says, pointing to the roof. "That's why I reckon we should front door it."

I nod, trying to listen to her, trying to acknowledge that her ideas are valid. "How do you propose we do that? My fear is that the guild is going to be hyper aware that there are contestants crawling the grounds. Won't we get caught trying to walk through the front door?"

"Not if we go in disguise."

I open my mouth to protest, only nothing comes out. Perhaps it's not such a bad idea after all.

"Okay, I support the concept of a disguise. You mentioned the roof, but we didn't examine the understructure of the building."

I rotate the model and flip it upside down.

"There," I point. "There are underground tunnels, too. This really was a fantastic purchase."

Bella folds her arms. "Do you feel clever, Professor?"

I glare at her. "My point is that I like the idea of a disguise, but boldly walking through the main entrance feels dangerous, more like a blunt force than tactical prowess. We can use some delicacy. The rules stated that getting caught is the fastest way to get disqualified from the challenge. Therefore, it's logical to conclude that we need to enter through the most tactical and discreet entrance."

Bella's face stiffens. I swear she's going to protest. But to my surprise, she gives me a sharp nod. "Fine. I don't disagree."

"Meaning you agree?" I frown.

"Don't push your luck."

I smile but continue. "Okay, we'll use disguises because it won't hurt to be dressed in architect uniform, or engineers or cleaner or something," I say.

"We could forge ID badges, too. I happen to know a great forger."

"Red?"

Her eyes widen. "How did you find out?"

"I saw her painting the other day. Incredible talent."

"Then it sounds like we have the start of a plan. Wow, I guess teamwork isn't that complicated after all." She winks and sticks her hand out to shake mine.

A figure appears behind me. I sweep my hand over the 3D model, making it vanish.

"Aww, would you look at that? The cheaters are making deals with each other. How cute," Alba Merrick snarls.

"What do you want?" Bella growls.

Gabe's lanky figure appears next to her. "Did you really think you could get away with it?"

"With what?" I say, already tired of this conversation.

"We want to know why you're cheating," Alba says.

My stomach rolls.

"No idea what you're talking about," Bella snaps.

Although, in theory, she does. Or thinks she does, because I let her believe that the trackers I'd released were me checking up on the other contestants. And while that's true, it's not for the reasons she thinks. This could get very messy fast.

Alba scoots her arse onto the corner of the table, leaning toward the pair of us. "Then why, pray tell, are we being invited to bid for a commission to create a distraction during the final challenge, hmm?"

Bella's brows scrunch. This is news to me. I'm as confused as she is.

"What commission?" Bella asks me.

I shake my head.

"It's being run through the Dark RuneNet. Invitation only," Gabe drawls.

"It's called the Great Breakout. Ironic huh?" Alba say. "But then, you already knew that, didn't you?"

The frown I had furrows into a deep scowl. "And what precisely do you think this has got to do with us?"

Alba looks at Gabe, who nods for her to continue. "Because we found your trackers."

Shit. My world grinds to a halt. The room spins. I underestimated them. I assumed no one would scan the competition system. That was a mistake.

Alba leans forward. "You're tracking our avatars in the competition, and there happens to be a commission out to create a distraction for the very same competition. You put it together."

Bella twitches beside me. She shifts her footing and steps closer to me.

"And what is it you want, Alba? Because you wouldn't be here unless you wanted something," Bella says.

"I want what I deserve."

"Which is?" I say.

"To win."

I laugh. "Not that I'm going to spout runic philosophy, but no one deserves to win, Alba. You earn it."

She glares up at me, folds her arms. "Throw the final."

Three little words. As if they're meaningless. As if we're not all here fighting with every cell in our bodies for the holy grail of prizes. For the accolade thousands dream of, and only one can take.

"You're out of your mind," Bella says.

"Am I? Or am I doing everything I can to win?" Alba says. Behind her, Gabe can't bring his eyes to meet ours. He doesn't agree with her.

"What kind of Royal Rune Master steals her way to the role?" Bella asks.

"The same kind who cheats," Alba spits.

Bella opens her mouth to give Alba a load of shit, but I place my hand on her arm, and she stops dead.

My mind races. I can't afford to get kicked out of this competition. I want to win more than anything. Getting kicked out for cheating, even if I didn't actually cheat, will fuck my reputation as much as Roman escaping will.

When have you ever needed anything more than an accusation to ruin someone? Bella's a living example of that with what Roman's association has done to her. Worse, if I'm kicked out, I can't investigate. I can't stop him from escaping. I need to prove that my work isn't faulty or that Roman can't escape my security systems or everything I've worked for will be ruined.

Bella can't push them on this. We have no idea how they'll react. No clue what they're capable of doing. No. We need to tread carefully.

"I'll admit to the trackers," I say, my mouth souring over the lie, but this is the better play, the only strategic option that will keep me in the game long-term. "But the commission isn't me."

This makes Alba falter, Gabe too. They glance at each other as if they're trying to work out what's the truth from a lie.

"Alright," Alba shrugs. "I'll buy what you're selling. But who then, are they trying to break out of jail? You don't create a commission called the Great Breakout unless that's exactly what you're doing."

Bella pales. "What are they asking you to do?"

"Create a diversion that draws people away from some old tunnels or something. I can't remember the details. I guess you'll have to bid for the commission if you're desperate for cash," Alba says.

Bella's eyes widen to orbs, but before I can ask what's wrong, Gabe pipes up. "Alba, we have a meeting."

Alba nods at him. "So you'll throw the final?" she asks, her voice high and perky, like this won't ruin both our lives.

"N—" Bella starts.

"We'll think about it," I say. Bella glares at me. But she doesn't know the truth of what's going on. Given her reaction, I'm now certain it's not her helping Roman. No matter what Morrigan says, it's time to tell her the truth. It's the only way I can see this competition through to completion without being discovered.

CHAPTER 21

BELLA

Once Gabe and Alba leave, Remy and I are the only ones left in the practice room. She paces up and down the main walkway between workstations, as the last of the sun sinks below the ocean horizon, showering the room in burnt orange hues. Somewhere deep in the recesses of my mind, I'm screaming.

Roman has asked me to steal blueprints for the tunnels. The same tunnels someone is commissioning a distraction for.

Which means without a shadow of a doubt, Roman is trying to break out of prison and he's using me to do it. I knew he was trying to use me, but now I know exactly what the shape of this setup is.

And right now, I have no way of proving I'm innocent. That fucking bastard promised me I just had to do this, and we'd be done.

And yeah, we will be done, because I'll be in prison for treason.

My stomach turns, my skin heats, and I'm not sure if I'm going to be sick or pass out.

No.

I need to calm the fuck down. This doesn't change a thing. I still have a plan. I am still going to get out of this. I just need to execute the plan. I find myself sat on the table, my fingers gripping the edge so hard my knuckles have whitened. A sharp cramp spears through my palm and I have to let go, but the ache grounds me back in the room. I take a deep breath and try to force the calm back in. I can handle this, I can handle this.

I notice Remy. Thankfully, she looks worse than I feel, and it's enough of a distraction to refocus me.

I get that she's upset she's been caught, but she was legitimately cheating. Her pacing becomes more agitated. The steps get shorter, the turns sharper.

I grab her hand, make her stop. Focusing on her, brings me back to reality.

"What's wrong?" I say, stroking my thumb over her skin.

Her eyes are as skittish as her pacing was. She licks her lips, checks the room. My eyes follow her movement.

"There's no one here. What's going on?" I say.

She rubs her forehead as if she's trying to wipe something clean. Her fingers leave a red mark she pressed so hard.

"Remy," I snap. "What the hell?"

She straightens, "I...I have to tell you something."

"Okaaayyy..." I say, drawing out the last syllable.

"Fuck," she says.

I put a hand on my hip, growing impatient. "I swear if you don't spit it out..."

"I'm going to tell you, give me a second. Look... There's

something... Fuck, you're not going to like this. But I need you to hear me out, and let me get all the way to the end before you get mad."

I raise an eyebrow. "I spend half my life mad."

"Exactly."

"Okay, fine. Go on." I fold my arms over my chest, waiting.

"I—I'm not cheating," she says.

And I laugh. I can't help it. "Of course you're cheating. You just admitted as much to the Merricks. Look, I appreciate you don't like the fact you've been caught. But you did get caught, Remy. You're going to have to deal with it. Don't start lying to me now."

She rounds on me, her eyes stern and serious. "Bella. I'm *not* cheating."

There's something so calm and firm in her tone that I find myself believing her.

"Then what are you doing? Because it sure as shit looks like you're cheating."

She falters, fine lines coat her face. She's worried. Wait.

If she's worried, then she's still doing something she shouldn't, even if that isn't cheating.

My eyes snap up to meet Remy's and for the first time, she stares at me with a tremor in her gaze. As if her world is breaking apart and she doesn't understand how to piece it together again. Or perhaps it's the lies unravelling and the jagged truth revealing itself.

Oh, fuck.

"You knew," I say, my voice a snarled whisper.

There's a horrendous pause; silence thick enough I can't swallow the air down. My heart stops beating and I wait and wait and wait for the truth. Is she helping Roman? I mean, it doesn't make sense. She jailed him. It can't be true.

I don't want it to be. The idea is a twisted, gnarled thing that I refuse to believe until she says it.

She tears her eyes away from me. It's a knife to my chest. I buckle a hand over my mouth.

"I'm sorry," she whispers.

"How did you know?" I have to hear it from her mouth. The ache in my chest ripens into a furnace. It builds and builds until it's ready to explode. "I said, how?"

She flinches. "The palace's security intercepted messages that indicated there was going to be a breakout attempt and that the games were going to be used as a cover."

"And..." I snap.

"And it was most likely Roman they were trying to break out..."

"*And*...?" I am shouting now because I need her to say it. To break my heart, tell me she was using me this whole time.

She wipes her face, her eyes looking anywhere but at me. "And that makes you the prime suspect."

My world shatters, pins and needles rush to my extremities, to my nose and lips, my fingers and toes. I can't breathe. I need to get out.

"I'm the suspect because... why? Because I was apprenticed to him?"

She nods.

"And you thought you'd what? Come and spy on me? Fuck the truth out of me?"

"That's not—I mean."

"Fuck, that's exactly what you're doing, isn't it?" I'm standing in front of her, an accusing finger pointed at her chest.

She takes my hand, pulls it away from her chest. The

heat between our palms is ferocious. I'm livid with her. I hate her more in this moment than I ever have, and yet... her touch does things to me. It short circuits my mind, rewires my thoughts.

"It's... I told you to let me finish," Remy says.

I shut my mouth.

She runs her hand through her hair. "Yes, I was sent here to spy on you. But I need you to know that I tried to defend you. I told them repeatedly there was no way you'd risk your freedom after Roman was jailed. I said that yes, you can be petty, and you have light fingers."

I pout, but I stay silent because she's not wrong.

So she continues. "Over and over, I told them, you're not the sort to commit treason."

I swallow hard; the realisation settling over me: it's me. She's defended me this whole time, but I'm the problem.

"I knew there was no way you would go back to Roman. Not after I erased the evidence of you working with him before."

My throat dries. But she continues this unrelenting truth that makes my insides shrink.

She takes my hand as she says, "Everything I've done has been to protect you."

I want to disappear inside myself. But something about the way she said team makes me listen a little harder.

"Team?" I say.

Remy sags, "We're friends. *Really* good friends. Morrigan, Stirling, all of us. We've been working together on various projects for months now."

Oh, fuck me. She's friends with the princess? I blink at her, words failing me as my blood runs cold. "What do you mean friends? What projects?"

"Crown politics mostly. Undercover things the crown needs doing but can't be associated with," Remy says.

"Fuck. The map? You helped the Queen repair the Borderlands?" I'm breathless.

Remy nods.

"I have a room at the palace. Well, in the cottage Morrigan stays in to be more accurate. The whole team does."

"So when you say good friends, you really mean the best of..."

Remy gives me a limp smile as she nods.

I am so fucked. The irony is that I actually am the one she's searching for. Or at least, the one Roman wants to take the fall.

I've been set up, led right to Remy, and there's not a single piece of fucking evidence to prove my innocence.

This is a mess. A tiny voice in my mind squeaks that I should confess. She's sent here looking for the culprit, and Roman's handed me to her on a plate. But she'd tell them, she would have to or risk her friendship with them. And right now, I look guilty as hell.

I'm the one who was apprenticed to him. I'm the one she protected after the magic importation fiasco. If I tell her Roman's blackmailing me into stealing the very blueprints he needs to escape, and that I have plans to steal them, then I am guilty. Even if I'm doing it to set him up in return. No. I'll steal them so no one else can. I'll prove my innocence first. Stop Roman getting his hands on the blueprints, and then I can tell her.

Isn't it ironic? I've fought my mother for years and after all this, she's right. My reputation, my connection to Roman, will be my downfall.

"Did you hear me? Earth to Bella," Remy says.

"Huh? Yes. I—"

"You're angry with me?"

"Obviously, I'm furious, Remy. You fucking spied on me. Lied to my face. Fucked me because why? You just wanted to get close to me? Those trackers were never about cheating. You were doing it to track my runic footprint."

My eyes well, but I refuse to cry in front of her. "How could you use me?" I growl, trying to cling to the rage rather than the agonising ache in between my ribs.

"The sex was never—"

"Never what?" I say, shoving a hand on my hip. "Never about fucking the hate into me? Never about fucking the resentment over my parents? The fury of all those times I beat you? The fact that I'm a legacy and you're what?"

"Bella," Remy snaps. "Don't. You're hurt and I'm sorry, but don't do this."

"Do what? Fling insults after you lied and tried to dig up evidence to jail me? I think that's the least I can do."

My finger jabs into her chest. Heat pools between us. My breaths are uneven. She looks down at me, holding my gaze, those worry lines etched beneath her eyes. Gods dammit, I can't stand the way she's holding me in her gaze. It makes me want to throttle her and kiss her. I want to steal her away and forget this whole mess.

"Don't ruin us. I'm begging you," she says and tilts my chin up. "I'm sorry. If I could have told you I would have, I wanted. But I couldn't. Not until I released the trackers and could prove you weren't in cahoots with Roman."

I slap her hand away, "Because asking me and believing what I tell you isn't enough?" The lie is sour on my tongue as I release it.

"That's not what I said."

"It's what you didn't do that's the problem."

Even as I say it, I know the awful truth. I'm such a hypocrite.

"Bella," she says, her voice a rumble in her chest.

"What?" I say, scarcely able to look at her. She pulls my chin around again. I can't breathe, I can't speak. Something wet rolls down my cheek. She wipes it away with her thumb. Where her pad caresses my cheek, tingles lay in her wake.

I hate that she has this power over me. The ability to stop my heart, to make my world fracture into new pieces, to make my heart race like it doesn't need my body. To make me feel safe enough when we're surrounded by lies and poison that I can cry.

She leans in. She must be able to sense the static between us. "I may have kept things from you about what I'm really doing here. But the sex... what I feel in here," she places my palm over her heart. "That was always true. I swear to you."

Her lips brush against mine, and the touch shoots straight to my pussy.

Dammit.

I want to hurt her.

I want to punish her for lying to me. But how can I when I know the truth of what I'm holding back?

I want to kiss her like this moment will never end and the truth will stay hidden.

"You swear?" I say, something unlocking inside me.

"I—," she brushes her lips against mine again. "Swear." This time, her mouth lingers a little longer.

My tummy furls into a tangle of butterflies, desire pools between my legs. "Prove it."

"Mmm, and how should I do that?"

"Fuck me like you hate me, Remy. Fuck me like you love

me, like you'll never lie to me again. I want you to fuck me like I'm the only one you'll ever fuck again."

Her eyes darken. She grabs me by the waist and lifts me onto the desk. Our papers and tools scatter and something clangs as it clatters to the floor. But I don't care, because the way she holds me in her gaze could set the palace aflame. Her expression is wild like the night and feral things. She looks as though she's going to consume me, and I don't want to stop her.

She cups my neck and steps between my legs, hitching my skirt up to my hips. I cross my ankles behind her arse, locking her into me. She leans in, her perfume strong even at this time of the evening. The scents of leather and bergamot and hints of vetiver wash over me. I close my eyes as she pulls me to her mouth and everything I was worrying about slips away.

She kisses me like she's possessed. Like I am her world, and my mouth is a prayer she can't stop singing. She moans into me as she holds me tight. My hands find her waist.

"I'm so sorry," she says.

Again and again. Between kisses, between tugging her shirt out of her trousers and sliding my fingers up her back.

Between my silent tears and all the regrets wrapping themselves around my soul. She whispers apologies and I take them and take them and take them. I use them to massage the guilt away like the fucking hypocrite I am. I need to stop thinking. Need to get out of my head. I dig my nails in hard enough to mark her skin. She hisses and breaks the kiss.

"Is that how we're playing?" she says.

"I'm not playing, Remy. This is my heart. I don't want to play anymore."

Her nostrils flare, her fingers find my tights, slide up my

thighs. She pokes at a hole that's usually covered by my skirt, then slips two fingers through it.

She pinches the nylon and yanks hard.

I gasp as my tights tear. She grabs the edges and yanks again and again. Until they're shredded and barely hanging on.

Then she gets on her knees in front of me, and I stop breathing. The sight of her between my legs, her hands on my knees, ready to take me, to own me and fuck me and undo me is too much. She pushes my knees apart, my skirt cinched at my hips, my legs carrying the tattered remnants of tights.

"Shame you're not wearing those slit knickers," she says grinning at me, and scooches my arse to the edge of the workstation.

"I'm sure you'll cope," I say.

She buries herself between my legs, her mouth showering my lace knickers with kisses. She swipes her tongue down the side between my thigh and underwear, and it elicits a moan. So close to my core and yet so far away. I push my legs further apart, desperate for her tongue to touch my cunt where I need.

"What if we're caught?" I say, glancing over my shoulder at the door. The room is empty, the darkness of evening drawing dimness into the practice hall.

"Then the lucky spectator will get to see what a proper fucking looks like."

I bite my bottom lip, excitement building between my thighs. Soaking the lace. Remy pinches the gusset and pulls it away, revealing my pussy.

And then she's on me. Her tongue ravishes my clit like a starved beast. She licks every bit of wetness away and draws her tongue down my slit like she's desperate for more.

Remy moans into my pussy, focusing short sharp strokes on my clit that wind my body so tight I have to hold back the whimpers in case I'm too loud for passersby. She breaks off, stands up between my thighs. She kisses me like she's never going to see me again and then slides a hand up my skirt and under the lace of my knickers.

"If I died with the taste of you on my tongue, I'd die a happy woman."

She pushes two fingers inside me, burying them so deep I have to grab her arm to steady myself as I cry out a moan of carnal pleasure. Every time she fucks me with her hand, I've forgotten how thick her fingers are. But gods do I love how full she makes me feel. She leans down to shower soft kisses and hard bites on my neck. I moan into her touch as she slides her fingers in and out.

"Ride my hand, Bella," she says, her words trickling warm breath down my chest. I do as she says.

She curls her fingers inside me, and it's almost too much. Waves of pleasure peel out from her fingers. She drives them inside me harder, faster. She slides her free hand around my waist to keep me upright on the workstation. My fingers dig into her biceps where I'm trying to stay up. My body shivers and trembles under the force of her thrusting and the ripples of molten pleasure pouring through my body.

"More. I need more," I pant.

I can't hold myself up anymore, even with her support. She lets me slide down and I settle onto my elbows, but even that is too much. I lay flat on the workstation. Something digs into my back, several more items crash to the floor, but I'm too far gone to check.

I slide my feet onto the desk, spreading me open so her mouth can return to my pussy. She sucks my clit fully into her mouth and I yelp as hot bolts fire through my thighs and into my breasts. She laps at my cunt with a bruising pace, her fingers matching with pumps that make my walls clench and my breath catch.

I grab the edge of the table as she winds me higher, as I bury the truth and let her wrap the lies I need to believe around my orgasm. I grind my hips against her face as she pushes me higher, harder, faster.

I slide my fingers into her hair and hold on as she tips me with one airless breath after another over the edge and my world comes apart.

I am completely spent and blissed out of my mind. The only tarnish in this moment is the shadow of reality on the horizon. But like the ocean, the horizon seems so far away, and I have convinced myself everything is going to be fine.

CHAPTER 22

REMY

The day of challenge two arrives faster than I'd like. Time is draining away. There's only a week left until the last challenge and every time I think I'm closer to catching the culprit, their digital signature changes. They encrypt another layer of rune cyphers, another layer of rune walls, or they disappear off the net altogether. The bugs I placed in the training room and corridors have come up with nothing. Likewise for the camera orb. And not that I think it's necessary to hack Bella's account, but I didn't even manage to do that. I'm failing at everything. That knowledge infects my mind, laces around my thoughts like a parasite. I'm not good enough, I don't deserve the reputation I have. And if I don't figure out what's going on, I'm going to be humiliated in front of the entire city.

But today is challenge two, and the team is convinced someone will try to steal Roman's prison blueprints. But this time, we're ready to catch the culprit. Scarlett and

Morrigan have added extra security around the vault containing the blueprints to all the city's houses without magic.

It's one of those days where the sun likes to lie to you. It's bright, masquerading as summer, despite the bite of winter in the breeze.

The carriage draws to a stop against the cobbled front of the Architect's Guild. The castle is enormous. Of course, we can only see the crenelated exterior building. The outside walls protect the other inner concentric rings. But as I step out of the carriage and inhale the sharp morning air, I close my eyes and picture the 3D model we had.

Bella is twitchy this morning, her demeanour skittish and flighty. I suppose she doesn't like knowing she was under suspicion, especially not now we're on site and she knows I'm hunting for a thief.

"You're going to be fine," Red says, gripping Bella's shoulder. She pulls her into a hug. "I'll be waiting for you, okay?"

As Red says those words, it's like she's really saying something else. But I don't have time to ponder it, I need to stay focused on the job today. I've set up a recording around the blueprints to Roman's prison to monitor any attempts at theft through records stored in the RuneNet. And the guild themselves will be monitoring the physical records. Hopefully, if anyone goes near any form of Roman's records then we'll get them.

In front of the Architect's Guild is a small stage and a plinth. Morrigan steps up to it and smiles as the last of the carriages pull up and deposit the final contestants, their family and friends. The courtyard of the guild is packed with people. It makes me nervous. I know there's added security but there are so many people here it's too crowded.

Crowds make for easy escapes and ghosts slipping between bodies. I told Morrigan we should ban the audience. But she argued that it would be too suspicious. We might make the culprit run or find another way in. She wanted it to look like all was running smooth so that we didn't alert them to the fact we were on to them.

And I understand her position, but for all the academic postulating and theorising, I have a bad feeling twisting in my gut like I've missed something. And sometimes you need to pay attention to your gut.

There has to be another layer I'm missing. But I spent the best part of the last two days chasing the digital ghost. It reminded me of when I was still an apprentice and how furious I would get with Marcel because I wasn't good enough to beat him. We used to play cat and mouse on the RuneNet. He was always pushing me harder, and further to outdo my previous hack, the previous build. Whatever it was, he always wanted me to do one better.

"Welcome, magicians. Before we begin, let me thank everyone who attended the first challenge. We're already seeing inventions and patents coming out of the patcher groups from the first challenge. This is very promising for our technological developments."

There's a smattering of claps that turn into whooping and hollering. Morrigan, pleased by the response, continues.

"Today marks the second challenge and by the end of the day, we will have just five teams left in the running for the coveted prize of Royal Rune Master."

There's another smaller ripple of applause from the magicians and families gathered. I glance at Bella, her eyes flick to mine.

Morrigan shifts on stage. "Today, we will pair each

team of two with another team. The first of those teams will need to break and enter the guild to steal blueprints for a prison. The second team will work with the guild's existing security, and their own skills and Rune coding abilities, to prevent the break-in attempt."

She pauses while Games Maker Eli and Marcel step in front of the plinth and spread their arms wide. Two twenty-foot screens fizz to life, hovering in front of the building.

"You'll be able to watch the teams on these screens and follow their progress. The winning team will be decided by knock-out. Either team one escapes with the blueprints or team two facilitates their capture." Morrigan nods to Eli.

He waves his hand and the screen zooms into colour, traversing the inside of the building and to the heart where, behind a vault door, sits a set of pink blueprints.

"These are the blueprints you're aiming to steal," she gestures at the screen.

Her eyes catch mine. A warning passes between us: *keep an eye on Bella*. It bothers me more than it should. I want them to back her, to accept her innocence. How can they not when I've monitored her every move on the RuneNet and she's done nothing? I don't know when I went from wanting to beat her to defend her, but we're here and my head is a mess.

Made more so by the fact she accepted my apology. I thought I'd lost her, and despite the awful lie I kept from her, she took me back.

They're wrong about her, I know it.

Now I need to prove it.

"We should talk about what happens in the final... not how we do it... but what happens when only one of us wins." She looks away and I know that she understands what I'm really saying is that if one of us wins, the other loses and I'm not sure either of us lose particularly well.

"What happens if I win?" she says.

I'm not sure how to answer that. "What happens if I win?"

She can't bring her eyes to meet mine.

"I don't want to lose you," I whisper.

"Nor I you," she says. "But this role... it means more to us than life itself. Are you going to choose me over the win?"

I swallow, my whole body heating with tension. I want to say yes. I do. But I don't know if I can.

"Would you? Could you still choose me if I win?" I ask.

But she doesn't answer. She looks away, slips her hand into mine, and turns back to the plinth.

CHAPTER 23

BELLA

We take our places on the east side of the guild. This is the entrance we both agreed on last night. It takes an hour for the first two teams to run; we were drawn third. So we wait.

Mostly in silence too, as if the ugly secret I'm keeping hangs between us. I consider telling her. I even get close, but as I'm about to confess and throw my fate into her hands, she passes me an earpiece.

"Here," she says and shows me how to place it in my ear. "Can you hear me?"

"That's bizarre," I say swallowing down the confession.

"Made it myself." She wears this smug grin that makes her eyes twinkle and a piece of my heart melt. "It's only in case we have to split up. We shouldn't have to. But you can't be too careful."

Eventually, Games Maker Eli appears around the curve of the guild. "Ready?" he says.

I glance at Remy; she nods at me. "As we'll ever be," I say.

Eli creates a RuneNet screen in front of him and a countdown timer appears. "In five. Four..." he mouths the last numbers, fingers up indicating the seconds. *Three. Two. One.*

I break into a run, wanting to get this over and done with as fast as I can. I threw up this morning, the anxiety of having to steal blueprints from under Remy's nose too much.

We're dressed in the guild cleaner uniforms. An addition we both agreed on after quarrelling over whether we should be in a cleaner or engineer uniform.

We reach a drain hidden behind a hedge. It takes both of our combined efforts to hook it out of the metal frame.

"I'll go first," I say and hop into the hole, hanging from my fingertips until my eyes adjust. I fall the few feet to the floor, landing in a crouch.

Remy plops down a second later and hands me an orb from her pocket and holds another herself. She rolls her hand over the top and it flares to life.

I do the same, and then she gives me her orb so she can pull her RuneNet screen up. It shimmers to life, her hands vibrating as the screen fills with lines of rune code. It shifts fast, and the sewage system appears on the screen.

"Down here," she says.

I stay in front with the orbs, and she directs from behind. We move left and right and right and left again so many times I'm dizzy. Admittedly, this is a longer route into the building than some of the other contestants chose. But we both agreed that we could get further into the heart of the building without being seen. Whereas some of the other's strategies may have been more direct, but also far more dangerous.

"Turn left there," Remy says as we approach a T-Junction. I veer left and climb up through a smaller tunnel pipe. The space is tight enough we have to crawl on our hands and knees. It makes my chest clamp and my breathing laboured. Even with the orb lights Remy has, the eerie darkness presses down on me. My breath hitches. Remy rubs my lower back. Or the part she can reach, anyway.

"Keep going, Bella, it's not far," she says.

My whole body tingles, my ribs are so compressed I swear they're going to crack. I can't breathe, my fingers are going numb. I need to get out. My breathing is uneven, panting short breaths. Static sweeps across my vision, my arms wobble. I'm going to pass out.

"Ten feet, Bella. Ten more feet."

I push as hard as I can, desperately trying to breathe slower, deeper. Finally, when I'm certain I'm about to black out, we spill into an underground chamber and my lungs inflate. I lie on my back, taking huge gulps of air.

Remy slides a hand over my shoulder. "Are you okay?" Her words are so tender I almost crumble beneath her touch.

"We don't have time, I'm fine." I'm not. But I am better now we're out of that godsforsaken tunnel.

Her eyes remain narrowed as she stares at me, but she doesn't protest because ultimately I am right. We don't have time. This challenge is timed and if we don't get to the blueprints quick enough, even if we get out, we won't win.

She nods her assent and points up. "That drain cover will lead us to the first garden ring between the outer building circle and the middle one."

"Let's get it open."

Together, we notch a metal hook into the cover and slide it open. She has a longer arm's reach, so she climbs out first and drops a hand back into the drain to pull me out.

The garden is small, only about fifteen feet wide. Tall bushes and shrubs and exotic flowers fill the space. The ground is made of gravel that crunches under our feet as we walk around the circular building hunting for the cleaners' entrance.

"Here," I say, as Remy catches up behind me. I push open a door with a sign that says caretakers only.

We both grab a cleaning trolley filled with brooms and buckets, and cleaning products and rolls of paper.

Remy consults the map of the guild on her mini RuneNet screen projection. "The lift is down the corridor and to the right. Three doors and the fourth is a lift."

We push the trolleys out the door and down the circular corridor. It has this strange dissonant effect; the horizon never shifts, we're always walking around a corner, never making progress. It makes my skin crawl. Goosebumps fleck up my arms and down my spine, and my stomach twists like we're being watched. And we might be. If I were on the other team, I'd have hacked into the orb cameras to watch us. But I'm still hoping the disguises will keep us camouflaged. I tug Remy's cleaner cap down further to hide her blonde hair.

"Thanks," she whispers.

We reach the fourth door and Remy pushes the button.

"Hello?" a man says.

I freeze.

"Hi," Remy answers, her voice infused with a calm I know she's not feeling.

"Who are you?" he says. He's wearing a security

uniform. The button around his port belly strains against the hole. His face is wide and kind, big blue eyes beam out at us. Shit, shit, shit.

"Cleaners, obviously. What does it look like?" The snark is out of my mouth before I can stop it.

Remy's eyes widen at me as she glances between us.

"Well, I can see that. Where's the usual guy?"

I blurt words before I can over think the response. "Off sick. Got a terrible dose of the shits. Apparently he—"

The security guy holds his hand up to stop me from speaking, as his nose wrinkles. "Right."

"I mean, I can call him if you want. He might be shitting his insides out on the loo as we speak, but you never know, he may have taken an orb into the toilet."

The guard's face is so scrunched I know I've won.

He shakes his head at me. "I don't need to hear more. Make sure you clean the bins on the third floor. They were left yesterday."

"Will do," Remy says as the lift door opens and she pushes her trolley in a little faster than necessary.

The lift doors shut and both of us sag against the wall.

"Close call," Remy says.

"Almost like using disguises was a good idea." I grin.

"Even during a break in, you have to be smug." She rolls her eyes, but her lips twitch like she's holding back a laugh.

The doors ping open on the third floor and we push the trolleys out into the hall. My back prickles. This floor is made entirely of glass; we're extremely exposed even in cleaners' uniforms.

We make a move, passing an art library, a stockroom and draw level with a drawing room.

"In there," Remy says to the drawing room.

We slip inside and on the opposite side of this vast room is a bridge and a security guard at the entrance.

Shit.

Remy glances at me, and we head toward the bridge, pushing between the huge white tables. Some are tilted up for people who want to stand, others have light boxes, some sets of chalk and pencils hovering in the air, waiting for their architect to return.

"Identification," the guard says.

Remy bends and contorts her fingers and swipes her hand over her badge. Unfortunately for me, I don't have that trick in my magical repertoire.

He examines the entirely fake badge and gives it a nod. "Yours?"

Balls. I'm going to have to improvise.

Actually, balls is a great idea. He realises I'm an intruder, his hand slipping to the orb attached to his hip, but it's too late. I drive my knee into his crotch. He buckles over and falls to the ground, groaning. I pull out a pin from my hair and jab it into his neck.

He blinks at me and then is out cold.

"Bella," Remy hisses. "What the fuck? I thought we weren't going to draw attention to ourselves?"

"Yes, well, you failed to teach me that little mirage trick, didn't you? So I had to go with the flow."

"Is he dead?"

"Don't be ridiculous. He's asleep and will be for a good few hours. And when he wakes, he'll have a nasty headache and probably a sore cock. Help me get him in the cupboard."

She grips him under the arms, and I pick up his feet, and together we scramble to shove him in the drawing cupboard. It takes too long, but he's dead weight and there's only two of us. Finally, sweating and panting, we slam the stationery cupboard door shut and return to our trolleys. I pick up my hair pin and slide it back into my bun.

"You're mildly terrifying. What if you accidentally stabbed yourself with that pin?"

I shrug. "Then I'd enjoy the wild sex dreams about you."

"You've had wet dreams about me?" Remy says, a hint of pink tinging her cheeks.

"We can act them out if you like."

"Yes. Definitely. But later. Move your arse, we have a challenge to win," Remy says and moves onto the bridge.

It's enclosed; the floor, the two walls and the ceiling are all made of glass. It makes my stomach twinge and curl into a ball when I glimpse the concrete below. I hate being this exposed, but there's nothing we can do. We have to make it to the inner sanctum.

We make our way across the bridge, but Remy stops a few meters from the end.

"What's wrong?" I say, grinding my trolley to a halt before I slam into the back of her.

"There's a field protecting the inner building. I can see it shimmering."

"Shit, let me try." I push in front of her, my hands already extended and vibrating. The lattice tattoos running up my forearms shine white and shimmer as runes burst to life and join in the air and a huge lattice forms before my eyes. It hovers, waiting for a command. I ball my fists and hold my knuckles together, pull my hands back and fling them forward. The lattice flies the final meters to the entrance and attaches like a leech onto the shimmering protection field.

Bolts of static and magic spark off the entryway. Something backfires and a sharp lance of pain rips through my tattoos, up my arms and into my chest.

"Fuck," I bark as I buckle to my knees.

"Bella," Remy's voice is strained.

"I'm okay, give me a minute." I recalibrate, send several lines of code into the lattice. Sweat breaks out across my forehead. My hands scream in protest as the ache of pressure builds until every bend and contortion is like fire. Nausea rolls in my stomach. I'm pushing too hard, using too much magic.

Something runs from my nose. I wipe my face across my shoulder and a line of blood stains my uniform.

Remy's face is lined with horror.

"I've got this, just. One. More. There." The lattice locks into place and the shimmering stops.

I collapse to my knees, and Remy is beside me in seconds.

"I'm fine honestly," I say. But if I look as pale as I feel, then I know she won't believe a word I'm saying.

She helps me to my feet.

This is it.

No turning back.

We need to break into the architect's vault, and I need to steal a set of tunnel plans while no one's looking.

She slips her hand into mine and I swallow hard. Her touch tingles like the warmth of safety and the chill of treachery, and my gut swirls.

But it's too late because we cross the threshold, and there, at the heart of the guild, is the safe and the fate of both of us lies within.

CHAPTER 24

REMY

I pull up the RuneNet screen and navigate my way to the Architect Guild's security system.

"Once I access their security, we'll be visible to the other team. They'll unleash everything they can on us," I say.

"I can bolster the bridge entrance if guards come. The lattice I made was only to get us in, not keep anyone out. But I can flip the coding to keep the guards out," Bella says and pushes her sleeves up, and aiming her hands at the entrance.

"Do it."

She creates another lattice in seconds. Her hands pull and weave runes in the air, each thread shining bright and turning a coppery colour as it locks into place.

"Done," she says as her eyes return to their normal colour. Her skin is pallid, she looks exhausted or like she's going to puke, she's clearly pushed too hard.

"We're almost through this," I say, knowing my words are useless. We still have the hardest part to come.

We examine the front of the inner sanctum vault. It has a giant wheel to unlock and open the door above an ancient safe dial.

"There's a force field layered over the door, too. It'll be connected to the RuneNet," Bella says.

I nod. "Got it. I see the code. We'll need to attack this simultaneously. But I wasn't anticipating the safe dial. How old is that thing?"

"But kind of genius when all of us magicians will be expecting runic security."

My mouth pinches, "I know, but a pain in the arse. Worse, I don't know how to break the analog part of the vault. I only know how to hack the force field."

"Good job for you that I'm an expert then." A smug smile peels across her lips as she rubs her hands together. Her middle fingers touch at the tips, slide over each other, and then her hands shift through a series of movements so fast I can't see.

A lattice forms in front of her. It's small and funnelled and she places it on the vault door. She swipes her hand over the sharp end of the funnel, cutting the end off. It disintegrates in the air. Then she places her ear to the blunted end.

"Perfect," she says.

"How do—"

"Roman. That man has more safes than I have runes. He's so secretive and I am nosy. If you listen to the internal mechanisms, you can crack the safe open, but it's a delicate job.I broke into fifty per cent of the safes."

"And the other fifty per cent?"

"He might've valued security, but the idiot used the same code for the other half of them: 10. 03. 1980."

"You said it like a date," I say, and the numbers run through my mind with an itch of familiarity.

"Easier to remember if I say it like a date."

"Marcel's birthday is the tenth of March 1980."

Bella's mouth falls open, her skin, already paled from exertion, goes ghost grey. Frown lines burrow into the space between her eyebrows.

"What are the odds?" I say.

"Remy," she says suddenly serious. "I don't believe in coincidences." Her voice is insistent like she's trying to tell me something. But she returns to the vault her face furrowed in concentration. I'm acutely aware we've been in the guild far too long already, so I return to the screen.

"Okay, so you're going to crack the dial code and I'll work on the force field. Ready?" I ask.

She nods.

"In three, two, one."

She places her ear against the funnel and her hand on the dial, turning it this way and that.

I focus on the RuneNet projection in front of me. Lines of code populate the screen as I hack into the external guild wall.

"Shit, they've seen me," I say.

A slew of attack runes appear on the screen. The team fighting us taking zero chances. One of the runes chomps through the main line of code, decrypting the primary Rune wall in the Guild's security.

"Fuck, it's disrupted my decryption rune."

I funnel more power into my runes, but the team defending is viciously quick. Another layer of my code is destroyed and this time there's kickback. I'm flung across the room, disconnected from the RuneNet, and my head smashes against the glass wall.

"Fuck! Are you okay?" Bella shouts.

Despite the dizziness and throbbing bruise forming on the back of my head, I wave her off. "Focus on the dial."

I cast back onto the RuneNet more determined this time. Those bastards are not going to win. But with each layer I recode, they take another layer out. This is a stalemate. But then there's two of them and only one of me.

Bella looks up, and I realise I can't do this without her.

"I need your help."

"What about a protection wall?" she says, turning the dial three times.

"Do it. I can't afford for them to destroy another set of runes."

Bella splits her focus. One hand and her ear still working the dial, she freehand creates a lattice and casts it into the RuneNet. Sweat runs down her temple. I re-create my decryption code and bolster it this time with an anti-hack. Bella's lattice swoops in and encircles my code and we're ready to go again.

"You really are magnificent. I hope you realise that." I focus all my attention on creating a set of runes to surround the lattice that will explode.

It works and a minute later Bella's unlocked the dial. Thirty seconds after that, I'm through the force field, and one of their avatars has been destroyed.

"Yes!" Bella shrieks as the final runes disintegrate and the force field evaporates.

We enter the vault. It's dim, and the air is musty and stale. There are rows and rows of shelves. Thankfully, the hardest part for us was breaking in. The prints sit on a table in the middle of the vault.

She holds her hands up. "You take them," she says and slides her hands behind her back.

I pull them out of the scroll holder and an alarm screeches to life.

"Fuck. *Run*," I bellow.

Bella sprints out of the vault. I race after her, a split second later, only to slam into an invisible wall. I find myself shot back ten feet and collapse in a heap on the floor.

"NO," Bella screams, skidding to a halt outside the vault door.

"Those bastards," Bella says. "The other team must have rewired the protective force fields and routed them to this door."

I spin around, scanning the vault, then pull up the RuneNet projection and the schematics of the Architect's Guild. Along the map of the vault, there's an air vent in the ceiling that will lead to the rooftop. I can get out that way. I rotate the screen and point at it.

"I can get out this way. You continue with the plan. I'll meet you out the back, where we dropped into the sewer system."

Bella's eyes are wide. Her chest rises and falls in a jagged rhythm. For one brief moment, Morrigan's voice echoes through my mind: don't let her out of your sight. I hesitate. This wasn't her fault. The alarm went off. That was part of the challenge, right?

Only there's something about the way she's looking at me, the way she's biting her lip, the slight tremor in her hands that seems like more that exhaustion. The first seed of doubt nestles in my gut.

"Okay," she nods. "Okay. Be safe."

She places her hand up to the force field and I do the same and then she's sprinting out of sight.

I run down the central alley of the vault and down a racking system. The air vent sits in the ceiling's corner. I climb up the racking, grip the vent and yank. It doesn't budge. Shit. I swing off the racking and use all my weight to pull the vent as hard as I can. It budges an inch and then drops out, and I crash to the floor.

My hands are cut, my elbow is as bruised as my head, but there's no time to dither. I scramble up the racking carrying the vent and haul myself up and inside, just as guards break into the vault itself.

I still my breathing and back away from the vent opening as the guards enter the vault and bark commands at each other to check various locations. Too bad bastards.

I can still hear the calls of frustration as I shuffle on my hands and knees all the way out of the vault and to the rooftop. I break out into the open air and breathe deep before climbing down the outside of the building. Foot over hands, I clamber down a drainpipe and sprint the rest of the way to our start line. Bella is running to meet me from up the side of the building.

Games Maker Eli smiles at us, "Congratulations. That was a fast time, too."

He shakes our hands, and I spot Red walking away from the direction Bella just came. I glance from Bella to Red, but Bella is beaming and jumping up and down on her feet, looking at the screen Eli is pointing to.

We're in first place. We beat the Merricks by an entire minute.

She leaps in the air, jumping into my arms. "We did it."

That we did. I glance back at Red, disappearing around

the curve of the Guild. But Bella pulls my face around and hugs me, still cheering and jumping. The way her arms cling to me like I'm the one filling her with joy makes everything else seem insignificant.

CHAPTER 25

BELLA

I meet Red at midnight. The sky is clear, but on the ocean horizon, black thunder clouds streak dark smears across the stars.

"Did you get it done?" I ask.

"Yes, but you owe me. That was tight," she says and hands me two envelopes. "This was mine. That's the original."

"Thank you. And for what it's worth, I owe you big. Whatever you want, consider it done."

"Be careful who you hand that kind of power to," she says, smiling.

But she's my best friend in the entire world. I'd give her the universe if she asked for it. I pull her into a hug. "Thank you for having my back."

We make our way back to Lantis Palace. She leaves me to return to her room and I descend the main building staircase into the bowels of the building and into the bar I met Marcel in.

I have a choice to make.

He's waiting for me. A drink in his hand, another parked on the table next to him—wine for me I assume. He's reserved seats in the pub's corner next to the fire. Its logs are burnt low. The odd ember gleams and floats up the chimney. There's nobody other than the barman left in here.

"Good evening, Marcel," I say.

"Bella," he says and slides the drink across the table towards me. He reclines in his armchair sipping what I guess is whiskey. "Did you secure what he requested of you?"

I nod. My fingers hesitate. I'm not ready to hand them off yet.

"Tell me about you and Roman. How did you end up hating each other?"

Marcel stiffens in his chair. He rubs his throat. "Ancient history."

"Humour me," I say and take a sip of wine.

He chortles, leans forward and says, "Okay, I'll bite and tell you how it started. I was the best translator of the old runic language when I was an apprentice. There was no one else who could come close to the accuracy I could reach."

I press my lips together, listening to every word he says.

He takes a deep breath and continues. "Roman, being the legacy he was, and with the eye for detail he has, was the second best in our cohort. Especially because he had a penchant for the old language, too."

"He really did," I say, remembering the lessons he forced me to take in addition to RARM classes.

He takes another sip of whiskey.

"Unfortunately for me, I am not a legacy magician. We were at the intercity security competition. Three days in, I was leading the competition. I was using the Runeastic Minor string code to make a grid system that was impenetrable to other forms of magic. There were fae there and people from a handful of other cities. Anyway, Roman decided to take it upon himself to steal my project. When I discovered what he'd done and tried to go to the Games Makers, who do you think they believed? A fellow legacy or me—some wannabe magician from the burbs of the city?"

Funny thing is, Roman tells this story in *exactly* the same way. Word for word.

"So all this was over one poxy competition? You both trained Remy and I to loathe each other," I ask.

That makes Marcel laugh so hard he throws his head back and clutches his stomach.

"Gods no. I said that was how it started. I worked hard for the position I'd reached and I wasn't about to let some privileged legacy brat steal my work."

"And there I was, thinking you were an upstanding magician."

He smiles, and it lights up his entire face, the dapple of grey around the side of his head offsetting the darkness of his eyes. He's quite handsome, objectively speaking. Not that cock has ever done it for me. Chests just aren't the same without a set of breasts.

"I never said that, Bella. I'm a scrapper. I never go down without a fight, and Roman unleashed the pettiest, nastiest side of me. I'm not proud, but it is what it is. So I lashed back at him. He punched harder. My old mentor used to say we fought like jealous brothers."

He laughs to himself. A soft chuckle of a thing, his eyes distant as he stares into the fire.

Marcel steeples his hands, turns back to me. "Resentments built, the punches got more brutal, the consequences more severe. It became a game between us. Hate... jealousy, whatever you want to call it, has a way of tracking scars through a person. It's why it's always better to let it go."

"But you didn't?"

"Neither of us did. Even into adulthood."

"What would you say if I told you Roman used to use your birthday as the security code for his safes?"

Marcel's eyes flicker wide. A strange warmth settles over his features, but as he shrugs and the expression sloughs off his face. But it was there. I saw it even if it was brief.

"I suppose I held little totems, old stone runes, silly things really. Items Roman had taken to competitions when we were apprentices. I'd steal them to spite him. Keep them to remind me of what I was trying to do. Who I was trying to beat." He looks up at me, holds my gaze. "Perhaps it was the same for him. A reminder of the one he hated more than anything else."

I chew over his words. I used to keep Remy's scores at competitions to compare her performance to mine. I liked to see how much she'd improved compared to me. I remembered every little detail about her scores, her performance, and her weaknesses. The more I reconcile what Marcel is telling me with my past, the more it makes sense. But I didn't keep those memories because I hated her, but because I was fascinated by her. Maybe if I admit it to myself... because a part of me always l... No, I'm not ready to admit that. And with that thought, I'm done with this conversation.

"So, I secured the tunnel blueprints. I'm sorry I had to change the rendezvous time. But we got here in the end."

"Don't worry, I'm just glad we could meet. That man cannot be allowed to escape," he says.

"I knew I was in trouble the second I got into the vault and all the blueprints were for modern castles and mansions. I had to track back through the guild to get into the older vault in order to find the old one. Did you know the tunnels predate most of our architecture?"

He smiles, "I did, as it happens. Apparently, there are skeletons down there from magicians who got lost."

"And those that got dragged down there during the vampire wars," I add.

He winces, and I cringe at the image too. That was a story I'd rather Red hadn't filled me in on, especially because her version was spectacularly gory. Her life is blood, she doesn't get queasy like the rest of us mere magicians.

"So the blueprints...?" Marcel says his eyes glint against the flickering flames.

"Right," I say, remembering why I'm actually here. "What exactly is it you're going to do with them?"

He leans back. "My thoughts were to use the fact princess Morrigan is here. Given her and Remy were the ones to capture and then jail him, if he truly is trying to break from prison, it is they who will need to know."

Here we go... come on Bella, lure the bastard in... "I want assurances you will keep my name out of this. I don't want Remy knowing."

He nods solemnly. "You have my word."

I slide my hand inside my coat. "Here," I say and hand over the packet.

"Thank you," he says, his shoulders sagging. "You can trust me. I will help you keep that bastard away. You have nothing to worry about."

He slides the envelope inside his jacket. I track every millimetre of the movement. The envelope vanishes and I swallow hard, hoping and praying to the High Magician that I made the right choice.

He shakes my hand goodbye. Our grip is tacky, but when he releases me, I realise it's not him that's clammy, it's me.

Fuck.

Deep in my mind, all I can do is scream: *what have I done?*

CHAPTER 26

REMY

Tonight, we party. Not only are we now top of the competition, but it's fun fair night. I used to adore the fun fair as a youth. My parents would save up all year and give us a bag of small coin to spend. There's even a firework display marking the start of the fun fair party at seven this evening. Stirling mentioned music and all sorts. To my delight, the rides and food stalls open at four, so we're heading down now.

There's a parade of magicians walking out of Lantis palace across the main bridge back to New Imperium. Above the beach, the Games Makers bought in architects to erect an enormous pier that stretches a couple of hundred meters into the ocean. Rollercoasters, fun houses and helter-skelters fill the pier, along with candy floss that turns your tongue rainbow colours, and other sweet treats.

I meet Bella and Red outside the palace in the courtyard at five to four.

"Ready?" I ask.

Bella is practically vibrating with excitement. She bounces on her tiptoes, her curls bobbing up and down with the movement.

Red, I note, is already holding a bottle of beer. She pulls two more from her back pockets. "I investigated early." She grins at me.

"Thanks."

We clink glasses and head down the bridge, following the procession of people. I spot Morrigan welcoming the magicians into the fair. She's surrounded by a crowd of adoring magicians, Scarlett and Stirling at her sides ensuring order. I leave them to it. Though Morrigan catches my eye, her expression narrowing as Bella walks into view.

I wish I could find a way to make her believe me when I tell her Bella is innocent.

"Where do you want to go first?" Red asks.

"Candy floss, we can't do anything without that. I want the magic stuff that crackles and makes you see everything in fifty colours," Bella says.

"Over here." I lead them towards a stand that sells candy floss and ice cream of all different flavours and a thousand variations of sweets, including my favourite rune stoppers.

"Ooh, chocolate rune shapes," Bella says, picking up three different flavours.

"Oh my gods, have you tried the salted caramel of this brand? It's amazing," Bella says and pays the seller. She swipes the chocolate and takes a giant bite out of the salted caramel rune. "Ohmmyygodths."

Red and I give each other the side eye as Bella practically comes over the chocolate rune.

"Don't look at me like that." She breaks what's left in

half and shoves one half in my mouth and the other into Red's mouth.

I don't have much of a sweet tooth, but holy shit, is this delicious. Sweet and salty right at the end. The chocolate melts on your tongue, the caramel bursts from the inside. I have to suppress the urge to moan in delight. Red isn't so successful. Her eyes roll shut and she groans.

"Told you," Bella says, her mouth curling into a smug pout.

I return to the seller and buy three more, one for each of us.

Once we've eaten enough chocolate we're all nauseated, we walk around the fair. Bella spots the Merricks. A roll of ride tickets trail out of Alba's back pocket. Bella's expression darkens.

"Back in a second." She strides up to Alba, knocks into her. If I hadn't noticed the ride tickets in the first place, I wouldn't have seen Bella's deft finger work. After a few cross words, Bella strides back to us, brandishing the roll.

"Bella," I warn.

"What?" she shrugs. "She deserved it."

Bella hands Red and I a third of the tickets each and keeps the remaining ones for herself. Bella has never denied her light-fingered touch. She's never hidden it, and never really used it to hurt anyone.

Why would Roman use Marcel's birthday as his safe code?

It's not just that though, it's the ghost avatar's code. The more layers of code I get through, the more the shape and flow of the runes feel familiar. Too familiar. Uncomfortably so. I only know one person who can create runes that delicate, that perfect and poetic. But there's no way it could be him. It doesn't make sense.

Red chooses the Ferris wheel. We share a car and as we climb to the highest point of the ride, all three of us fall silent. The sun is setting. An orb of fire liquifying and warping as it plunges into the ocean. The surface glistens like a blanket of sparkling gems and, in the centre of the bay, Lantis palace stands like a giant palatial glacier. The sun sends wings of orange and burnt claret to bleed over the palace windows, making the structure appear to melt. Enormous blue turrets lance the sky with Runic Games flags. Last, the six bridges to the six realms stretch further than the eye can see into far-off lands with magic that addles my mind trying to comprehend.

"Wow," Bella says.

"Really wow," Red replies.

"It's stunning," I say.

When the Ferris wheel docks back at the bottom and we're let out, it's my turn to choose. They glance at me, expectant.

"House of Mirrors," I say, determined.

Bella groans. "But they make me look weird."

"That's the best part. Let's go pretend we're twelve again and pull stupid faces in ridiculous mirrors," Red says.

Bella huffs, but she can't mind too much because she leads the way, winding us through the fair. The smell of cooking chestnuts and the sweet stench of popcorn and hot dogs wafts around us.

"Madame," Bella says and gestures for me to enter the house of mirrors first.

I take over leading and give the ride operator three coins. He holds open the door and all three of us step inside.

Red buckles over instantly. "Oh, oh, my word." She's wheezing, tears falling down her face.

I glance at the mirror she's pointed at. I expected them

to warp and bend our bodies, but these mirrors are enchanted.

Standing before us are three pixies with the most enormous nostrils I've ever seen. Red is tall, taller than me and stick thin with a nose that covers three quarters of her face. Bella is even shorter than normal, a nose that sticks up vertically with gigantic nostrils and I... Oh my gods. I look bizarre. I'm far shorter than Bella—my normal tall stature shrunk to a foot high. My face is all nose. Like, literally, I don't even have eyes or a mouth. Bella is bent double, gasping and laughing at my pixie figure, and I can't help but join her for the ridiculousness of it.

Red wipes tears from her eyes and says, "Come on, I want to see what else there is."

She grabs my hand and I take Bella's and we trail through the house of mirrors, room after room showing us with bulbous bellies or enormous feet or only an inch wide. Some of the mirrors transform us into krakens and fairies, but the fun ground to a halt when we walked into a room and the mirrors made us appear like vampires.

Red stops dead, her face turning ashen like the projection in the mirror.

Bella stiffens. "Forget it, Red. Let's go. I didn't know they had stupid mirrors like this."

The air chills. Red is frozen on the spot. She raises her fingers, brushes her skin and lips. A hardness that reminds me of the steely desire for vengeance crosses her expression.

"Red," Bella whispers. She reaches out to touch Red's arm. Red flinches as their fingers meet.

"Come on, let's get out of here," Bella says and tugs her away.

Red leads the way, her expression distant and vacant.

We wind through a maze of mirrored rooms, but Red is no longer paying attention. She's just blindly walking. I try to search for the way out, but every direction I turn are dozens of repeating reflections. It's disorienting. My heart palpates in my chest, my fingers and toes numbing as waves of hot, then cold wash over me. I want to get out.

Bella pulls me aside. "Are you okay?"

"It's a lot in here."

She nods. "It was fun for a bit, but I want to get out now, too."

Having her near me, her hand sliding into mine calms my heart rate enough the tingling abates.

Red turns the corner and vanishes.

"What happened to her? I knew she hated them, but... what was that?" I say.

Bella glances in the direction Red vanished. She chews the corner of her bottom lip. "That's not my story to tell. You'll have to ask her."

We catch up to Red as she shoves open a door and we walk into a circular room made entirely of mirrors.

"Woah," I breathe.

The door closes behind us and my gut lurches. It's impossible to see where it is. Every wall, the floor and the ceiling are made of mirrors. We're trapped in an infinite box, endless repeating images of ourselves stretching far into the glassy void.

"Anyone else as uncomfortable as I am right now?" Bella says.

Red raises her hand.

"This is crazy," I say, staring each and every way in the room. "It's like we're a kaleidoscope."

Every inch of mirror swirls and twists, pieces of our bodies, a head here, an arm, a torso. All reflected and refracted off each other until we're a myriad of moving pieces spinning and turning.

It's beautiful and horrifying and my chest is so tight I can't breathe. How will we get out? It's a mirrored prison designed to confuse.

I stop dead.

An idea forming.

My eyes track the mirror in front of me, above me, below, and to the side. In each one, I'm reflected back, an identical mirrored copy.

"This is how we win," I breathe.

CHAPTER 27

BELLA

"What do you mean, this is how we win?" I say, staring at the kaleidoscope of mirrors around us.

Remy spins around, facing us both. "I'll need Red for this too. What's the biggest thing you've ever forged?" she asks.

"Er..." Red looks from Remy to me. I nod at her to continue.

"Well, I once forged the image of a pet dog, which was threaded into mirage magic."

Remy shakes her head. "Way too small. Do you think you could apply your skills to forging objects?"

Red scratches her temple, her face scrunching. "I don't see why not. I can apply the same methods to different materials."

Remy paces up and down the mirrored room. "Okay,

okay, and what if it wasn't an object at all? What if it was a simulated room?"

Red's eyes narrow. "Theoretically, that would be easier. I could mimic the physical properties without using half my blood to create something tangible."

I realise where Remy is going. "You genius," I say.

Red glances between Bella and me, her face a crumple of confusion. "What's going on?"

Remy puffs her chest out. "What's going on is that I am, as Bella has informed you, a genius. We don't need to create an impenetrable security system if we can create a system that traps imposters."

I smile or try to. But Remy's eyes glint at me, hungry for more, for winning and victory. How am I going to get around this? I'm so close to securing the evidence. But I still need the culprit to make a wrong move in order to trap them.

Remy stands prouder. "The system needs to be impenetrable long enough to stop the Games Makers hacking in, right? We'll trap them in a mirror hack thinking they're in ours. Meanwhile, our prison is safe, and we wait for the timer to drain."

"Okay, let me get this straight, we're creating a mirror prison and seamlessly overlay it on the real one?" Red's forehead is lined in concentration.

"Yes, once we know what prison we're assigned, that's exactly what we'll do. But more broadly, if you can teach us the forging magic, we could recreate Roman's prison and trap whoever is trying to break him out inside a mirror prison security grid. They'd think they were hacking the real thing, when really they're giving us all the evidence we need to convict them," Remy says and she's bouncing as she paces up and down.

"I'm happy to help," Red says.

"Then we have a plan," Remy says and holds out her hand. Red takes it and shakes, and I roll up next.

I hesitate before sliding my hand in. Trying, pleading with my mind to find a justification that would work, a logical argument that I could give right now to make her believe me. But I come up with nothing. No, the only thing I can do now is dig deeper, stick with the plan, and wait for the culprit to make their next move. Then I'll have the evidence I need to prove I have nothing to do with this bloody breakout. My plan will work. It has to.

My hand slips into hers. "I guess we do make a great team after all."

Red spends all night training us to use basic blood magic in the apartment. We have less than a week to learn to forge, build a simulation and get the transitions seamless enough it's indistinguishable to reality.

A tall order if we had a month, let alone less than a week.

"So we're agreed. We use Remy's idea of a secondary mirror prison for the challenge. And then my suggestion of setting up a trap in the tunnels to capture the culprit trying to break Roman out?" I say, holding my breath. It's taken me all night to coax Remy towards the idea, but finally we're here.

"Yes, I'm going to take this to Morrigan and the team. It makes total sense. The tunnels lead to all the major mansions and castles in the city and have connections to every city in the realm. There's no better escape. They could walk out of the city and no one would know, great idea guys," Remy says.

"Especially given none of the vampires use them anymore. Only the occasional hunter coming to visit a friend," Red grins.

"Exactly," Remy says.

"And we'll work together, use my lattice as the cage and your forging Red to make it appear like the tunnels and—"

"And my precision security grid to trap them inside," Remy finishes.

My shoulders sag in relief.

"Again," Red says handing me a needle.

"Ugh, my finger is sore," I protest.

"Didn't take you for a whiner," Red says, winking at me.

"How dare you—" I say and shove my rapidly bruising and swollen mess of an index finger in her face.

"Well, why don't you use a different finger to draw blood, dummy?"

"Because then she'd have a hand like this," Remy says and gestures at herself. Her fingers are decidedly less red than mine, but every single one of her pads looks sore.

"Honestly, what sort of magic needs blood to work?" I moan.

"The powerful kind. I'd like to see your runes do this."

I huff at her. "Is that a challenge?"

She raises an eyebrow at me. "Again."

I snatch the needle off her and jab it in my middle finger. I grit my teeth as a bead forms on the end.

"Infuse it with your runes and bind it to the lattice," Red says.

I shut my eyes, feel for my magic, letting it rise to the surface. Runes appear in the air, the beginnings of a lattice forming in front of me as I weave and thread symbols, stitching and sewing piece by piece. I bring a rune in front of me and allow the bead of blood to sink onto the surface of the rune. It hisses. A ribbon of steam peels off the symbol.

"I don't think I'm doing this right," I say.

"Oh trust me, this is much better than you were doing at three o'clock this morning when nothing was happening," Red says.

"I *did it*!" Remy shouts as the rune hovering in front of her glows bright and then washes red instead of its usual coppery colour.

"Yes, Remy!" Red shrieks, jumping up and giving her a high five. "Now weave that into your RuneNet server code and we should be able to start building."

I slump down on the sofa, frustrated.

"You going to quit?" Remy says.

"Go fuck yourself Reid."

Remy laughs, "Now that's the Bella I recognise. I mean, if you're not capable of doing it..." She shrugs at me.

My blood boils. How dare she doubt my ability. I get that I didn't score like her when we were kids and my parents bought my way into RARM but that doesn't mean I'm not as good as her now.

I jab the needle into my middle finger again, harder this time. It hurts like a bitch and makes me bite down suddenly from the pain; I catch the inside of my cheek and draw more blood. Which, in turn, makes me even angrier.

Fucking Remy. I'll fucking show her who's the best at Runic magic. Me. That's fucking who.

I draw my magic up, fire runes out faster than before, weave a micro lattice in front of me, and then instead of bringing the central rune out to meet me, I walk up to it.

Smear the blood running down my finger over the central three runes.

And would you look at that?

They tremble and change, the coppery bronze shivering into a deep rouge. My lips pull into a smug smile.

Remy smiles, "Bravo Bella, I knew you couldn't resist the bait."

"Oh fuck off," I snap, but Remy comes over and pulls me into a hug. "Proud of you." She leans down and kisses the top of my head.

Red coughs. "I am here."

"Yes, oh holy blood mother and wise one. And we're very grateful too," I mumble over Remy's shoulder.

"Shall we regroup this afternoon? I'm exhausted and could do with catching some sleep," Remy says.

Red waves goodbye and lets herself out of the apartment.

I glance over at the balcony, the ocean view, the first hints of sunrise on the horizon. I open the doors and lead Remy out onto it. There's a sofa in the corner, and a set of table and chairs, but otherwise the space is clear.

The air is cool, though warmer than I expected at this time of night. There's no bite. Almost like a storm is brewing, and the atmosphere is swollen, warm, and sticky with it.

"Watch the sunrise with me," I say.

She takes a seat on one of the table's accompanying chairs and pulls me down into it to sit on her lap.

I curl into her, and for a while we sit there, watching stars wink out and the black turn to grey. Eventually, the grey turns to a watery yellow. As the sun rises, a blaze of oranges and reds adorn the sky in swathes of liquid cloud streaking the morning across the horizon.

"It's beautiful," Remy breathes in my ear.

"Isn't it?" The ocean's surface glistens like rubies and diamonds and all the treasures you wanted as a kid.

"I never thought I'd end up here," I say.

"At the runic games?" Remy adjusts our position, and I hook my legs over her crossed ones.

"No. Here... with you." I point at her chest.

She smiles, slides her hand around my neck, and pulls me in for a kiss.

"Makes two of us."

"I still think about that night," I say and run my fingers over the sides of Remy's shaved hair. It bristles like a brush under my touch. I have the urge to rub my hand back and forth, but I hold it in.

"The night on the rooftop when you stole a kiss from me?" she smirks.

I huff at her. "Does it please you to think that?"

"What if it does?" she pouts her lips at me.

"Do you remember the other kiss? The one by the lake?" I ask.

"How could I forget?" she says and bends my palm up to kiss my hand. "Did I ever tell you the Merricks tried to sabotage my project at that competition?"

I gasp. "Those bastards."

She presses her lips together and nods. "Planted an inverted rune into my network."

"Ugh, those viruses are a bitch to fix."

"Neither of us did well at that competition, I seem to remember," she says.

"Yes, well, you stole a kiss from me that night, and I had to masturbate so hard my hand nearly fell off. Gods, I hated you for that."

Remy's face crumples at my confession. She laughs so

hard her head rocks back and I jiggle up and down on her lap.

"Oh, fuck off," I mumble, but I'm smiling too. And then I'm laughing at the memory of a sexually frustrated nine-teen-year-old me whacking one out at the handsome and most hateful version of Remy.

"I hated you because I wanted to fuck you. Because you kept me on my toes at every competition. Because you were better than me, then, and I knew it, even if my pride wouldn't let me admit it," I say.

She stops laughing suddenly. "Bella, there is no better here. We're a team and I think you're incredible. You weave runes in indestructible security meshes that I only dream of doing. Don't underestimate yourself."

She pauses, lifts my hand between us. "However, I'm afraid I am deeply disappointed about one thing in particular..."

"Oh?"

She nods at me, sullen and forlorn. "I'm devastated I didn't get to see you masturbate over me."

"I see." A bolt of excitement pulses through my clit. Her eyes darken, her lips part, her expression fills with lust as if she can sense the pleasure in me.

Oh gods. Is she really going to make me do this? Even the image makes my knickers wet and stick to me.

"Get on the sofa," the words are so hungry they're growled.

She pushes me off her lap, and I walk over to the sofa, sitting on the edge. Remy turns her chair to face me and sits down, reclining in it. She crosses her foot to her knee and leans her elbow on the arm of the chair, resting her chin on her fingers.

I glance up at the balcony above.

"What if they look down?" I say.

"It's too early. And if they do?" she shrugs. "They'll enjoy the same view I'm about to."

"Remy," I squeak.

"Take your knickers off, Bella."

"Remy," I whine, but I don't really mean it. I want to protest just to be a brat. Not because I want this to stop. A part of me wants to get caught, or wants the threat of it, at least.

"Bella. Take. Your. Knickers. Off." Her words are slow and controlled and each one winds me tighter. Soaks my knickers further. Fuck, I want this. I don't care if anyone sees. It's not only the balcony above us. I look behind me, glance over Remy's shoulder. There are balconies all the way around this side of the palace. Anyone could come out this morning and watch. And that idea winds me tighter.

I slide my hand up the skirt of my dress and shift until I slip my knickers under my bum and down my thighs.

I hook them over my ankles and tug them off. Balled in my fist, I fling them. They land on her face. When she pulls them down, she's grinning.

"I'm keeping these. Now, hoist up your dress. Show me that pretty pussy of yours."

I do as she says, drawing my dress over my knees and pushing it under my belly, holding it in place. But I keep my legs firmly shut, knees pressed tight together.

"Bella," Remy says, a warning in her tone.

Fuck, I love it when she gets all bossy and demanding. I suppress a squeal and instead embody my inner brat.

"Mmm?" I purr.

"Only good girls get orgasms. If you don't show me that pretty little cunt right now, I will edge you into oblivion until you're begging and pleading with me to let you come. Do you understand?"

Fuck, fuck. I wonder if she could talk me into an orgasm without even touching me? If I open my legs, she's going to see the excitement glistening over my pussy.

I inch my knees open. But slowly. On my terms. I can play as hard as she can. When my thighs part and she can see how soaking I am, she sits up and rests against the back of the chair.

"Touch yourself," she demands.

Two little words that make my body melt. I bite my lip, slide two fingers into my mouth, and coat them with saliva. Then I lower my hand between my thighs and down to my clit.

"Keep going. I'll be back. I want to hear your moans from the kitchen. Oh, and you're not allowed to come," she says.

She slips back inside the house as I run my fingers between my folds, drawing them through the slickness. I find my clit rubbing and circling until it swells beneath my touch.

"Are you imagining me between your thighs, Bella?" Remy calls from the kitchen.

I wasn't, but I am now.

I lean back on the sofa, stretching my legs wider apart so I can access all of me. I imagine her head pushing my thighs apart, her tongue in place of my fingers.

She returns with a tumbler of what I assume is alcohol and sits down facing me, swilling the glass.

"I didn't say stop."

I hadn't realised I had. My fingers move again. But Remy frowns.

"Stop. Come here."

I pout but do as she says.

"Get on your knees," she demands. "Turn around."

When I'm facing the sofa, she leans into my ear. "This won't do. I want to watch you touch yourself naked." Her fingers find my spine and undo my zip. Then she brushes the straps off my shoulder and the dress falls to the floor.

"Back to the sofa," she says, but holds out a hand so I can get up. The only thing I'm wearing are my heels. The warmth from the stormy morning air caresses my skin. I kick my hips out just enough I hear the inhale of Remy's breath as she watches me walk to the sofa.

I sit back down and return to the position I was in. My fingers rubbing at my clit. All the while, Remy sits back in her chair watching, drinking and saying nothing.

Her calm demeanour is enough to drive me wild. I want a rise. Need her as affected as I am. I slide my other hand between my legs and find my hole, slipping a finger inside.

That, at least, gets a rise out of her. Her nostrils flare as she leans forward. I push my finger in and out until I feel my walls tighten and the shimmering edge of pleasure building inside me.

"What are you imagining I'm doing to you?" she says.

"I'm imagining you naked, licking my cunt while I'm fucking yours." I close my eyes, let my words do their work.

As my first throaty moan escapes, she can't take it anymore.

"Enough," she says.

And when I open my eyes and see her standing over me, she's naked. Winner.

"Get up," she says, and slides on to the sofa. When she's laid down, she looks up at me. "Sit. Here." She points at her mouth.

I grin but climb on top of her, placing my thighs on either side of her cheeks. She grabs my arse and lifts me into the position she wants. Our eyes meet, and the sight of her beneath me between my thighs makes my insides combust. She lunges for my pussy, swiping a wet swipe down my middle.

"Fuck," I moan.

She strokes again and again. Sucks my clit into her mouth and holds it there and I swear I almost die as pleasure blooms as my clit swells under the pressure. She releases me and draws heavenly laps over my pussy.

She nudges my arse, encouraging me to rock back and forth to allow her tongue to reach all of me. I ride her face until my thighs are burning and I'm shaking from the effort of staying upright. She lifts me off her head and helps me rotate onto my front. I lay flat on her stomach. I shift my arse back and spread my legs to let her access my clit. She doesn't waste a second and latches onto my pussy immediately.

I drop my head between her thighs and sweep a lick between her folds. Her tongue stops resting on my clit.

"More," she says. And so I give her exactly what she wants. Lapping and ravishing her pussy until she soaks my mouth and chin. I shift my body weight and hook my arm between her legs. It's awkward, but this way I can make her pussy mine.

I push a finger inside her and she arches under my weight. "Fuck, Bella," she says as I continue to slide my finger inside her.

She continues to lick my clit, but the movements are more jerky now and the harder I thrust my finger inside her, the more sporadic her mouth becomes. She wraps her arms around my thighs as if holding on to me will help her hold on to the orgasm. But I have other plans. Her tongue is hard and fast, then soft and slow.

Her pussy tightens around my finger. Her walls grip me so hard I have to angle my body again to keep pumping.

The erratic rhythm on my clit shouldn't make the pleasure build, but it does. I can scarcely concentrate as my clit throbs under the constant worshipping of her tongue. Her pleasure builds with mine. She moans between every swipe of her tongue on my pussy and I do the same.

My mind fractures. The delicious taste of her. Every thrust of my finger. Her hips tilting as she grinds into me. Waves of tingles radiate out and rush around my body as she runs delicate fingertips down my back. Her pussy clenches against my finger. My clit pulses deeper, harder as the pleasure winds me tighter—winds both of us tighter. Together we pant, gasps and soft moans and whispered names drifting off into the morning air.

"I'm so close," I moan into her thighs.

"Me too," she says.

And so together, as the sun climbs above the horizon, our mouths ravishing one another, we tip over into the ecstasy of pleasure, moaning each other's names. I swear as I fall into the orgasm, I lose my sight, the release so high and blinding I gasp as she swipes one more lick over my tingling pussy.

When it's over, I rearrange our bodies until I'm cozied into her side. She wraps her arm around me and pulls me up so I can reach her mouth.

She kisses me, slow and lazy, her lips soft and swollen from sex. She tastes of me, as much as I taste of her.

She pulls back, and I run my fingers through her hair, staring up into her eyes. Words bubble up, forming on my tongue, pressing and shoving their way out.

My heart hammers in my chest as I realise I don't want to fuck this up. I don't want to lose her, to lose the way we are with each other.

I don't care what my mother says, I'm not marrying anyone. I want Remy. I want her more than I want anything else. Maybe even more than I want to win this competition. And that is terrifying.

"What's wrong?" Remy says, a line forming between her eyebrows.

"I—nothing." I close my mouth, trapping those three little words that mean too much, that change everything.

"Don't hide from me. Tell me what's in there." She places a kiss in the middle of my forehead.

But I can't.

I might be falling for her, but I can't tell her until I know I'm safe.

"I'm just tired," I say, the lie tasting bitter where those three little words were sweet.

I will tell her.

I will.

Just not this morning. I kiss her and get up off the sofa, picking my dress up and disappearing inside. All the while my heart hammering inside my chest.

How the hell did I fall for Remy Reid?

CHAPTER 28

REMY

Exhausted, I force myself to stay awake until Bella is snoring softly in the bedroom. I need to find the team and tell them the good news. I slip out from Bella's grasp and tuck the duvet over her. It's mid afternoon so the team are bound to be somewhere in the palace.

I find Morrigan in the royal quarters. They're in the penthouse of the palace—an apartment shared by all the royals from the six cities. Thankfully, there's a lift at the entrance. No royal worth their crown is going to climb the hundred floors to get there, no matter which city they're from.

The lift doors open to a lavish open plan suite with a jaw dropping view of Lantis ocean bay. Walls and corridors behind me lead to bedrooms. The white tunnels covered in six pieces of stunning art, one from each of the cities. The penthouse is a palatial suite dripping in opulence.

In front of me, the walls are all glass with a one-hundred-and-eighty-degree view of the ocean. We're high enough I can see the shadow of other lands in the distance. The bridges stretch like ladders to the horizon.

I step down into the living room, which comprises enormous plush sofas, statues and more artwork, tables and sculptures dripping in gems. In the middle of the room, Morrigan sits nestled into Stirling's arms. She spots me as soon as the lift doors ping shut. Her face is so grave it sends a shiver down my back.

Opposite them, Scarlett and Quinn sit, their heads bent together, whispering.

"Hey guys," I say, my voice as chipper as I feel. It jars against the expression Morrigan is wearing.

Scarlett and Quinn snap to attention. Morrigan sits up, her face turning stone cold.

"Remy," she says and somewhere beneath the stiffness is the warmth I recognise. But it's buried deep and my stomach turns like I'm going to be sick. Something is wrong.

Very, very wrong.

"What's happened?" I ask.

Morrigan rubs her face, gestures to the armchair between the two sofas. I sink into it, my chest tightening with every second she continues to stare at me like I murdered someone.

"You first," Morrigan says. "What have you found?" Only she says it like she already knows.

"Well, I... It's less what I've found and more that I worked how to stop the breakout," I say. But the giddy excitement I had on the way up ebbs away as Marcel steps into the room.

Stirling stands and indicates he can take her seat. "Let's give them a minute, shall we?" she says.

Scarlett and Quinn follow her out. Quinn gives me a look of pity and I wonder what the hell is going on.

"There's something you need to know," Marcel says.

Morrigan's lips are paper thin. She can't bring herself to look at me, and I realise that whatever Marcel is about to say is going to break a piece of me.

He pulls out an envelope and slides it across the coffee table towards me.

"What is it?" I ask.

"Open it," he says.

I slide the papers out, scan the page, and my world bottoms out. I know before he starts speaking what they are and who they came from. But I have to ask. I have to follow through and hear the words or I won't believe it.

"Where did you get them?" I ask, my voice a whisper.

"Where do you think?" he says.

I turn away, my eyes sting but I don't want to let the tears fall in front of him. I stare at a seagull perched on the edge of the balcony outside the windows until I can get my heart rate under control.

"Bella?" I breathe.

"I'm sorry, Remy," Morrigan says, and she moves to a seat nearer me so she can place her hand on mine. But I pull away. I don't want to be touched right now. I can't handle the tenderness.

I didn't want to believe it was true. Yes, she's a thief. Yes, I knew what she'd done with Roman's imported magic. But her heart was in a good place, or at least I assumed it was. To being the best. To earning the reputation she desperately craves.

Why? Why would she break him out? She told me she was done with him. And when she did, she was adamant, like I've never seen her before. Why would she lie about that then, to help him again now? Why would she tell me we could use the tunnels to trap him? It doesn't make sense.

"She stole the blueprints to the tunnels for him," Marcel says.

"How did you get them?" I ask.

"I overheard her talking to a man. I saw the exchange of envelopes for coin."

No. My stomach lurches. I'm such an idiot. Of course, she was telling me to create a mirror of the tunnels. A fucking mirror she could steal, send the palace team into while she got Roman out using the real tunnels.

I want to laugh; sheer hysteria. She well and truly played me. She was always working for him. I can't believe I was letting myself fall for her. My chest spasms, bile claws at my throat.

"If you saw the prints given to that man, how have they come to be in your possession?" I ask when my voice is calm enough to be steady.

His face turns grave. "I paid twice what Roman was paying him in order to secure the prints."

"The crown will reimburse you, of course," Morrigan says.

"If we have the prints in our possession, then this is all hearsay. How are you going to gather evidence that she's working for him?" I ask.

"We need your help," Morrigan says. "We're organising a raid right now. But we need you to go back to the apartment and keep her in there until we can formally arrest her. You did your job, Remy. This is a good thing. We suspected it was her. It was just a matter of securing the final piece evidence to slot into place."

"If she's working with him, then she has to have had

communication with him, right?" Marcel says, his face bunching with concern.

"We're going to raid the apartment and hope that we can find whatever or however she's communicating with him as evidence," Morrigan replies.

"And if you do?" I say.

"Then she'll be arrested, jailed, and tried for treason."

My throat is so thick I can't speak. I was a fool. What a clever web of deception.

Marcel's face droops, his eyes soft. "I'm sorry, Remy. But given this overwhelming evidence, I felt it was only right I told you myself. I wouldn't have forgiven myself if you'd been embroiled and she made you the scapegoat."

I frown. "You suspect she was going to make me the scapegoat?"

He shrugs. "I can't be sure of anything. You might not be my apprentice anymore, but I will always be your mentor. It's my duty to care for you, even now."

I hang my head, willing the sting to vanish. The ache settles in my heart and shatters it like glass. A thousand pieces of a future I'll never have evaporate inside me. Hope and dreams unspool, a hardness like granite replacing them. I'll never trust her again. She needs to pay. When my features are neutral, I glance up.

"What do you need me to do?"

CHAPTER 29

BELLA

I regret staying up all night the minute I roll over. The sun leaking in through the window no longer has the yellow tinge of dawn, but the thick warmth of sunset. I've woken up on edge. I pull up my RuneNet, check my evidence files. Even looking at it winds every muscle of my body tight.

"Hnnmghh," I groan as I roll over and smash my face into the pillow, the RuneNet screen bouncing to the other side of the room before evaporating. I am going to end up awake all night at this rate. I suppose at least Red can train us and then let us loose on practicing for as long as we stay awake.

Remy's side of the bed is cold. I don't know when she left, but she's been gone a while given how cool the sheets are. I get up and rifle through my suitcase for some clean joggers and a hoody. Clean clothes options are running low, I'll have to do some washing. I find what I'm after, but something is out of place.

I pull on the clothes and head to the kitchen, but I freeze as I step out of the bedroom.

Remy is on the sofa in front of the coffee table, a number of folded notes laid out in a neat little row. The wax seals broken. I can tell, without turning to check, they're my notes. The ones that were tucked in my suitcase.

The ones Roman has been sending me.

No.

Fuck. I forgot to hide the fucking notes.

I shift to the open plan living room. Remy's face is hard, expressionless. So unlike the woman I know, the Remy I've fallen for. Her ice white hair seems harsh against the rigid lines of her jaw and the cold, lifeless eyes she's harbouring.

My chest cracks, a cavernous, gaping chasm of pain slides between my ribs and buries itself in my heart. Time slows, the world mutes, the ocean waves dull, my heart speeds up and slows down as if it's choking and racing all at once. And my vision tunnels on Remy and only her. The way she's staring at me, as if I'm nothing. As if I'm already dead to her. It makes my knees want to buckle and beg to explain.

I step forward, but she holds out her hand to me. "Don't."

One word, four letters and my world crumbles.

She tuts at me. As if I've already answered something for her. But I haven't. She only knows what she thinks is true and that so rarely is the real story.

"Let me ex—" I start.

"Stop," she says. Her commanding tone I've grown to love is frozen through. Hate fills every syllable and that breaks another piece of me.

"I don't want to hear anything other than the answer to my questions," she spits.

"Remy, please." This time, I fall to my knees.

But her expression remains stoic and empty of everything I love.

"Are these notes from Roman Oleg?" she says, picking each one up and putting them into a neat pile where all the edges line up.

My eyes close, I put my head in my hands. I don't want to answer because any answer I give won't be enough. I need her to let me explain. When I meet her gaze, my whole face is pleading with her.

"Rem—" I start.

"Answer the fucking question, Bella." She growls the words out.

There. She swore, and I know her well enough to recognise the crack in her stubbornly calm demeanour. Calm words covering the storm inside. She can't hide from me. This is hard for her. Which means there's hope, even if she's furious now.

"Yes," I whisper. The word is bitter on my tongue. It turns my insides liquid. A worm of cold loops around my spine, suffocating all my thoughts. What if the last three weeks don't matter and she won't listen to me? What if she never speaks to me again? What if my plan fails?

Remy glances at the floor as if I'm too disgusting to look at. She places her index finger in the middle of the pile of notes.

"Are you working with Roman?" she says, each word pronounced with icy precision.

"What? No. Of course not." I shuffle forward until I'm on my knees at her feet. "Remy, please listen to me, this isn't wh—"

She finally meets my eyes, and the chill that sweeps through me makes my entire body shiver. It doesn't matter what I say, she's already made her mind up. I reach up, place my hand on her knee. She smacks it away.

I cup my hand in my palm, not because it hurts, but because my heart does.

"So you didn't steal tunnel blueprints?" Remy says.

I close my eyes. I worried this would happen when I made the choice to do it. But I still have one card to play. I need her to listen.

I open my mouth and close it. This has to be done carefully. It's the only card I have left. "I need you to trust me. To listen to everything before you make a judgment." I replay the same words she said to me in the practice room, hoping it works.

She huffs at me, stands up from the sofa and walks towards the apartment door.

She rounds on me. "Marcel showed me, Bella." She's shouting now. "He showed me the fucking blueprints. So stop lying and tell me the damn truth."

I go death-still. I take three enormous breaths, trying to steady myself. "What did he say?" I ask.

"He overheard you talking to some guy. Saw the exchange of envelopes and coin. And as a loyal subject of the crown, he bought the blueprints to Morrigan."

"No," I breathe, my face crumpling in confusion. That's all a lie. That's not how it happened.

Remy sags. "Honestly, I'm exhausted. I've been awake for almost two days. I need to know. Did you steal the blueprints?"

"Yes. Bu—"

"It's over." She opens the door, and the world explodes in a flurry of bodies and sounds and confusion.

Assassins thunder into the room, metal grinding against metal as they draw swords. I'm thrown to the floor.

Two assassins pile on top of me, my body crushed under their weight as I'm flung onto my stomach, my arms wrenched behind my back and fastened into cuffs. Shouts fill the apartment. Instructions bellow out to guards. Chairs fly across the room, the fruit bowl spills, cupboards flung open. Guard after guard piles into the apartment, tearing through our belongings.

Hunting like bloodhounds. For what, I'm not sure. Evidence, I suppose. I might have fucked up leaving Roman's notes in my suitcase, but I wasn't dumb enough to leave my ace in here. I will not go down for this. No matter what, I can still play one last card.

Someone hauls me to my feet by my cuffed hands. Pain shoots through my shoulders as my body weight threatens to pop a joint out.

"Remy," I scream.

But it's too late. She's long gone from the room. A tall assassin enters the room. She looks like the woman Red knows. Stirling was it? It's not her, this woman's hair is longer, but the similarity is uncanny. They have to be twins.

"Bella Blythe, you're under arrest for treason for the crime of aiding and abetting of a known traitor to the crown."

"I didn't do it," I say. But this woman doesn't care.

"That's not for me to judge. You'll be brought before the crown and tried in due course," she says.

I need to do something, anything, to try to get her to listen before it's too late. Even if I go down for this like Roman no doubt planned. I need Remy to know it wasn't me.

"Are you the sister of that woman always with Morrigan?" I ask, desperate to try to find an in.

"Stirling is my twin, yes," she says.

"What's your name?"

She glares at me. "Not that it's relevant, but Scarlett."

"Listen, Scarlett, you know her, don't you?" I ask as a uniformed assassin shoves me forward and forces me to walk.

"Who Morrigan?"

"No, Remy."

She nods as I'm shoved harder towards the door.

"You have no reason to trust me, no reason to believe anything I'm saying. But I didn't do this. Please tell her. Tell her I get what this looks like, but it wasn't me."

Scarlett shakes her head, pity turning her eyes down. "The evidence is weighted against you, Bella."

"It is. But I know who is behind this, and I can prove it."

That makes Scarlett falter. "Wait," she says and grabs the biceps of the man shoving me through the door.

"Tell me what you know and we can arrange a plea deal."

I laugh. Like a plea will stop me from being sent to prison for the rest of my life. No matter what, I'm fucked now. So I might as well take Roman down with me. That bastard set me up after everything I've done for him. I'm not letting this go.

"Remy. I'll only talk to Remy."

Scarlett tilts her head to examine me. "If you're playing us, you'll only make it worse for yourself."

"I'm not."

She nods once. Curt, precise. "Okay. I'll see what I can do."

And then I'm shoved into the hallway, pushed and tugged with fingers that dig into my arms and bruise.

I'm cajoled and yanked and nudged until we reach the lift and descend into the darkened bowels of the palace.

Apparently, I'm not being taken to the city prison, or at least not yet. The lift opens into to the dank underbelly of the palace. My ears pop and we're deeper under the palace than I've been before. The stone steps are damp, the air is musty and stale like stagnant water. We walk along the dim corridor, a chill seeping further into my bones with every step I take.

Fire lanterns hang between barred cells. They're all empty. They can't have used the palace dungeon in years. There are no windows, no ways out. Only cell after cell after cell. Fear prickles up my neck, seeps into my bones.

The guard stops when we reach the end of the corridor and pulls out a set of iron keys. He unlocks the cell, the metal key clanking in the lock. The door screeches as he pulls it open. This is not a well-used prison.

The door clangs shut, sealing me inside the cell.

I turn around and grip the bars, my cuffs clattering metal against metal. "Please don't leave me here," I beg.

But the guards laughs in my face and then spits on the floor through the bars. "Traitor."

And just to taunt me, he hangs the cell door key on an iron hook opposite my cell so that I can see my escape and know I'll never be able to reach it.

His footsteps echo all the way up the corridor, his feet splashing through the shallow puddles, his heeled boots clacking against the stone slabs, the noise a rhythmic beat that sounds far too much like the sound of death and fate coming for me.

I step back from the cell bars and retreat into the corner of the cell. I curl up against the wall, damp and cold burrowing under my skin, the hope ebbing away one layer at a time.

CHAPTER 30

REMY

I drank myself to sleep. Slept all night and half the following day. I'm not proud of it, but it was a coping mechanism. Not wanting to process the lies, the betrayal or the way my heart keeps stuttering like it can't quite beat right anymore. Like I can't catch my breath when she's away.

But I can't love a traitor. I won't.

She always had a thin line between what she viewed as right or wrong, but I believed she kept that line intact.

I was wrong. So fucking wrong.

Now, the final challenge and therefore the breakout attempt is three days away. I need to take the paltry skills I amassed from Red's teachings and create fake versions of the tunnels and weave them into the RuneNet.

The next thing I need to do is to create a mirror prison security grid. I can't have whoever Bella's working with hack Roman's actual prison. I won't take the risk. Therefore, I'll recreate a mirror version. That just means I need a simulation program to allow a seamless switch between the challenge prison system and the mirror one. The same simulation program can overlay on the tunnel forgery, too. I sag, a little relieved I have a plan: forge a digital version of the tunnels, create a mirror version of Roman's security grid, create a simulation for a seamless transition between reality and the RuneNet simulations.

I knead my temples, runes and code strings running through my head. If I can't make the transition between Roman's actual RuneNet security grid and the mirror one seamless, none of this works. I need to get the magic fuelling the simulation overlay right or they'll break Roman out and walk away instead of walking into my trap.

But with only three days, a glorious hangover smashing my brain and no one to help me create. What if I can't do it? This seems like one challenge that is insurmountable.

But I don't want to give Bella the satisfaction of beating me, not this time. Not when my reputation is at stake. She could have crippled everything I hold dear. If Roman gets out, my security fails and my business goes bust. I'll lose everything.

No. I need to win this fucking competition and capture Roman in the process.

I climb out of bed. It's lunchtime, but I'm too queasy to eat. Instead, I make coffee and head to the living room. I nearly jump out of my skin when I see Quinn curled up on the sofa.

She unfurls herself like a cat.

"Hey," she says.

"Hey yourself."

"Do you remember me bringing you home last night? It was super late. I crashed on the sofa, hope that's okay?"

I scratch my head, trying to remember, but last night is a haze and then black.

"Did Scarlett send you?"

Quinn shrugs. "She said that you were remaining very calm about the whole thing, but she doubted very much that you were. So I figured I'd find you."

"She asked me if I'd consider talking to Bella and I calmly lost my shit."

Quinn's lips twitch.

"That was when I went to the bar. Is that where you found me half cut?" I ask.

She nods and rubs the sleep out of her eyes, gets off the sofa, takes the mug of coffee out of my hand, and slurps.

"Ugh. I hate coffee. But thanks," she grumbles and sits back down taking another sip.

I return to the kitchen and make a new one and when I get back, she's sat cross-legged on the sofa and I slot in next to her.

"They made a right mess in here," she says, glancing around the apartment.

"Horrendous, I don't even have time to clean it up. Not if I'm still going to stop Roman."

"You have to."

"Don't you think I'm aware of that?" I snap a little too sharply.

Quinn looks away.

"Sorry, I didn't... Fuck, I'm sorry, okay? This is a lot."

She leans her head on my shoulder. "I understand. Why do you think I'm here? Listen. I'll tidy the apartment. You figure out how the hell to trap Roman."

"You'd do that?"

"Of course. You can't work in a mess. I've been to your flat, remember?"

I drop a kiss onto her head. "Thank you."

"But first, you're going to tell me how your heart is doing," she says.

I stiffen under her. She must sense it because she sits up. "Shit, you did fall for her..."

I can't look at Quinn.

"Remy...?" her voice is all high and screechy. It hurts my head.

"Doesn't matter, does it? I thought she was someone she wasn't."

Quinn shuffles back on the sofa to see me. "You don't believe that."

"I'm furious. No matter what, she stole those blueprints after Roman asked her to. What does that tell you?"

"It tells you she's a thief. But did you ask her why she did it?"

"Well. I—"

"No then," Quinn gives me a patronising glare.

I take a big gulp of coffee to avoid having to answer.

"What can she possibly say to defend herself against the fact that Roman wants to use the tunnels to escape, and she stole the plans for him? It's black and white, Quinn."

"Please. You're cleverer than that. Nothing is ever black and white."

A good researcher looks at an experiment from all sides. But my heart hurts and I'm not interested in hearing it. Even if Bella had her reasons, she's gone too far. I risked everything to keep her out of jail the first time.

I broke the law for her.

"Does Morrigan know you have feelings for Bella?" Quinn asks, draining the dregs of her coffee.

"I doubt it. I avoided telling her. Do you know the funny thing?"

"You always liked her?" Quinn says, a smirk nestled in the corner of her mouth.

"How do—"

"Come on, Remy. We didn't date for long, but we've always been friends. Bella drove you insane. She was all you'd talk about for weeks after a competition. There's never really been anyone else. Haven't you wondered why you couldn't hold down a long-term relationship?"

"I..." but the words fade because if what she's saying is true, then it makes everything much worse. "Fuck."

"Let's get you cleaned up and back to work. I'm not Bella, but I can help you. We have the rest of the team, too. I can get them around."

"While I appreciate that, none of you can work rune magic. It's not going to help."

She presses her lips together and nods, then she sets about the room, picking up chairs and stacking papers into piles.

I head for a shower and get myself feeling half human. Once the water has drained the dirt away, the headache has mostly eased too.

I return to the living room, and Quinn has made me a sandwich and another coffee. The apartment is considerably tidier than it was this morning.

"I'm going to head to our apartment and get showered and changed. I'll come back and check on you later. Okay?"

I see her out and set to work. First, I push the sofas to the edge of the room. I rearrange the furniture, piling chairs on top of each other. The coffee table next, moving every item until there's an enormous rectangle of space in the apartment.

I hold my hands out, pull my magic from deep within, and let it seep into my skin. My hands fly through spells I've cast a million times. I repeat the movement once, twice, three times. But still I'm not satisfied. Three huge RuneNet screens hover in my living room. I connect them, fuss over their position, add a fourth, until it's just right.

Finally, I have a setup that works. Four huge hovering screens, one on each side of the rectangle of space. Now I can work on multiple pieces of Rune code at the same time. I can watch the magic work while I write other codes. This will work.

I throw my hands out, letting the magic flow and cast onto the RuneNet.

Next, I need to review Roman's prison code. I access my data files and pull out the source code to Roman's security grid. It makes me groan. It's a complex system and I now need to rewrite it as a mirror. I figure maybe *I* don't need to do the work. I could create a Rune string that would replicate and mirror the code automatically. But I'd need to write that Rune program. Still, more efficient than doing it, precise rune by precise rune. I stop short, fuck; I sound like Bella. Her voice trickles through my mind: *Gods, Remy, this is waaaay more efficient than a precision laser.*

I push up my sleeves, shaking thoughts of her away and get to work. My hands vibrate in front of me, Runes spinning off and attaching themselves to other runes. Lines of code writing and connecting with each other.

The afternoon slips while I work. I lose all sense of time, minutes drifting into hours. By evening, my body aches, my head hurts, and I realise the only thing I've eaten and drunk today are the coffees Quinn made and the sandwich. I sit down and decide to order something up to the room.

But as I collapse into the plush cushions, my body grows heavy. A fifteen-minute nap won't kill me. I pull up a mini screen of the RuneNet in front of me, intending to set an alarm. But before I hit save, my eyes have already rolled shut.

I wake with a start, head still leaning against the arm of the sofa. My neck is stiff from the horrendous angle I slept at. My body hurts worse than yesterday, aching in places I can't quite identify.

A tingled panic settles into my limbs as I realise I lost an entire night. The last challenge is now only two days away. I can't waste a single second of today.

Quinn arrives with Stirling shortly after I'm up and dressed and sipping coffee.

"Have you visited her?" Stirling asks as I hand her a mug of milky coffee and Quinn some herbal shit from the cupboard.

"No. I need to focus on winning this challenge and getting my program written so we can capture Roman. There isn't time. I'll deal with her after."

"And how is the program going?" Stirling asks.

"I'm behind. I need three people to pull off what I'm trying to do and probably three weeks. Not forty-eight hours and a single pair of hands. But here we are."

"Can we help?" Quinn asks, taking a sip of her fruity tea.

"Not unless you can forge digital simulations or write a code, that's going to create a transition simulation th—"

"I'm going to stop you there," Stirling says. "Of course I can't help. I'll bring food."

"I'll pop in later, okay?" Quinn says, and the two of them finish their drinks and leave me to it.

I set the code I wrote last night going on one of the

screens. It works on a private server no one has access to other than me. On one half of the screen is the original prison security code. The other side is empty, or it is briefly until the program initiates and mirrored runes appear, slowly filling the lines of code.

The next job is forging digital versions of the tunnels. I pull up the blueprints for the tunnels Marcel gave me and scout around the house for a needle.

This is how the rest of the day goes. Me trying and failing and getting a little better at building a digital version of the tunnels.

It's excruciating work. By the time midnight rolls around, I have a pathetic attempt at a tunnel that looks more like a cottage hallway.

This isn't working, but I don't know what else to do.

I collapse in bed, drained, my fingers throbbing from being stabbed so frequently with a needle and squeezed for drops of blood.

Tomorrow I'll only have twenty-four hours until the challenge and as it stands now, I'm no closer to being able to win or catch Roman.

I fall asleep with the knowledge that I'm fucked. Knowing that I need help and the only two people that can help either won't or can't.

I close my eyes with thoughts of Red and Bella, with an ache drilling between my ribs that follows me into my dreams. She plagues me even when I sleep. I worry about where she's being kept. I worry that she's going to be tried and executed as a traitor.

I need to make sure we catch Roman. As sleep takes me, I have this twisting in my gut.

What if I'm wrong? What if I've missed something?

CHAPTER 31

REMY

That's how I wake up—convinced that something is missing. I've been with Bella for most of the time we've been in the competition. She snuck the blueprints out during challenge two because she wasn't with me. But the ghost tracker I installed showed nothing untoward on the RuneNet.

I head to the living room and the four screens I created. I recheck the data. Her avatar is, as I suspected. Not suspicious, no unusual activity, and nothing to suggest foul play. I pull the tracking records and load the ghost onto the screen beside Bella's.

I run one more deconstruction rune over the two avatars. Finally, the ghost avatar cracks and the source code appears on screen.

I examine the source runes for each. What I find is surprising. Morrigan suggested the ghost avatar could be the same person trying to throw us off the scent. But the source runes behind the ghost's avatar couldn't be more different to Bella's. Her coding is brash. The runes hashed together and laced into meshes—so her sledgehammer style.

The deeper I hacked into the ghost's avatar code, the more precise it got. This inner core is exquisite. It's delicate, woven like poetry, like the old language. It's nothing like Bella. I'm not sure Bella is even capable of spelling runes like this.

The more I scrutinise the differences between the avatars, the more convinced I am that they're not the same. No, I sniff to myself. These are reminiscent of the type of code Marcel would cast.

I cast onto the dark RuneNet and hack my way into the commission the Merricks mentioned. Whoever it is, they want someone to blow the tunnels at a particular time. And as if by magic, there's the ghost avatar's signature.

I frown. If Bella is in jail, how can her avatar be active? I'm being ridiculous. It must be residual. Some kind of glitch.

I glance at my watch. Shit. There isn't time to sort it now, though. I have less than 24 hours to finish building the simulation and mirror tunnels.

I spend half the day attempting to forge and code, but by the time the afternoon rolls around, I'm sweating, red-faced and kicking a chair across the room.

No matter what I do, I can't get the fucking simulations or the forgeries to stabilise. The forgeries are better than they were when I started, but they're nothing like Red could create and even they aren't stabilising. Even if they were passable as reality, I can't get them to hold. The minute I place myself inside the simulation, they flicker and destabilise, and I have no idea why.

I need a break. I pull up a different RuneNet screen and

navigate my way to Bella's RuneNet. To my surprise, her account isn't as locked down as normal. I wonder if she was accessing it shortly before she was arrested?

I rifle through her files. I'm not sure if I'm looking for evidence to convict her or save her.

I stumble upon a set of financial files. Strings of transactions. As I scan the names, my blood runs cold. It's Roman's bank. And there are hundreds and hundreds of deposits into Marcel's account.

I slam the RuneNet shut. I can't look at it. Fuck. I need to get out, clear my head, it's swimming with awful possibilities and I don't know what's worse: the fact I was wrong about Marcel or wrong about Bella. Bile claws at my throat, I put my head in my hands. How could I fuck this up so terribly?

My eyes shift to the coffee table and the tunnel blueprints. I'll walk through the tunnels, clear my head and then I need to work out what the hell I'm going to do with this evidence.

Fifteen minutes later, I've entered the tunnels under the palace. I'm holding the blueprint a couple of hundred meters into the tunnels. I veer left and come to an abrupt halt.

I glance at the map and back up to the tunnel.

"What the fuck?" I say. The blueprint says this tunnel leads at least a hundred meters down here before leading to a T-junction and out under the ocean towards Sangui city. But this tunnel has a split into three different tunnels.

It must be a recent addition, though I thought no one

used these. I can't imagine why they would have new tunnels.

I track back to the beginning and decide to go right this time instead of left. Two turns in, I hit a dead end. I glance down at the map. It's supposed to bend right and then give me two tunnel options.

"What the fuck is going on?"

Frustrated, I head back to the start of the tunnel and find Red leant against the entrance.

"I wondered when you'd come down here," she says and her face relaxes as if she were holding days of tension.

"I've spent the last three days trying to make the plan work, and I can't."

"Why didn't you ask for help?" She says.

"Who was I going to ask? Bella's in jail. You were... I had no idea where you were, but you're her best friend and I put her in jail. I assumed you'd be pissed about that."

"I wasn't pleased."

"Exactly," I say.

Her face crinkles. "Out of curiosity. What's the problem with the system?"

"The system isn't stable. The forgeries aren't accurate enough. I can't do it on my own."

"Almost sounds like you need a lattice framework to hold the simulations to. Would that stabilise it?" Her eyes glimmer in the dim tunnel and dart to the prints in my hand and something dislodges. Why would Red be down here looking for me? I scrutinise the map again, over my shoulder at the tunnels, and back to Red.

Oh fuck. "You forged them," I say, holding the blue-prints up.

"There she is..." she nods. "You need to talk to her. There's so much you don't know."

Fuck, fuck, fuck. I've spent so long focused on getting to the end of this challenge I've missed the things right in front of me.

"But they took her back to the city," I say.

"No, they didn't. She's been in the dungeons below Lantis the whole time."

My jaw flexes at the image of Bella trapped in a dungeon. I wonder whether they have looked after her, whether they've fed her.

"I can take you," Red says.

All I can do is nod.

We wind our way into the depths of the palace, deep under the ocean bed. The air is damp, the stone walls claustrophobic as they press in on us. Red hurries us down the last steps and into a dim-lit dungeon.

There's a guard sat on a chair by the entrance. He stands, his brow furrowed in confusion.

"You can't be down here," he says.

"Oh, but I—" Red stumbles over a stone, her body tipping and flying towards the floor. The guard dives to catch her, Red's hand swings around, and she opens her balled fist, blowing rouge dust in his face.

The pair of them fall to the stone floor. Red groans, but he lays still. I rush over to her and haul the guard's heavy body off her.

"Do I want to ask what that was?"

She winks at me as I extend my hand to help her up. "A little blood-powered sleeping powder."

I shiver as we step through puddles of water and pass empty cell after empty cell. The odd lantern hanging on the wall does nothing to warm the frigid air.

Red stops and points to the end cell. "She's in there."

"Thank you," I say and move the final few feet to the end of the corridor.

I don't say anything at first. Bella is in the corner, shadows curled around her like blankets. She's shivering, her lips blue. She's lost weight, her hair is limp, the curls fuzzy. I'm instantly nauseous at the state of her. How could they treat her like this?

She glares at me, her eyes bright with fury even shrouded in darkness.

"I'm sorry," I say. Because what else can I say? She's in this mess because of me.

"Go fuck yourself, Remy," she snarls and turns away from me.

"I didn't know."

"You still don't. You never gave me a chance to explain."

"I confess, I'm an arsehole."

"Oh well, okay then, I'll just forgive you, shall I? Fancy spending three days in this cell with water and whatever the fuck they think gruel is."

"How about we forgive each other?" I say, stepping close to the cell bars.

She makes a huffing sound.

"I'm willing to admit I fucked up, but you lied to me, too. I told you I was hunting Roman, yet you didn't tell me he was contacting you. You stole those prints, and not once did you let me in on what you were doing."

"I didn't help Roman," she says and turns back to face me, unravelling herself and standing up. She wobbles on her feet, weak and paler than I've ever seen her. She stumbles her way to the cell door.

"I am not the one helping him escape. He was trying to blackmail me into it. But it's not me. I know who it is."

I shake my head. I don't want to confront this. The

avatar's rune style, the birthday safe code. But it doesn't make sense. Rationally, the pieces add up, but it can't be possible.

"Who is it?" I say.

Her hand wraps around mine over the bar. Her fingers are frozen, but I can't let her out, not yet, not until she convinces me of her innocence. Because if I trust her, and release her before Morrigan and Calandra approve, then I'm just as much a traitor to the crown as she is.

"Marcel."

I grit my teeth, my whole body railing against her words. That man was like a father to me. He took me in, cared for me, trained me. He was nothing but supportive and kind and caring. The idea that he's behind the breakout makes no sense. My heart trembles, breaking all over again. My eyes sting. I desperately don't want to hear this, but deep down, I've been putting the evidence together. My throat is thick, a lump aching every time I swallow.

"But he hates Roman," I say.

"Why do you think I went to him?" Bella says, her teeth chattering between her pale lips.

Even though it's the most inappropriate time, I want to kiss the warmth back in.

She continues. "I went to Marcel for help. I figured there's no one who hates him more than me. But fuck, I couldn't have been more wrong, Remy. He's been lying to us, they both have. I'm sure of it now. There's something going on that we don't understand."

There's a jingling of metal behind me, then something cold and hard presses into my free hand. I glance from Red down to my hand. It's an iron key.

"I'm going to keep guard. If you're going to use that, don't take forever. I have no idea when the shift will change over, and that sleeping powder doesn't work forever," Red says and heads back towards the exit.

Bella's eyes slide to my hand. She takes a deep breath and continues. "I asked him to protect me because I knew he hated Roman. He told me he would. But that I should do what Roman said. I questioned him. But he was convincing. He said that I needed to lead Roman on, that it was the only way to get evidence and catch him red-handed. Otherwise someone else would steal them and then we'd never catch him. It... it made sense, and I panicked."

"But you gave him fake blueprints, didn't you?" I say, glancing at Red, who nods confirmation.

"It was a test," Bella answers.

"One he failed." My voice cracks on the last syllable.

"I'm so sorry. He was your mentor. I knew you wouldn't believe me."

I want to deny it, but how can I when she's right?

"How did you know?"

"So many reasons. The book, Marcel gave it to you, but Roman gave it to him. I could read the inscription because Roman used to write using that code all the time."

I lean my forehead against the rails.

"They're brothers?" I say and a hot tear rolls down my cheek. My soul cracks. It's a strange dichotomy to still love a man who's broken your heart. I want to gouge the affection out, score the memories of him from my mind. Was any of our life true?

Bella wipes her thumb across my cheek. "Just before the bank hack, Red made this offhand comment about following the money. So that's what I did. Hacked Roman's accounts... found the patterns in his transactions. Then there was the vaults and Roman's security code."

"I'm a fool," I say.

"If you were, then so was I."

"What happened with the maps?" I ask.

"In one of the notes, Roman asked me to steal them. I was in a tough position. If I didn't help him and he got out, he'd come for me. If I did help and I was caught, I'd go to jail. So I stole the blueprint and used it to set him up."

"How did you do it?" I ask.

"I had Red create two sets of blueprints.."

"If he was so convincing, why did you give him the fake prints?"

"Because I told him about Roman's safes and the code. And there was this expression he pulled and I couldn't place it. Not at the time. But I get it now."

"What was it?"

Bella laughs, a nasty little sharp thing. "He said *'perhaps it was a reminder of the one he hated more than anything else.'*"

I raise an eyebrow. "Who keeps totems of the people they hate?"

"Exactly. But who do we keep the belongings and trinkets of?" she asks and grabs the cell door with both hands, her face strained as she stares at me.

I swallow hard, thinking of the book Marcel had given me of the old language. The spine frayed and falling apart, the pages so ancient I'm afraid they'll dissolve into dust soon.

"The ones we love." I whisper.

"How different are love and hate, really?" she says.

"But why?" I say.

She shrugs, then adds, "They're brothers. Or at least half brothers. I suspect Marcel wasn't treated well and Roman tried to make up for it. Bastard children don't go down too well with high-ranking legacies. It's a reputational hazard. Gods, I sound like my mother."

I lean my forehead against the cell bars.

My mind wanders back to the book Marcel gave me. The way the runes were so intricate and perfect in there. As an apprentice, it was a skill I could only aspire to.

"I deconstructed the ghost avatar," I say as I push off the cell and slide the iron key into the lock. I pause.

"And?" she says, her voice light as if hope is seeping back in.

"Your avatar's source code was so different from the ghosts. It was exquisite, honestly. Used the old language, archaic runes that were precise and elegant..."

"And?" she said.

"And there's only one person I've ever known skilled enough to use archaic runes like that."

"Marcel?" she asks.

I nod. I fall silent as her eyes glaze over like she's lost in a memory.

"You know the funny thing?" she says.

"What?"

"Roman was always keen on me learning the old language too. He used to send letters in the old language. I never thought anything of it. I figured it was a quirk of his."

"But you think they were always communicating?" I ask.

"It's the only conclusion I can come to. I suspect they have a strange and twisted relationship. Brothers who love each other as much as they hate each other. Who seethe with jealousy for the life of legacy one has and the life of freedom the other had. But it's all a guess. We won't know unless we ask them," she says and her hand slips through the bars to hold my mine—the key cool in my palm.

Red appears. "It's time. The guard is stirring. You need to decide. Who do you believe, Remy? Bella or Marcel?"

And that is a question I never thought I'd face.

CHAPTER 32

BELLA

The key grinding in the lock is the most glorious sound I've ever heard. I lean on Remy as we tiptoe out of the dungeon. I'm weak. My body throbs from the cold that I'm sure will never leave my soul. But with every step further away from the cell, I stand a little straighter, hurt a little less.

Red leads the way. She uses the tunnels and the palace schematics to sneak us through some dodgy passages, into the guest suites, and right to her room. "You can't go back to your room tonight. Not when they realise you're out. I gave the guard a second dose of the sleeping powder, but it won't keep him under all night," Red says.

"What now?" I say.

"Now we lay a trap. Marcel thinks the plans you gave him are legitimate. If he is the one working with Roman, then they'll use those to plot their escape routes. We use one of the fake turns that leads to a dead end to trap him in a simulation."

Red and I are silent. We share a surreptitious glance. Then, I say, "Remy... it is him..." My voice is soft. I have to take this slowly. I can't imagine the heartbreak.

Remy shakes her head. She folds her arms around her stomach and rocks forward. It's her mentor, her ache, but fuck does it feel like someone slid a knife between my ribs seeing her this way.

She takes a deep breath and once she's steady; she says. "I... I know. But... It's going to take a minute for me to accept it."

I squeeze her hand.

"We need to finish the forgeries, merge them with the simulation, and get ready for the challenge tomorrow."

Red jumps up. "I'll get food and supplies. It's not safe for you to leave the room, Bella."

"Wait, let me show you the forgeries I've made so far," Remy says, drawing out her RuneNet screens and casting on.

She pulls up the lines of code, but Red shrugs at her.

"Red can't read the code," I say.

"Right. Sorry." Remy adjusts and casts several more runes out until the simulation forms around us. Fuzzy at first, but it sharpens and grows more intense the longer Remy casts, the more runes she throws at it.

"There, that was as far as I got," Remy says.

We're stood in a dingy tunnel. The light is dim. She's got the lanterns right, but the colours are off, the proportions aren't quite right.

"The look and accuracy needs work, but I've been mapping off the wrong blueprints anyway," Remy says, the exhaustion clear in her voice.

"Not wrong if we want to trap them. He'll carry the wrong blueprints into the simulation."

"You're extraordinarily terrifying," Remy says and for the first time in three days, I laugh.

"Red, give me the real maps. We need to overlay the two and find a room or a dead end we can use to cage them in," I say.

She disappears into her bedroom and returns with the real blueprints laying them on the living room table. She leaves us to strategise and heads out to get food.

Remy glances up at me, lines burrowing into her forehead. "Should we talk about us?"

My lips purse. "We've both fucked up."

"I'm sorry I didn't listen. I should have believed you. There was too much evidence against you, and with the pressure from Morrigan... The need to protect my reputation. I had to be sure. I had to."

I reach out and take her hand. "It wasn't just your reputation at risk, Remy. You literally saved my ass from prison. Do you really think I'd throw that in your face? I told you if I don't win this competition, I'm going to be married off to some gods awful lord to produce heirs. And that stopped me from letting you in. I was terrified you wouldn't believe me if I told you..."

Remy pulls her hand out of mine, her fists balling. "You can't marry a man. How can she expect that of you?"

"I don't want to, but given everything that's happened. Given I'm a fugitive... that choice seems trivial now."

"We can't let that happen, Bella..."

I smile. "One thing at a time. I still smell like dungeon and, to be honest, I'm terrified that this task is too big for" —I look at the clock hanging on the wall— "seventeen hours."

"I'm a fraud. Some supposed academic genius. How did

I not piece this together? I should have come to you soon-
er," she says.

"Bitch please. You are every bit the genius your reputation says you are. And then some. We can do this, but we
need to do that thing we're not too great at..."

"Teamwork?" she asks her face crinkling with laughter.

"Exactly."

"Oh, well, we'll have no issues then," she says and we're
both laughing. We laugh because we're delirious and
exhaustion makes laughing funny. We laugh because we're
terrified, because we're determined, and because both our
mentors are fucking liabilities. It's a solid ten minutes
before we calm down. Both of us have laughed so hard tears
streak our faces and our bellies hurt.

"You should shower," Remy says finally.

And I reckon it might be the greatest thing she's ever
said to me. I leave and drench myself in the hottest water I
can stand, closing my eyes for a full minute of bliss. I steal
some of Red's pyjamas, as nothing else of hers will fit. By
the time Red is back with two bags of takeout from the
canteen, Remy and I are poring over the tunnel plans. We
assess the work she's already done and once we're fed, all
three of us are pumped for an all-nighter.

By three o'clock in the morning, we're a mess. I've had
three nose bleeds from the strain of overusing magic. Red
is paler than usual. She's had to use so much blood to get
the level of forgery to indistinguishable from reality that
she's passed out once already. Her hands are a mess of
scabs and swollen tips, and Remy has thrown up twice. She
coded too fast, burned too hot and hard. Her body gave
out, and she puked over the balcony and promptly blacked
out.

It's not going well.

"We can do this, right?" I say as I mop a fourth nosebleed.

"Sure?" Red says. Though she looks anything but sure and it definitely sounded like a question.

I smear another line of blood away. "What's left?"

"Only the transition," Remy says. "We need to make sure that the move from them walking through the real tunnel into our simulated tunnel is seamless."

"Run it. Let's see how it works," I say.

The three of us crowd around Remy's screen, where she's displaying a map of Lantis Palace.

"Marcel will be on the RuneNet server downstairs. He'll disconnect and make his way directly into the tunnels using this door. Based on the fake blueprints, this is their meeting point and the fake and real prints match to that point."

"Okay, so we lead them where?" I ask.

"Here," Remy points to a location one tunnel down. "It's a dead end in the real tunnels, but we can make the simulation appear to continue and then trap him inside a lattice cage."

"Red, can you work with me on smoothing the forgery of the blueprint as they're moving through the simulation?"

"I...I don't know how much more magic I can use tonight," she says.

I glance over. Red is spectacularly pale. We've pushed her too far. My chest tightens. Gods forbid anything happens to her because of us.

"Don't look at me like that Beatrice, a little blood loss isn't going to put a Hunter like me down," she says and throws a sofa pillow at my head.

"Rest. I'll go to Quinn, see if she has some herbs that will boost your iron. You've lost a lot of blood," Remy says.

"We need to talk about something else..." I say.

Remy hesitates. "What's wrong? Please tell me there are no more confessions I need to worry about?"

"No more confessions... But we need to go to Princess Morrigan."

"No. All things considered, that is legitimately the most terrible idea you've had. She'll arrest you all over again," Remy says, her eyes wide as orbs.

"If what we're building works, it's proof I'm innocent. As are the financial records on my RuneNet."

"She's right," Red says, yawning. "Plus, there's no way to get her out of here and connected to the Rune Server without being seen. We have no choice."

"I'm deeply uncomfortable at this prospect," Remy says.

"Can you think of an alternative?" I ask.

"Also no," Remy says, her shoulders dropping.

"Then we agree?" I ask. Both Red and Remy nod, though Remy seems reluctant. I hand Red a pillow and lay a blanket over her. Within minutes, she's snoring softly.

"How do we actually trap them?" I whisper to Remy, once Red has passed out.

"I coded the simulation to automatically record their RuneNet activity. Every step he makes, the minute he approaches Roman's security grid, he'll be recorded. We just need him to attempt the hack, and he's signing his own death warrant."

"So Roman is never going to escape?" I ask.

"That is the plan. I'm going to use our simulation program to transfer Marcel into a fake version of Roman's prison. We need him to think he's hacked the real one, otherwise he won't go into the tunnels."

"Okay, and once he's in the tunnels?"

"We'll that's the interesting part. I hacked into that commission the Merricks told us about."

"And?" I ask.

"The task is to bomb the tunnels. Shut off access from the palace."

"Shit," I say, "As if we needed any more reasons to go to Morrigan. We'll need her guards to scour the tunnels. We can't let a bomb go off. It could endanger the palace's structural integrity."

Remy runs her hand through her quiff. She looks as exhausted as I feel.

"That's where we need your cage in place with the simulated version of the tunnels. I know Marcel. If he has any doubt over its authenticity, he'll bolt. And these tunnels give him access routes to all six cities. If he runs, he'll disappear forever."

"Then we better make sure he doesn't."

CHAPTER 33

REMY

We decided it wasn't safe to take Bella out of the apartment without having spoken to Morrigan. Which is how Morrigan ends up flush-faced and in the living room of Red's Lantis Palace apartment at seven o'clock in the morning.

Stirling is at the dining room table, her legs kicked up onto the top as she plucks grapes from Red's fruit bowl. Red is on one sofa with Quinn, who is spooning a tarry black substance into her mouth. With every mouthful she swallows, the colour runs back into her cheeks. Though the expression she pulls gets more puckered and violent.

"That truly is the most awful shite I've ever had the displeasure of eating," Red whines as she accepts another spoon.

"Well, you clearly feel better, with the amount of moaning you're doing," Quinn says, heaping a final mound of black whatever it is onto the spoon.

Quinn packs up. "I need to get you a follow-up bottle. I have something in my room, but I forgot to bring it. Come with me, it won't take long." Quinn helps Red up and the two of them head out of the apartment.

"They're fake?" Morrigan repeats for the third time.

I turn my attention back to Morrigan.

But it's Bella that answers. "That's right. I had my suspicions that something was wrong and Red is a forger. So she whipped up a new set of blueprints and that's what you're holding. The ones Marcel gave you. The real ones are there." Bella points at the table and the piece of paper under Stirling's foot.

Morrigan tuts and walks over to the table, slapping Stirling's foot off and picking up the prints. "Let me get this one hundred per cent straight." She's pacing up and down between Bella and me with the prints in hand. "You went down to the dungeon last night and broke her out? Put a guard to sleep and have been in here all night finishing a simulation that you are planning to use to trap Marcel?" She comes to a halt in front of me. Her expression matches her severe fringe. I swallow the doubt down.

"That is correct," I say.

"But you need to do this at the same time as being in the competition?"

Bella answers this time. "One, we both still want to win. And two, if Remy isn't in the competition, then Marcel will know something is wrong, and we may not secure the evidence we need to prove he's helping Roman."

"Yes, but Marcel knows we've arrested Bella. He's going to think she's in prison. I can't just let her out and into the competition," Morrigan says.

"I can help Remy remotely. And be in a secure, guarded location if you'd like. I'm willing to hand myself back into your custody. That's why we brought you here. We needed you to know that I'm on your team."

"We also need something," I say.

"Which is?" Morrigan tilts her head at me.

"We need to ensure that Roman's prison is chosen as our hack prison in the challenge."

She inhales, her eyes widening.

"Without that, we can't run the mirror simulation as effectively," I add.

Morrigan's lips thin into a line as severe as her fringe as she rounds on Bella. "Know that I am not doing this for you. But for Remy. I owe her an awful lot. So if at any point I think you're lying, I will send Scarlett after you. If Roman escapes, I will send Scarlett after you. If you cannot gather sufficient evidence to convict Marcel... I will send—"

"Scarlett after me. I understand. Don't fuck up." Bella strides up to Morrigan and takes her hand, giving a polite curtsey and kisses her knuckles. "And... I hope that when this is done, maybe we can be introduced again.... Fresh start and all that."

Bella gives a sweet smile, but Morrigan bristles before then relaxing. "I want a conviction, then we discuss everything else. Stirling, I need to go gather some guards. Will you come with me? We need to find Scarlett and send a squad of assassins to Roman's prison, just in case. After, I need to start the last challenge."

Stirling puts the fruit down and moves to Morrigan's side. "I'll find Scarlett."

"Bella, I will inform the guard to stay with you until you have proof secured. Should you succeed, you're free to go. Your other misdemeanours will be... pardoned."

Stirling guides Morrigan, slipping a hand to her lower back and the pair of them disappear out of the apartment.

In silence, Bella and I stand staring at the door where Morrigan just was. Bella reaches out and slides her hand into mine, the soft pad of her thumb stroking my hand.

"Remy," she whispers.

"Don't say it. Don't fucking say it," I say.

But she will because in order for the mirror simulation to run effectively, convincingly, it has to be run simultaneously.

"We need to choose," she says.

I fire a vicious stare at the door.

I slam my fist into the table. I grab it, cradling the pain like the salve it is.

"There is no choice. Stopping Marcel, preventing Roman from escaping is far too important," she says.

I'm silent. So she continues. "If we don't choose, the mirror won't run, and then there's no way to prove I'm innocent."

"I get that," I say, my voice withdrawn. Bella turns away from me and slumps onto the sofa.

"I'm sorry," I say. But I'm wasting my words. There's nothing either of us can do. The part of me that cares for her wants her to win the role. The part of me that needs to prove I'm worthy needs to win.

"If we do this, we're sacrificing the challenge win," she says.

"So you're okay with the Merricks winning? Neither of us will ever be the Royal Rune Master," she says.

"I'm okay with you not being in jail."

She huffs at me, that perfect little pout forming.

"My other concern is your mother. She threatened to marry you off. I can't—. I won't let you be forced into a marriage," I say.

"She won't."

"How can you know that?"

"Because I'll face the consequences of saying no. Whatever they may be. I choose you, Remy. I choose saving us.
And if that means sacrificing the win, then that's what we
have to do. I'll be free. You'll still have your business. And
we'll still have each other... if that's what you want?"

"It is."

"Then let's take this bastard down," she says.

CHAPTER 34

REMY

Two hours later, Bella is tucked into a room off the balcony circling the RuneNet server room. A guard stands at the door, preventing Bella from leaving and anyone else from getting in.

"Can you hear me?" I say adjusting my earpiece.

"Like the maniacal overlord controlling my mind that you are? Yes, Remy. I can hear you," Bella says.

I glance up, my eyes brushing the door before returning to the RuneNet Server in front of me. The familiar concentric circles, one set above and one below, containing the mainline into the RuneNet. Glorious threads hang like silken ropes between the two sets of circles. Rune symbols float on the lines, shimmering and travelling so fast the untrained eye can't keep up.

Around the server, there's a circular table ready for the remaining four other teams and me—a solo contestant, or so the rest of them think. One last chance to cast on and compete for the role of Royal Rune Master.

On the other side of the table are the Games Makers. Eli, Marcel, and a couple of others I've not dealt with. Eli and Marcel will go head-to-head against the remaining teams.

Morrigan makes her way to the balcony. She opens her arms wide and silence descends on the room.

"Magicians, contestants, honoured guests, friends and family." She looks down at us, up at the balcony opposite where families sit watching and waiting for the results and at the guests on the balcony seats behind her.

"Today marks the end to another magnificent competition. I am excited to see what wonderful new security inventions the remaining teams have developed. We've already had many come from the first two competitions, and a number of patents submitted too."

There's a smattering of cheers and claps from around the balcony.

Morrigan starts again. "There will be a winning team. There will also be an individual from that team who will win the coveted role of Royal Rune Master as decided by their performance throughout the contests. Let the games begin."

She claps and the light shifts in the room. We're plunged into darkness and then spotlights appear on the RuneNet server, the table and seats for the contestants.

Alba Merrick sidles up next to me. "Too bad for Bella. But these challenges have standards, and they can't let any old trash in..."

"That fucking whore. If I were down there, I'd give her a piece of my—" Bella hisses in my ear.

"Quiet," I bark.

Alba recoils.

"Great comeback, Remy," she rolls her eyes and saunters off to take her seat next to Gabe at the table.

Soundproof viewing screens come down over the balcony separating the watchers from the contestants. This is to ensure silence during the contest.

Games Maker Eli heads to the table and a glass bowl filled with white cards. Each card is a prison. He plucks one from it and hands it to Gabe who reads it.

"Prison Lanceforth."

The prison appears on the screens, and Gabe and Alba take their places at the table. The Games Makers are given thirty minutes to hack their security. Either they hack the security in that time and Alba and Gabe lose, or they don't and the Merricks win their round. Points will be awarded for the complexity and difficulty of their security system and the number of layers the Games Makers break through, amongst other things.

The thirty minutes drag because the Merrick's session runs predictably smooth. They use a shifting rune cypher, combined with a basic mesh.

It's an effective, if unoriginal, idea. Bella and I discounted it for its rudimentary code. I'm amazed the Games Makers didn't hack it. Which leads me to wonder why they haven't. I pull out my RuneNet screen and cast on, trying to be as discreet as I can.

I scan the tracking code and locate Marcel's public avatar and then search for the ghost avatar, or maybe I should say Marcel's real avatar. And I realise why the Merrick's are having an easy time with it.

Marcel is already using his ghost avatar to hack Roman's security.

"Er. Fuck," I mumble.

"What?" Bella breathes in my ear.

"He's already on the prison. Can you initiate counter security? Throw as much lattice magic as you can spare at the prison perimeter. We can't afford him to hack the prison grid before we're on the server."

"On it," she replies.

I send her access code to the Rune source codes for the perimeter and then watch on my screen as I see additional layers of security added to Roman's prison. I glance at Marcel, who swears under his breath, and seeing the reaction in real time makes little pieces of me break.

Even though I knew, there was some part of me still clinging to the hope it wasn't him. A line of sweat covers Marcel's upper lip. The silver and pepper hair around his ears dapples as he sweats under the pressure of two simultaneous hacks.

The Merrick's challenge ends. So does the next, and the next. There's only one more set of contestants before I jump in.

"Bella," I growl down the earpiece. "He's through another lattice."

"Yes, I'm well aware of that, but I'm running on an hour of sleep, very little food, and three days in a dungeon. I'm doing my best here. I'd like to see you helping."

"I will as soon as these contestants are out of the way," I say.

Marcel must be growing frustrated because he diverts his attention to the prison and Eli barks at him to focus.

"Sorry," Marcel says, wipes his brow and refocuses on the team's security in front of him. Thankfully, that buys Bella some time to embed another lattice. I don't think Marcel has realised that we're live patching. The way Bella is feeding the lattices into the security grid, it makes it look like an intelligent algorithm shifting and adapting to Marcel's moves. It's actually rather genius.

Marcel gives a frustrated grunt, and the contestant's

security dissolves on screen. He's through. Their turn is over. Which means...

"It's time," Eli says to me.

I turn to Red. "Go be with her."

She groans in my ear, but she squeezes me tight. "Just so we're clear, you are buying me the most expensive bottle of Sanguis Cūpa that there is when this is over. Then we're getting shitfaced and I'm going to spend the night threatening to kill you if you hurt my bestie again."

I laugh and squeeze her back. "I would be honoured."

She leaves and makes her way to the balcony. I wait for the last team to leave the server arena area, take a deep breath and make my way to the table.

This is it.

"Hey, Red," Bella says in my ear and some of the tension eases out of me, knowing Red's in there and our little team is ready to go.

"Contestant, are you ready?" Eli says.

"I am."

"The Games Makers will have a five-minute time penalty due to your solo status. Do with those minutes what you see fit."

The screens drop over the balcony, sealing the guests off from our view. For a brief moment, I can't breathe. My chest clamps tight, and I want to run. I can't do this. I am about to destroy the greatest mentor I ever had.

I can feel Marcel's gaze boring into me, but I can't bring myself to look at him. I'm too exhausted to keep the pretence up.

I focus on casting on to the RuneNet server. I reverse engineered Marcel's avatar to hide Bella in the system.

I see her pop up as a blip in the code of the prison. I chance a quick glance at Marcel, but he hasn't noticed.

Good. Playing him at his own game.

I sit back and let the five minutes roll. We've planned and prepped. All we need is for Marcel to engage and we can attack.

"Games Makers hack in *three*. Two. One," Morrigan says.

My focus becomes a precision point. Marcel is viciously quick. He fires runes into the system. Lines of my precious code dissolve before my eyes, faster than I can patch them.

I load up my second screen because I need to see what his ghost avatar is doing. Goosebumps fleck down my spine as I realise he's diverted all his magic to the ghost avatar. And his attack is brutal. He's destroying lines of code at an insane rate.

"Remy, stop fucking about and help me. I need you to initiate the mirror before he actually hacks through the prison grid," Bella whines in my ear.

"I'm. Trying," I say through gritted teeth. "But I'm haemorrhaging magic, trying to keep him out of the challenge version and back up the real security grid. I don't have enough to switch him into the mirror."

"Distraction, you need a distraction," Red says in my ear. "Divert his attention back to the challenge for a second. Use the time to push all your magic into the overlay."

"Yes! That's exactly what we need. Thank you, Red," I say. "Bella, you remember those exploding runes?"

"The ones you swore I was never allowed to use, you mean?"

"The very same. Thread them into the challenge system."

"You're sure? It's essentially suicide for our avatars. What if we blow the bomb before he finishes the hack? We won't get the proof we need."

"Doesn't matter. We're not actually going to explode the bomb."

"Huh?"

"Don't attach the trigger rune. If you send it out without a method of exploding it, it becomes a distraction without the problem..."

"Why Professor, you are devious."

I smirk as I glare at my screen, my hands straining against the force of vibrations.

"Do it, Bella, deploy the biggest one you can. I can't hold him off any longer."

The Rune bomb rushes onto the screen, a tiny little star-shaped symbol that swells fast. It sucks lines of rune code into its orbit. It charges across the challenge screen, sweeping and absorbing every rune in sight.

"What the hell?" Marcel's growl echoes from across the room. His ghost avatar goes still as his attention is pulled from Roman's security grid back into the challenge.

"Deploy counter measures, raise the rune wards," Eli bellows. They know how dangerous rune bombs are. If they don't protect themselves, we'll destroy their avatars and win the challenge.

"*Now*, Remy. Execute the mirror now."

I pull back every ounce of magic I have and surge it into the mirror overlay. My hands throb with the pressure. Sweat slides down my back, but this is it. This is the moment we've been working toward.

"I can't hold it," I breathe through gritted teeth.

"I've got you, I'm adding a stabilising lattice," Bella says in my ear. "Change over in three... two..."

I push the last gust of magic I have into the mirror code as it slides into place like a puzzle.

"*Yes!*" Bella and Red's voices shriek through my head.

I flinch as the earpiece whistles, sending a horrendous squeal through my head.

"It's not over yet," I whisper. "Focus."

"Decommissioning rune bomb, Sir," Bella says.

"Bella," I growl. "Don't make me punish you. What did I tell you about good girls?"

"Remy," she gasps. "How inappropriate."

And despite the fierce level of concentration. Despite how exhausted we both are, I smile because she's here, because we're making this sacrifice together. And that is so unexpected it makes me fall a little harder.

Fuck. I am so in love.

"He's moving back to the ghost avatar," she says, bringing my attention back to the server.

"Following. He's in the final layer of security in both systems. I don't think he's noticed. I don't want to celebrate too soon, but it appears we're going to pull this off."

Bella goes silent. And I do too.

The future both of us have held sacred disappears before our eyes. We don't need to speak; we need to keep up the appearance of trying to stop him, but this is the moment we stand back and let it happen.

And how do you quantify that loss?

How can I explain what it means to let go of the dream that has kept me awake for a decade? Kept me pushing through the darkest parts of the night? How do I describe the visceral agony that's ripping through my body, knowing that I am choosing to let go of the one thing I've always wanted? My childhood dream, my hopes, my desires, the future I've already lived a thousand times in my mind.

I can't.

It's a death. For me and for her.

And that is why we're silent. Because there are no words that can ease the pain.

We stand and grieve as Marcel hacks the last three rune strings, and our dream of Royal Rune Master evaporates.

My throat is thick, a heavy knot lodged in the back of my mouth.

Two rune strings.

In my ear, Bella's breathing is fast and staccato. I know she's trying to control the tears. It hurts. It hurts so much.

One rune string.

No one prepares you for the agony of loss. But losing something and choosing to let go are two very different things. One is taken away, the other given up.

Here, in this moment, I stand passive, and allow the last rune in the last string to evaporate, exploding in a whirl of a thousand particles, along with my dreams.

And I am crushed.

CHAPTER 35

BELLA

I push the tears down. I don't want to give Marcel my tears as well as my dreams. But witnessing my chances of winning vanish hurt more than I'd expected. I thought I was ready, prepared. But everything I've dreamed of is gone and I have no idea what my life looks like without the role of Royal Rune Master.

"He's disconnected from the challenge," Remy says in my ear. Her voice low and cracked like she's struggling not to cry. I don't want her hurt, but knowing we're in this together helps.

She continues talking. "The room is being cleared. Everyone's heading to the award room. The Merricks won. Alba topped Gabe by a single point. Anyway, a guard is heading your way. Get down here as fast as possible. We need to initiate phase two."

"Where is he?" I ask.

"Heading towards the tunnels."

Another guard meets us at the entrance to the RuneNet server room. "I've cleared the room. You're safe to enter."

Morrigan is standing by the circular table at the foot of the server. She's wringing her hands.

The door opens, a guard points out where the stairs are, and Red and I race down to meet Remy as she's casting back onto the server.

"And you're sure the actual prison wasn't damaged?" she's asking Remy.

"Well, he compromised the security grid before we were able to transfer him onto the mirror grid."

Remy's arms slide across the screens, her hands awash with magic vibrating in rings around her fingers, runes flying off and into the server.

She turns to Morrigan. "But we're okay. As soon as he was on the mirror grid, I reverted to backing up the actual security grid. Its integrity is already back at eighty per cent. It won't fall, not before I can get it back to one hundred."

Morrigan hugs Remy. "Thank gods. Thank you, Remy, I've been terrified he'll get out."

"I told you I wouldn't let you down," she says, rubbing Morrigan's back.

Remy pulls a new screen up. Video footage from orbs placed in the tunnels last night flash up on the screen.

"Now, we wait. Bella created a lattice last night that is a remote link up to the RuneNet. And then Red here," she inclines her head in Red's direction. "Used her forg—er painting skills to make it look like the tunnel. It's invisible to the naked eye."

I bounce on my tiptoes, still buzzed at how realistic it came out. "He'll walk through it and be instantly transported into the RuneNet. It will shift the boundaries of his reality and he won't even realise. He'll be lost walking around virtual tunnels forever."

"And his physical body?" Princess Morrigan asks.

I smile at Remy. "We built a cage out of a combination of the same coding in Remy's security grid perimeter around Roman's prison and my lattices. The two bonded together are extremely strong."

Remy holds out her hand for a high five and I slap it. We did good. Remy turns to the screen. She shifts between different orbs until she finds Marcel.

"He's approximately one hundred feet from the lattice," Remy says.

Morrigan beams at us. "Well, Red, was it?"

Red nods and holds out her hand. Morrigan clasps it and places her other hand over the top. "Imperium city is in your debt. On behalf of the crown, I thank you for your service. If there's anything we can do to help you in the future, please don't hesitate to ask."

Red lowers her head in deference and Morrigan turns to me. "I guess this means I owe you an apology... and your freedom."

"Thank you, your highness. I'm deeply grateful you were generous enough to give me the opportunity to prove my innocence. I appreciate that not everyone has that privilege."

"Something tells me we need a fresh start... I'm assuming I'll be seeing a lot more of you." Her eyes flick to Remy.

"Oh. Well. I. Umm," I stutter, realising it's not my place to tell Remy's friend what we are or aren't. Hell, I don't even know what we are.

Remy points to the screen, oblivious to the conversation Morrigan and I were having.

"Marcel's walking into the cage in three. Two. One..."

All four of us stare at the screen, waiting. All four of us stop breathing. Remy pulls an orb camera recording from the other side of the lattice into focus, but Marcel never appears.

Remy slaps the desk in triumph. "We have lock in." She sags into the challenge chair in front of the desk and rests her head in her hands. "It's over," she mumbles.

"Hi," Morrigan says to me, her expression brighter and more open than it's ever been. All the formality, the rigid firmness and royal demeanour evaporates. "I don't believe we've met. I'm Morrigan, and you are..." She holds her hand out to me.

"Bella, Bella Blythe," I say, confusion rippling through my expression.

"Well, it's a pleasure to meet you, Bella. Remy's a good friend of mine."

"Umm, guys" Red says. Everyone's eyes swerve to Red. But her gaze is locked on the screen.

It's glitching.

"SHIT," I throw my hands out, casting onto the RuneNet server as fast as I can. Remy does the same. Morrigan and Red stand back, giving us space.

"What's happening?" Morrigan says, the quiver in her voice betraying the calm tone.

"The simulation glitched. I can't be sure if he's aware —" I start.

"How do we contain this? Morrigan, where are the guards?"

"There's only a couple left. We sent the majority of the force to the prison in case Roman escaped."

Remy digs in her pocket and chucks Morrigan her orb. "Call Scarlett, get her back here *fast*. She should have her bike. If we can't get this under control, Marcel will realise he's in a sim and start hacking his way out from the inside. Then we're in trouble."

"I'll send the guards I have into the tunnels. I can't afford for him to escape and attempt to free Roman again," Morrigan says.

Remy and I glance at each other. This is about as far from good as it gets.

"If he escapes, I can help. I'm a trained Hunter," Red adds.

"Fuck," I growl, spotting the screen. "He's becoming more erratic. Doubling back on himself in the tunnels."

"We need to stall him long enough to get assassins here," Remy says.

I rub my face, praying the exhaustion leaves me long enough for my brain to function. Nothing comes to mind.

"I have to go in," Remy says.

"What do you mean *in*?" I ask, my voice trembling because I am entirely sure I know what she means, and it's way too dangerous.

"You need to load me into the simulation. If you go in, he'll realise he's in a simulation," I say.

"I won't go in as myself... Red, how fast could you forge a 3D model of a person?"

"Do I know what this person looks like?" she says.

Remy sweeps a hand across the screen, and images of Roman appear.

"Remy, you can't," I say. "What if he realises it's you? What if he realises you've trapped him and you're caught inside the simulation with him?"

"Bella, I need you to swear to me you'll keep me in the simulation until Scarlett is back. Do not let me out, no matter the risk, no matter the cost."

Morrigan pipes up then, "She's right. It's too dangerous if he escapes."

I grab Remy and pull her into a hug. "I can't lose you too, not after everything we've been through."

"You won't." Remy plunges her lips onto mine, kissing me like it's the first time. Like I'm her fairytale princess, her craving, and her paradise. This is the rooftop all over again. But this time, when she kisses me like it's the end of something and the start of everything, I crack. A tear slides down my cheek because this kiss doesn't feel like hello. It feels like goodbye.

I dig my fingers into her arms, desperate not to let go. But it's too late, her mind made up. When she pulls away, she makes a space for Red, who's sweeping her fingers over her palm and slicing deep. Blood wells in the cup of her hand.

Remy draws a digital avatar of Roman out. She breaks it down to its source runes and pulling them out individually to allow Red to douse her blood on each individual rune.

"You need to work faster, guys. We're running out of time. He just doubled back again. He's returning to the start," I say, glancing between the pair of them and the screen.

Red's face is scrunched in concentration. She cuts deeper into her palm. I wince as blood pools in her palm and she smears it over Remy's runes. The two of them move together, drawing and sculpting.

"Done," Red says and sways a little on her feet.

"Thank you, Red," Remy says, squeezing her shoulder.

Red smiles, but she's pasty, and I'm seriously concerned about her ability to use any more blood magic.

"Red do you r—"

"I'll be fine. Hell, I'll take another holiday when this is over."

There's no more time. Remy disconnects from the server. "Bella, you control the simulation from here," Remy says.

"Scarlett and Quinn are on their way," Morrigan says.

Remy leans down and kisses me. When she pulls away, she whispers, "No matter the cost. Promise me..."

"Remy, please."

"Promise."

I close my mouth because I can't say the words, but I nod, my eyes stinging.

And then she's gone. My two favourite people running towards the most dangerous man in the city.

CHAPTER 36

REMY

R ed and I race through the tunnels, feet pounding the ground until my lungs burn and my thighs ache.

"We're here," Red says, pulling me to a walk.

"If I don't come out of this alive..."

Red shakes her head. "Don't, because if you don't come back, I'm pretty sure Bella is unhinged enough to blame me and then stab me in my sleep over it. So for the sake of both of us, please... come out the other side."

I laugh. It's delirious and hysterical, but I laugh and then Red does too and the pair of us are standing in a dark tunnel laughing like idiots.

When I get control of myself, I hug her. "It was great to meet you."

She shrugs out of my grip and punches me on the shoulder. "Don't do that. Don't say goodbye. Just hurry up and get control of him."

Bella's voice crackles in my ear. "Remy, you haven't got long."

I squeeze Red's shoulder and leave, stepping around the corner. The lattice is invisible. I can barely see it and that's only because I know it's there.

I take a deep breath, step forward and into the lattice. There's an imperceptible flicker, like a lantern flame in a breeze, and then nothing. It's as if I'm still in the tunnels.

My stomach rolls because I realise I'm not and yet my brain is telling me it didn't work because the forgery is that good. The dissonance makes me queasy.

"Damn," I say. "This is a total head fuck." I glance down at my hands and suck a sharp breath in. It's not my pale thin arms and chunky fingers.

I'm looking at a man's hand, hair on the knuckles. My stomach rolls again, nausea climbing into my throat. The dysphoria is intense. I want to pull my skin off. Climb out of my body and scream until I'm sick. But there's no time. Footsteps grind to a halt in front of me.

"You made it," Marcel's voice rumbles through the tunnel.

"Marcel," I say, the voice as alien as the body I appear to be in. My hand automatically reaches for my throat, the Adam's apple hard where my neck is soft.

There's a moment of hesitation. I'm not sure if Marcel is going to attack because he knows this is fake or if he's taken aback to see me.

"Brother," he says and swings his arms out to greet me.

"Brother?"

Marcel pulls back frowning, "You say it like a question. I haven't heard you question it since we found out all those years ago."

"Not a question. I just didn't expect to get out. I spent weeks alone... I..."

"You lost faith in me?"

"Never," I say, Roman's tones singing out.

"The isolation messing with your mind," Marcel says, but his eyes narrow and I know I'm on dangerous ground.

I nod.

"Remind me," he says and slaps my arm. "Where was it we first met..."

I laugh, a chortle of a thing. I try to make it sound natural, but there's a forced falseness underneath it. "Can we get out of here? I want to start fresh."

"In good time, brother."

The tunnel around us shifts. The glitch is far more obvious in here. I swallow hard.

"Was that—" Bella whispers in my year.

"Yes. Yes, of course. I'm just eager to be free," I say to Marcel, hoping Bella understands.

"Got it," Bella says.

"Only... you are free, aren't you...? Remy."

He draws his hands back and launches a forcefield of runes at me. The blow is savage, knocking me several feet back.

I smack my head on the tunnel floor, my face landing on a rock. Shit. I wipe a hand over my cheek, smearing blood and pieces of Roman's face off. Oh god, the forgery of his body is failing too.

I weave a shield of runes, blocking the rune burst as he fires at me. The force as it hits the shield throws me back another few feet.

"REMY," Bella shrieks. "I'm pulling you."

"NO," I snap. "Where is Scarlett?"

"Five minutes out."

"You do not pull me until she's in the tunnel. Do you hear?"

The ground rumbles and shakes so violently, both of us are knocked off our feet as a loud explosion rips through the simulation. The integrity of the forgery slips as static glitches roll around us.

"What the fuck?" I say, picking myself up.

But it's Red's voice that comes through. "There's been an explosion. I... I'm injured, but it's not serious."

"The fucking commission, I say. Tell Morrigan to send guards, palace staff, anyone she can get down to the tunnels. We need them clear," I scream orders as Marcel picks himself up again.

He charges at me. But I'm up and on my feet, blocking his fists flying at my face. I grab his shoulders. He didn't expect it and it throws him off balance as I drive my knee into his crotch.

He collapses to the floor, coughing and groaning.

"After everything I did for you," he spits.

"You're trying to break a traitor out of prison, Marcel. What did you expect?"

"I expected loyalty. I expected you to understand."

"Understand what? He's a fucking traitor to the crown."

"He's my brother, Remy. And he always looked out for me. Despite the fact our parasitic cunt of a father abandoned me because I was his bastard child. I thought you, of all people, would understand what it's like to be treated like shit by them."

"Roman is one of them, Marcel. Don't you get it?"

"He's nothing like them," he spits the words and kicks out, knocking my feet out from under me. I hit the floor on my side, the air bursting from my lungs. I gasp, winded. As he pulls me underneath him.

He yanks me up and shoves me hard into the ground. "You ungrateful piece of shit."

He punches me in the face. Pain radiates out as I jerk from the impact and blood splatters across the dirt.

I wriggle under his grip, but he grabs me by the throat and squeezes. Panic leeches into my bones. I can't breathe, I can't move under his weight. I'm not a fighter, not like Scarlett. This is it. It's all over.

"Fight," Bella screams in my ears. "You fucking *fight*, or I swear to gods, Remy, I will kill you myself."

I don't want to. All I can see is the smattering of grey stars and I'm exhausted.

Bella cries my name with such pain I can't stand it.

I reach deep, clutching at the last of my strength and magic and force my hands up between his, shove all my power through my arms and outwards as I draw my knee up between his legs. He lurches forward and I snap his grip from my throat and drive my fist up towards his chin. His teeth crunch together as he topples back to the ground and the simulation shudders.

The tunnels flicker in and out.

"Pulling you out now," Bella says.

There's a flash of light. I'm blinded by it. My hands snap to my face to cover my eyes as darkness descends over us. I flinch as I crawl over rocks expecting another blow to land, but it never comes.

Arms slide under me and help me to my feet.

"You're safe now," Red whispers in my ear.

"Don't move, or I'll cut you in half," Scarlett says.

I squint against the darkness as Scarlett cuffs Marcel.

I sag against Red, exhausted.

It's finally over.

EPILOGUE

BELLA

It's a strange twist of fate to find ourselves back in the tunnels two days later. We're in a small group, Scarlett and Remy at the front, six assassin guards in a formation ring around Roman, another six guards in a defensive ring around Marcel. Behind them Morrigan, Red and I walk huddled together.

We traipse through the wreckage of the explosion. The young magicians foolish enough to take the commission blew the wrong section of tunnel. There were still consequences, of course, collapses, structural integrity damage. Red had an enormous stone crush her foot. Quinn says it's a hairline crack and she'll be fine, but she was lucky to be wearing boots or it would've been worse. Red got a few facial cuts from stray rocks that hit her, too. But Quinn's patched and stitched those and said if she keeps applying her balm, they won't even scar given a couple of weeks.

"Are you sure you're comfortable with this? I'm aware you typically hunt them," Morrigan says to Red.

Red nods. "There are ways and means. The academy will see to it that your wishes are fulfilled."

Morrigan grips Red's hand and squeezes. "Thank you. We owe you a great debt."

Remy halts the group in a cavernous circular room. Cool air circles us, and around the room are six tunnels, one leading to each city.

The two groups of guards separate and stand next to each other. Morrigan proceeds to move in front. Roman's eyes meet mine. I want to look away. The force of his stare turns my stomach. His dark eyes tell me everything I need to know and so much more I don't.

The disappointment, the fury it all pools in his dark eyes.

"Roman Oleg. Marcel Corbin. You are both convicted of treason under the sovereign law of New Imperium. I sentence you to banishment."

Red steps forward, and Morrigan shakes her hand.

"You are banished to serve as blood bags in Sangui City. You will be sent to the Academy of Hunters and subsequently gifted to one of the vampire houses. You will never return to New Imperium. The vampires will drain you until such time as they see fit to dispose of you. Do you have any final words?"

Marcel sneers but remains silent.

"This isn't over," Roman says.

Morrigan steps up to the ring of guards and into one of the gaps. Her face is violent, her sneer exquisite. Fuck, I wouldn't want to get on her wrong side. I silently thank the High Magician she was generous with me.

"Yes, Roman. It really is. You will never hold my crown. Never hold my heart. Never, ever hold power again. And in fact, you'll never see the sun or wield magic or step on

Imperium land again, either. You have underestimated me too many times. And now my city and I will be rid of you for good."

He lurches forward, but stumbles against the heavy chains binding his feet and hands and lands on his knees. Morrigan smiles, a sharp and sinister expression.

"Fuck you, Morrigan."

Morrigan sniffs but ignores him. "I do hope to see you again, Red. You are welcome to visit this city whenever you please. We are in your debt."

I step forward and pull Red into a hug. "Love you," I say.

"Love you too," she squeezes me back. "Let's not leave it too long next time."

"Whenever you need me, okay?"

She rubs my back, releases me, gives Remy a hug, and nods to Scarlett.

"Let's go," Scarlett says, and the group march off, Red hobble-jogging to the front.

"Will Scarlett be okay?" Remy says.

"Red won't let anything happen to her," I reply.

"She's only going as far as the border. Red is having academy Hunters meet them at the entrance to the city. She'll be back before the day is over."

"That's it then?" I say.

"I guess so," Remy says.

"What now?"

"Well," Morrigan says. "I have a dress fitting for a wedding in a few months' time. I should like to extend you an invitation, if you're the forgiving type."

"I'd be honoured," I smile.

The following day, our bags packed, we're standing outside Lantis Palace waiting for Remy's carriage, when Alba Merrick walks past. I stiffen.

Remy slips her hand into mine and squeezes it. "We chose this," she whispers.

That we did. I take a deep breath and hold my hand out.

Alba startles. "Oh," she says, hesitates and then softens as she slides her hand into mine.

"Congrats, Alba," I say. I open my mouth to add something, but Remy squeezes my hand. I glare at her, but she shakes her head. Probably for the best, I'd have only added some kind of insult or back-handed compliment. Gods, being nice is exhausting.

"Thanks." She smiles, and to my surprise, Alba's sharp, birdlike features are quite sweet when she's not scowling.

Alba leaves as my mother appears. I was aware mother had come to the last challenge, no doubt causing mayhem, trying to find out where I was.

Her mouth is pinched, her hair drawn back into a severe bun. She scans Remy up and down. "Ah yes, the Borderling."

"Mother," I bark, stepping up to her. I won't stand for this shit, not anymore.

Remy places a hand on my arm and smiles, as polite and professional as always. "Mrs Blythe, a pleasure to meet you."

"The feeling isn't mutual. Now, Bella do come along. I have a meeting for you with Lord Longville. We've arranged a marriage contract, and the ceremony will be in six weeks."

"Yes, see. About that... the answer is no," I say.

Mother flinches. Her brows furrow so deeply they meet in the middle.

"I beg your pardon?"

"You heard me. The answer is no. I'm not marrying some reprobate lord. I'm not going to allow you to use my womb as your personal baby maker."

"Bella," she snaps her voice high and strained. I'm amazed a pack of dogs don't come charging into the palace courtyard. "You will come with me immediately. Or... Or..."

"Or what, Mother?"

She bristles, wipes her skirts down and refocuses on me. "Or I'll disinherit you."

I laugh, because I don't care. This was always what it was about: the family reputation, inheriting money, the aesthetics of being a legacy. And I don't give a shit. I'll make my own money. I'll build a new reputation, and I'll do it because I'm free of her, her expectations and her fucking reputation.

"If that's what you need to do, Mother... I think I'm okay with that."

Remy slips her hand inside mine and squeezes. "Ready?"

I nod.

"Goodbye, Ma, say hi to dad for me," I say and follow Remy into the carriage.

Remy shuts the door on mother's squawking. I can still hear her as we enter the bridge, screaming my name and begging me to come back.

But I won't. I'm never going back home. I'll find my way, whatever that looks like.

"I've arranged a barbecue tomorrow. I want you to meet my friends."

"I think I've already done that. Haven't I?"

The carriage rocks as we trundle over the bridge, heading towards New Imperium.

"You have. But I think we need to start again, don't you?"

"Tell me about them, the real them. Not the guard or negotiator. But what they're like as friends," I say and lean into her.

"Would you believe Scarlett and Quinn used to hate each other?" she says, laughing.

"No."

"Mmhmm. Oh, and I should probably confess I dated Quinn for like a couple of months when we were teenagers."

"You dated your friend?" I say, lifting off her shoulder and raising an eyebrow. "You're such a cliché lesbian."

She laughs.

"What about Stirling and Morrigan?" I ask.

"Well, they had a rough time of it. It's complicated. I'll let them tell you over a drink tomorrow. But we're all super excited because Morrigan is going to be announcing her official marriage to Stirling in a few weeks. First same sex royals in New Imperium history. And now you're invited to the wedding."

"And then there's you..." I say.

"And now you..." she replies. "I never got a chance to ask Red about her story. About why she hates vampires so much."

"Don't worry, I have a feeling she'll tell her story soon enough."

I slide my hand into Remy's, worries settling into my gut. "What if your friends don't like me?"

"They will." She leans down and kisses my nose.

She pushes a curl behind my ear and grazes her mouth over mine. Her smell, leather and bergamot and the softest trace of vetiver drift in the air. She smells delicious and I am starving.

Her hand slides between my legs.

"We can't. The carriage walls aren't soundproof," I whimper.

"Then you'll have to be quiet, won't you?"

"Oh no, not this time."

I slide off the seat and between her knees. I lean forward and unbuckle her trousers. Her eyes glimmer and darken as lust pools in her gaze. She hitches forward and I pull her trousers and boxers off.

"What do I get if I make you come?" I purr.

"Good girls get whatever they want, Bella. You know that."

I run my nails along her thighs. It makes her nostrils flare as she inhales and rolls her head back. I lunge for her pussy, not wanting to waste a single second of being with her. There's time to make love, time to worship each other, but I am so tired and so desperate to drown in her. I just want to fuck. Hard and fast. I want to lose myself in her body.

I lick down her pussy, sliding my tongue between her folds. She groans loud.

There's a knock on the carriage wall. "Everything alright, Miss?" the driver's voice says.

I stifle a laugh.

"Ye-es," Remy says as I thrust a finger inside her.

She looks down at me, glaring. "Bella." My name in her mouth is filth. It's a growl and a promise.

I press my mouth to her clit and swipe my tongue over it in an unrelenting rhythm. She grips the seat; her knuckles whiten.

I slide a second finger into her pussy, and she gasps but

manages to stifle most of the noise. Her hands find my curls, she grinds my mouth against her cunt, and I take it. I take all of it, all of her. I drink down every drop of excitement as she rides my face and whispers my name.

Whispers how she's going to fuck me until I can't walk. How she'll fuck me until I plead with her to stop the orgasms. Until I accept she owns me in the bedroom. Until I swear all my orgasms are hers and that I'll never look at another woman.

And I want it all. Want to swear to it all.

Her pussy drenches my fingers as I slide in and out, her words liquid lust to us both.

"You have me," I moan against her. "Always. Forever. I'm yours."

Her walls clench my fingers as I rub against her g-spot. She whimpers and tips over into bliss. She takes a moment to come back to me, but as she blinks at me, smiles.

"I will never love another woman," she says and tugs me by the waist to slide between her legs. Her hands reach around my back to find the zip in my dress and tug it down.

"If I'm honest, I think you stole my heart that night on the rooftop," I say.

She pulls my dress down, leaving me standing in the carriage naked. She lowers me onto her lap, facing her. Her fingers slide against my pussy, palming my clit, running two fingers through my excitement.

"You know, I used to wonder about the alchemical formula for love," she says and trails kisses down my neck and over my nipples.

"Gods, you're such a nerd, Remy. Maybe you should research it at Imperium University."

"I considered it funny enough."

"But you've decided against it?"

She nods, kissing the top of my breast.

"I don't need to anymore."

"And why's that?" I say and slide my hand between her naked thighs. I want to touch her as much as she's touching me.

She breathes in deep, running her tongue over my chest. I close my eyes and soak up every ounce of her, knowing I'm never going to let go. Her fingers push inside me as she rocks me against her, and I drift into the molten bliss of pleasure.

She looks up at me. "Because I've figured it out. It's you, plus me and the rest of eternity."

Want to read Red's story? Don't miss out on Red's spicy enemies to lovers vampire romance by getting exclusive release news here: rubyroe.co.uk/signup.

Last, reviews are super important for authors, they help provide needed social proof that helps to sell more books. If you have a moment and you're able to leave a review on the store you bought the book from, I'd be really grateful.

About the Author

Ruby Roe is the pen name of Sacha Black. Ruby is the author of lesbian fantasy romance. She loves a bit of magic with her smut, but she'll read anything as long as the characters get down and dirty. When Ruby isn't writing romance, she can usually be found beasting herself in the gym, snuggling with her two pussy... cats, or spanking all her money on her next travel adventure. She lives in England with her wife, son and two devious rag doll cats.

instagram.com/sachablackauthor
tiktok.com/@rubyroeauthor

Printed in Great Britain
by Amazon